SUPERMAN
of Smallville

Art Baltazar
& Franco

SUPERMAN CREATED BY JERRY SIEGEL
AND JOE SHUSTER. BY SPECIAL ARRANGEMENT
WITH THE JERRY SIEGEL FAMILY.

LAUREN BISOM Editor

STEVE COOK Design Director - Books

AMIE BROCKWAY-METCALF Publication Design

BOB HARRAS Senior VP - Editor-in-Chief, DC Comics

MICHELE R. WELLS VP & Executive Editor, Young Reader

DAN DiDIO Publisher

JIM LEE Publisher & Chief Creative Officer

BOBBIE CHASE VP - New Publishing Initiatives & Talent Development

DON FALLETTI VP - Manufacturing Operations & Workflow Management

LAWRENCE GANEM VP - Talent Services

ALISON GILL Senior VP - Manufacturing & Operations

HANK KANALZ Senior VP - Publishing Strategy & Support Services

DAN MIRON VP - Publishing Operations

NICK J. NAPOLITANO VP - Manufacturing Administration & Design

NANCY SPEARS VP - Sales

DC Comics, 2900 West Alameda Ave.,
Burbank, CA 91505

Printed by LSC Communications,
Crawfordsville, IN, USA.

7/26/19. First Printing.
ISBN: 978-1-4012-8392-6

Library of Congress Cataloging-in-Publication Data
Names: Baltazar, Art, author, illustrator. | Aureliani, Franco, author,
    illustrator.
Title: Superman of Smallville / Art Baltazar and Franco.
Description: Burbank, CA : DC Comics, [2019] | "Superman created by Jerry
    Siegel and Joe Shuster." | Summary: "Can Superman keep Smallville from
    going to the dogs?"— Provided by publisher.
Identifiers: LCCN 2019009477 | ISBN 9781401283926 (pbk.)
Subjects: LCSH: Graphic novels.
Classification: LCC PZ7.7.B33 Sw 2019 | DDC 741.5/973—dc23

PEFC Certified

This product is from
sustainably managed
forests and controlled
sources

PEFC/29-31-337   www.pefc.org

TABLE OF CONTENTS

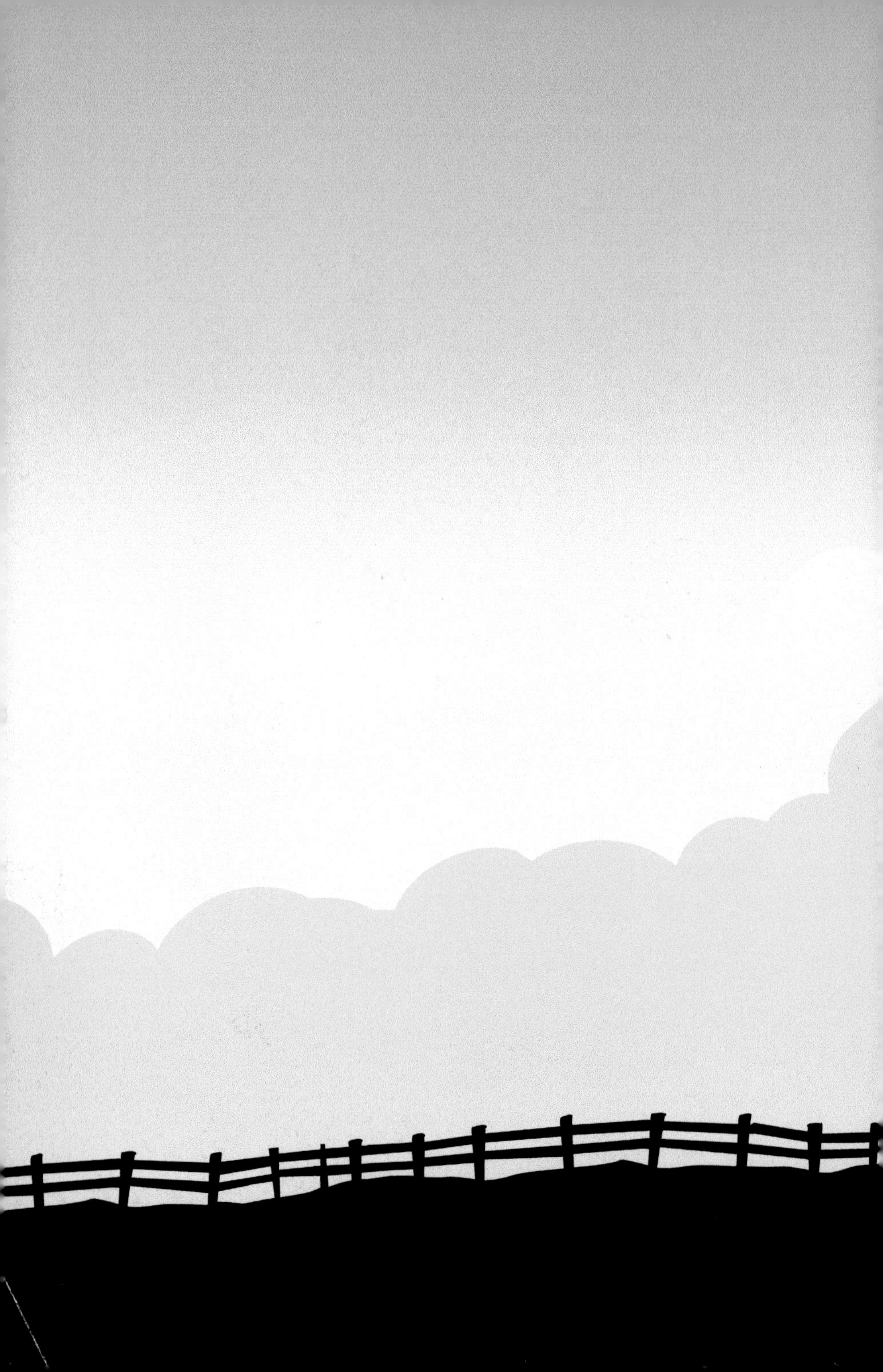

CHAPTER ONE

CALL ME

SUPERMAN

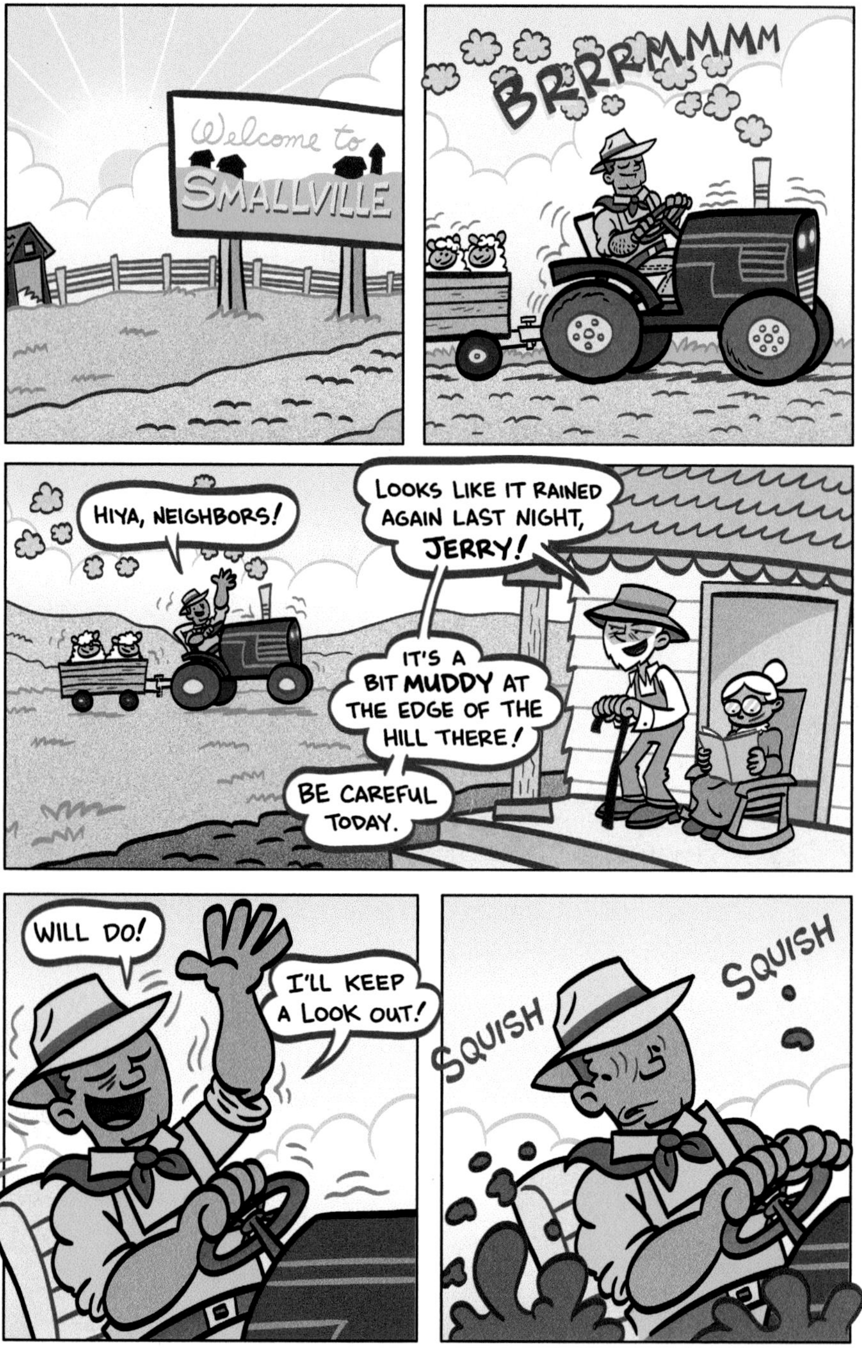
Welcome to
SMALLVILLE
BRRRMMMMM
HIYA, NEIGHBORS!
LOOKS LIKE IT RAINED AGAIN LAST NIGHT, JERRY!
IT'S A BIT MUDDY AT THE EDGE OF THE HILL THERE!
BE CAREFUL TODAY.
WILL DO!
I'LL KEEP A LOOK OUT!
SQUISH
SQUISH

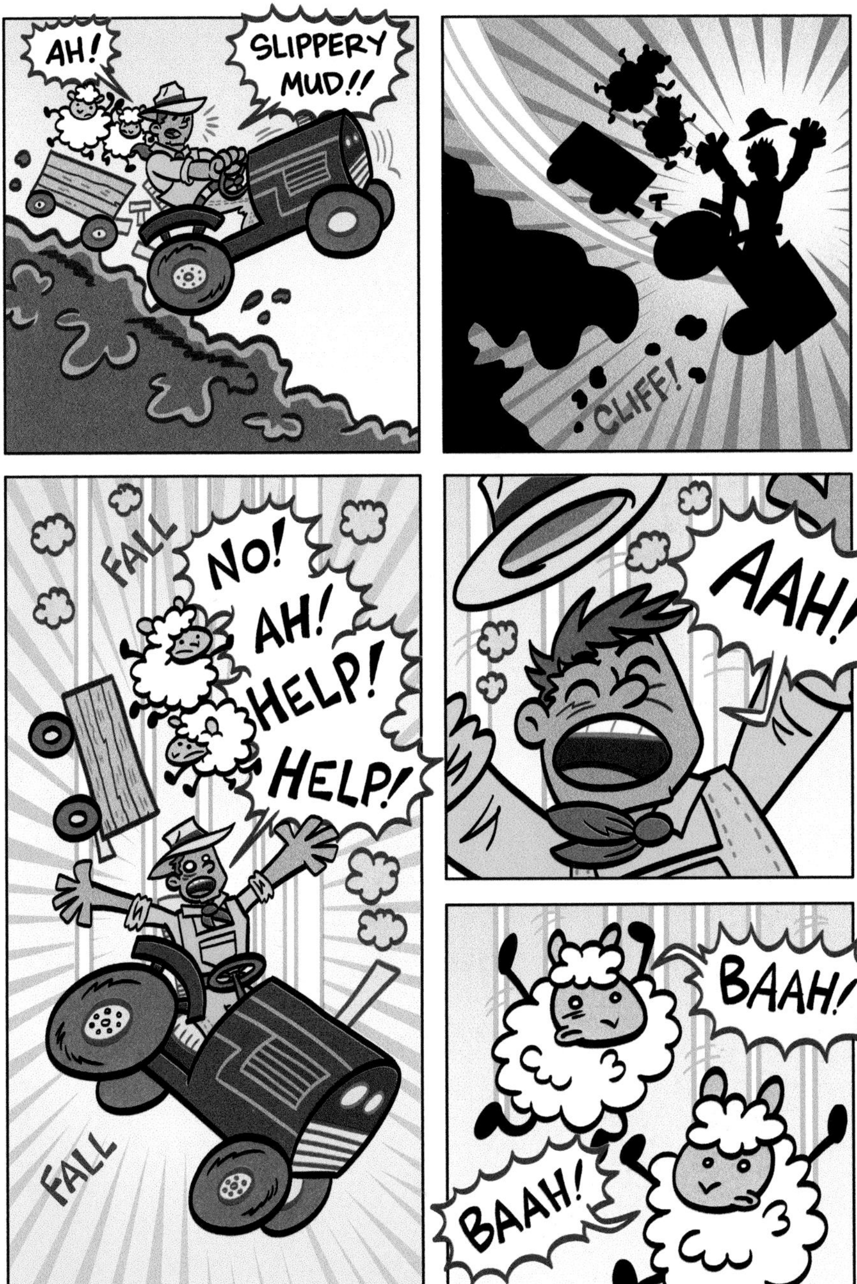
AH!
SLIPPERY MUD!!
CLIFF!
FALL
NO!
AH!
HELP!
HELP!
FALL
AAH!
BAAH!
BAAH!

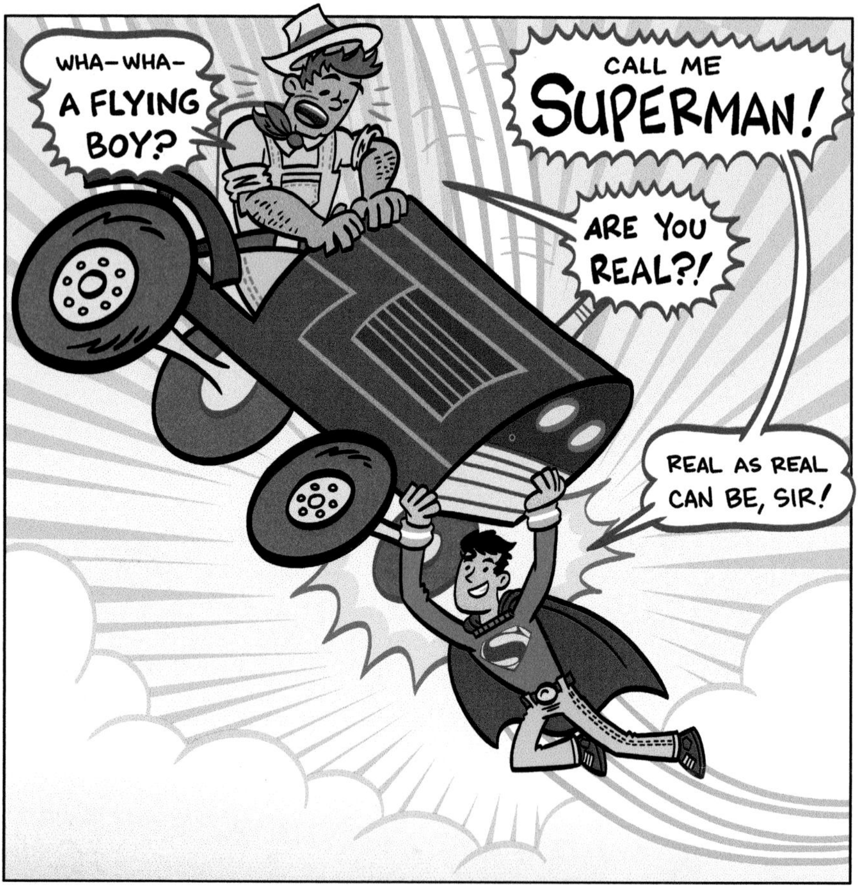
WHA-WHA- A FLYING BOY?
CALL ME SUPERMAN!
ARE YOU REAL?!
REAL AS REAL CAN BE, SIR!

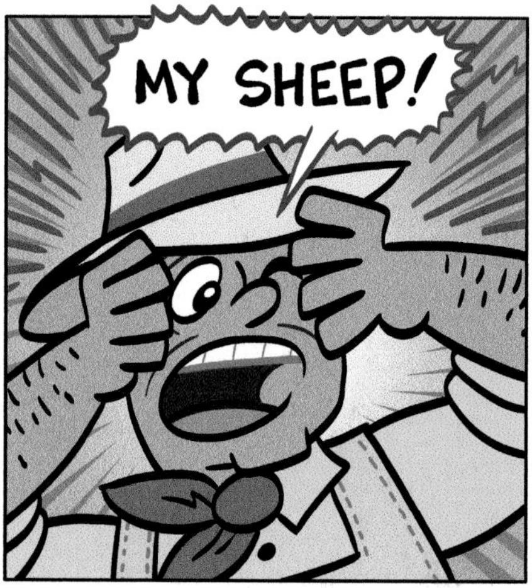
MY SHEEP!

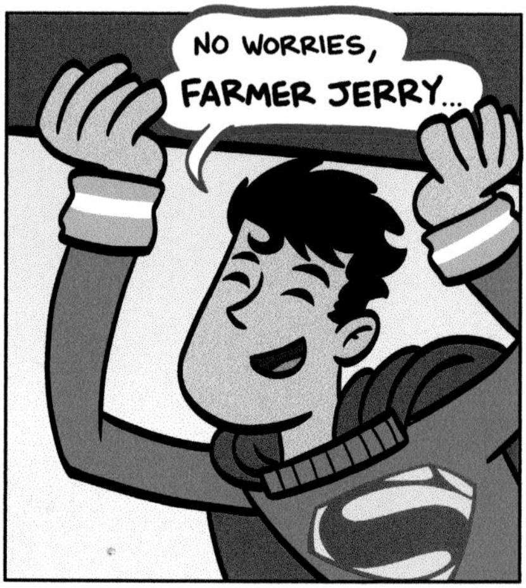
NO WORRIES, FARMER JERRY...

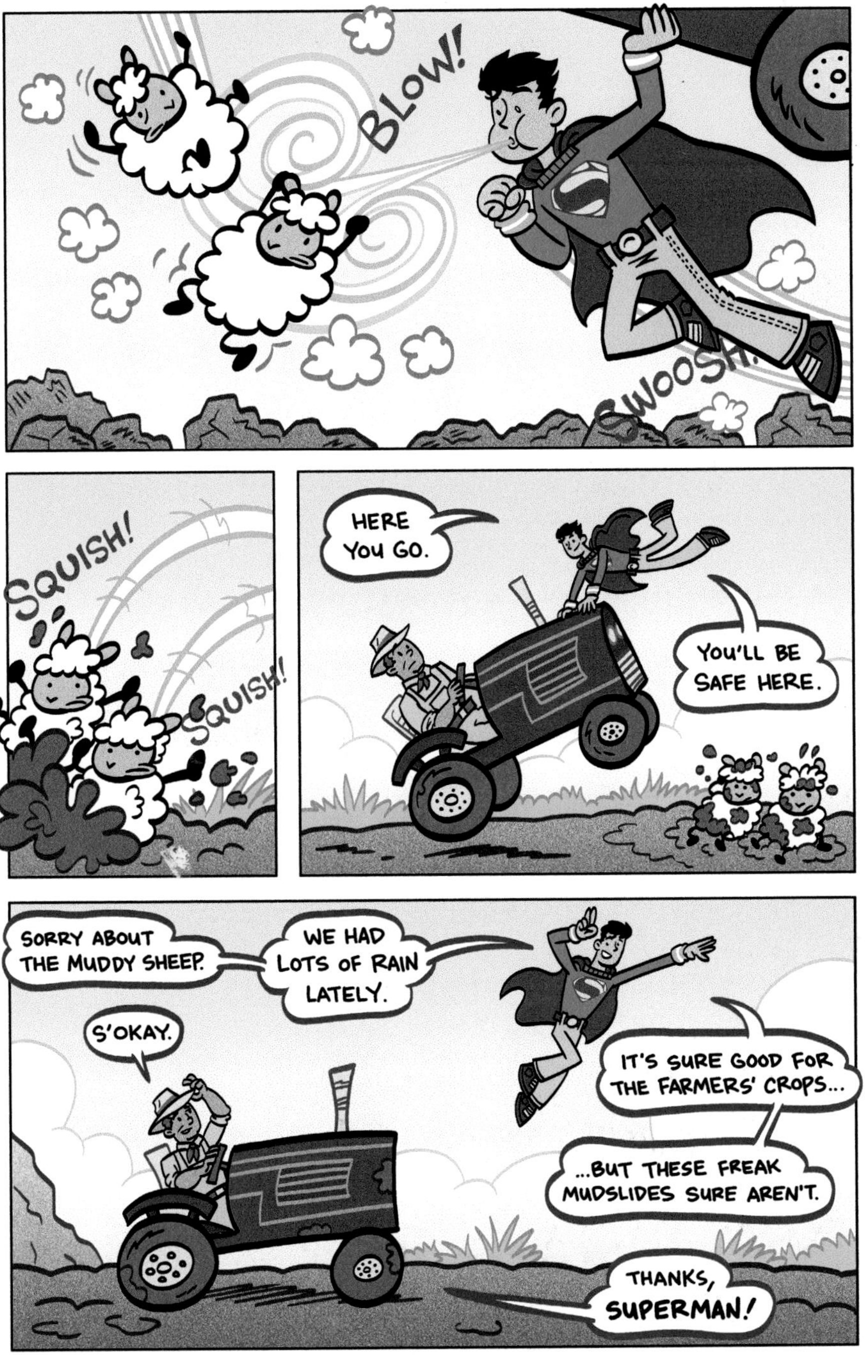
BLOW!
SWOOSH!
SQUISH!
SQUISH!
HERE YOU GO.
YOU'LL BE SAFE HERE.
SORRY ABOUT THE MUDDY SHEEP.
WE HAD LOTS OF RAIN LATELY.
S'OKAY.
IT'S SURE GOOD FOR THE FARMERS' CROPS...
...BUT THESE FREAK MUDSLIDES SURE AREN'T.
THANKS, SUPERMAN!

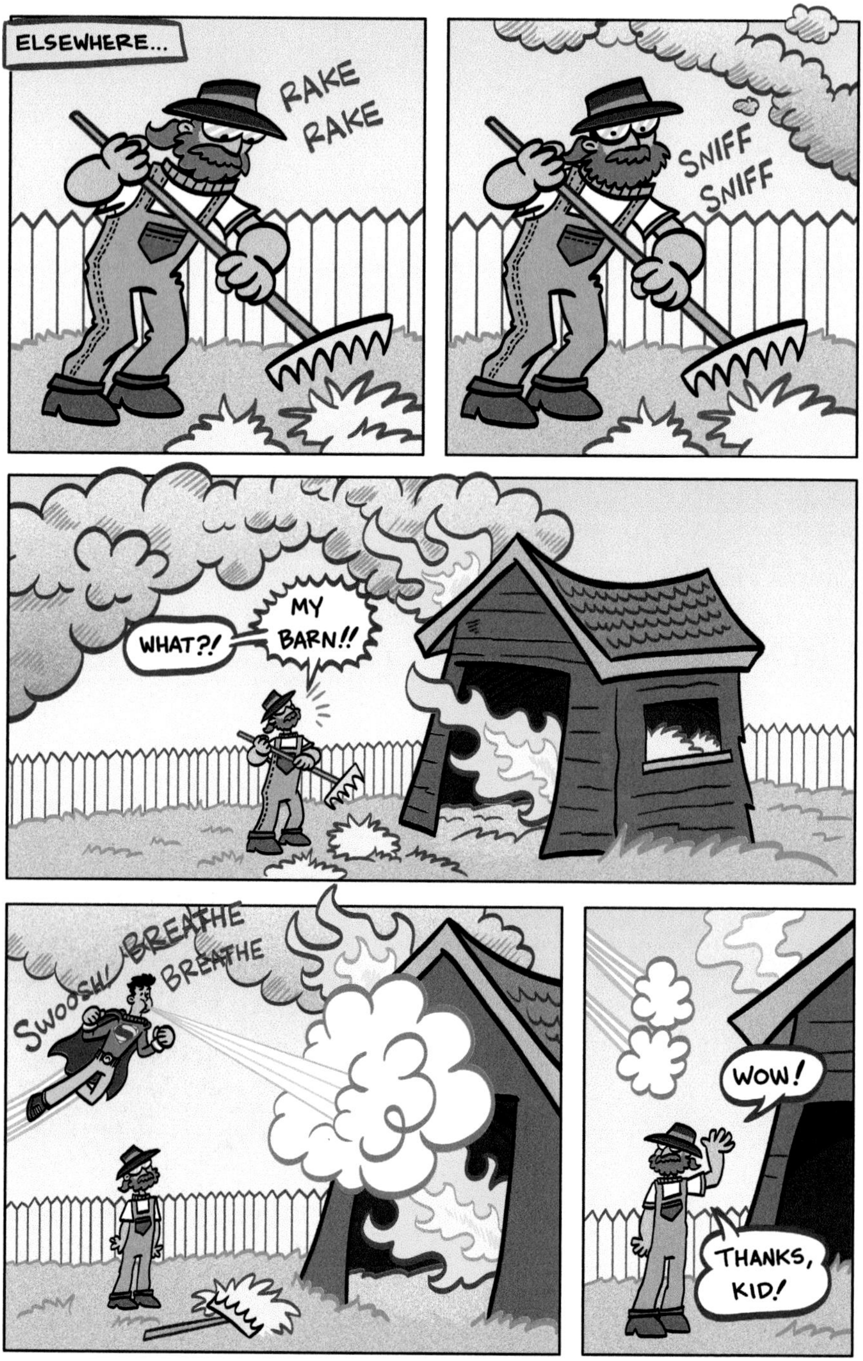
ELSEWHERE...
RAKE RAKE
SNIFF SNIFF
WHAT?!
MY BARN!!
SWOOSH!
BREATHE BREATHE
WOW!
THANKS, KID!

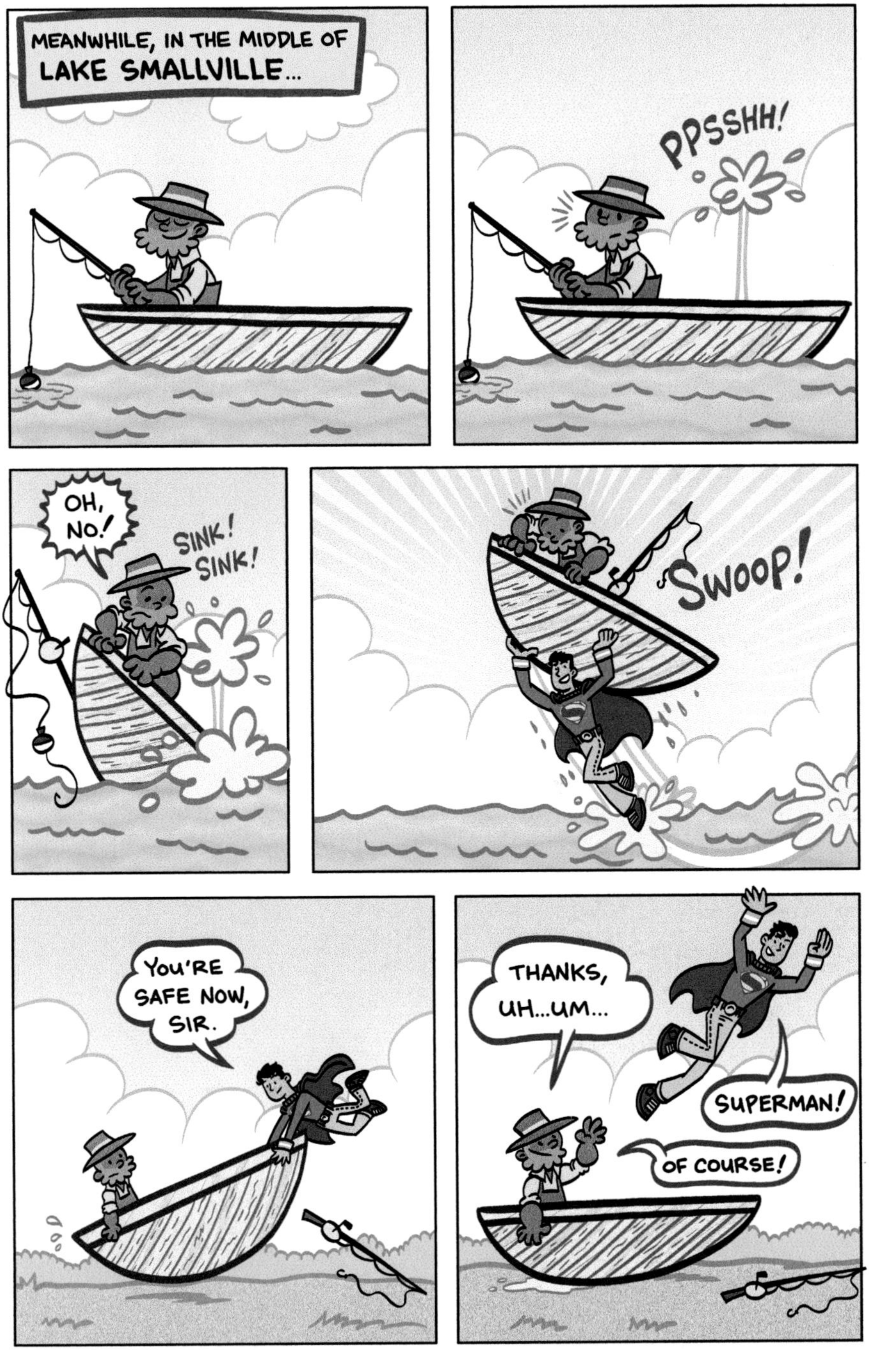
MEANWHILE, IN THE MIDDLE OF LAKE SMALLVILLE...
PPSSHH!
OH, NO!
SINK! SINK!
SWOOP!
YOU'RE SAFE NOW, SIR.
THANKS, UH...UM...
SUPERMAN!
OF COURSE!

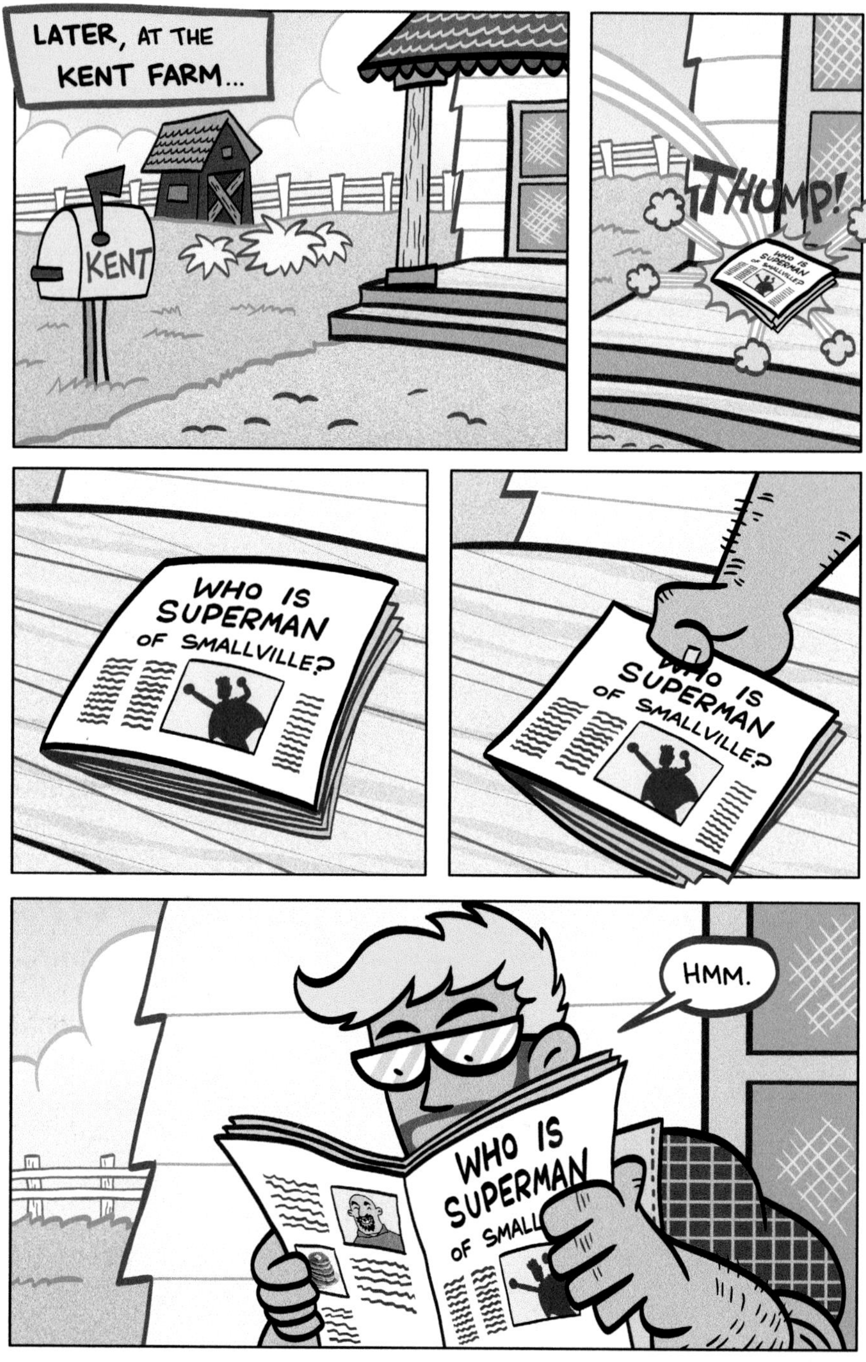
LATER, AT THE KENT FARM...
KENT
THUMP!
WHO IS SUPERMAN OF SMALLVILLE?
WHO IS SUPERMAN OF SMALLVILLE?
WHO IS SUPERMAN OF SMALLVILLE?
HMM.
WHO IS SUPERMAN OF SMALL

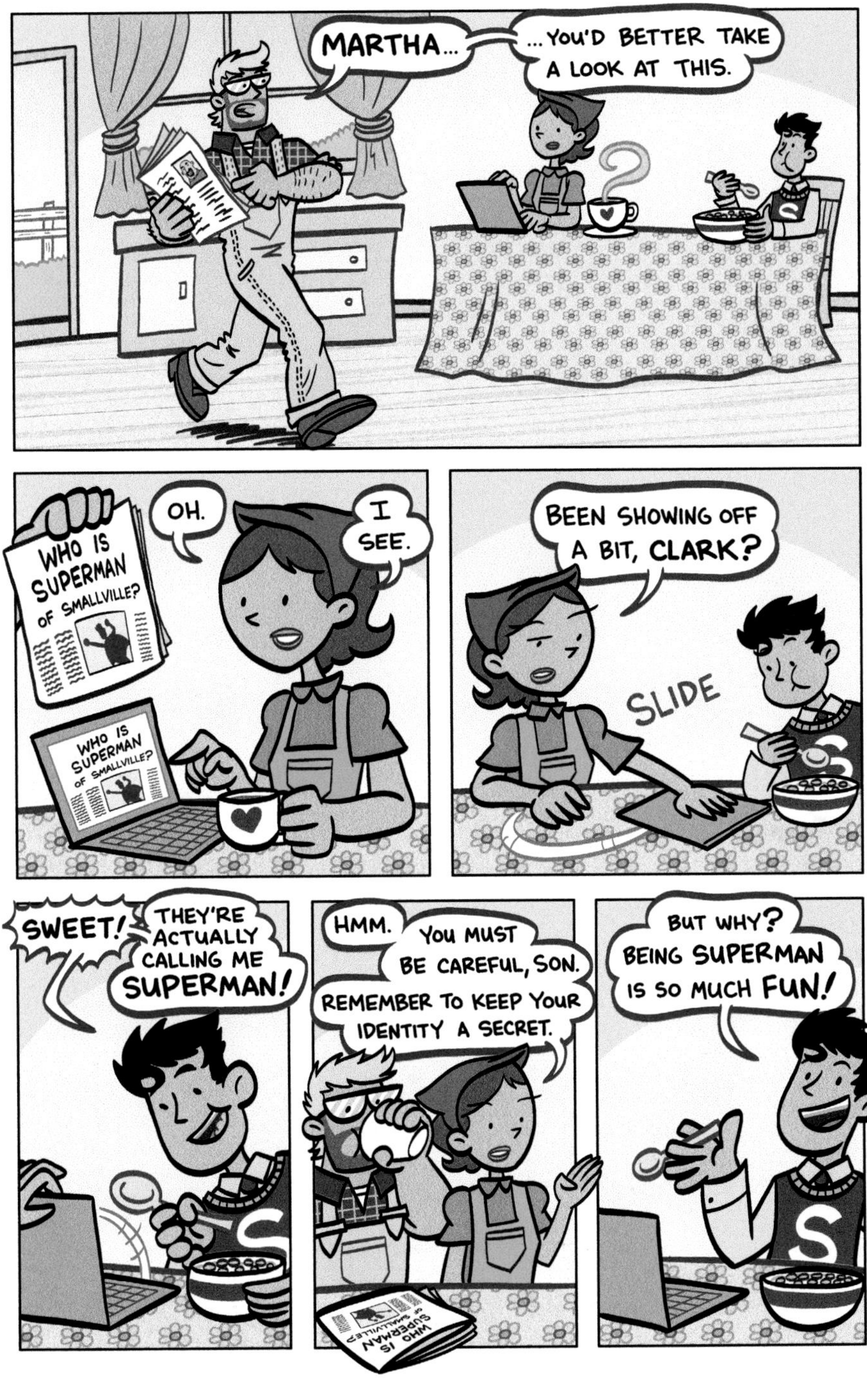
MARTHA...
...YOU'D BETTER TAKE A LOOK AT THIS.
WHO IS SUPERMAN OF SMALLVILLE?
OH.
I SEE.
WHO IS SUPERMAN OF SMALLVILLE?
BEEN SHOWING OFF A BIT, CLARK?
SLIDE
SWEET!
THEY'RE ACTUALLY CALLING ME SUPERMAN!
HMM.
YOU MUST BE CAREFUL, SON.
REMEMBER TO KEEP YOUR IDENTITY A SECRET.
WHO IS SUPERMAN OF SMALLVILLE?
BUT WHY? BEING SUPERMAN IS SO MUCH FUN!

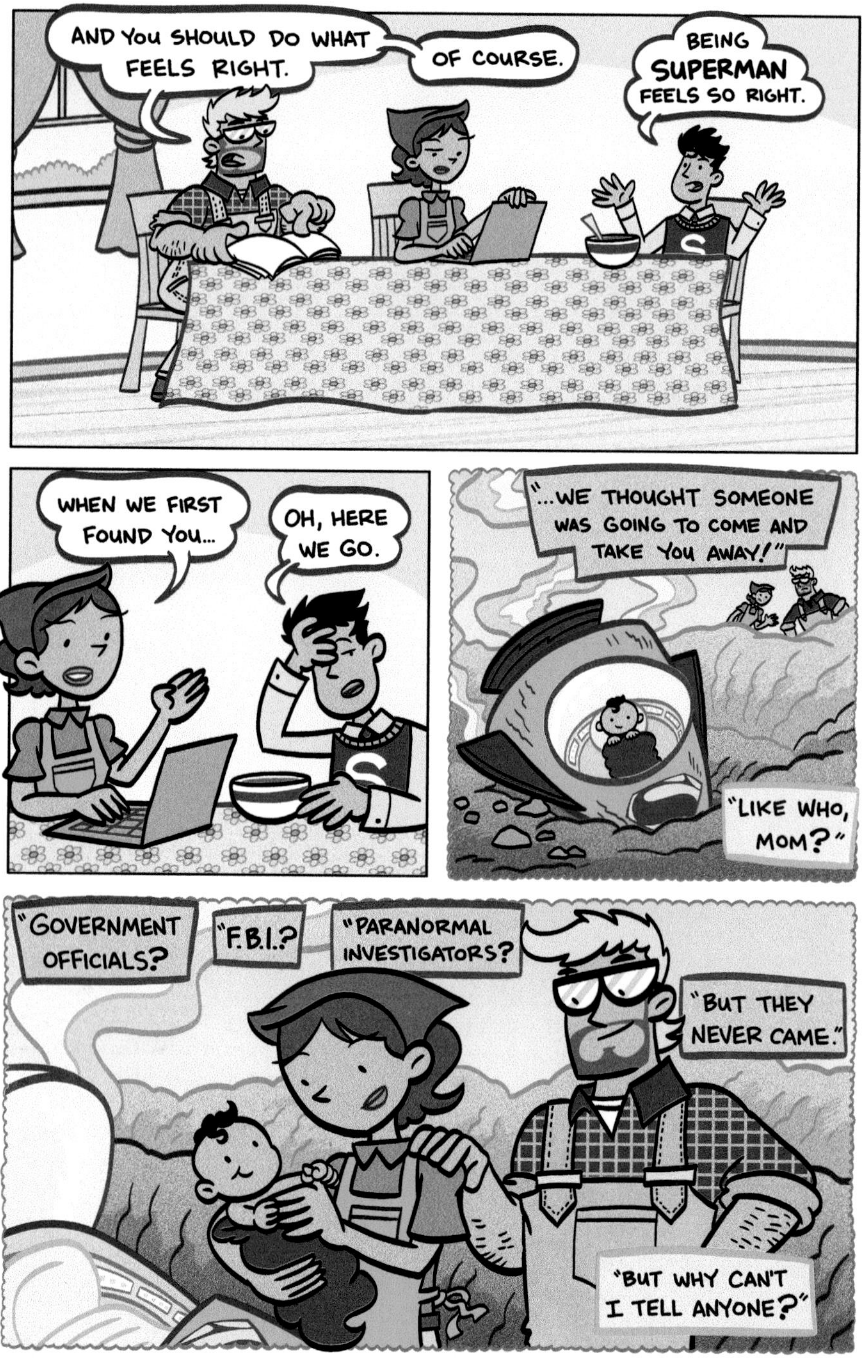
AND YOU SHOULD DO WHAT FEELS RIGHT.
OF COURSE.
BEING SUPERMAN FEELS SO RIGHT.
WHEN WE FIRST FOUND YOU...
OH, HERE WE GO.
"...WE THOUGHT SOMEONE WAS GOING TO COME AND TAKE YOU AWAY!"
"LIKE WHO, MOM?"
"GOVERNMENT OFFICIALS?
"F.B.I.?
"PARANORMAL INVESTIGATORS?
"BUT THEY NEVER CAME."
"BUT WHY CAN'T I TELL ANYONE?"

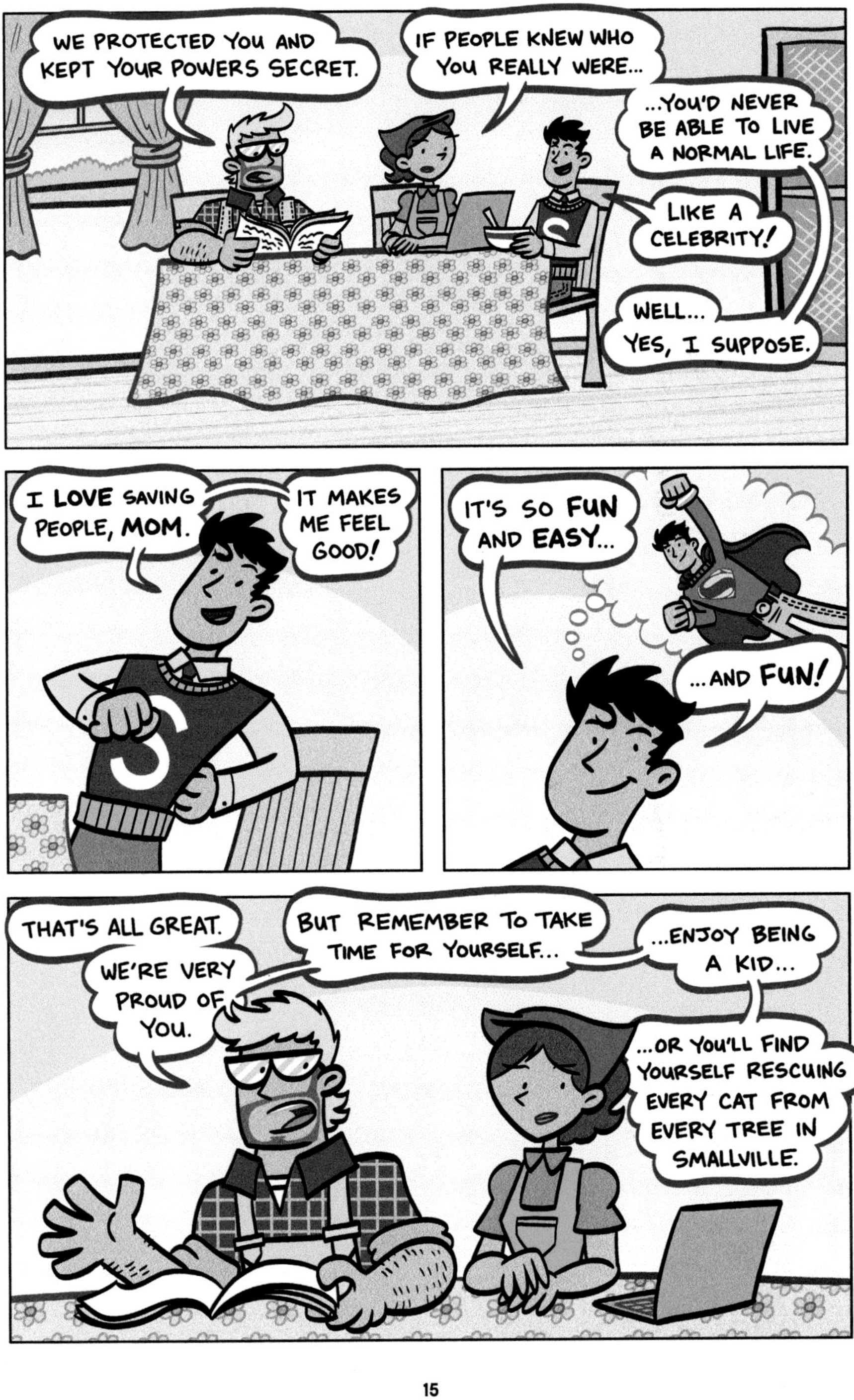
WE PROTECTED YOU AND KEPT YOUR POWERS SECRET.
IF PEOPLE KNEW WHO YOU REALLY WERE...
...YOU'D NEVER BE ABLE TO LIVE A NORMAL LIFE.
LIKE A CELEBRITY!
WELL... YES, I SUPPOSE.
I LOVE SAVING PEOPLE, MOM.
IT MAKES ME FEEL GOOD!
IT'S SO FUN AND EASY...
...AND FUN!
THAT'S ALL GREAT.
WE'RE VERY PROUD OF YOU.
BUT REMEMBER TO TAKE TIME FOR YOURSELF...
...ENJOY BEING A KID...
...OR YOU'LL FIND YOURSELF RESCUING EVERY CAT FROM EVERY TREE IN SMALLVILLE.

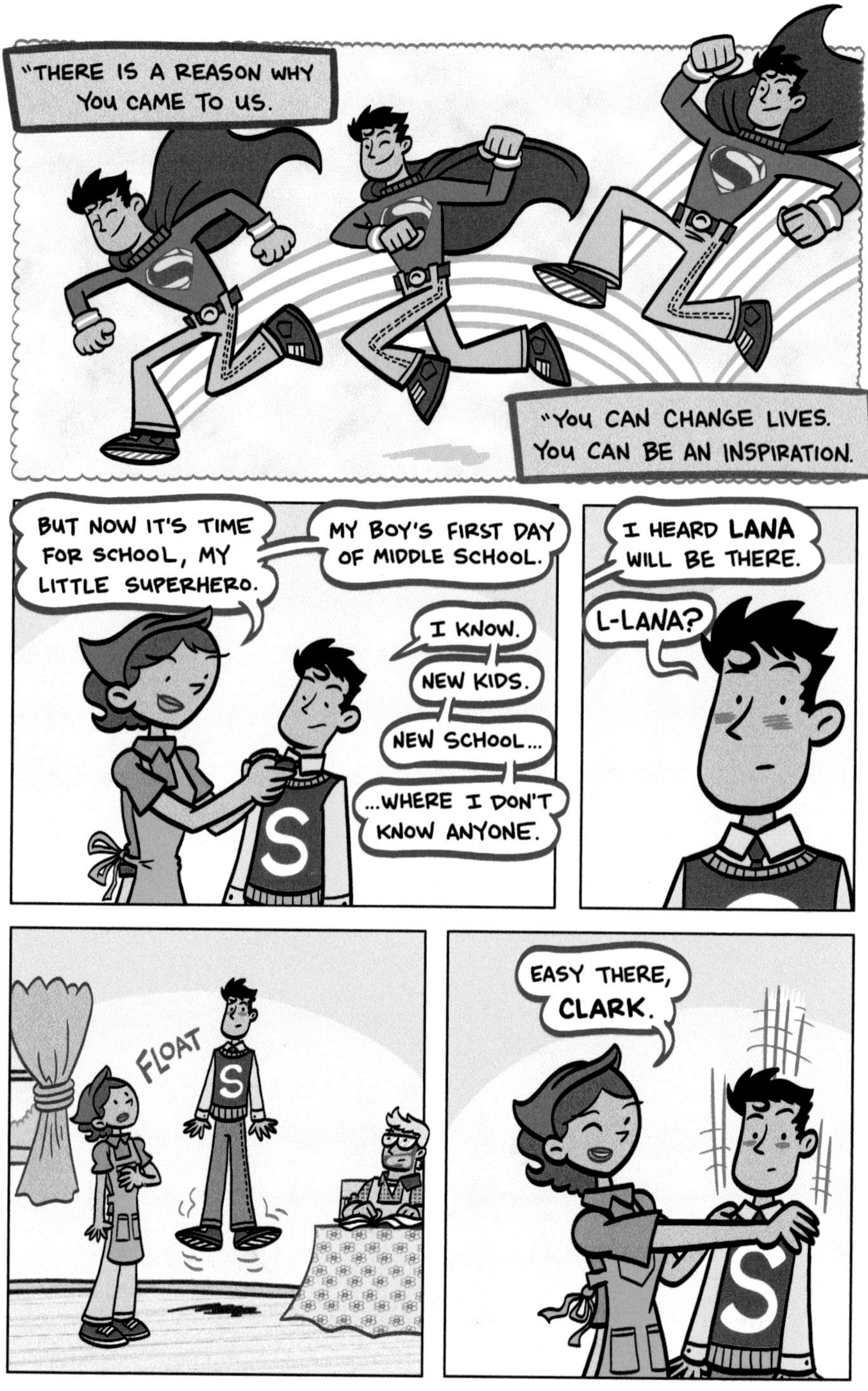
"THERE IS A REASON WHY YOU CAME TO US.
"YOU CAN CHANGE LIVES. YOU CAN BE AN INSPIRATION.
BUT NOW IT'S TIME FOR SCHOOL, MY LITTLE SUPERHERO.
MY BOY'S FIRST DAY OF MIDDLE SCHOOL.
I KNOW.
NEW KIDS.
NEW SCHOOL...
...WHERE I DON'T KNOW ANYONE.
I HEARD LANA WILL BE THERE.
L-LANA?
FLOAT
EASY THERE, CLARK.

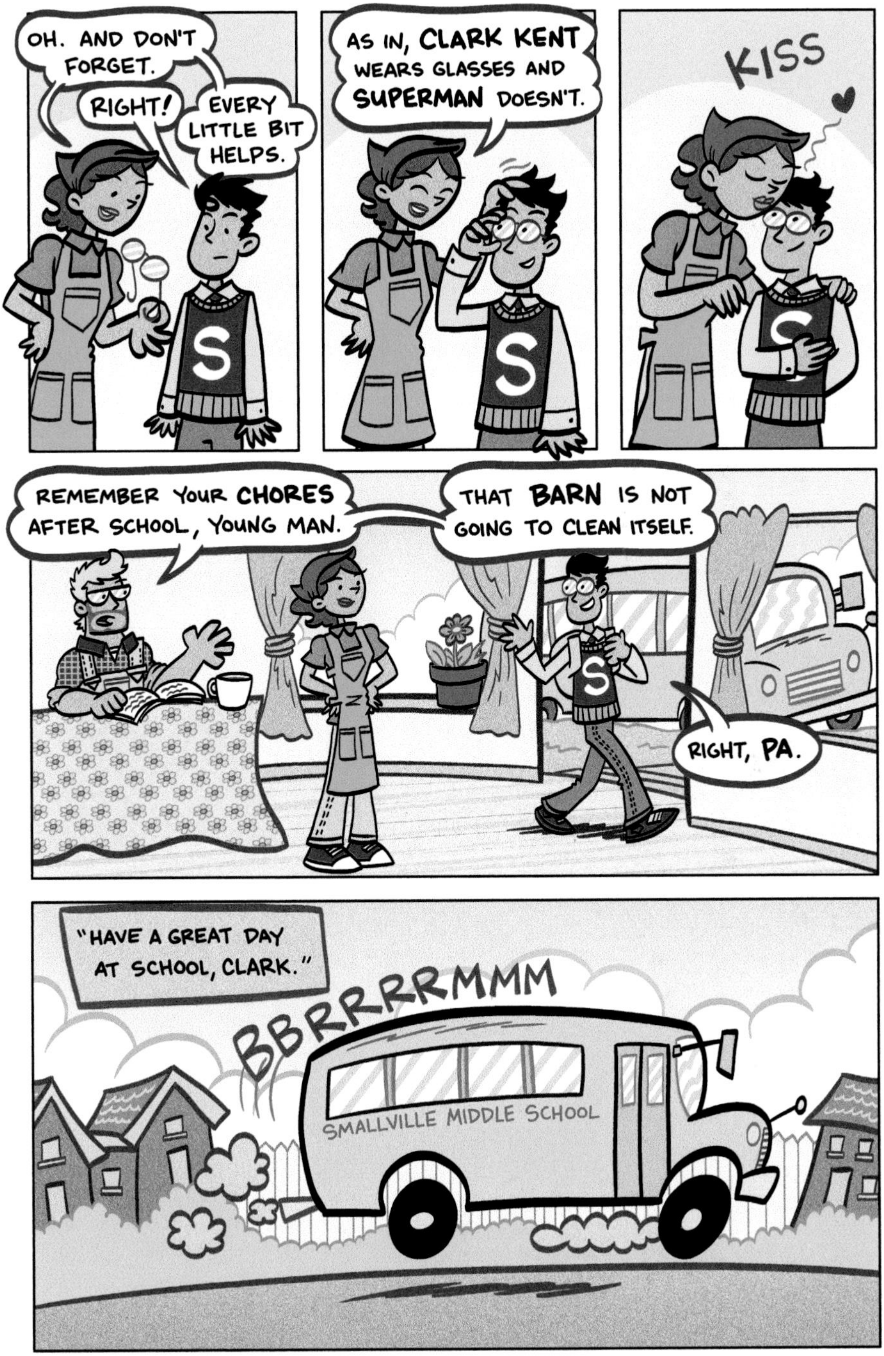
OH. AND DON'T FORGET.
RIGHT!
EVERY LITTLE BIT HELPS.
AS IN, CLARK KENT WEARS GLASSES AND SUPERMAN DOESN'T.
KISS
REMEMBER YOUR CHORES AFTER SCHOOL, YOUNG MAN.
THAT BARN IS NOT GOING TO CLEAN ITSELF.
RIGHT, PA.
"HAVE A GREAT DAY AT SCHOOL, CLARK."
BBRRRRMMM
SMALLVILLE MIDDLE SCHOOL

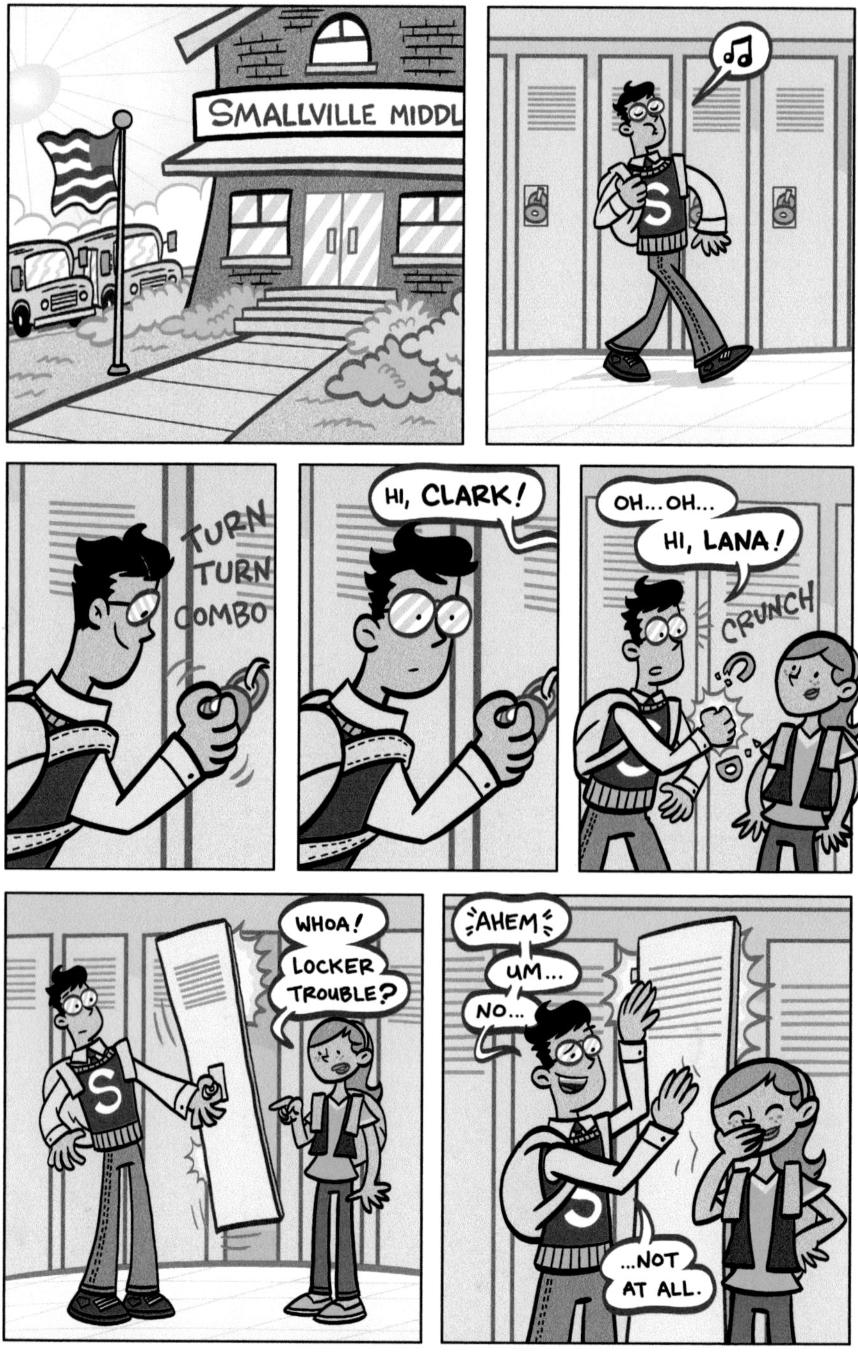
SMALLVILLE MIDDL
♫
TURN
TURN
COMBO
HI, CLARK!
OH...OH...
HI, LANA!
CRUNCH
WHOA!
LOCKER TROUBLE?
AHEM
UM...
NO...
...NOT AT ALL.

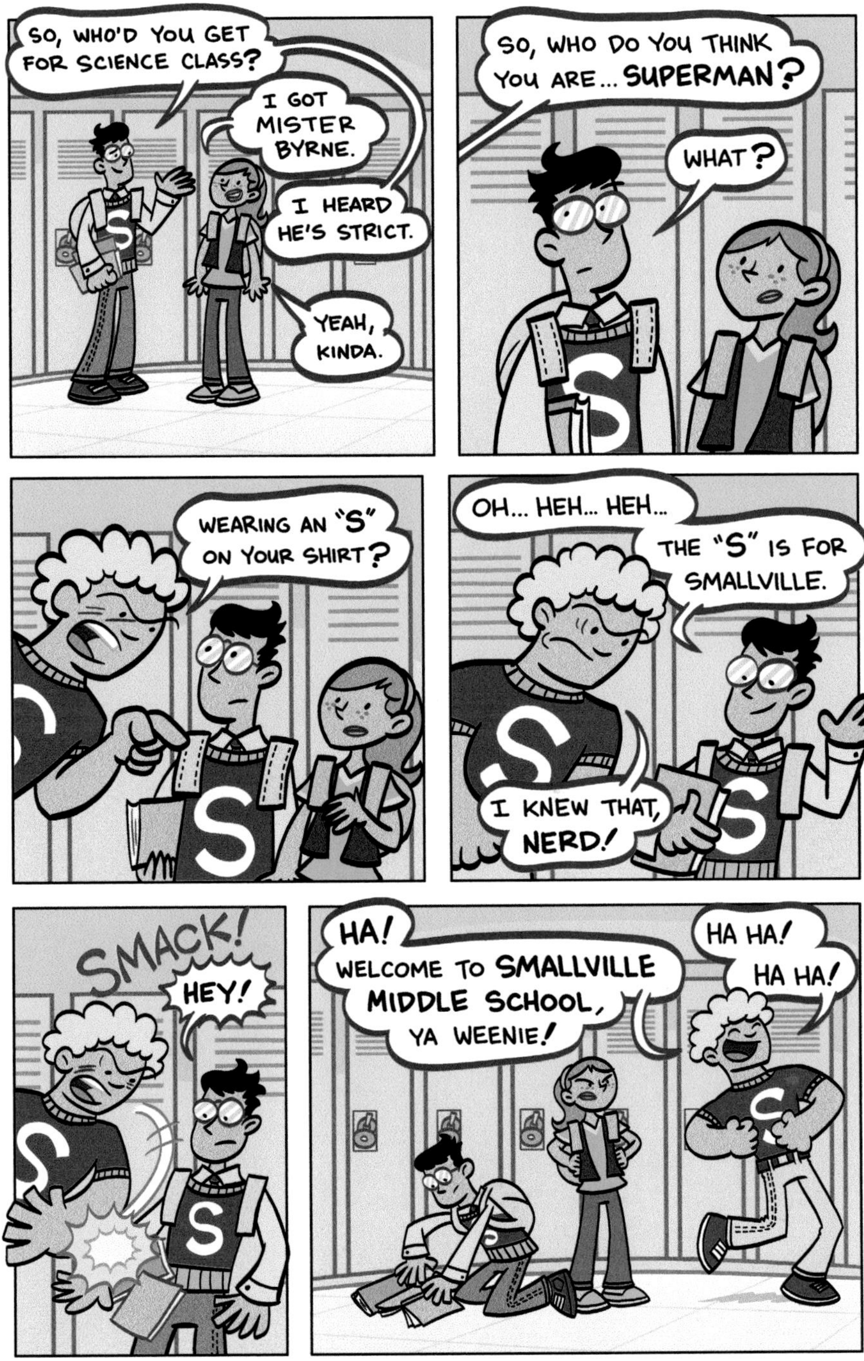
SO, WHO'D YOU GET FOR SCIENCE CLASS?
I GOT MISTER BYRNE.
I HEARD HE'S STRICT.
YEAH, KINDA.
SO, WHO DO YOU THINK YOU ARE... SUPERMAN?
WHAT?
WEARING AN "S" ON YOUR SHIRT?
OH... HEH... HEH...
THE "S" IS FOR SMALLVILLE.
I KNEW THAT, NERD!
SMACK!
HEY!
HA! WELCOME TO SMALLVILLE MIDDLE SCHOOL, YA WEENIE!
HA HA! HA HA!

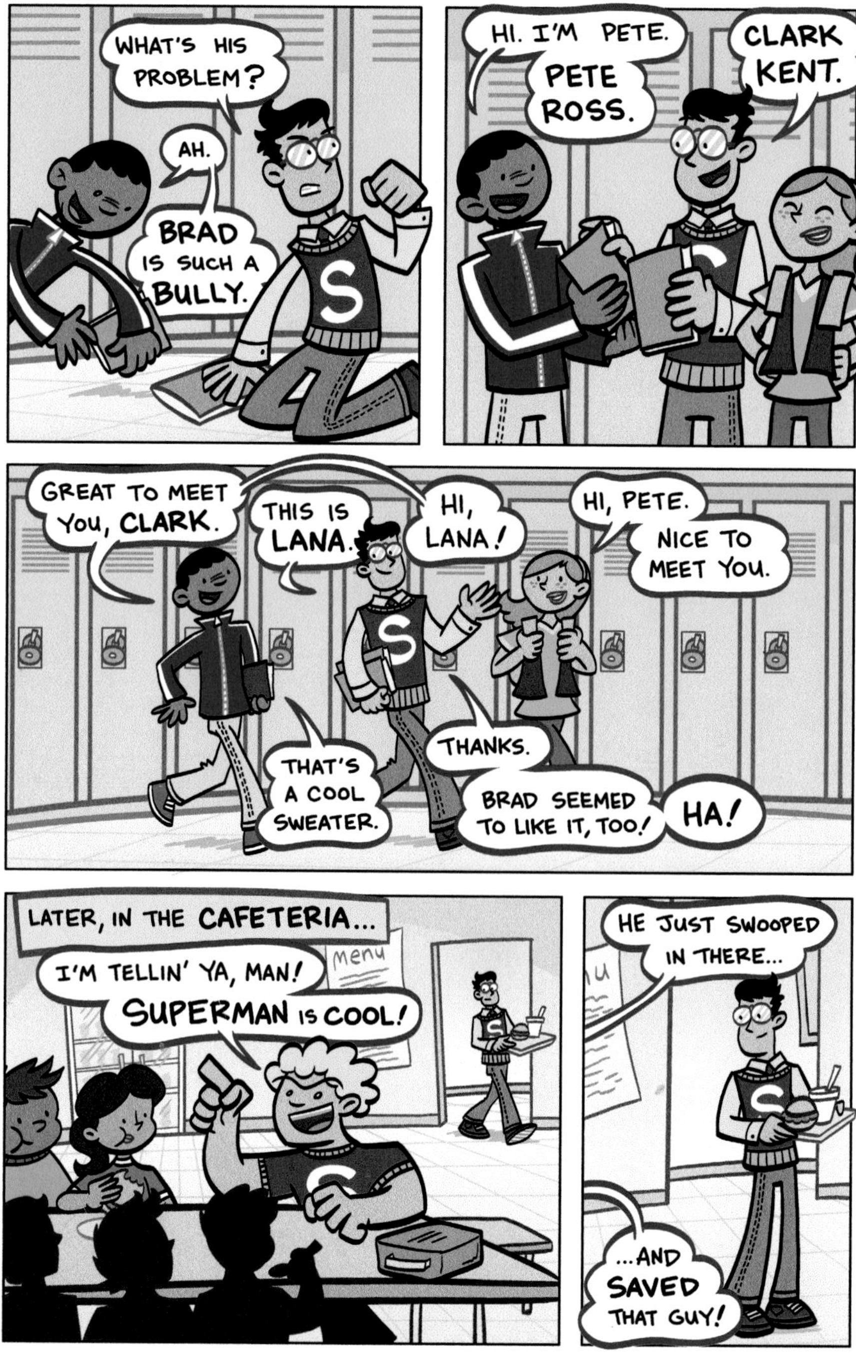
WHAT'S HIS PROBLEM?
AH.
BRAD IS SUCH A BULLY.
HI. I'M PETE.
PETE ROSS.
CLARK KENT.
GREAT TO MEET YOU, CLARK.
THIS IS LANA.
HI, LANA!
HI, PETE.
NICE TO MEET YOU.
THAT'S A COOL SWEATER.
THANKS.
BRAD SEEMED TO LIKE IT, TOO!
HA!
LATER, IN THE CAFETERIA...
menu
I'M TELLIN' YA, MAN!
SUPERMAN IS COOL!
HE JUST SWOOPED IN THERE...
...AND SAVED THAT GUY!

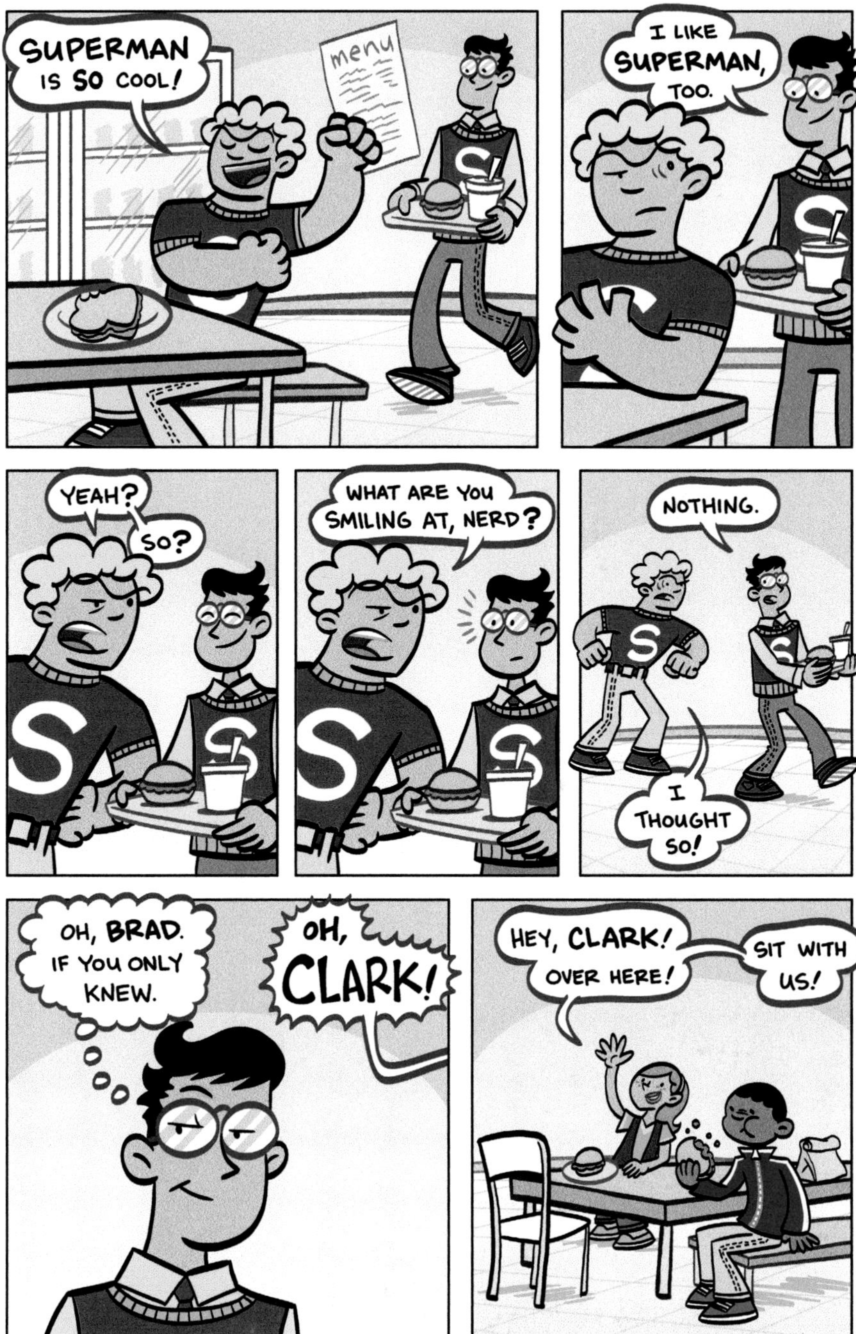
menu
SUPERMAN IS SO COOL!
I LIKE SUPERMAN, TOO.
YEAH?
SO?
WHAT ARE YOU SMILING AT, NERD?
NOTHING.
I THOUGHT SO!
OH, BRAD. IF YOU ONLY KNEW.
OH, CLARK!
HEY, CLARK! OVER HERE!
SIT WITH US!

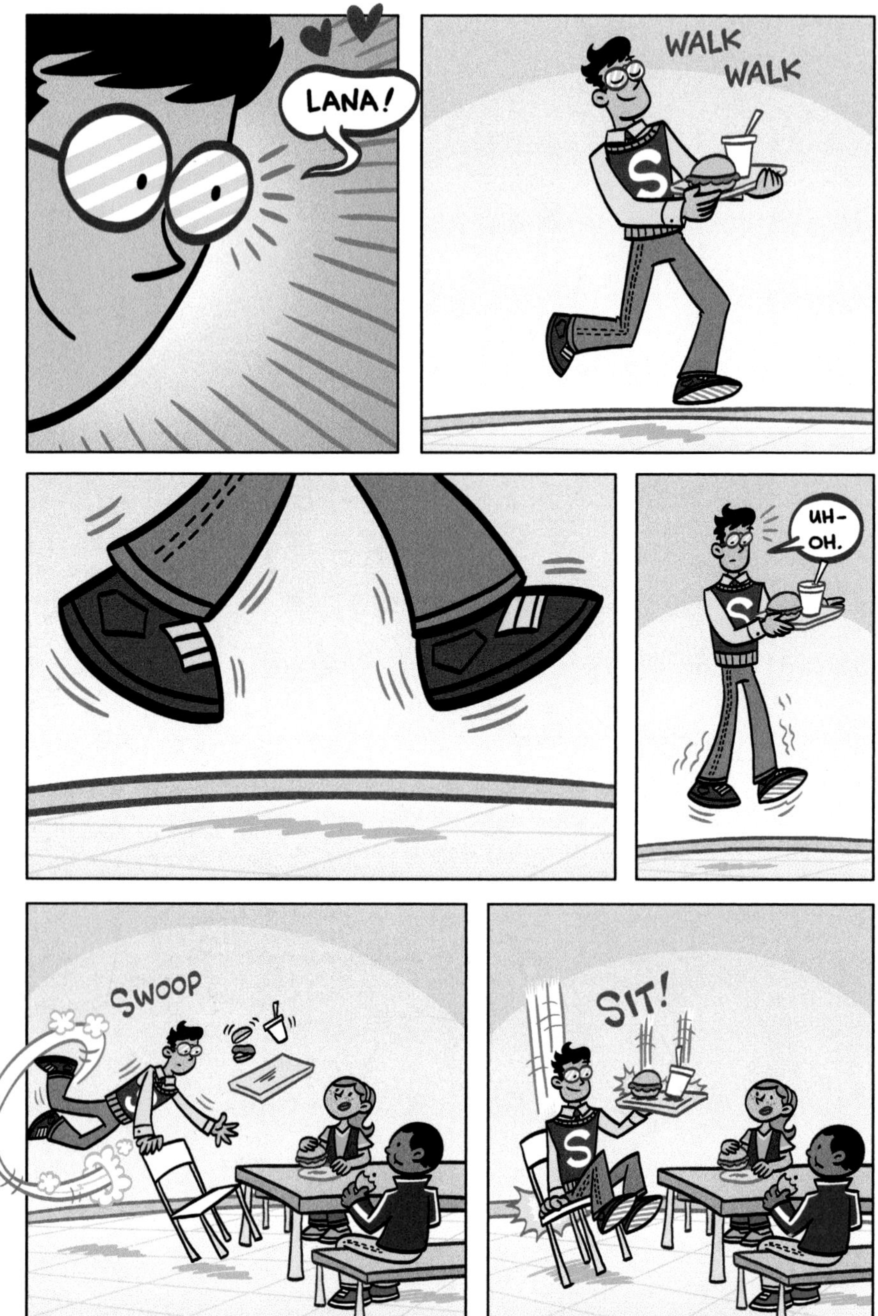
LANA!
WALK
WALK
UH-OH.
SWOOP
SIT!

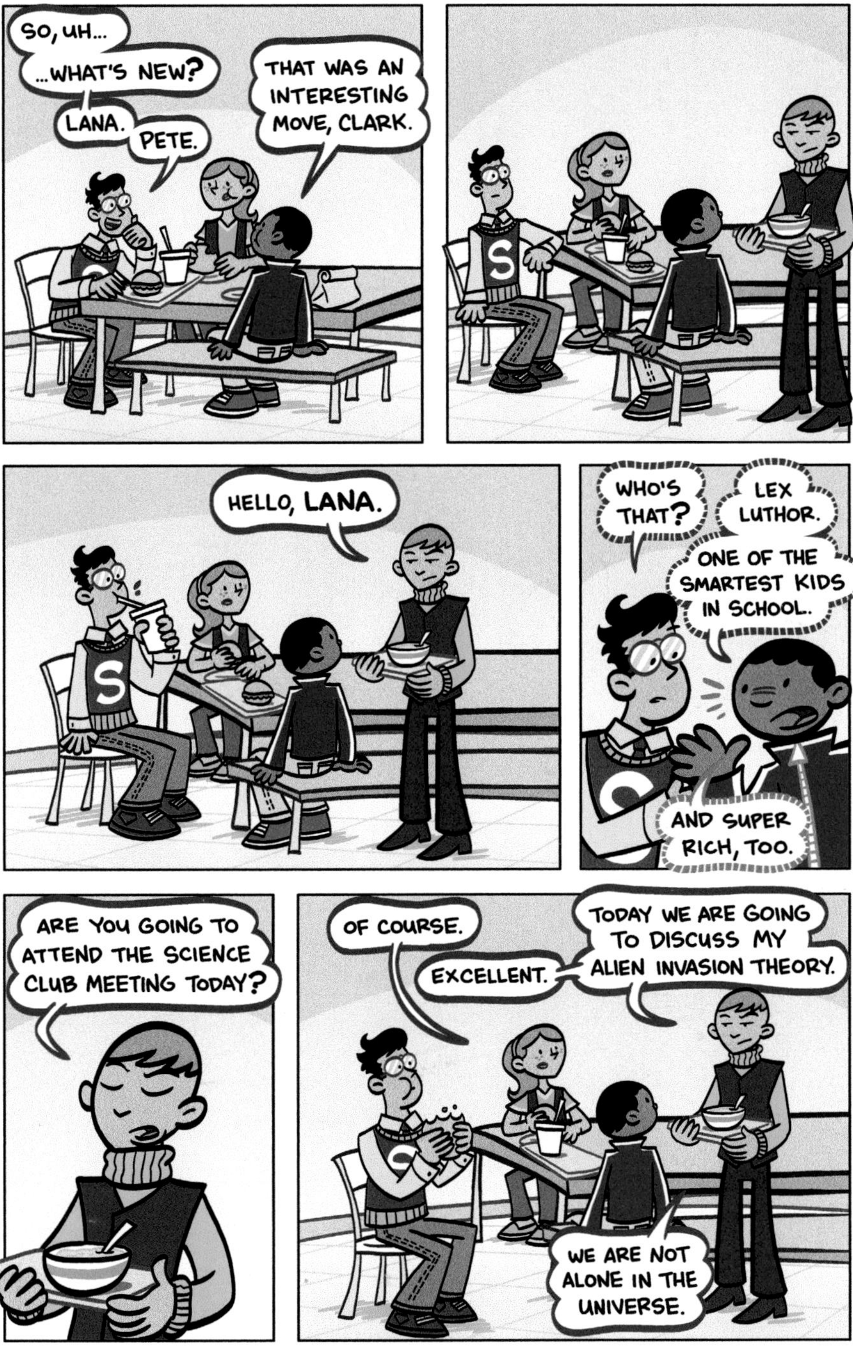
SO, UH...
...WHAT'S NEW?
LANA.
PETE.
THAT WAS AN INTERESTING MOVE, CLARK.
HELLO, LANA.
WHO'S THAT?
LEX LUTHOR.
ONE OF THE SMARTEST KIDS IN SCHOOL.
AND SUPER RICH, TOO.
ARE YOU GOING TO ATTEND THE SCIENCE CLUB MEETING TODAY?
OF COURSE.
EXCELLENT.
TODAY WE ARE GOING TO DISCUSS MY ALIEN INVASION THEORY.
WE ARE NOT ALONE IN THE UNIVERSE.

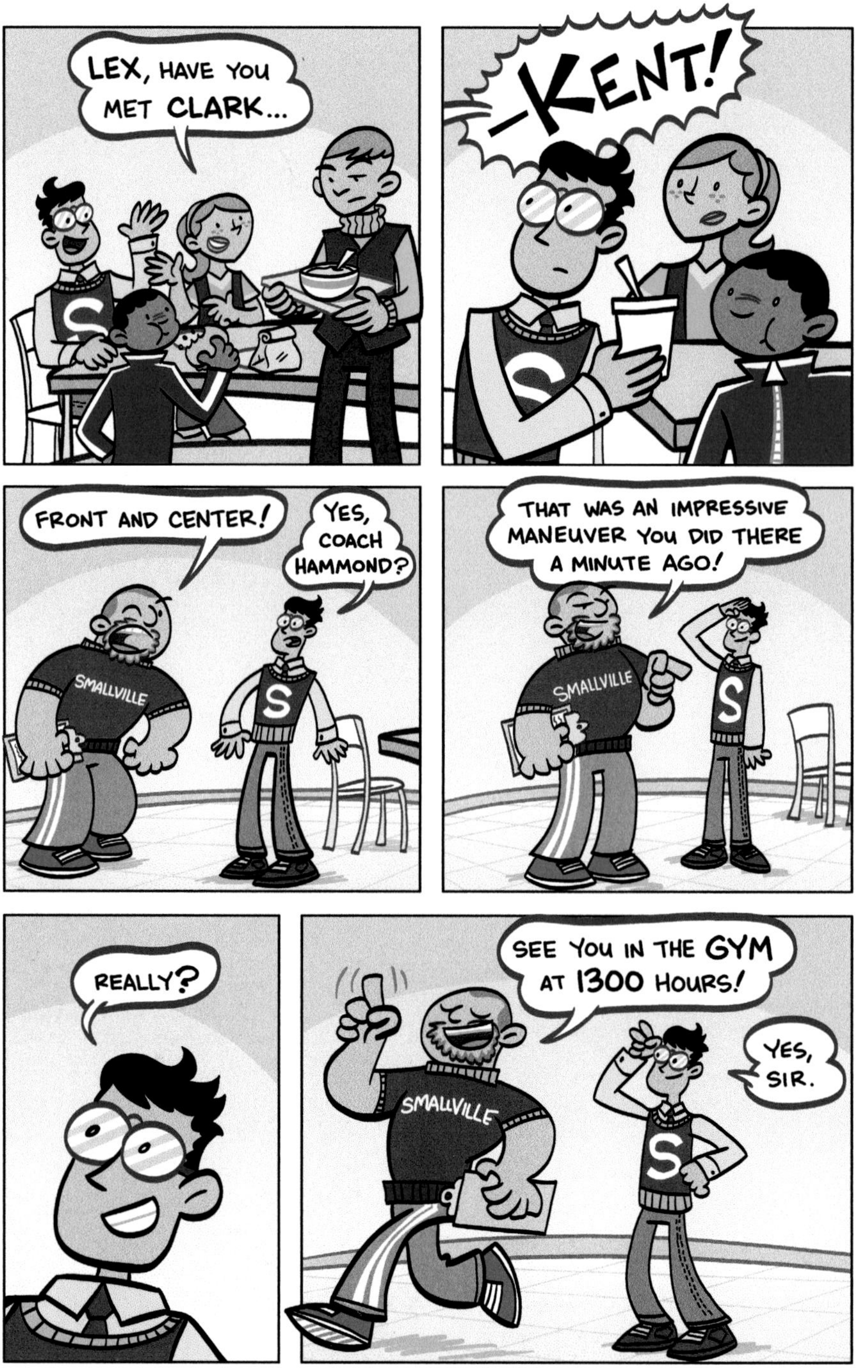
LEX, HAVE YOU MET CLARK...
-KENT!
FRONT AND CENTER!
YES, COACH HAMMOND?
THAT WAS AN IMPRESSIVE MANEUVER YOU DID THERE A MINUTE AGO!
REALLY?
SEE YOU IN THE GYM AT 1300 HOURS!
YES, SIR.

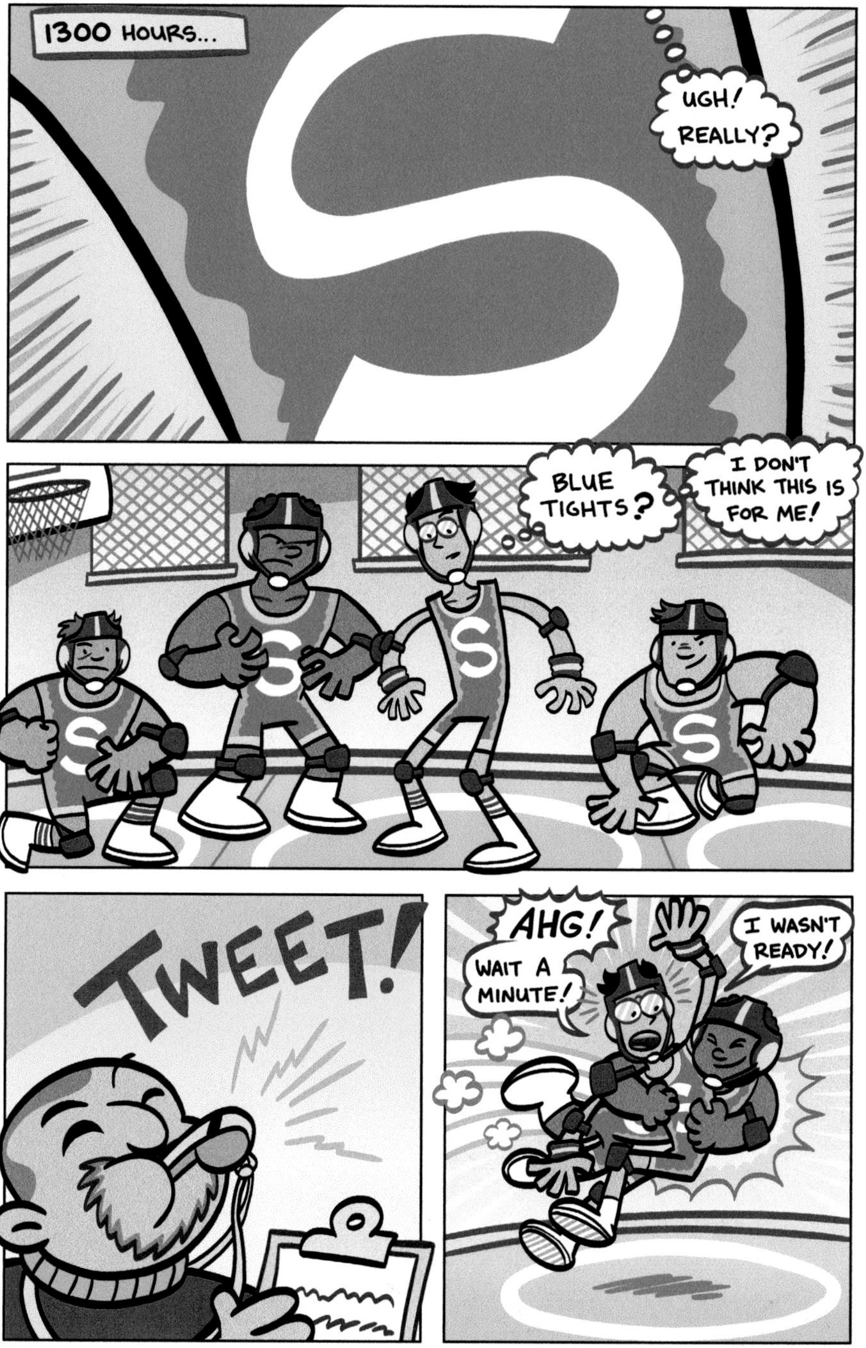
1300 HOURS...
UGH! REALLY?
BLUE TIGHTS?
I DON'T THINK THIS IS FOR ME!
TWEET!
AHG!
WAIT A MINUTE!
I WASN'T READY!

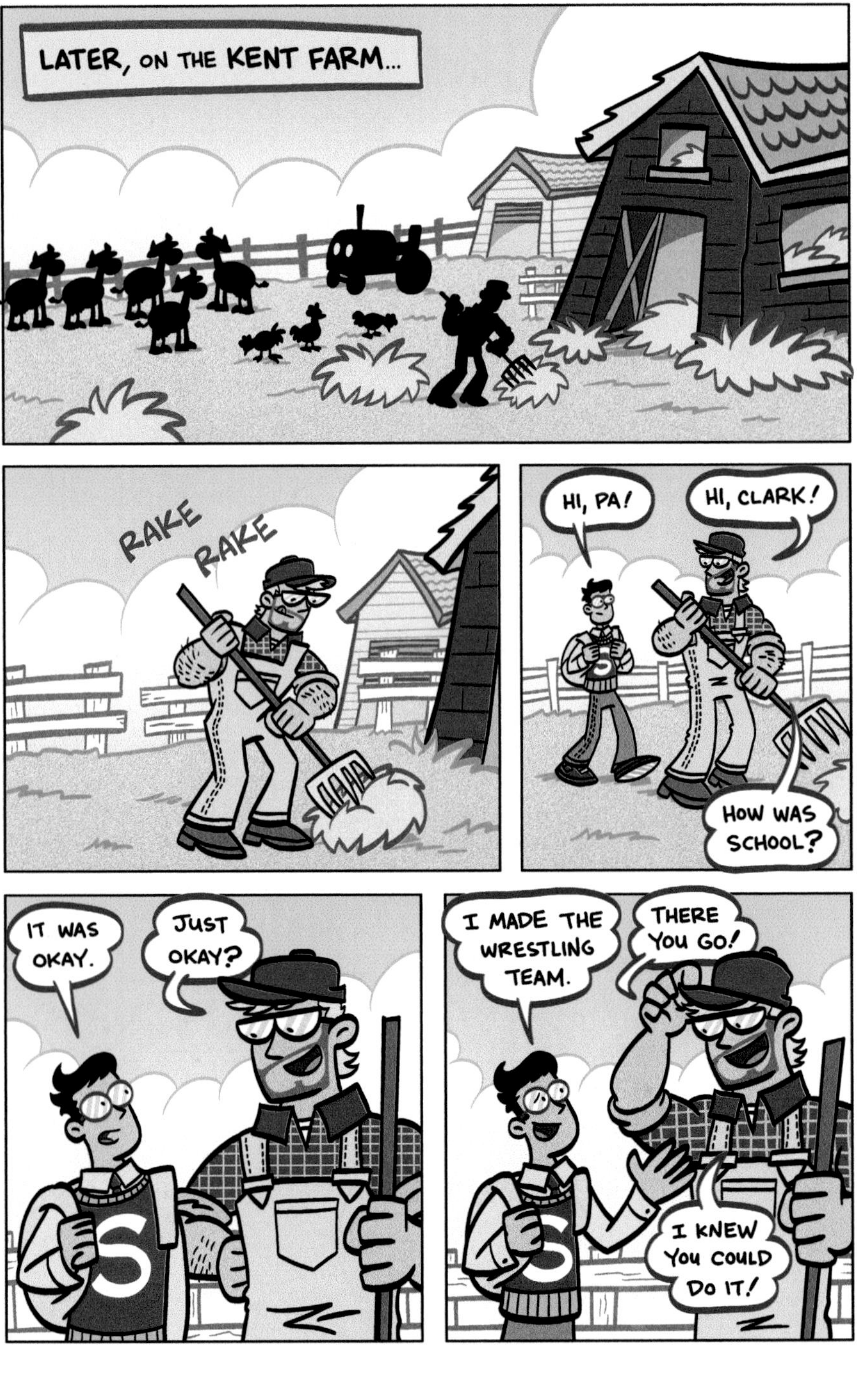
LATER, ON THE KENT FARM...
RAKE
RAKE
HI, PA!
HI, CLARK!
HOW WAS SCHOOL?
IT WAS OKAY.
JUST OKAY?
I MADE THE WRESTLING TEAM.
THERE YOU GO!
I KNEW YOU COULD DO IT!

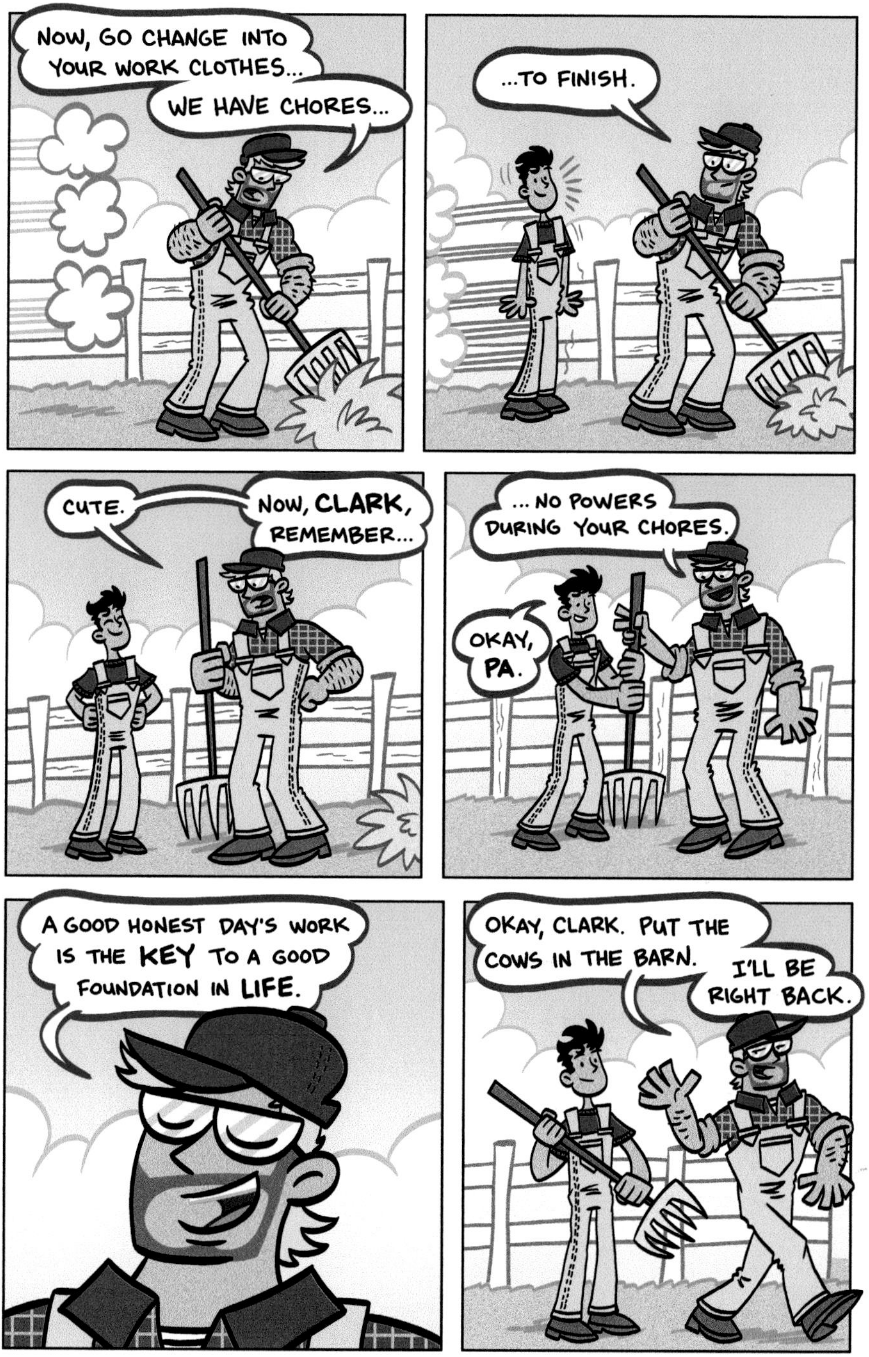
NOW, GO CHANGE INTO YOUR WORK CLOTHES...
WE HAVE CHORES...
...TO FINISH.
CUTE.
NOW, CLARK, REMEMBER...
... NO POWERS DURING YOUR CHORES.
OKAY, PA.
A GOOD HONEST DAY'S WORK IS THE KEY TO A GOOD FOUNDATION IN LIFE.
OKAY, CLARK. PUT THE COWS IN THE BARN.
I'LL BE RIGHT BACK.

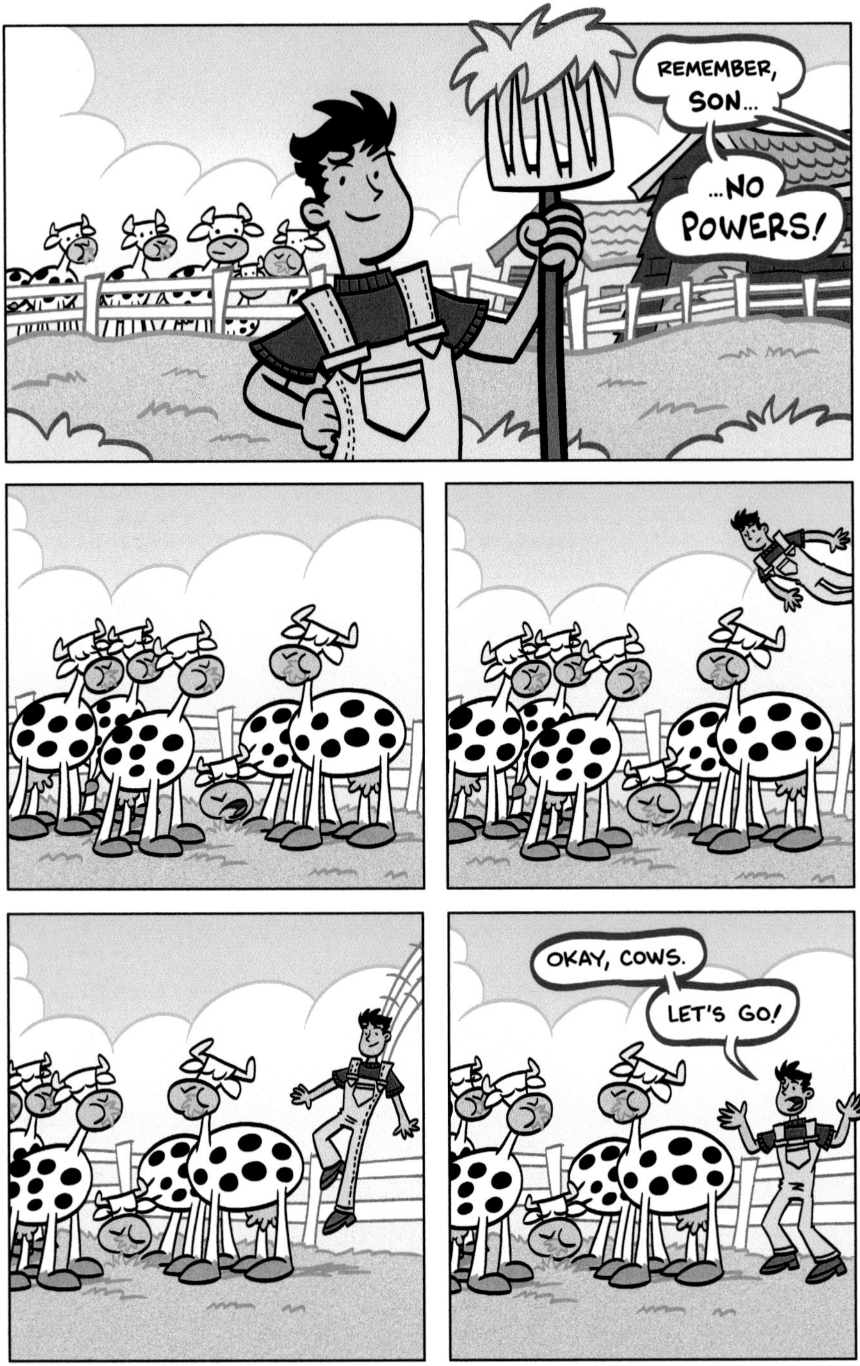
REMEMBER, SON...
...NO POWERS!
OKAY, COWS.
LET'S GO!

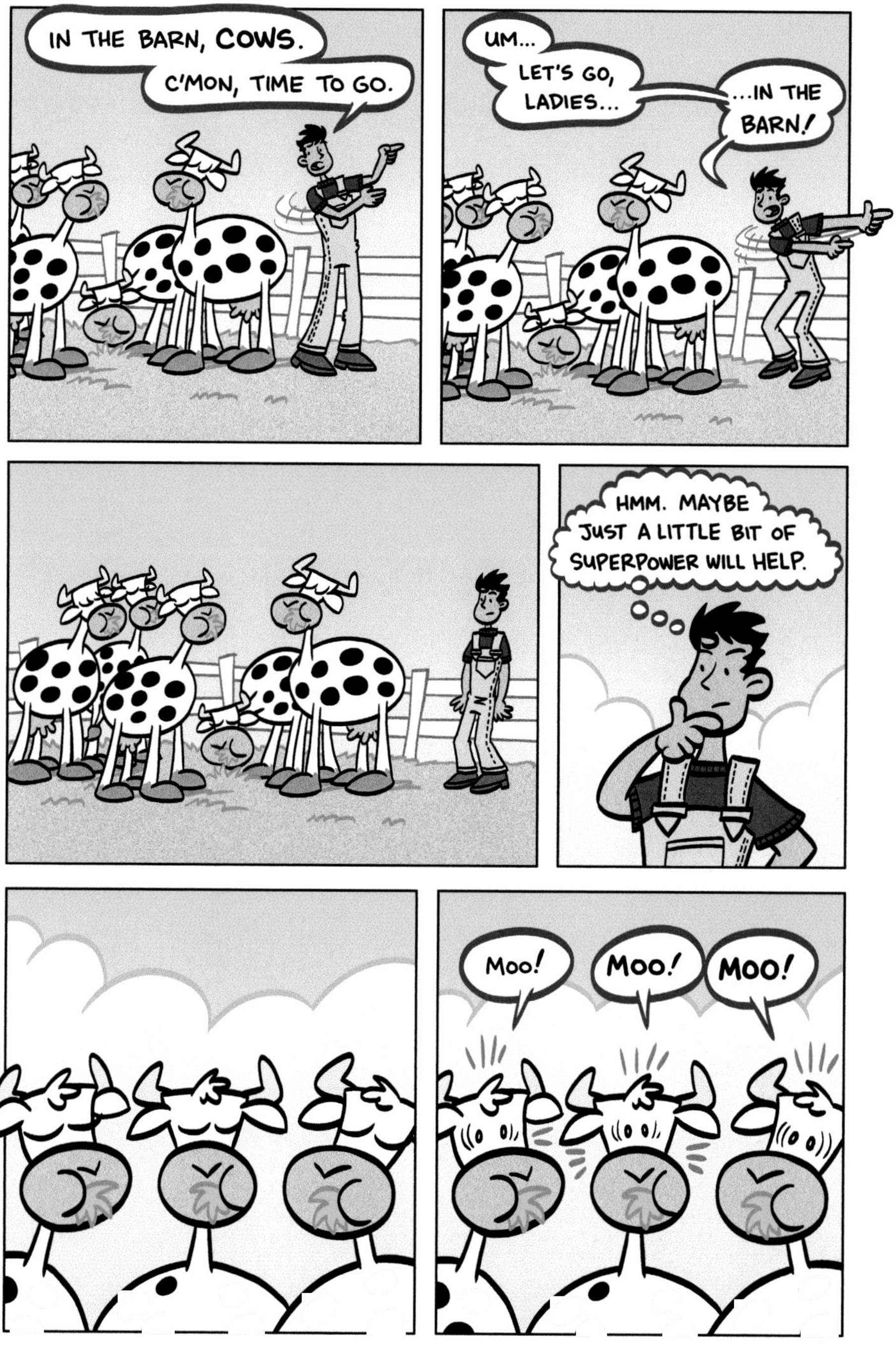
IN THE BARN, COWS.
C'MON, TIME TO GO.
UM...
LET'S GO, LADIES...
...IN THE BARN!
HMM. MAYBE JUST A LITTLE BIT OF SUPERPOWER WILL HELP.
Moo!
MOO!
MOO!

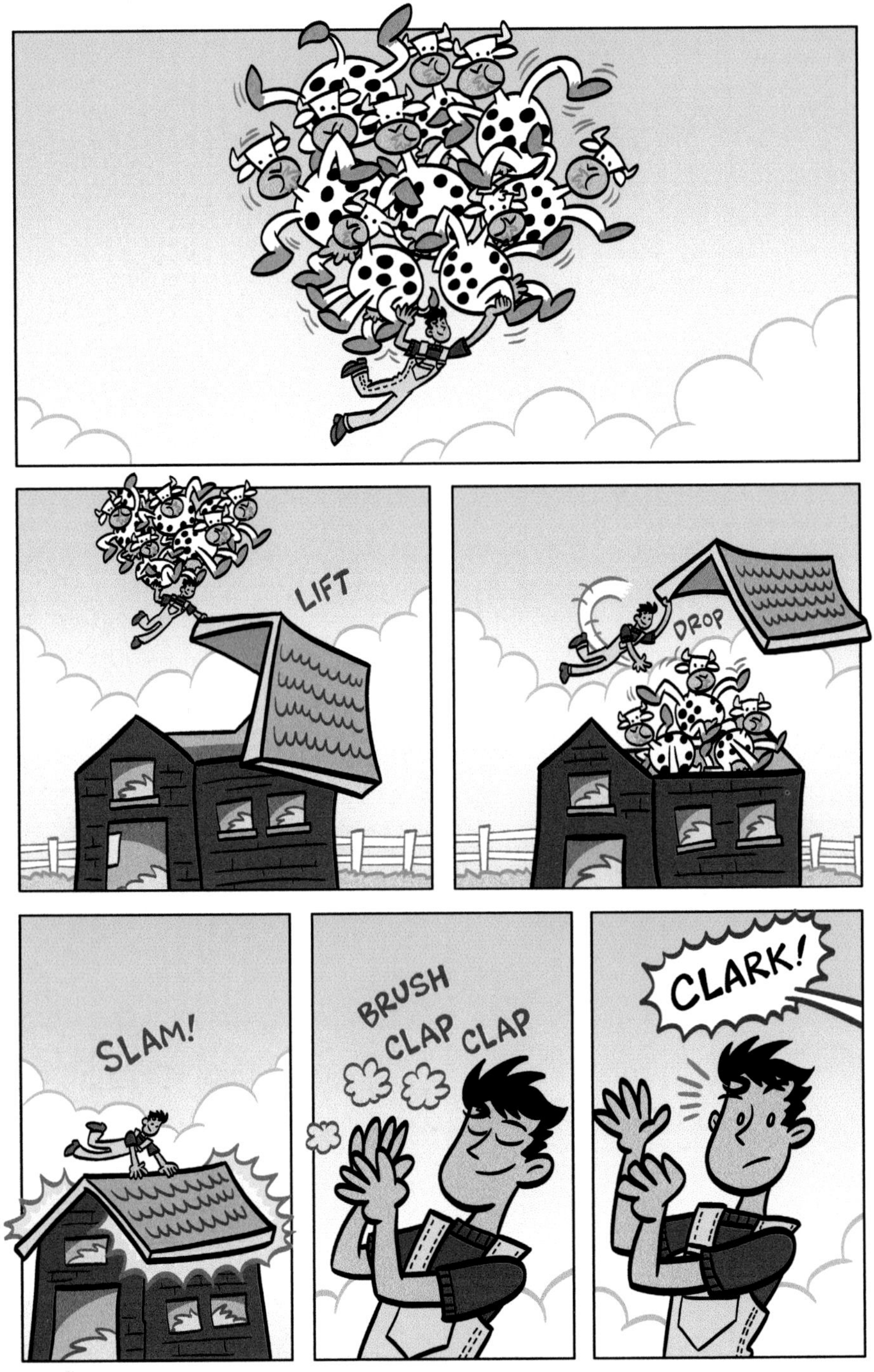
LIFT
DROP
SLAM!
BRUSH
CLAP
CLAP
CLARK!

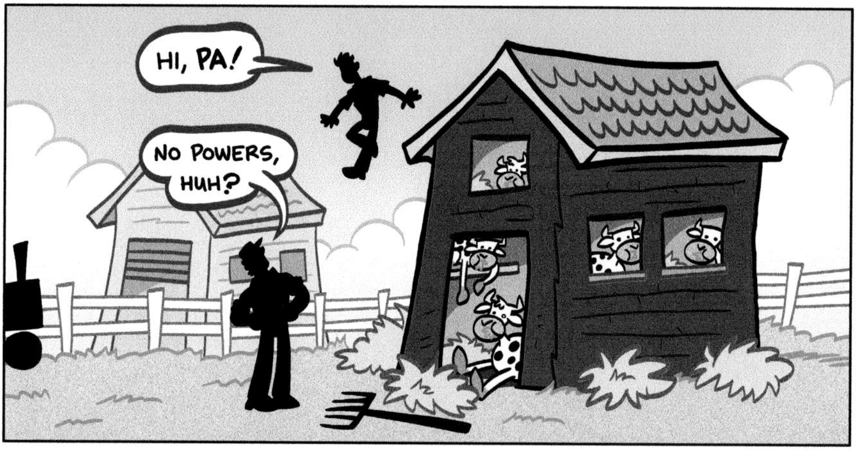
HI, PA!
NO POWERS, HUH?

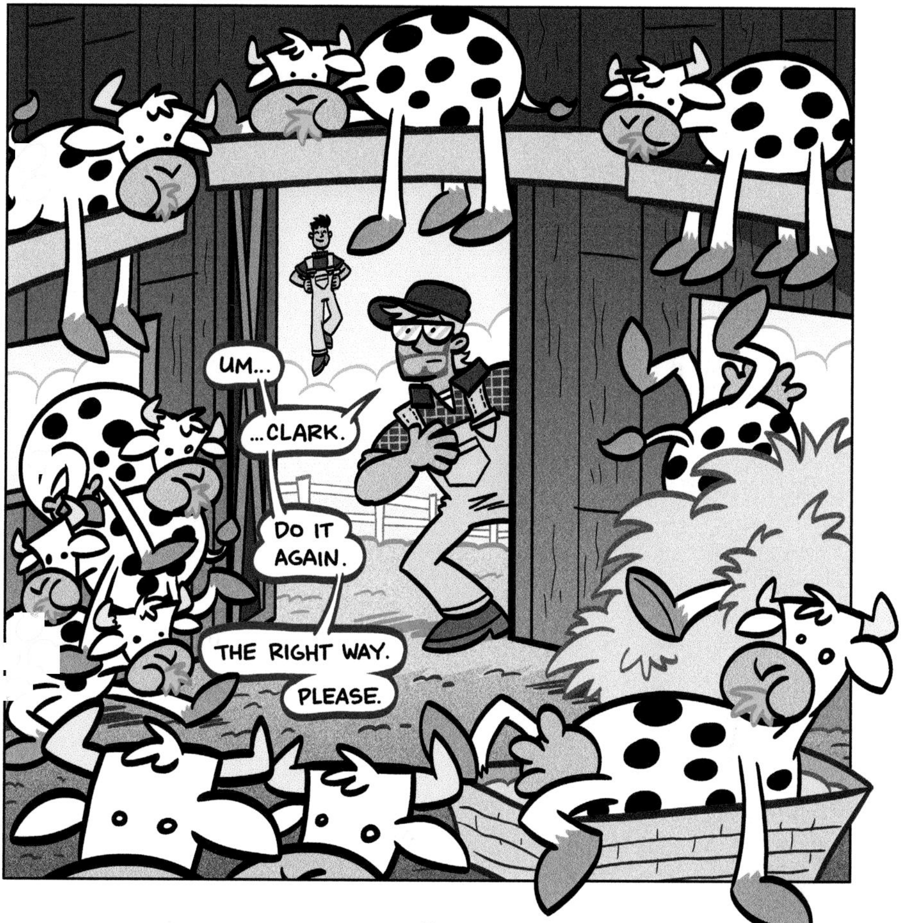
UM...
...CLARK.
DO IT AGAIN.
THE RIGHT WAY.
PLEASE.

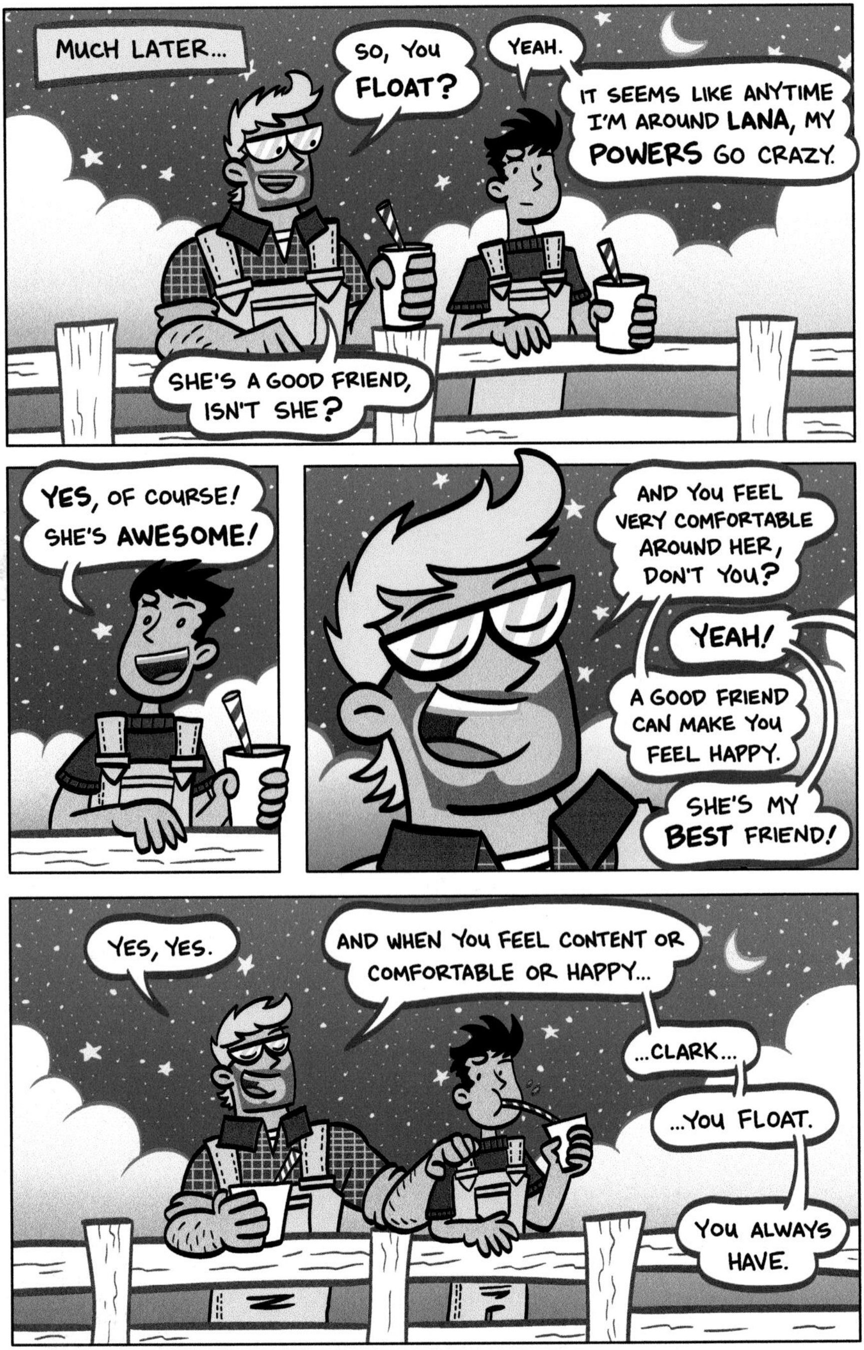
MUCH LATER...
SO, YOU FLOAT?
YEAH.
IT SEEMS LIKE ANYTIME I'M AROUND LANA, MY POWERS GO CRAZY.
SHE'S A GOOD FRIEND, ISN'T SHE?
YES, OF COURSE! SHE'S AWESOME!
AND YOU FEEL VERY COMFORTABLE AROUND HER, DON'T YOU?
YEAH!
A GOOD FRIEND CAN MAKE YOU FEEL HAPPY.
SHE'S MY BEST FRIEND!
YES, YES.
AND WHEN YOU FEEL CONTENT OR COMFORTABLE OR HAPPY...
...CLARK...
...YOU FLOAT.
YOU ALWAYS HAVE.

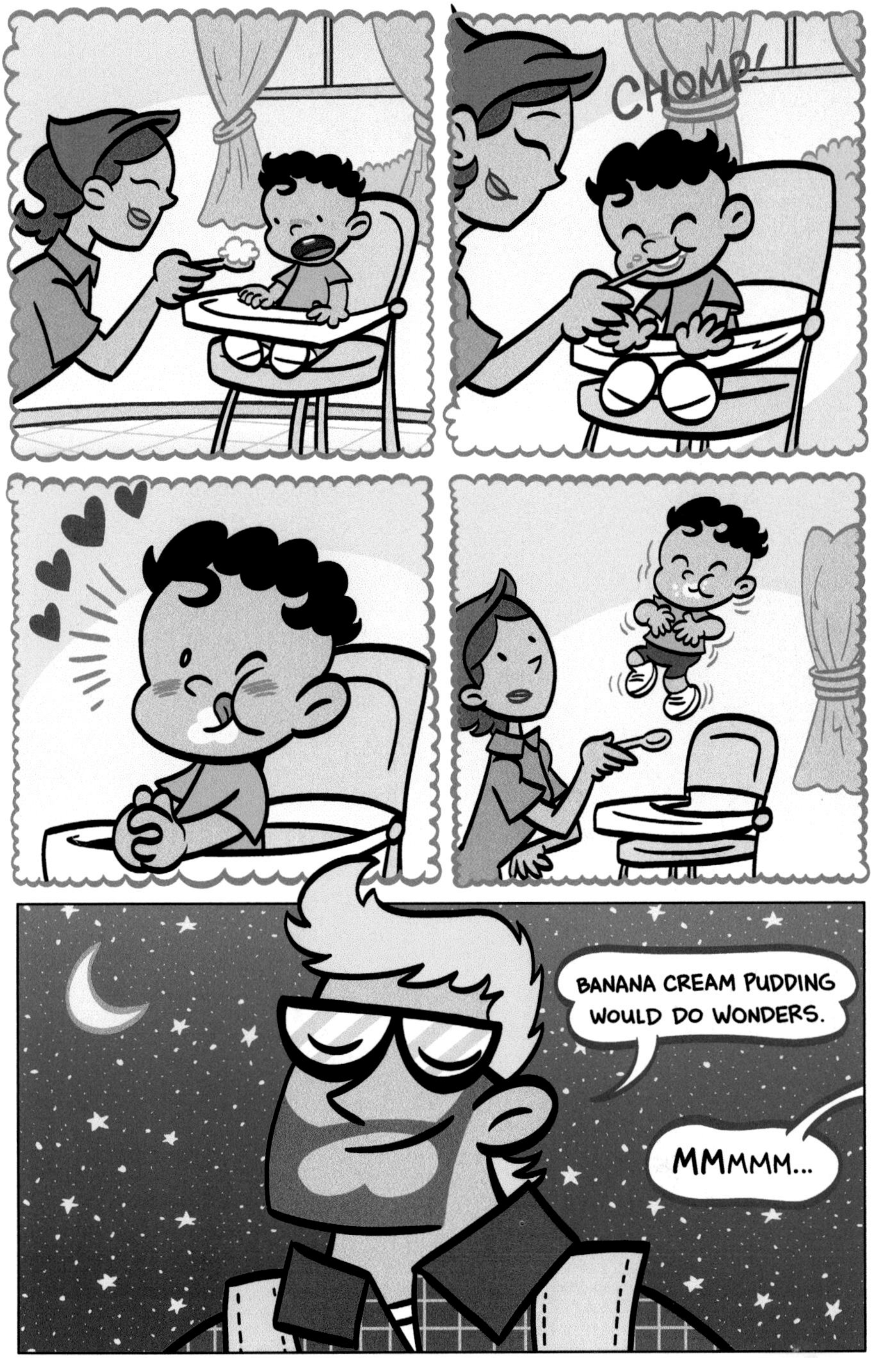
CHOMP!
BANANA CREAM PUDDING WOULD DO WONDERS.
MMMMM...

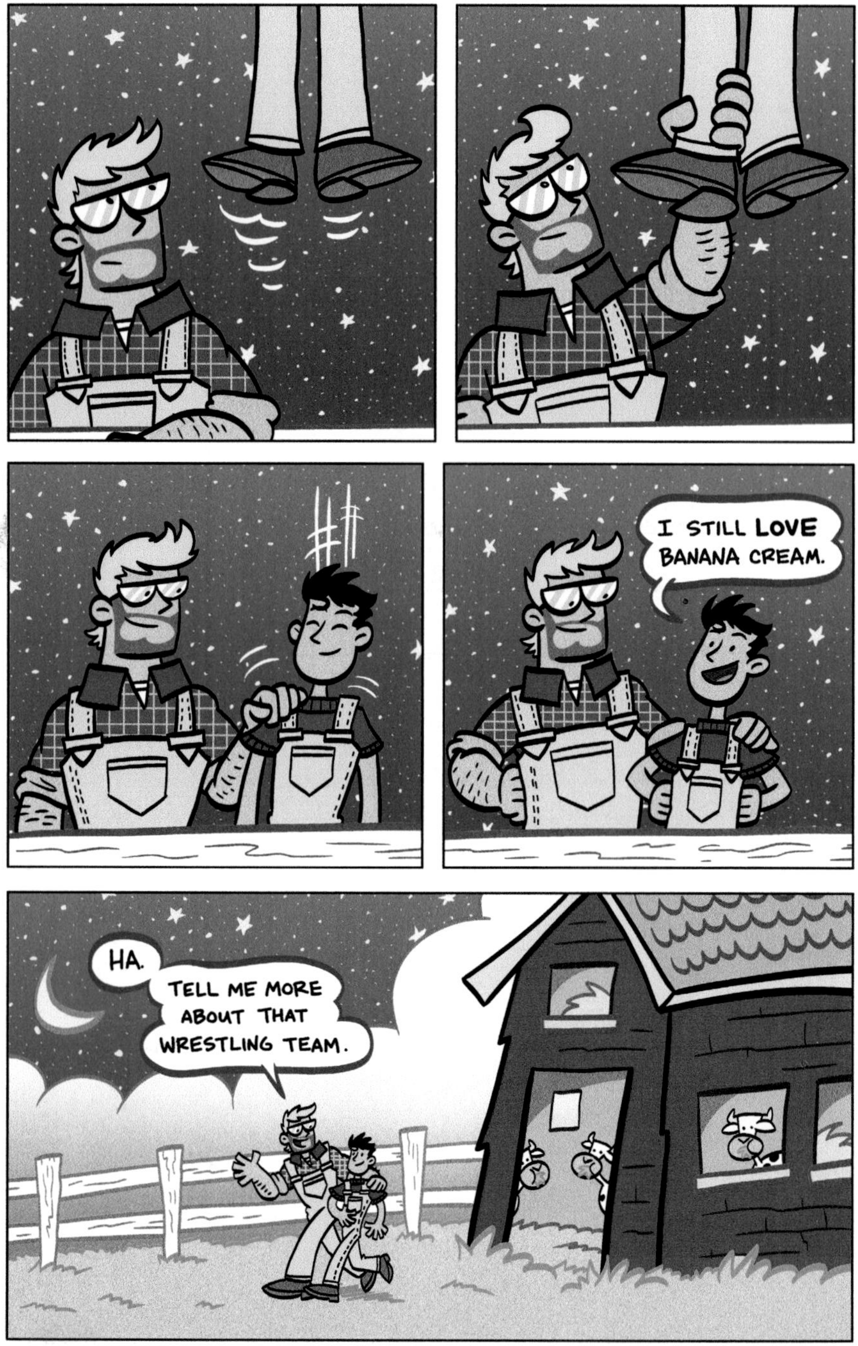
I STILL LOVE BANANA CREAM.
HA.
TELL ME MORE ABOUT THAT WRESTLING TEAM.

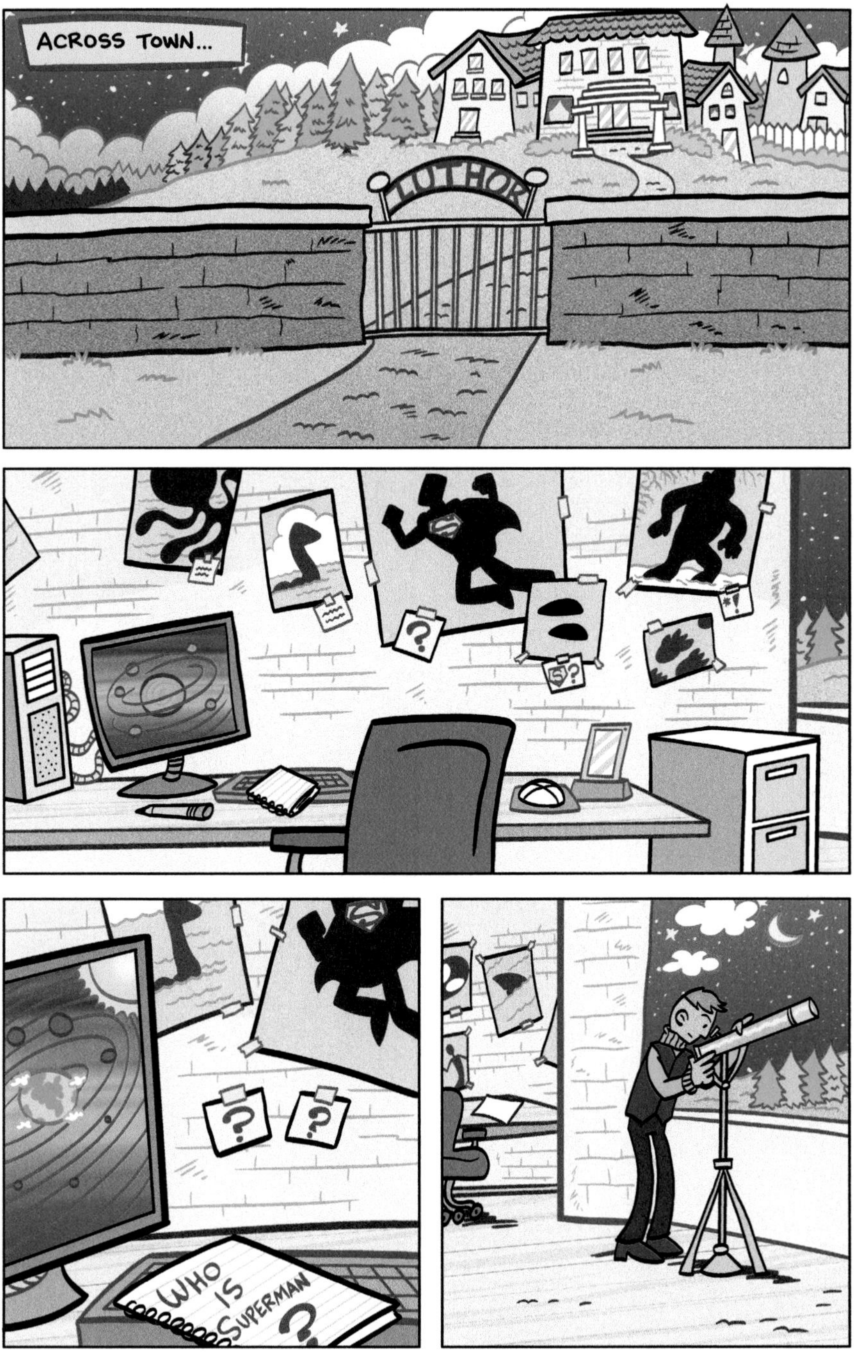
ACROSS TOWN...
LUTHOR
WHO IS SUPERMAN ?

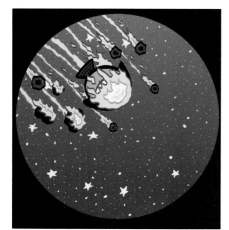

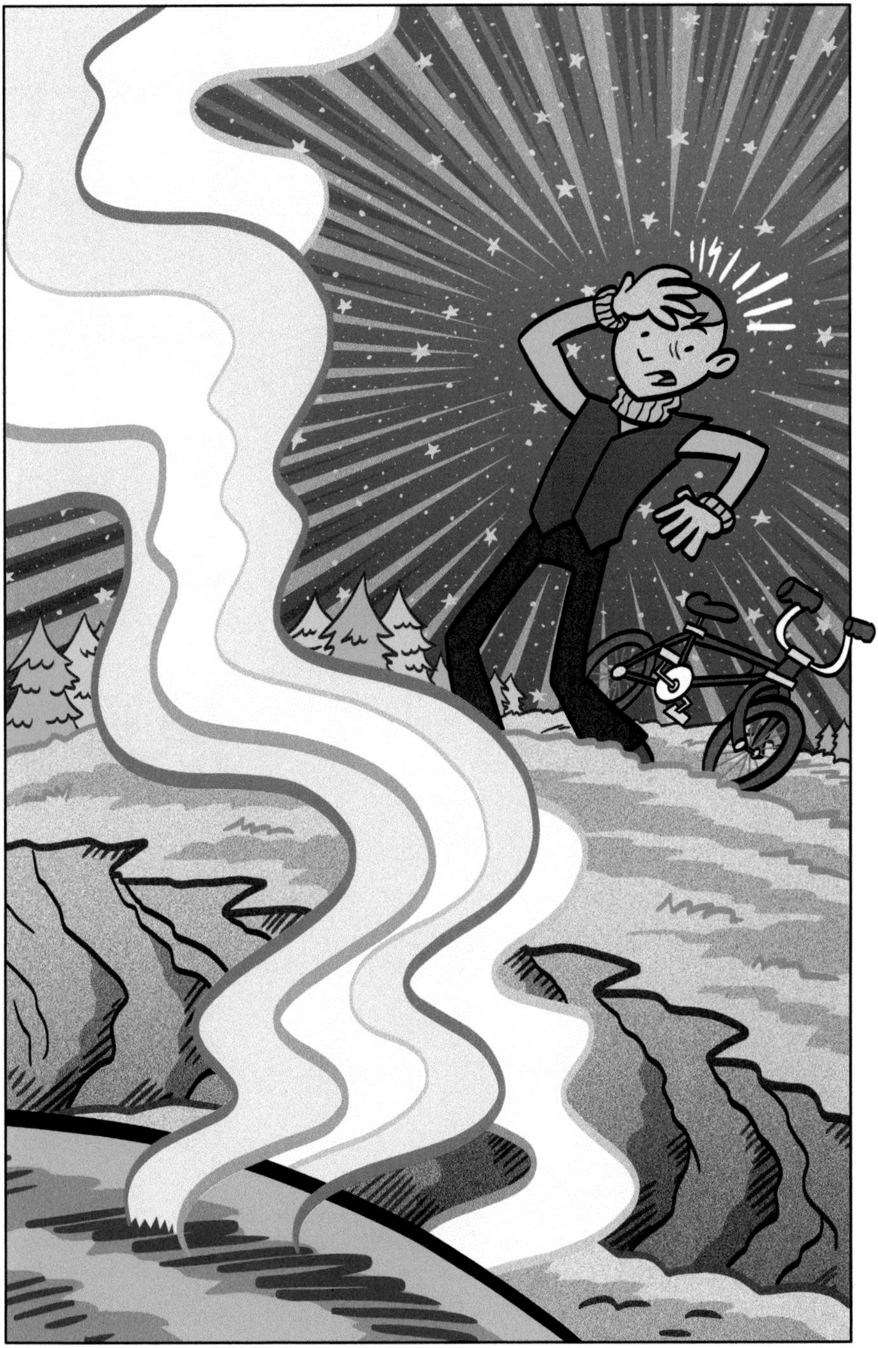

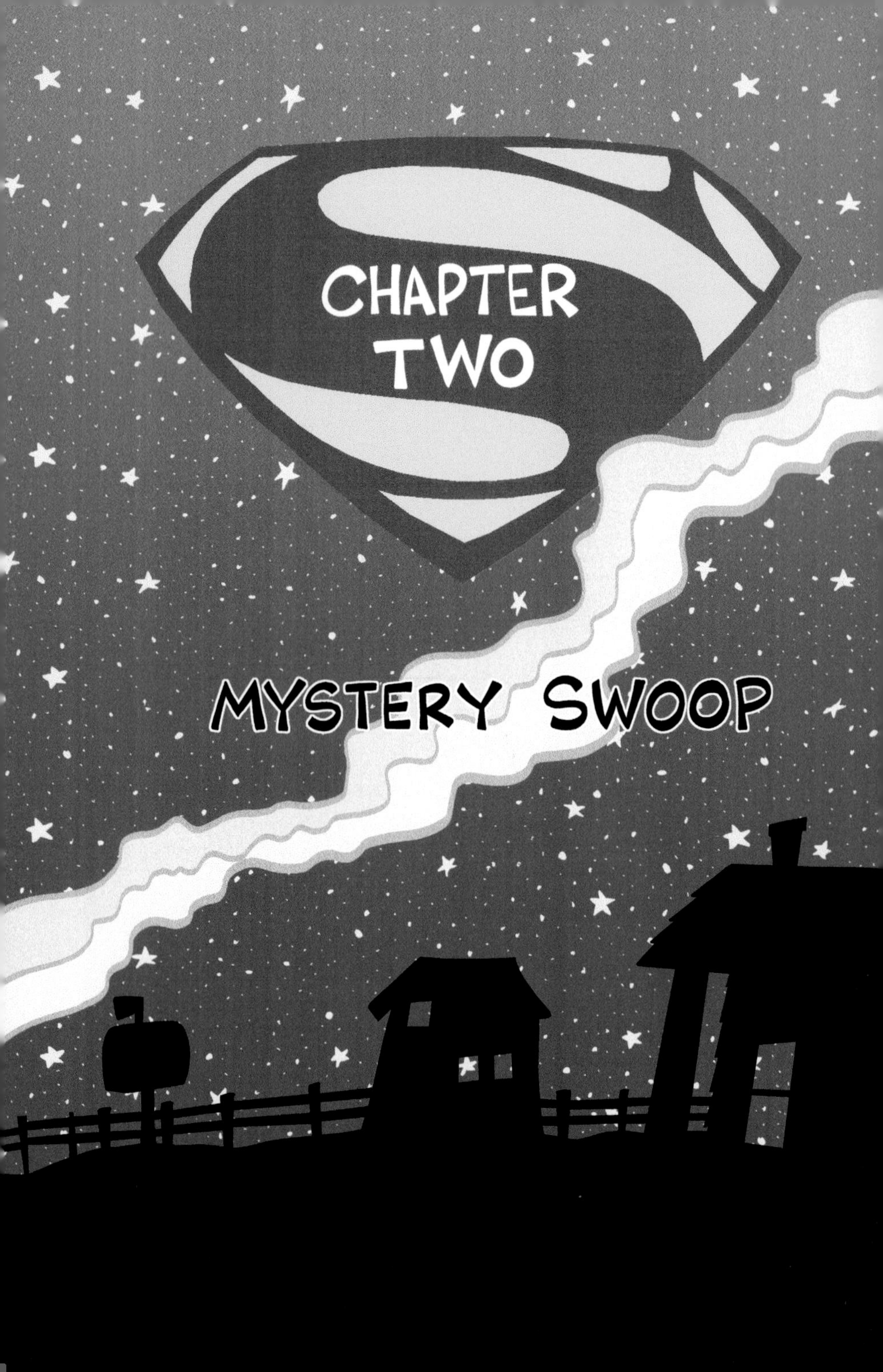
CHAPTER
TWO
MYSTERY SWOOP

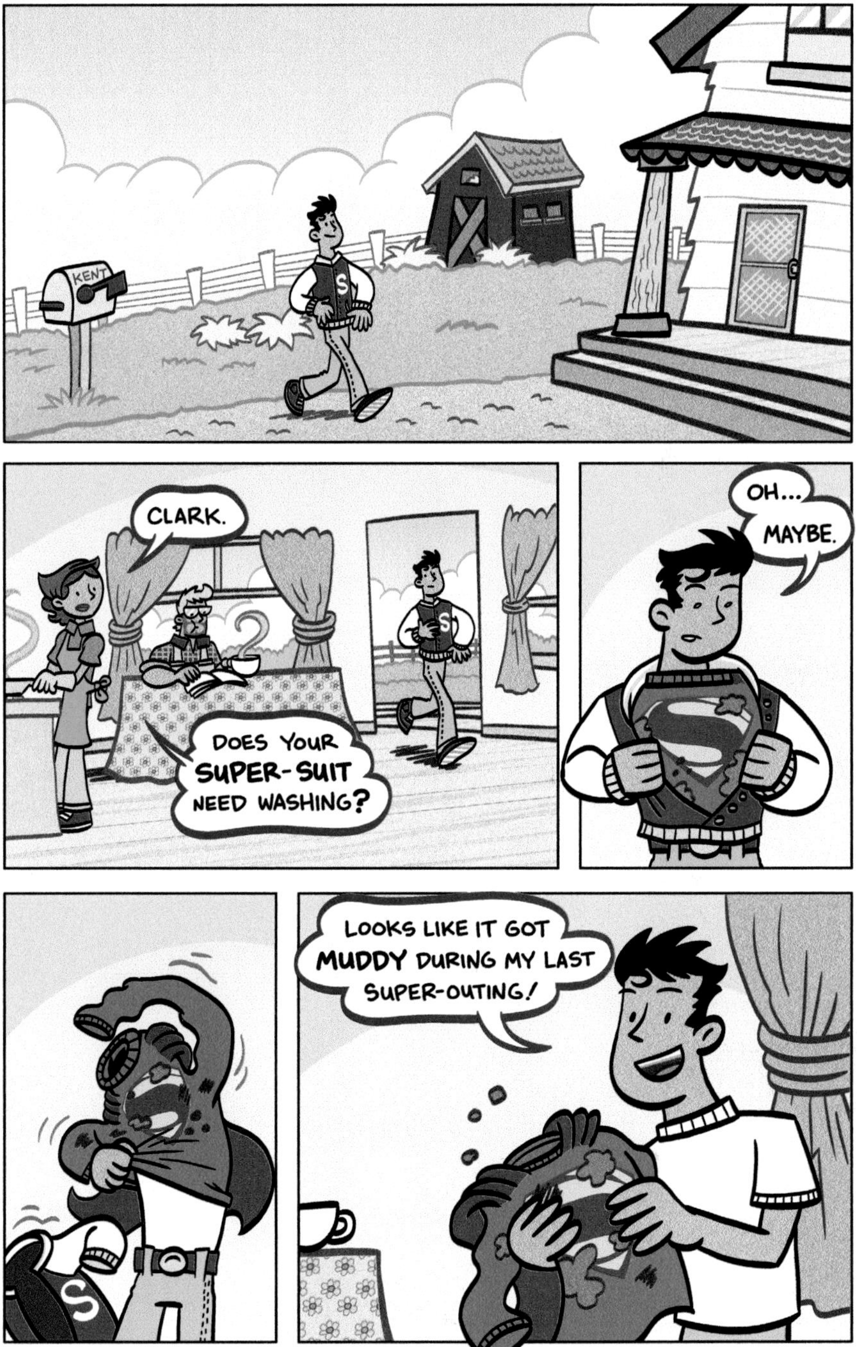
CLARK.
DOES YOUR SUPER-SUIT NEED WASHING?
OH... MAYBE.
LOOKS LIKE IT GOT MUDDY DURING MY LAST SUPER-OUTING!

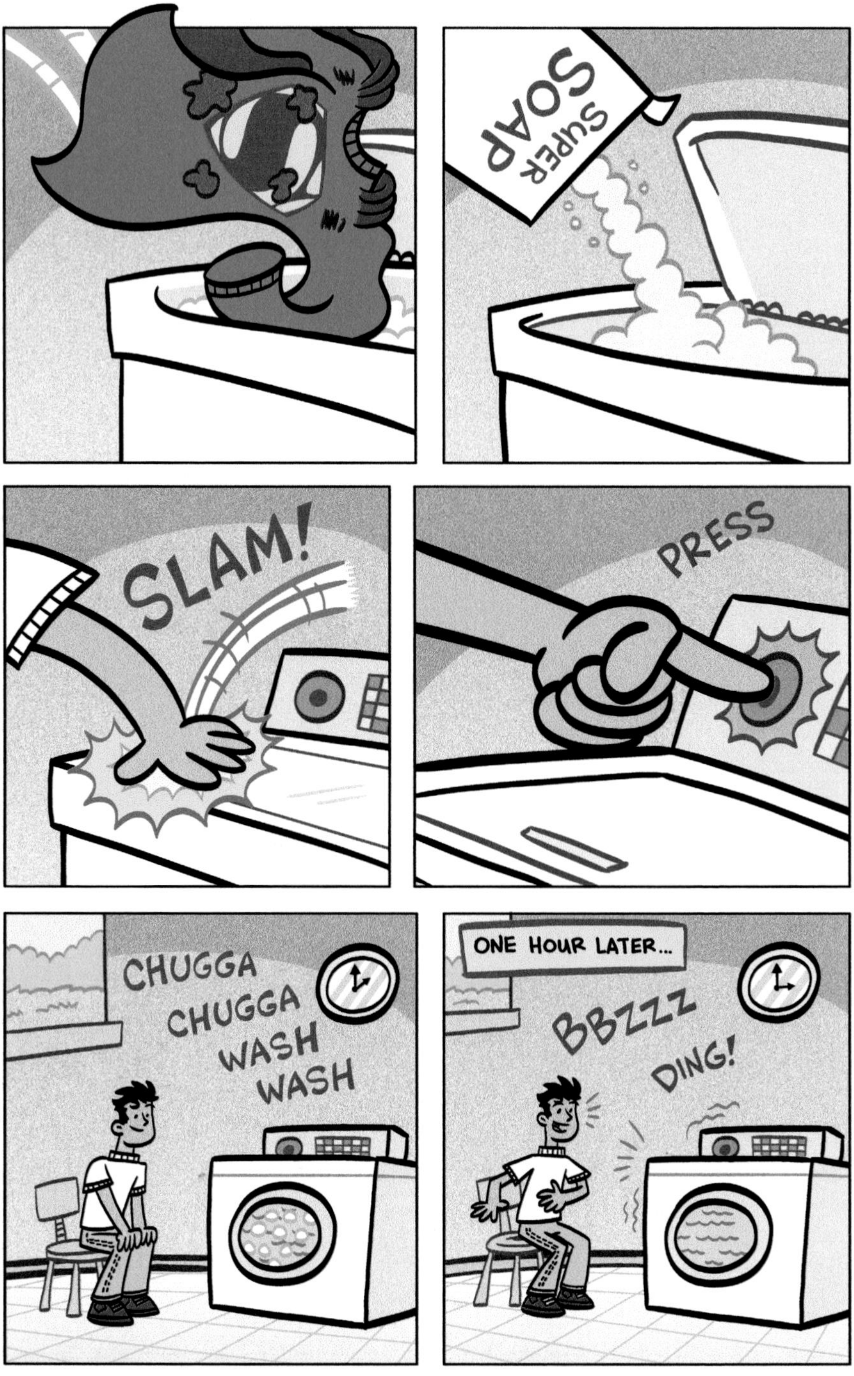
SUPER
SOAP
SLAM!
PRESS
CHUGGA
CHUGGA
WASH
WASH
ONE HOUR LATER...
BBZZZ
DING!

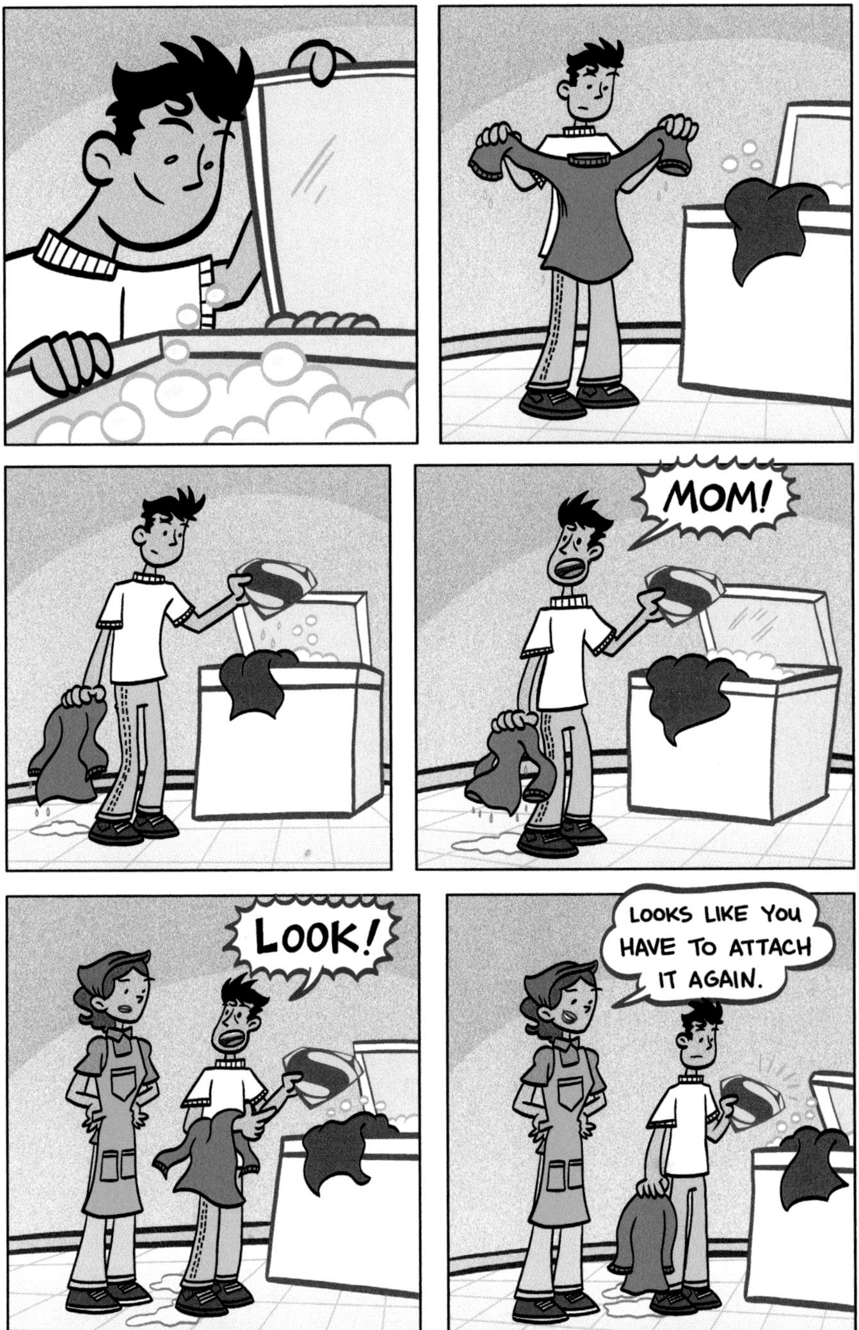
MOM!
LOOK!
LOOKS LIKE YOU HAVE TO ATTACH IT AGAIN.

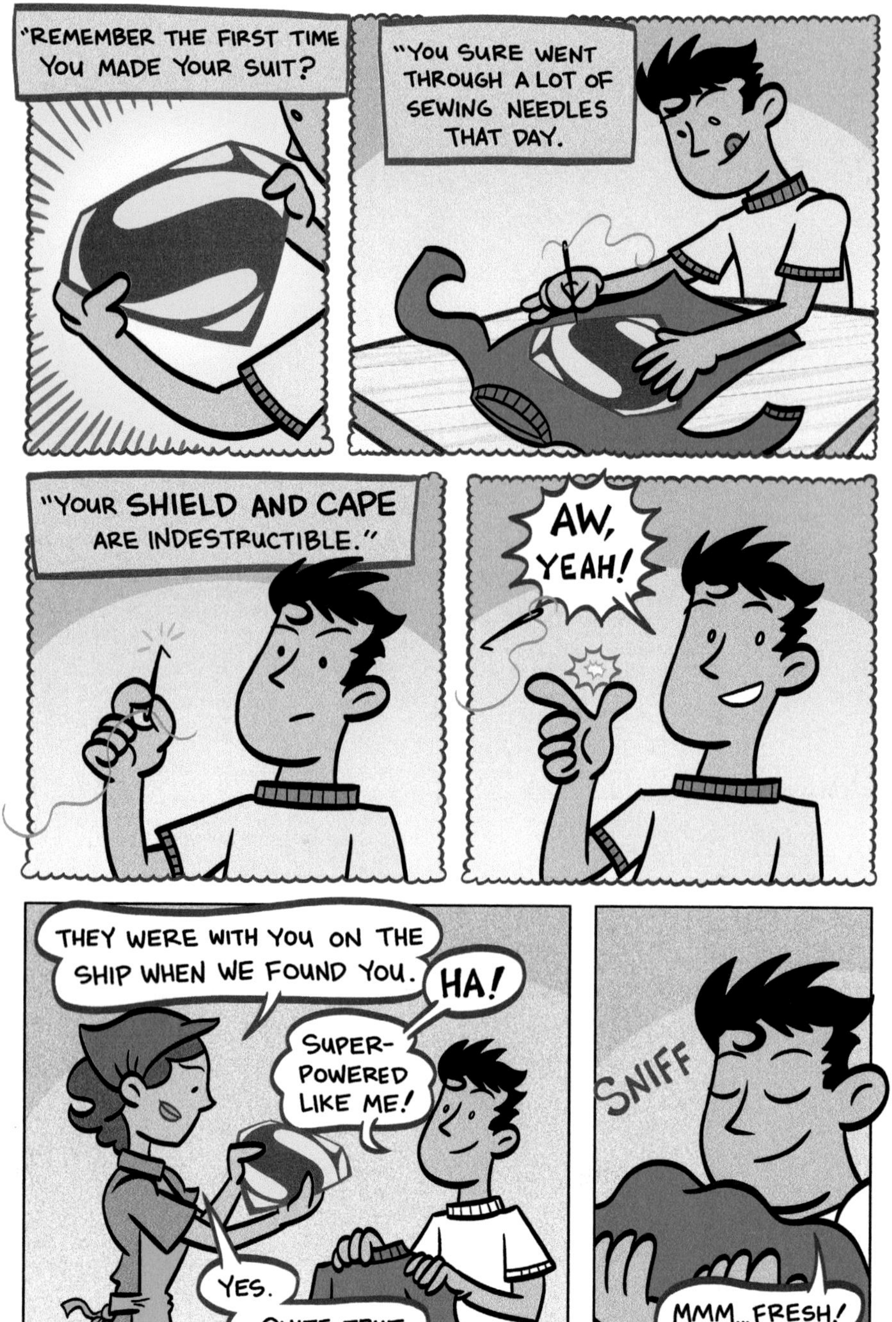
"REMEMBER THE FIRST TIME YOU MADE YOUR SUIT?
"YOU SURE WENT THROUGH A LOT OF SEWING NEEDLES THAT DAY.
"YOUR SHIELD AND CAPE ARE INDESTRUCTIBLE."
AW, YEAH!
THEY WERE WITH YOU ON THE SHIP WHEN WE FOUND YOU.
HA!
SUPER-POWERED LIKE ME!
YES.
QUITE TRUE.
SNIFF
MMM...FRESH!

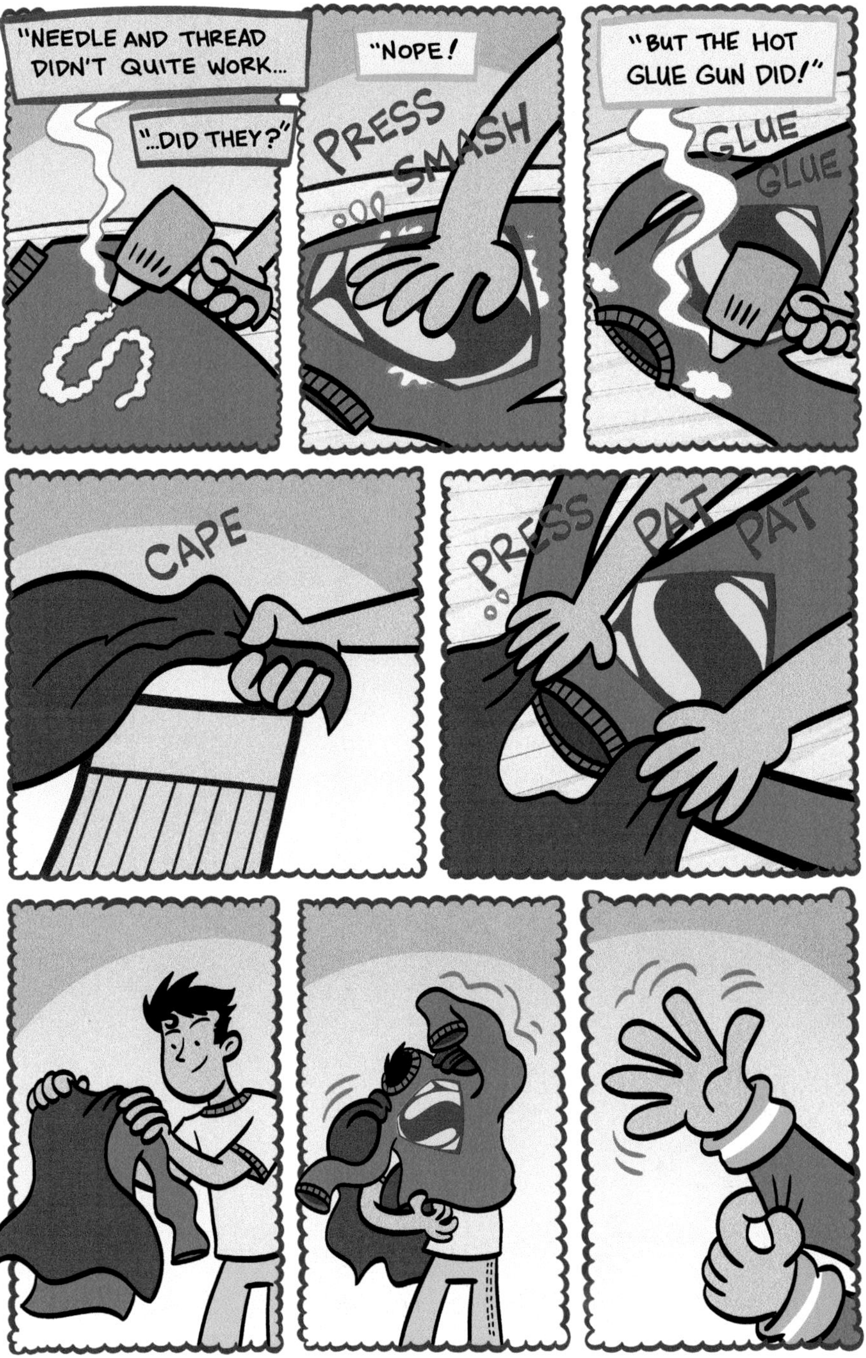
"NEEDLE AND THREAD DIDN'T QUITE WORK...
"...DID THEY?"
"NOPE!
PRESS
SMASH
"BUT THE HOT GLUE GUN DID!"
GLUE
GLUE
CAPE
PRESS
PAT
PAT

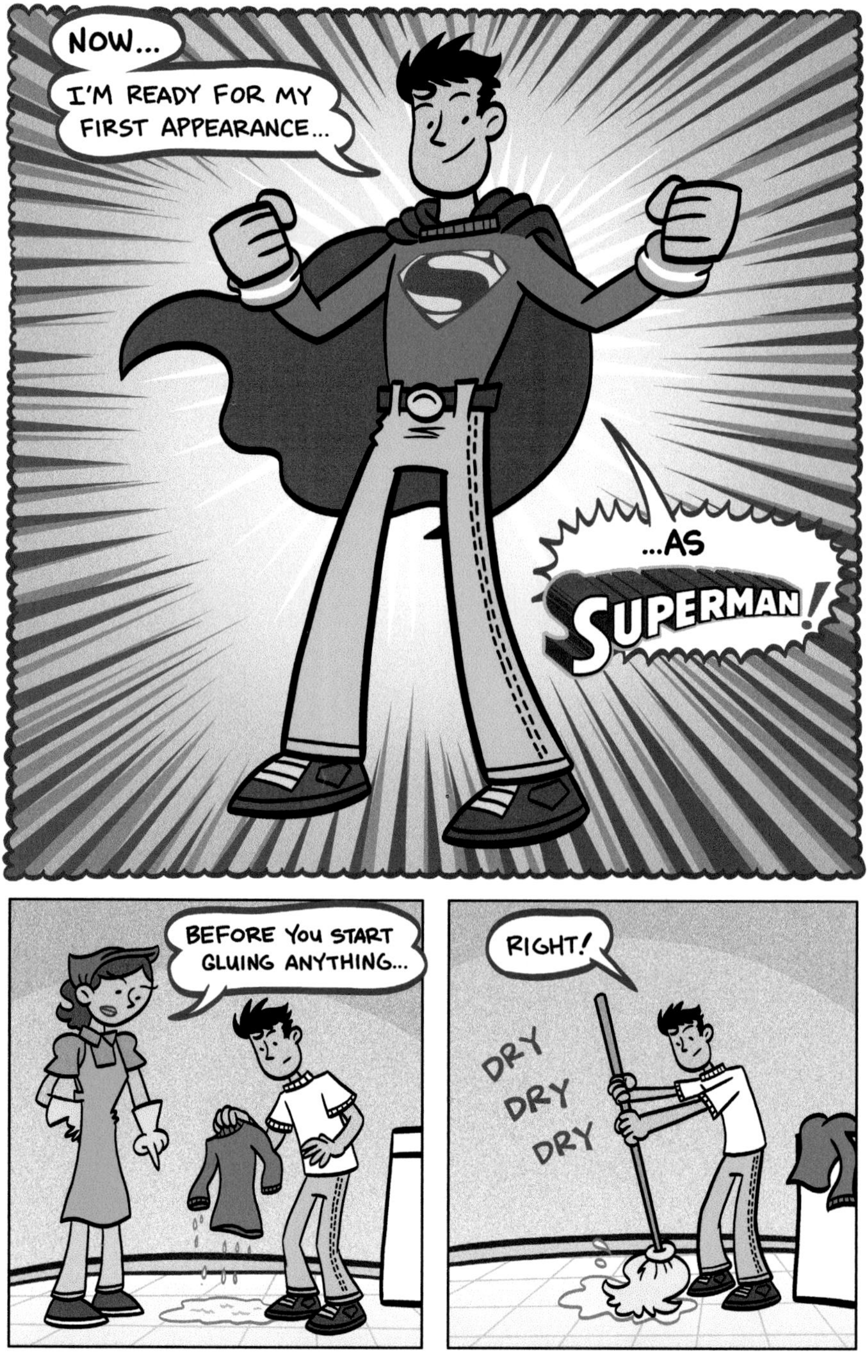
NOW...
I'M READY FOR MY FIRST APPEARANCE...
...AS
SUPERMAN!
BEFORE YOU START GLUING ANYTHING...
RIGHT!
DRY
DRY
DRY

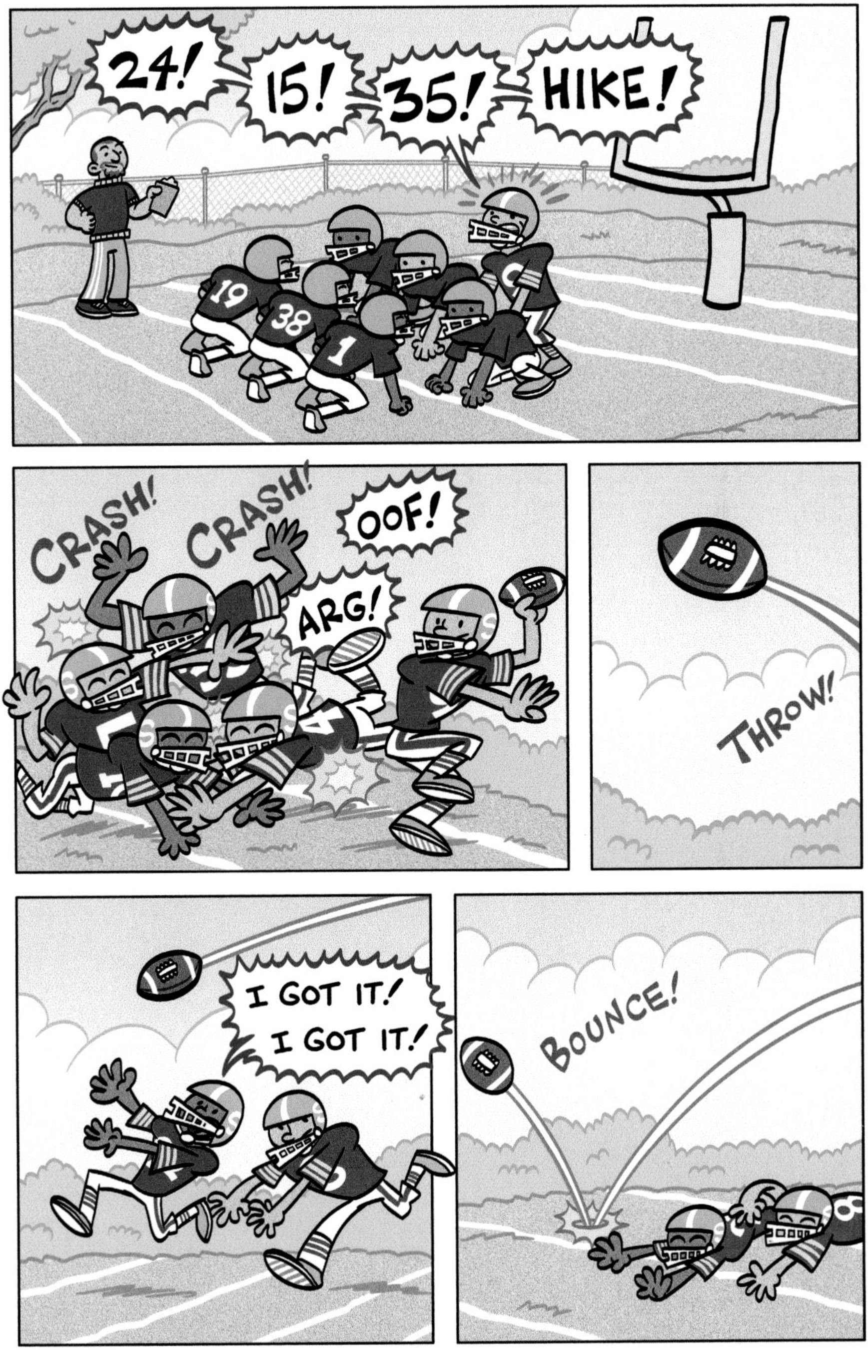
24!
15!
35!
HIKE!
CRASH!
CRASH!
OOF!
ARG!
THROW!
I GOT IT!
I GOT IT!
BOUNCE!

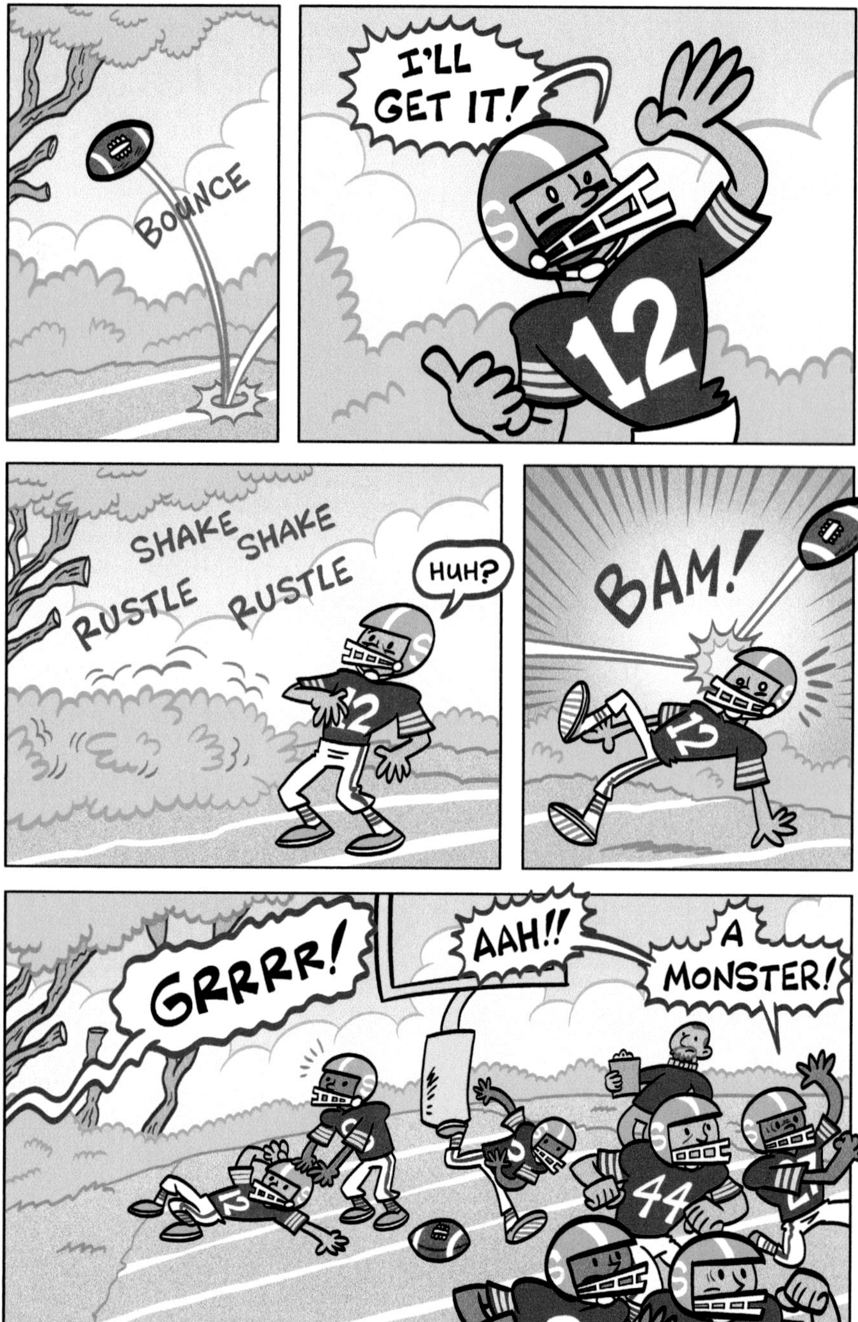
BOUNCE
I'LL GET IT!
SHAKE SHAKE
RUSTLE RUSTLE
HUH?
BAM!
GRRRR!
AAH!!
A MONSTER!

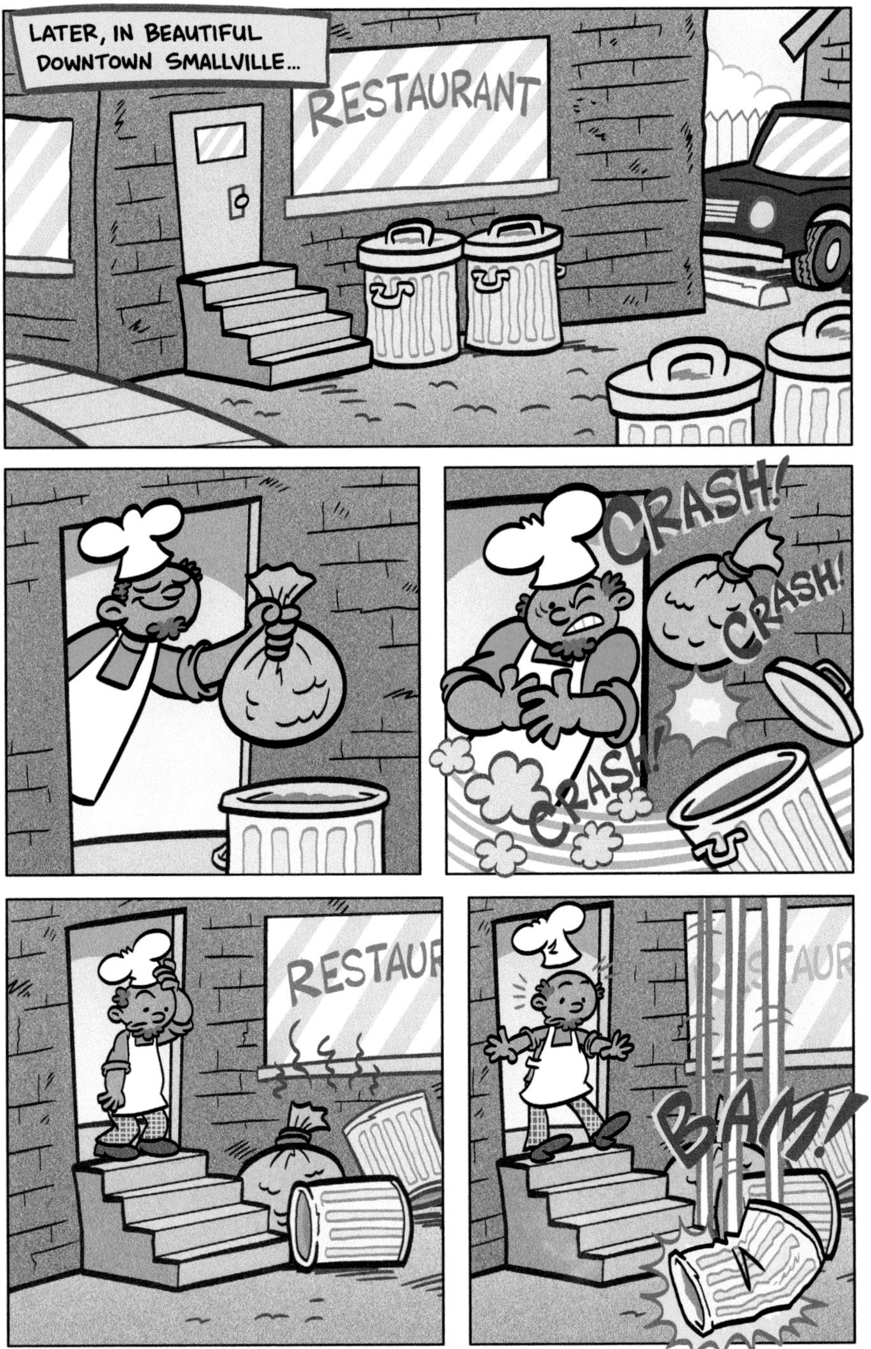
LATER, IN BEAUTIFUL DOWNTOWN SMALLVILLE...
RESTAURANT
CRASH!
CRASH!
CRASH!
RESTAUR
RESTAUR
BAM!

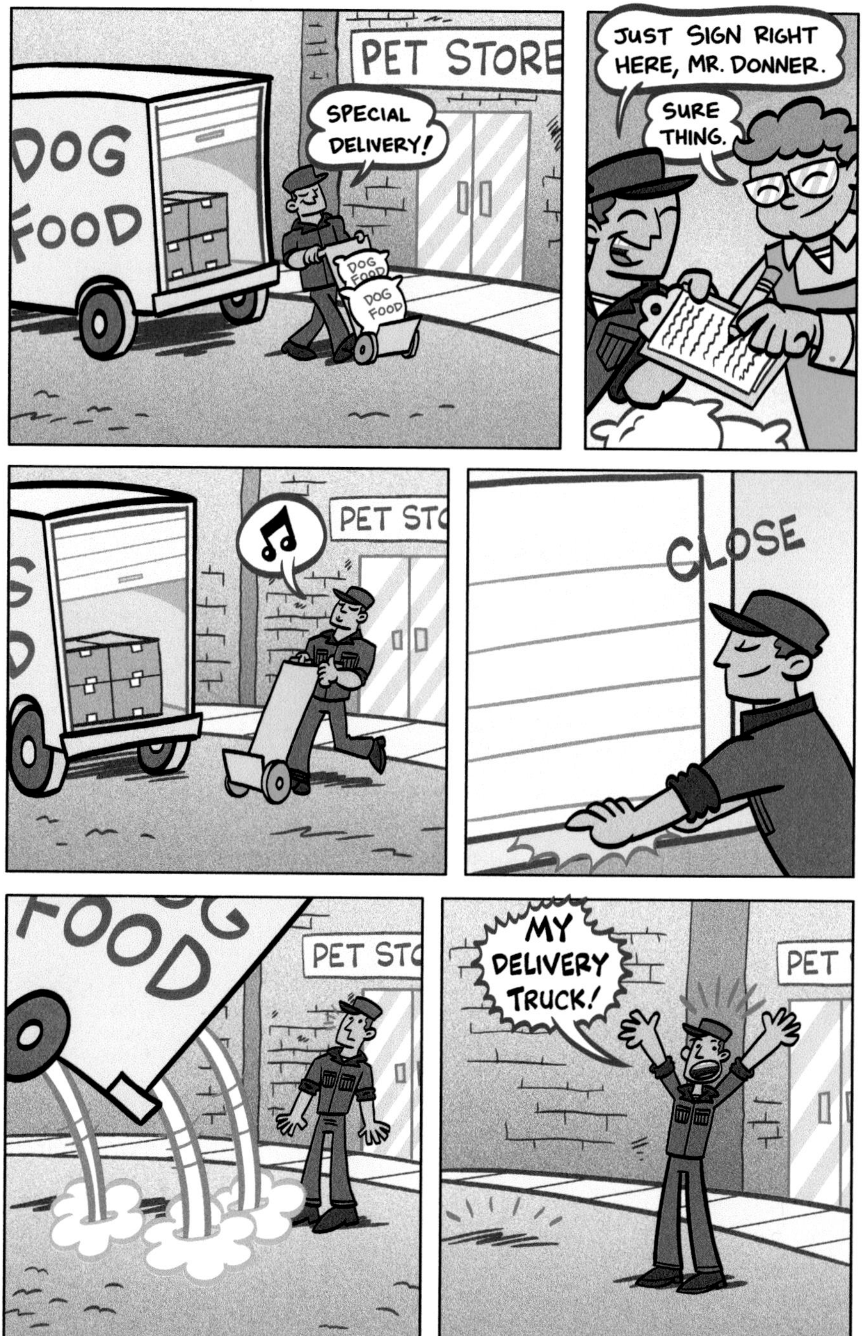
PET STORE
DOG FOOD
SPECIAL DELIVERY!
DOG FOOD
DOG FOOD
JUST SIGN RIGHT HERE, MR. DONNER.
SURE THING.
PET STO
CLOSE
FOOD
PET STO
MY DELIVERY TRUCK!
PET

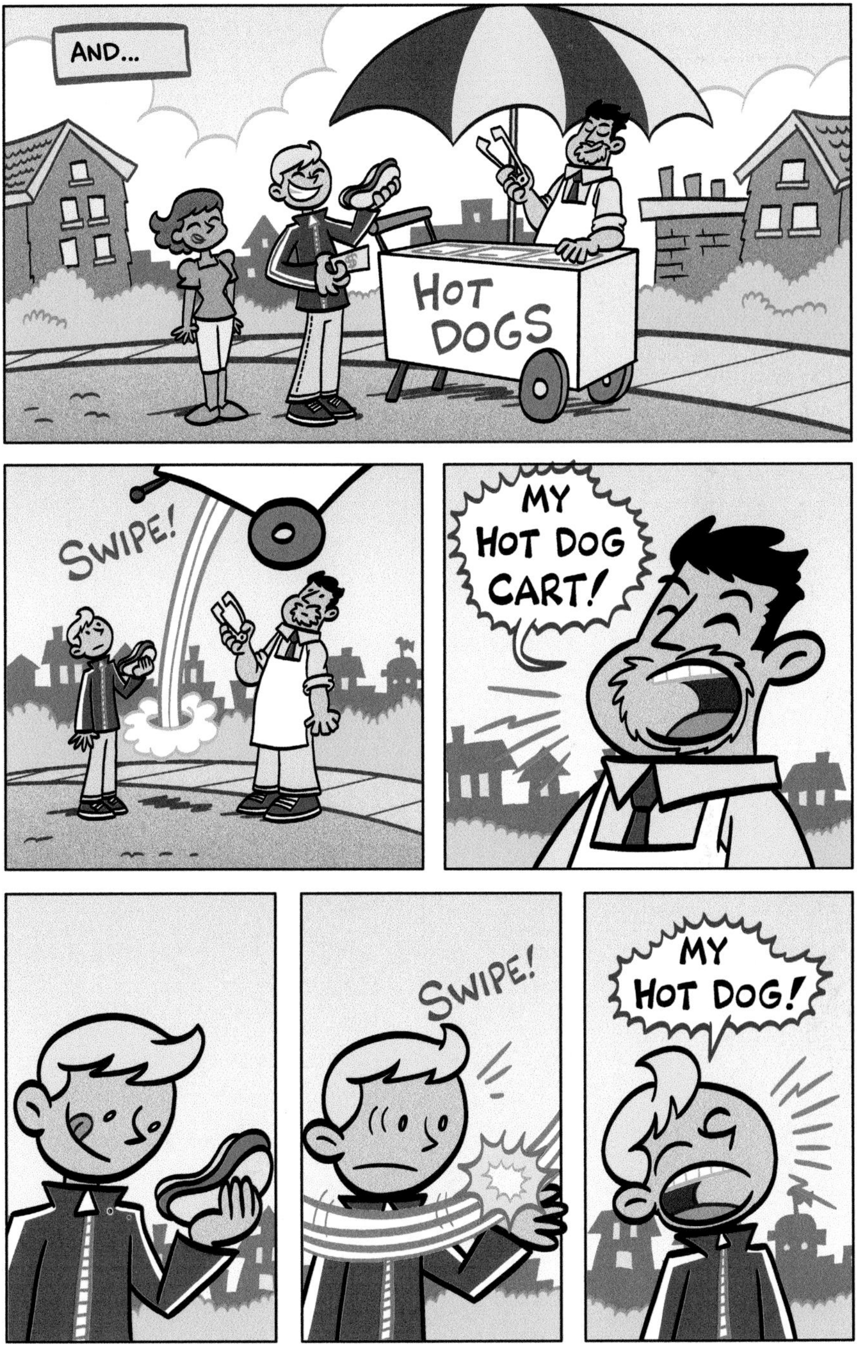
AND...
HOT DOGS
SWIPE!
MY HOT DOG CART!
SWIPE!
MY HOT DOG!

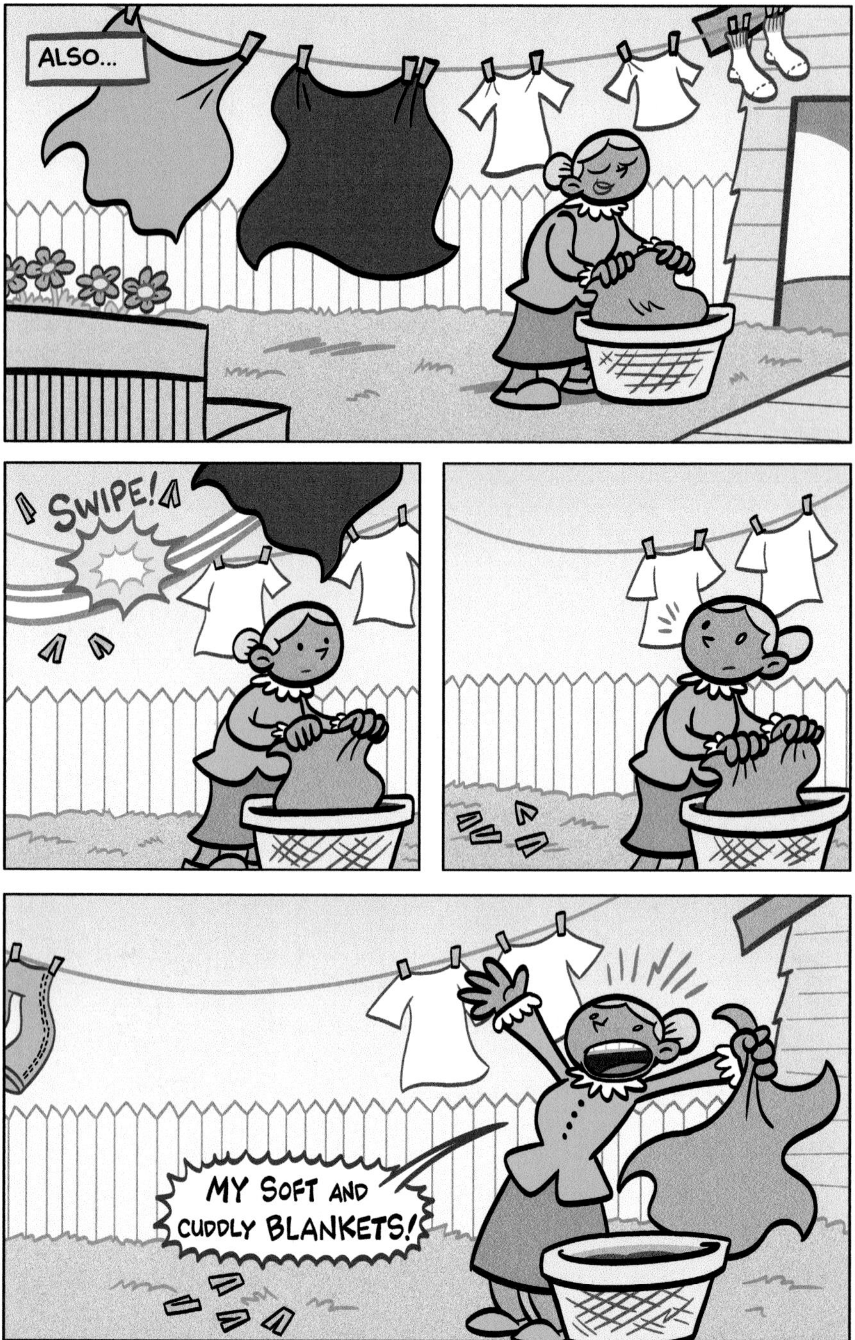
ALSO...
SWIPE!
MY SOFT AND CUDDLY BLANKETS!

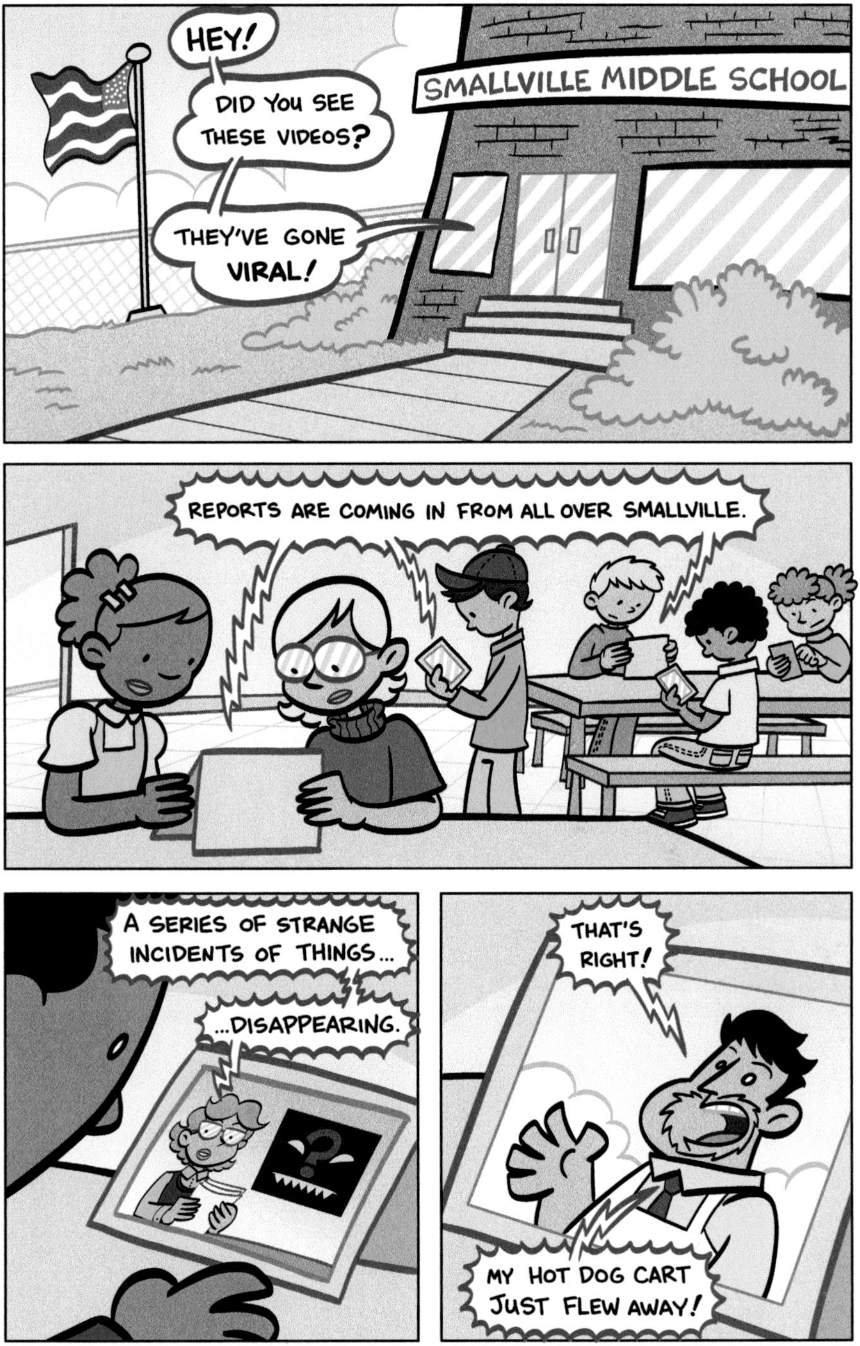
HEY!
DID YOU SEE THESE VIDEOS?
THEY'VE GONE VIRAL!
SMALLVILLE MIDDLE SCHOOL
REPORTS ARE COMING IN FROM ALL OVER SMALLVILLE.
A SERIES OF STRANGE INCIDENTS OF THINGS...
...DISAPPEARING.
THAT'S RIGHT!
MY HOT DOG CART JUST FLEW AWAY!

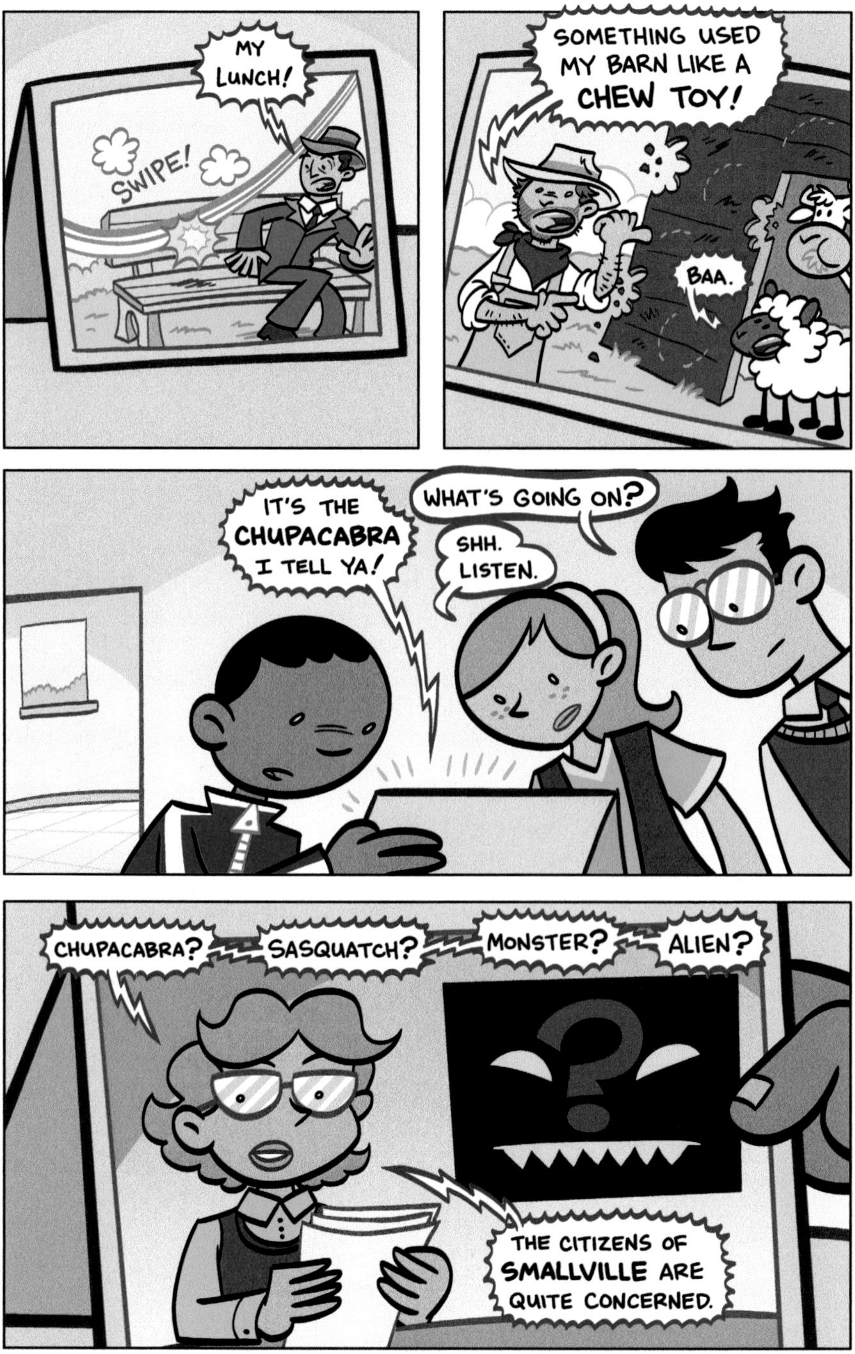
MY LUNCH!
SWIPE!
SOMETHING USED MY BARN LIKE A CHEW TOY!
BAA.
IT'S THE CHUPACABRA I TELL YA!
WHAT'S GOING ON?
SHH. LISTEN.
CHUPACABRA?
SASQUATCH?
MONSTER?
ALIEN?
THE CITIZENS OF SMALLVILLE ARE QUITE CONCERNED.

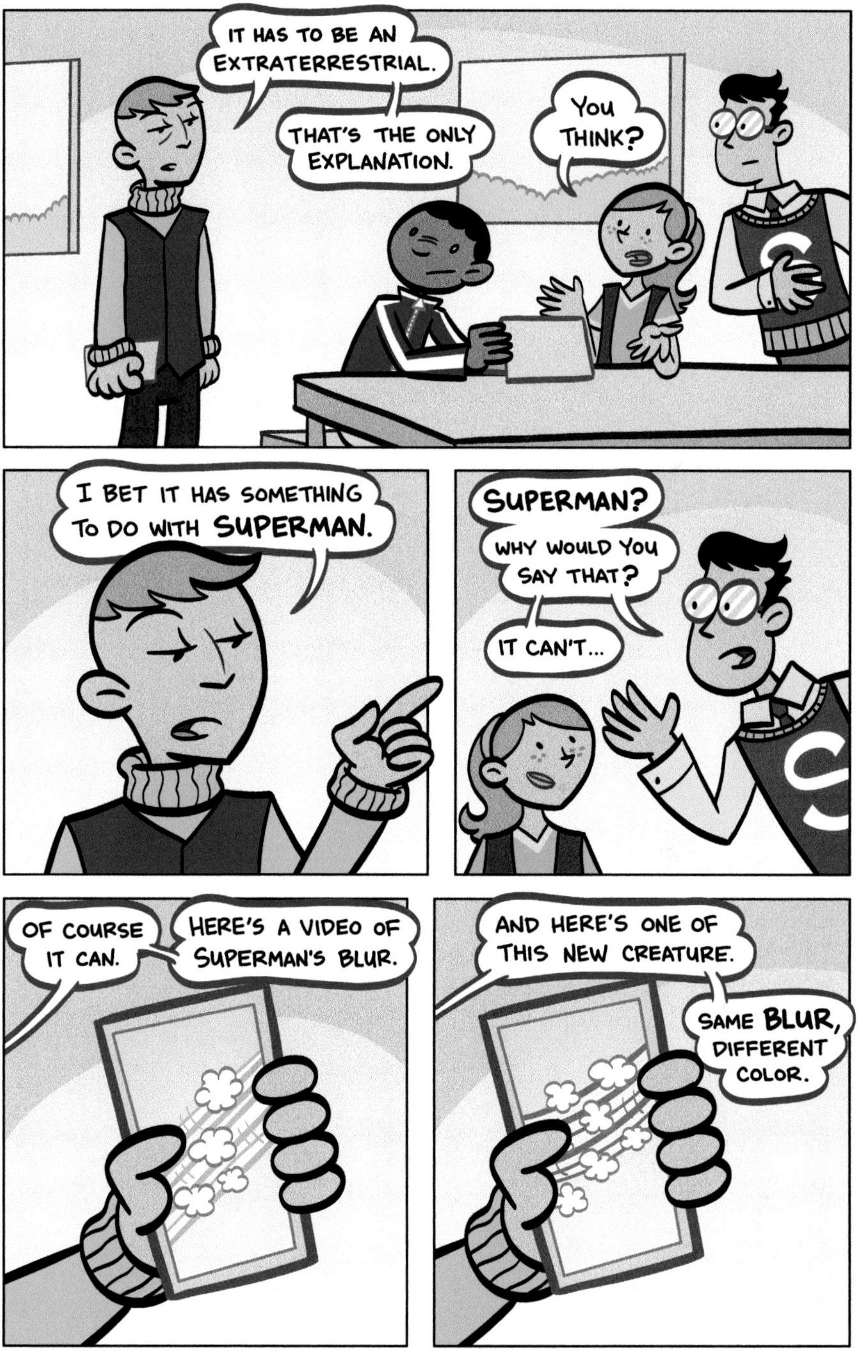
IT HAS TO BE AN EXTRATERRESTRIAL.
THAT'S THE ONLY EXPLANATION.
YOU THINK?
I BET IT HAS SOMETHING TO DO WITH SUPERMAN.
SUPERMAN?
WHY WOULD YOU SAY THAT?
IT CAN'T...
OF COURSE IT CAN.
HERE'S A VIDEO OF SUPERMAN'S BLUR.
AND HERE'S ONE OF THIS NEW CREATURE.
SAME BLUR, DIFFERENT COLOR.

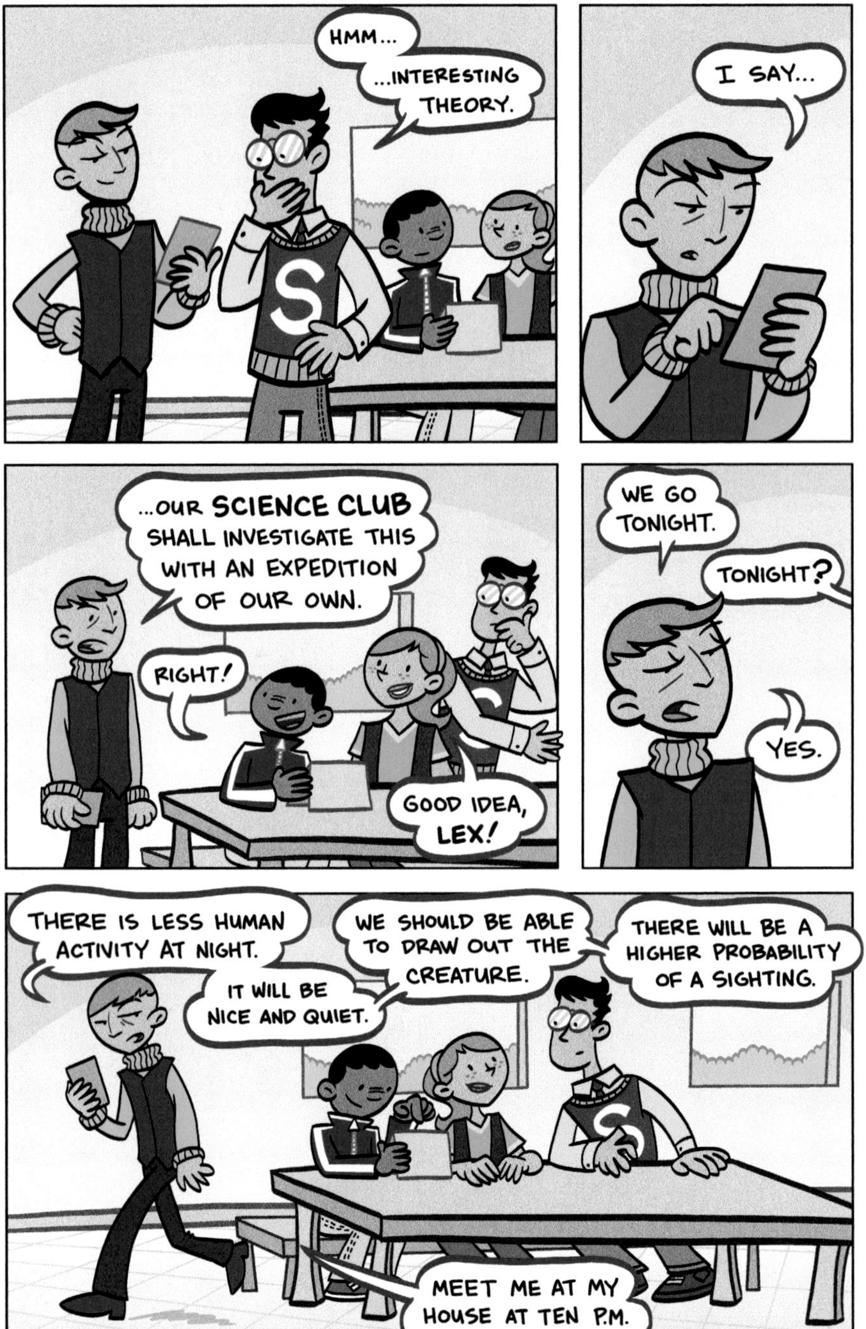
HMM...
...INTERESTING THEORY.
I SAY...
...OUR SCIENCE CLUB SHALL INVESTIGATE THIS WITH AN EXPEDITION OF OUR OWN.
RIGHT!
GOOD IDEA, LEX!
WE GO TONIGHT.
TONIGHT?
YES.
THERE IS LESS HUMAN ACTIVITY AT NIGHT.
IT WILL BE NICE AND QUIET.
WE SHOULD BE ABLE TO DRAW OUT THE CREATURE.
THERE WILL BE A HIGHER PROBABILITY OF A SIGHTING.
MEET ME AT MY HOUSE AT TEN P.M.

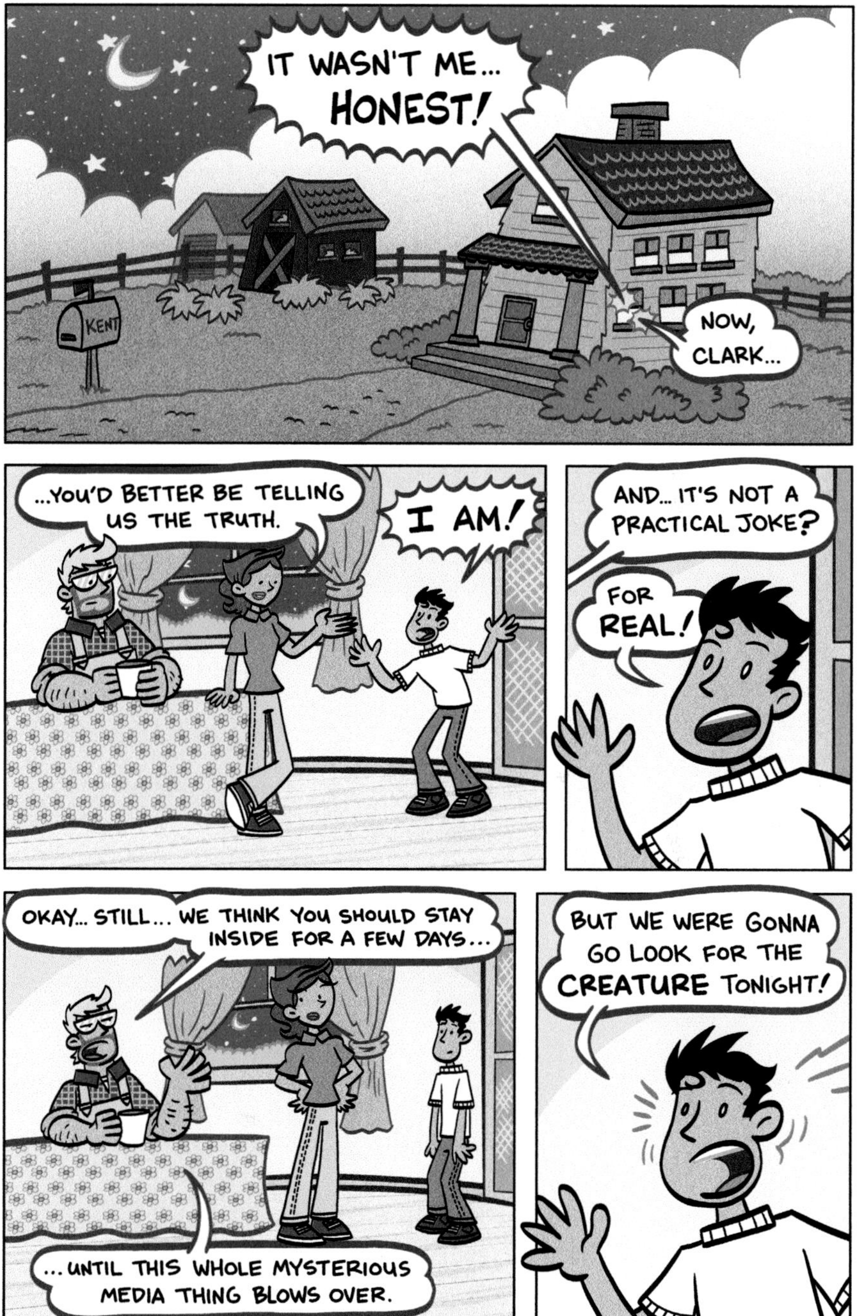
IT WASN'T ME... HONEST!
NOW, CLARK...
...YOU'D BETTER BE TELLING US THE TRUTH.
I AM!
AND... IT'S NOT A PRACTICAL JOKE?
FOR REAL!
OKAY... STILL... WE THINK YOU SHOULD STAY INSIDE FOR A FEW DAYS...
...UNTIL THIS WHOLE MYSTERIOUS MEDIA THING BLOWS OVER.
BUT WE WERE GONNA GO LOOK FOR THE CREATURE TONIGHT!

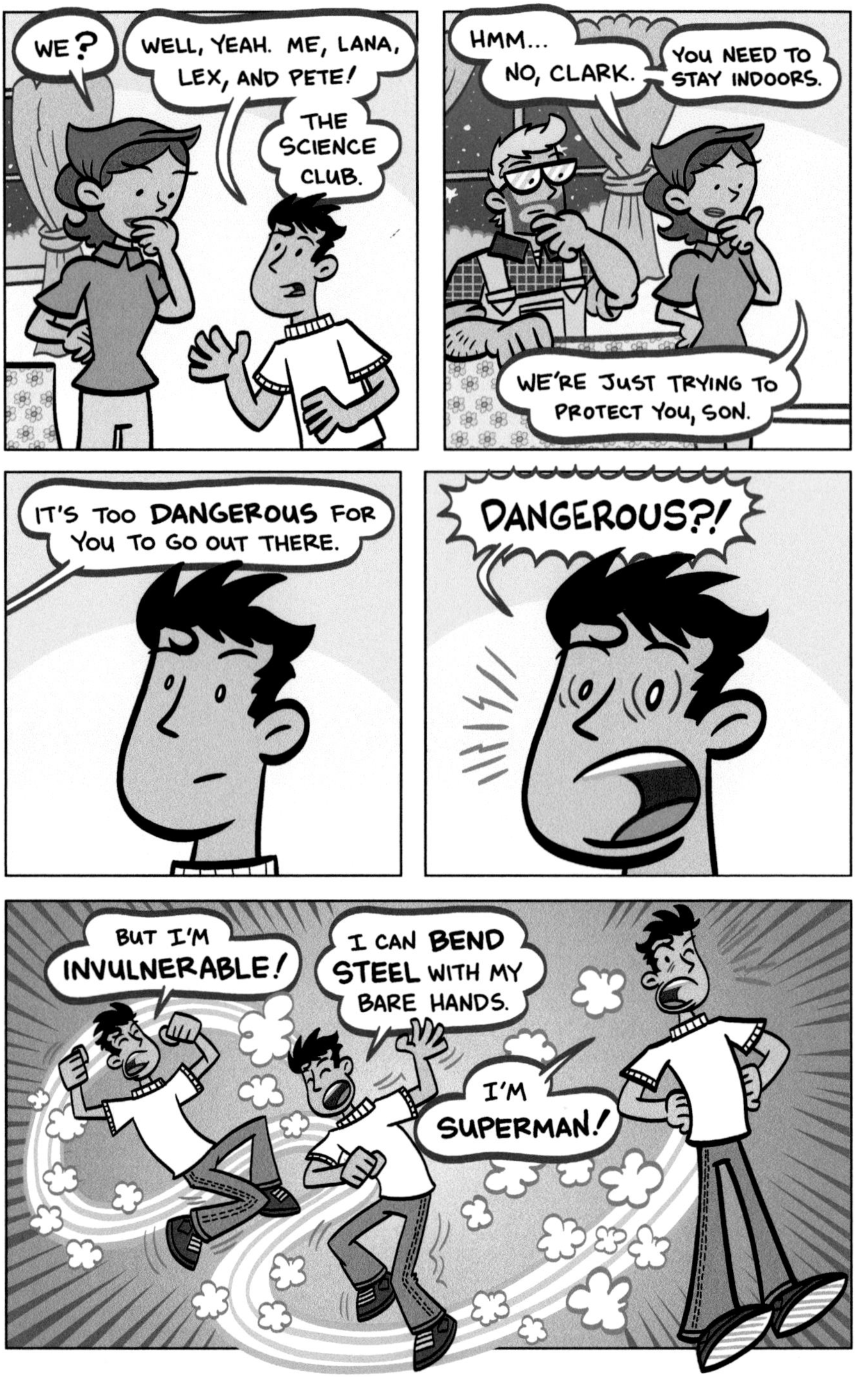
WE?
WELL, YEAH. ME, LANA, LEX, AND PETE!
THE SCIENCE CLUB.
HMM...
NO, CLARK.
YOU NEED TO STAY INDOORS.
WE'RE JUST TRYING TO PROTECT YOU, SON.
IT'S TOO DANGEROUS FOR YOU TO GO OUT THERE.
DANGEROUS?!
BUT I'M INVULNERABLE!
I CAN BEND STEEL WITH MY BARE HANDS.
I'M SUPERMAN!

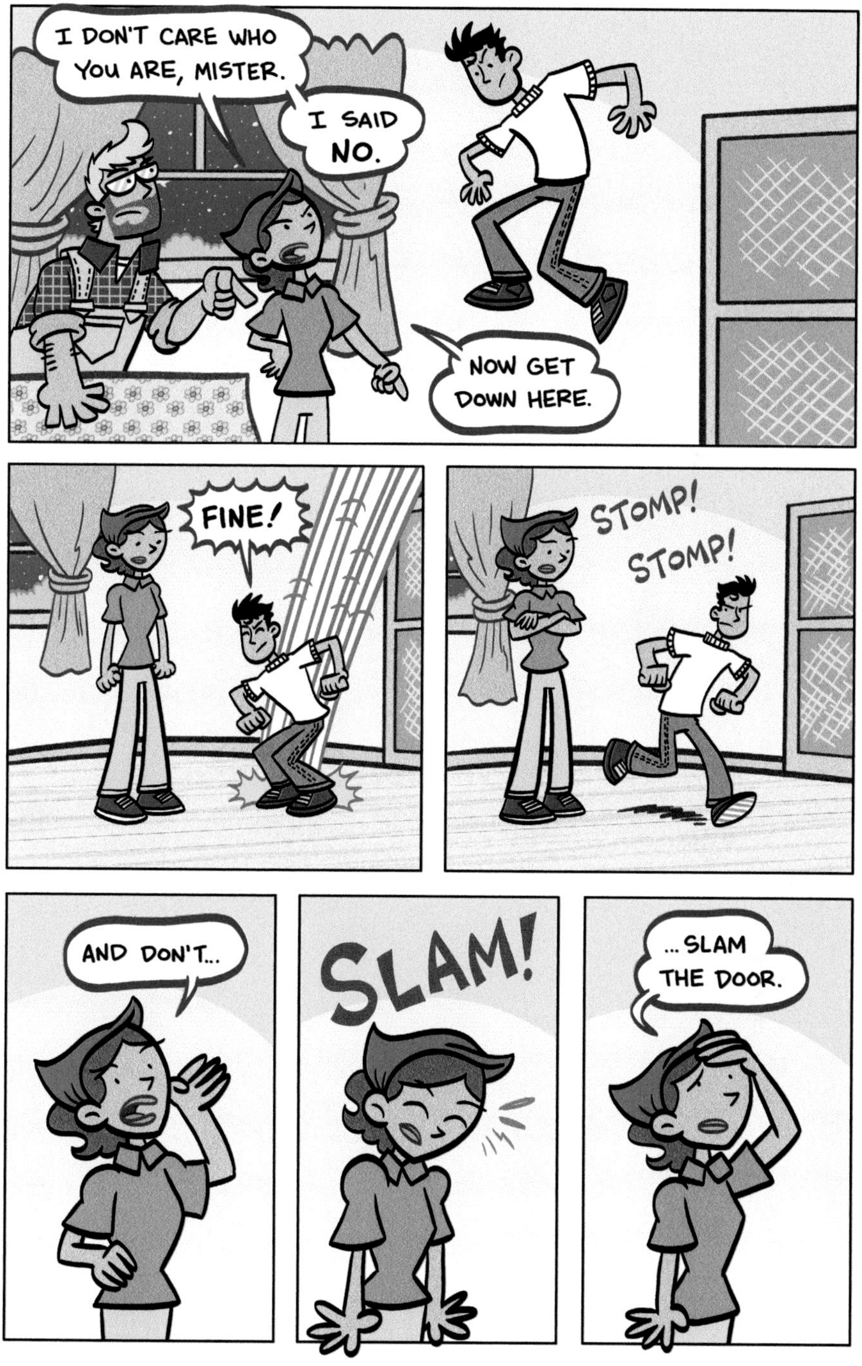
I DON'T CARE WHO YOU ARE, MISTER.
I SAID NO.
NOW GET DOWN HERE.
FINE!
STOMP!
STOMP!
AND DON'T...
SLAM!
...SLAM THE DOOR.

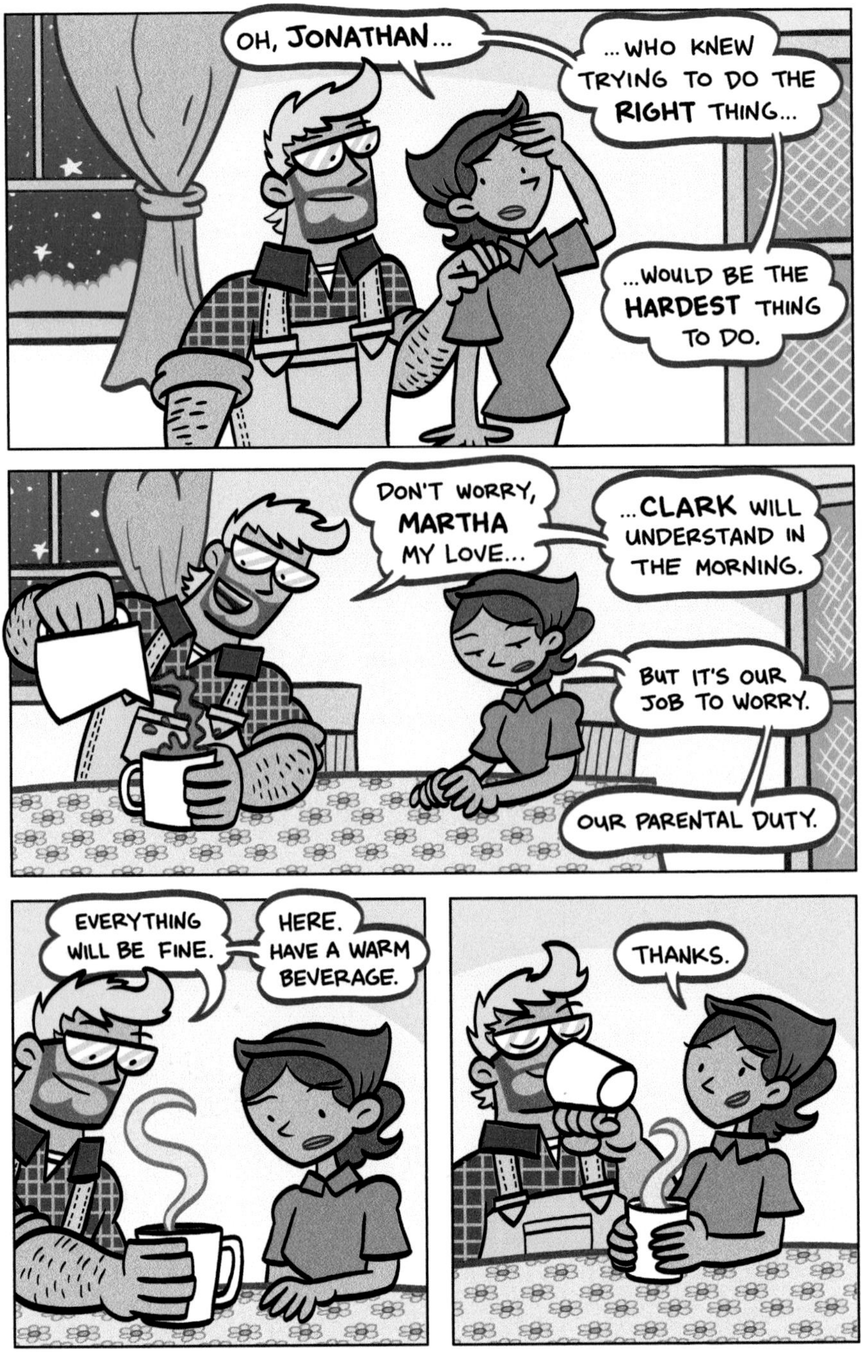
OH, JONATHAN...
...WHO KNEW TRYING TO DO THE RIGHT THING...
...WOULD BE THE HARDEST THING TO DO.
DON'T WORRY, MARTHA MY LOVE...
...CLARK WILL UNDERSTAND IN THE MORNING.
BUT IT'S OUR JOB TO WORRY.
OUR PARENTAL DUTY.
EVERYTHING WILL BE FINE.
HERE. HAVE A WARM BEVERAGE.
THANKS.

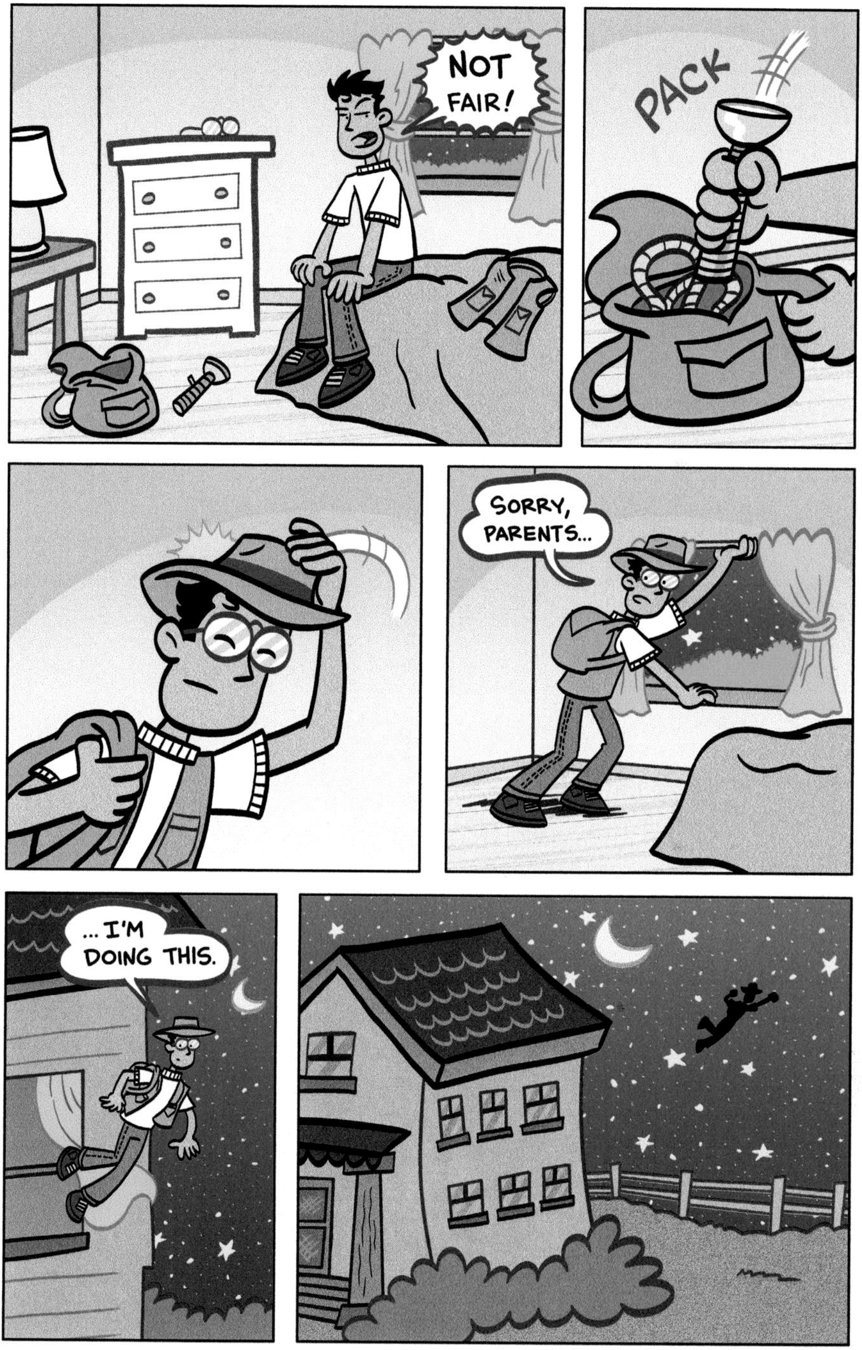
NOT FAIR!
PACK
SORRY, PARENTS...
... I'M DOING THIS.

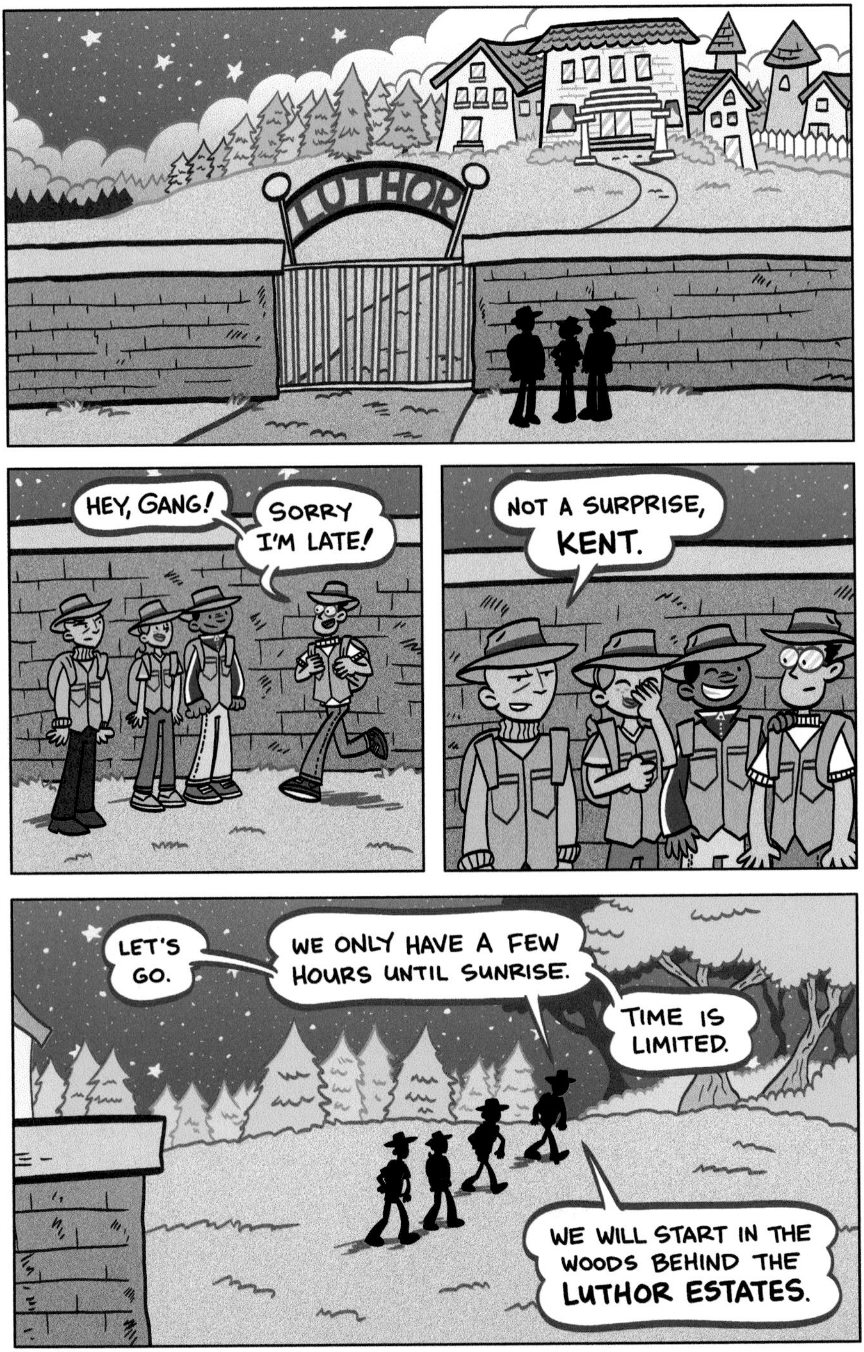
LUTHOR
HEY, GANG!
SORRY I'M LATE!
NOT A SURPRISE, KENT.
LET'S GO.
WE ONLY HAVE A FEW HOURS UNTIL SUNRISE.
TIME IS LIMITED.
WE WILL START IN THE WOODS BEHIND THE LUTHOR ESTATES.

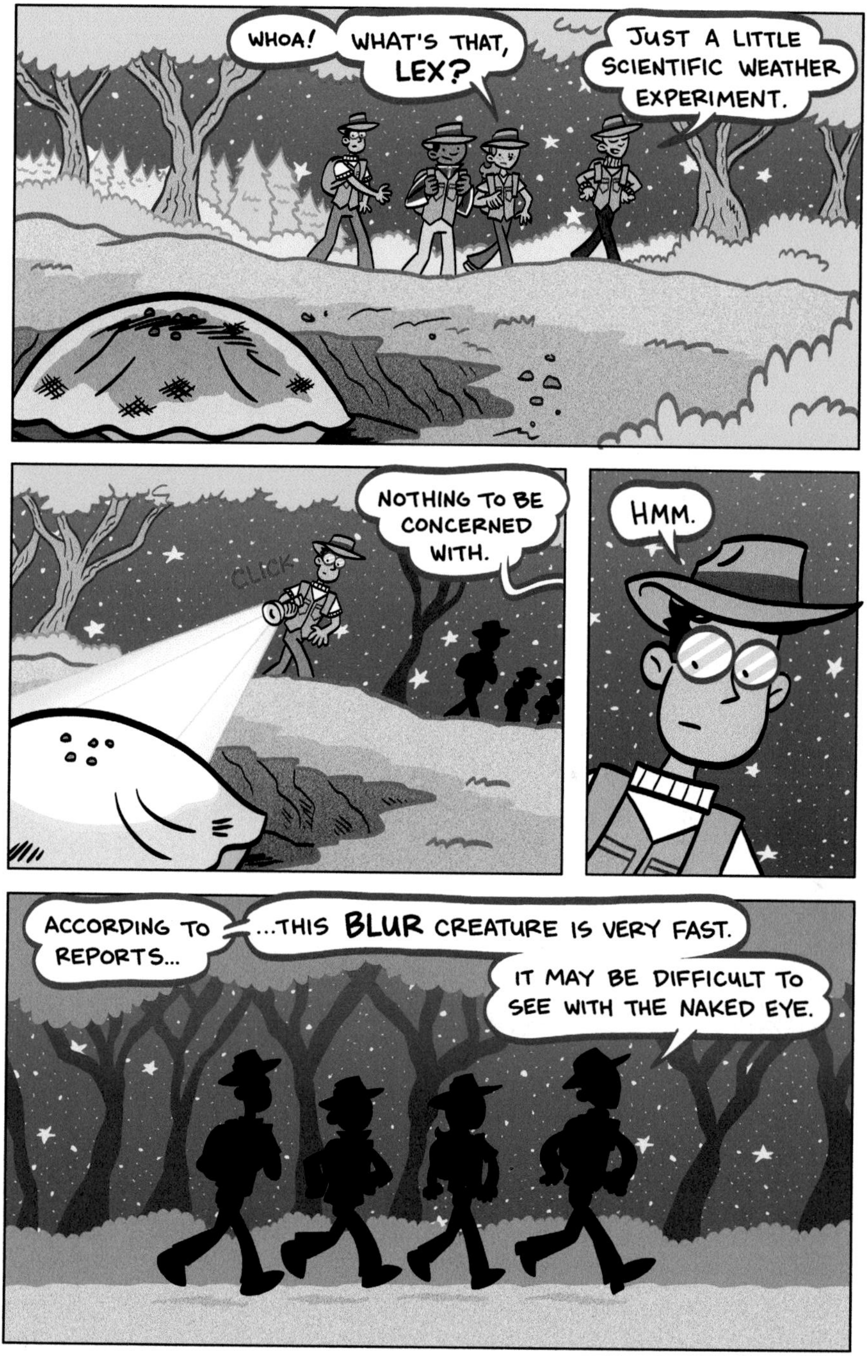
WHOA!
WHAT'S THAT, LEX?
JUST A LITTLE SCIENTIFIC WEATHER EXPERIMENT.
CLICK
NOTHING TO BE CONCERNED WITH.
HMM.
ACCORDING TO REPORTS...
...THIS BLUR CREATURE IS VERY FAST.
IT MAY BE DIFFICULT TO SEE WITH THE NAKED EYE.

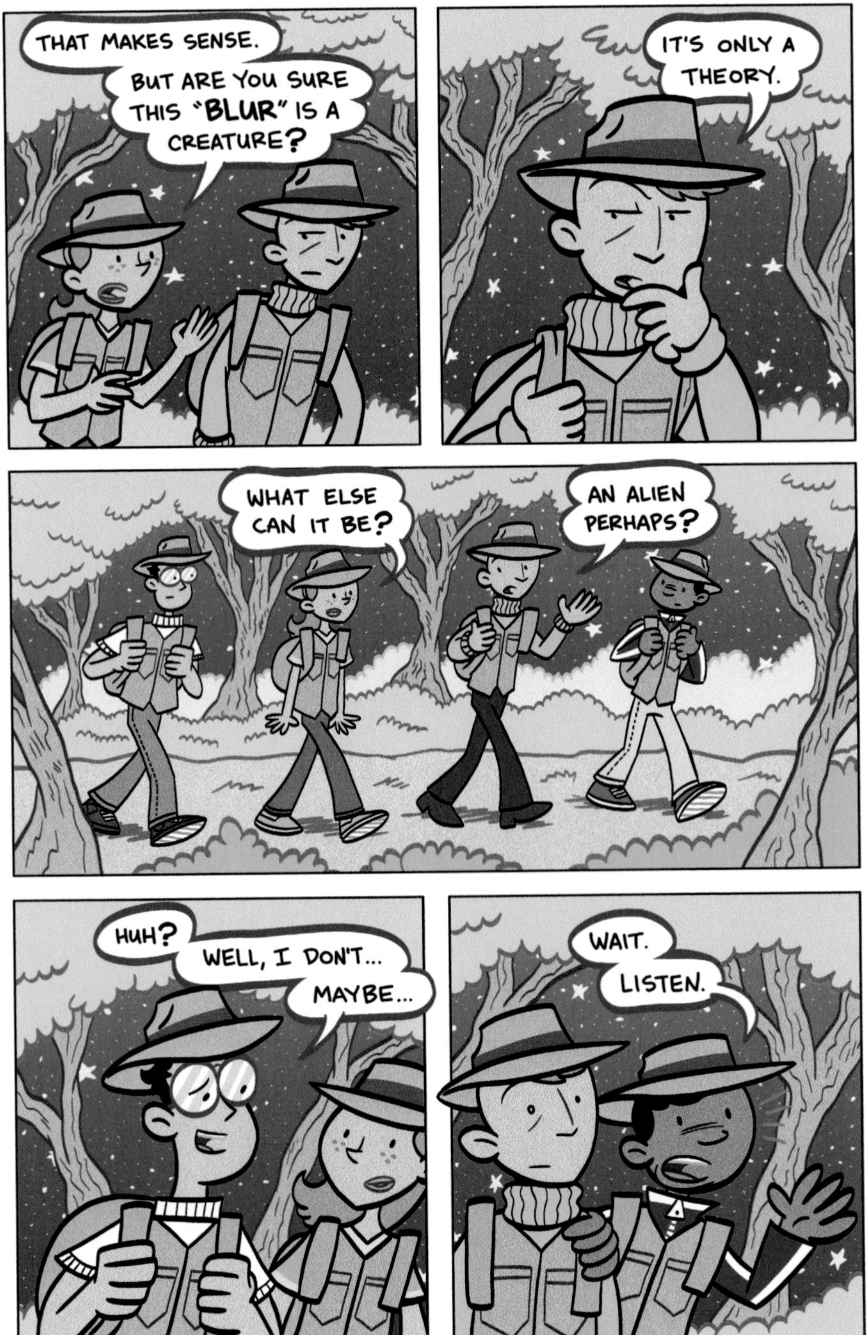
THAT MAKES SENSE.
BUT ARE YOU SURE THIS "BLUR" IS A CREATURE?
IT'S ONLY A THEORY.
WHAT ELSE CAN IT BE?
AN ALIEN PERHAPS?
HUH?
WELL, I DON'T...
MAYBE...
WAIT.
LISTEN.

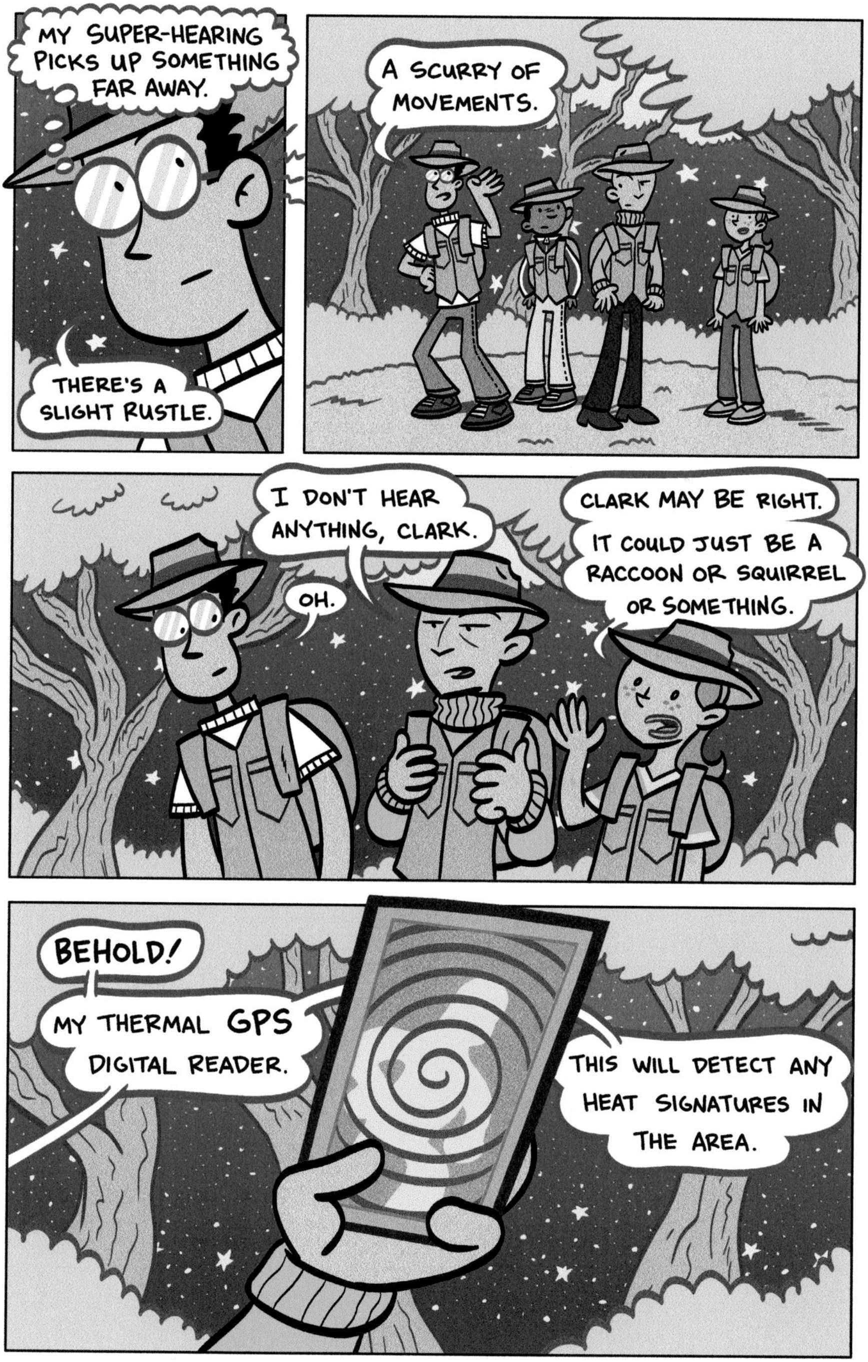
MY SUPER-HEARING PICKS UP SOMETHING FAR AWAY.
THERE'S A SLIGHT RUSTLE.
A SCURRY OF MOVEMENTS.
I DON'T HEAR ANYTHING, CLARK.
OH.
CLARK MAY BE RIGHT.
IT COULD JUST BE A RACCOON OR SQUIRREL OR SOMETHING.
BEHOLD!
MY THERMAL GPS DIGITAL READER.
THIS WILL DETECT ANY HEAT SIGNATURES IN THE AREA.

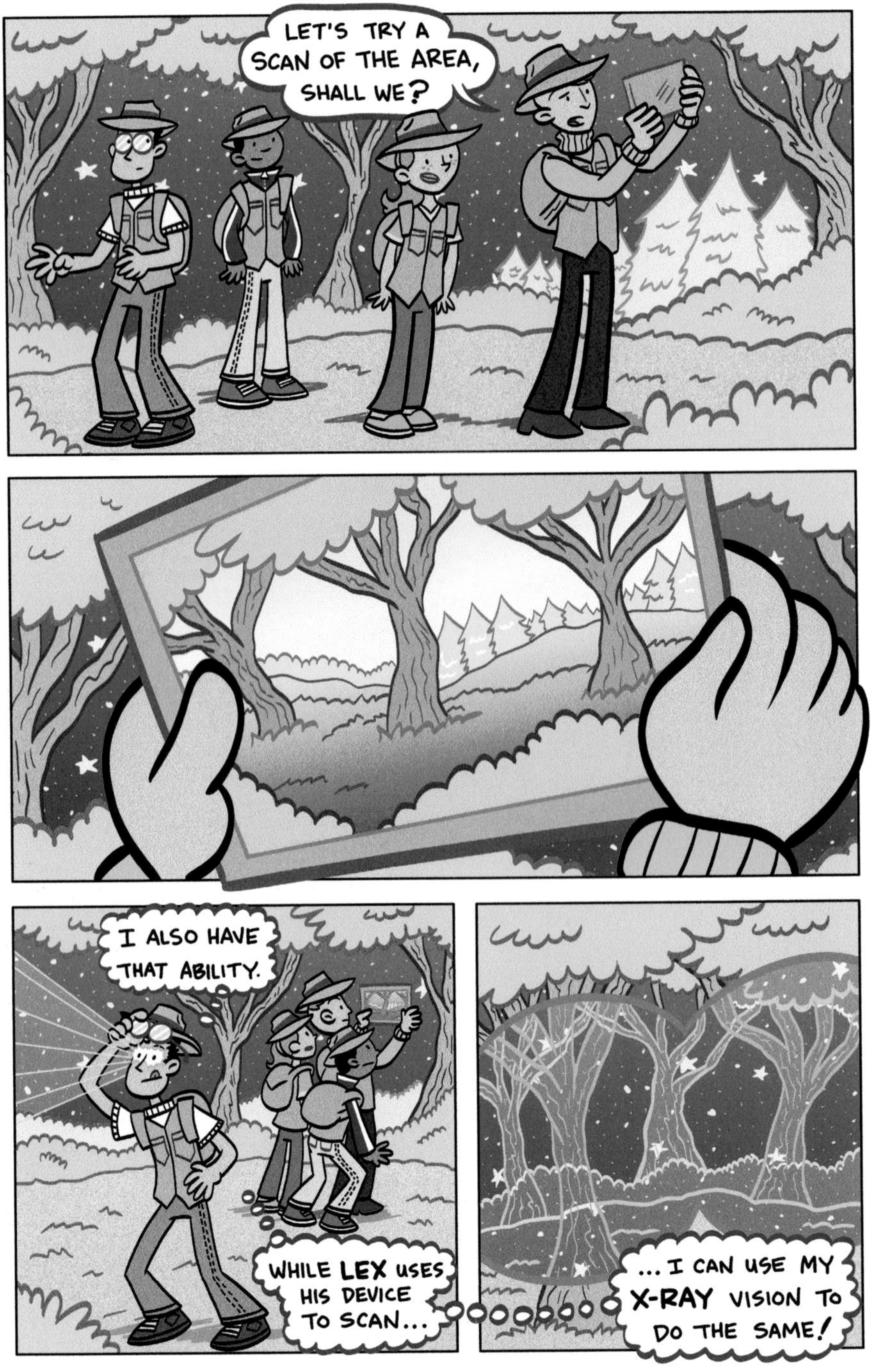

LET'S TRY A SCAN OF THE AREA, SHALL WE?
I ALSO HAVE THAT ABILITY.
WHILE LEX USES HIS DEVICE TO SCAN...
... I CAN USE MY X-RAY VISION TO DO THE SAME!

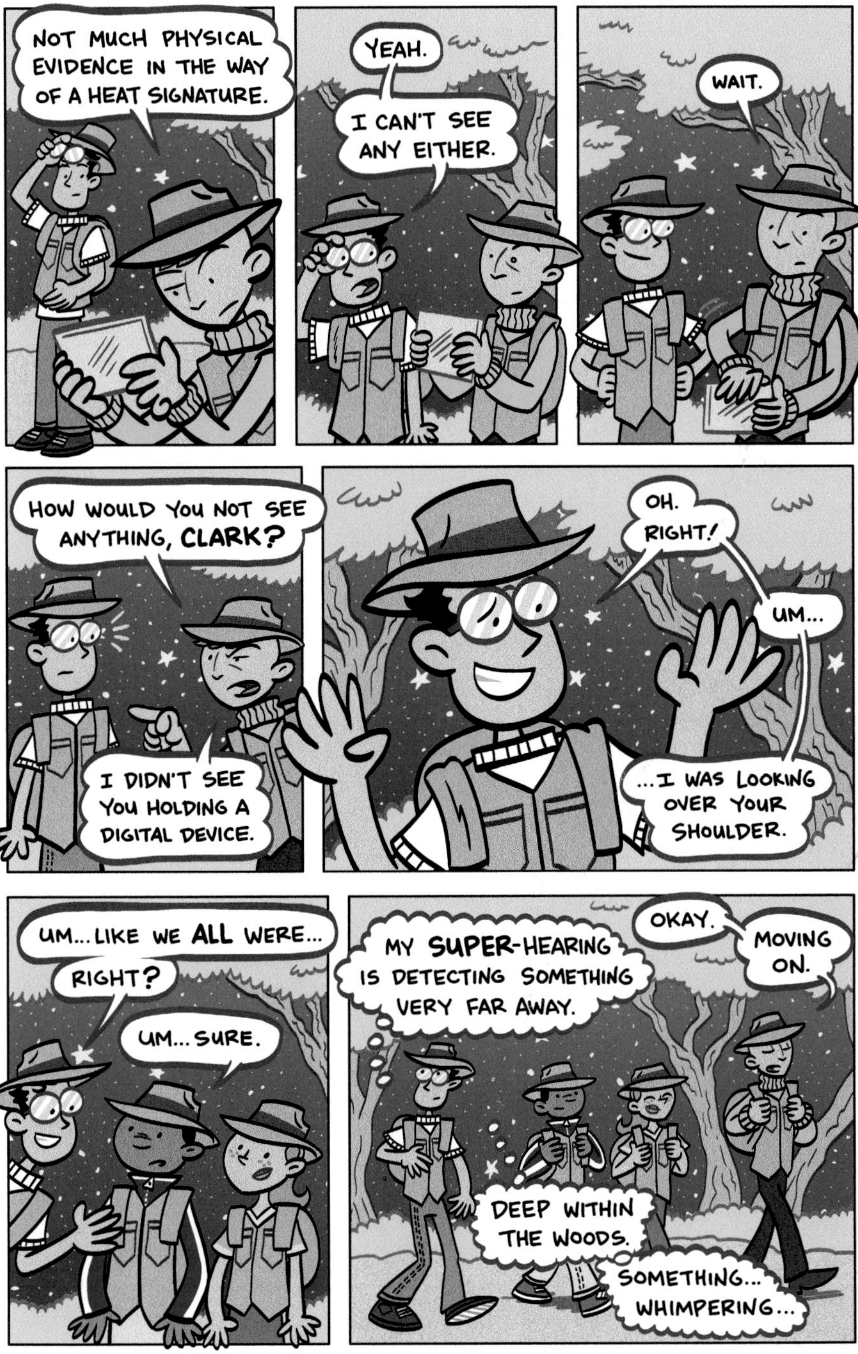
NOT MUCH PHYSICAL EVIDENCE IN THE WAY OF A HEAT SIGNATURE.
YEAH.
I CAN'T SEE ANY EITHER.
WAIT.
HOW WOULD YOU NOT SEE ANYTHING, CLARK?
I DIDN'T SEE YOU HOLDING A DIGITAL DEVICE.
OH. RIGHT!
UM...
...I WAS LOOKING OVER YOUR SHOULDER.
UM... LIKE WE ALL WERE...
RIGHT?
UM... SURE.
MY SUPER-HEARING IS DETECTING SOMETHING VERY FAR AWAY.
OKAY.
MOVING ON.
DEEP WITHIN THE WOODS.
SOMETHING... WHIMPERING...

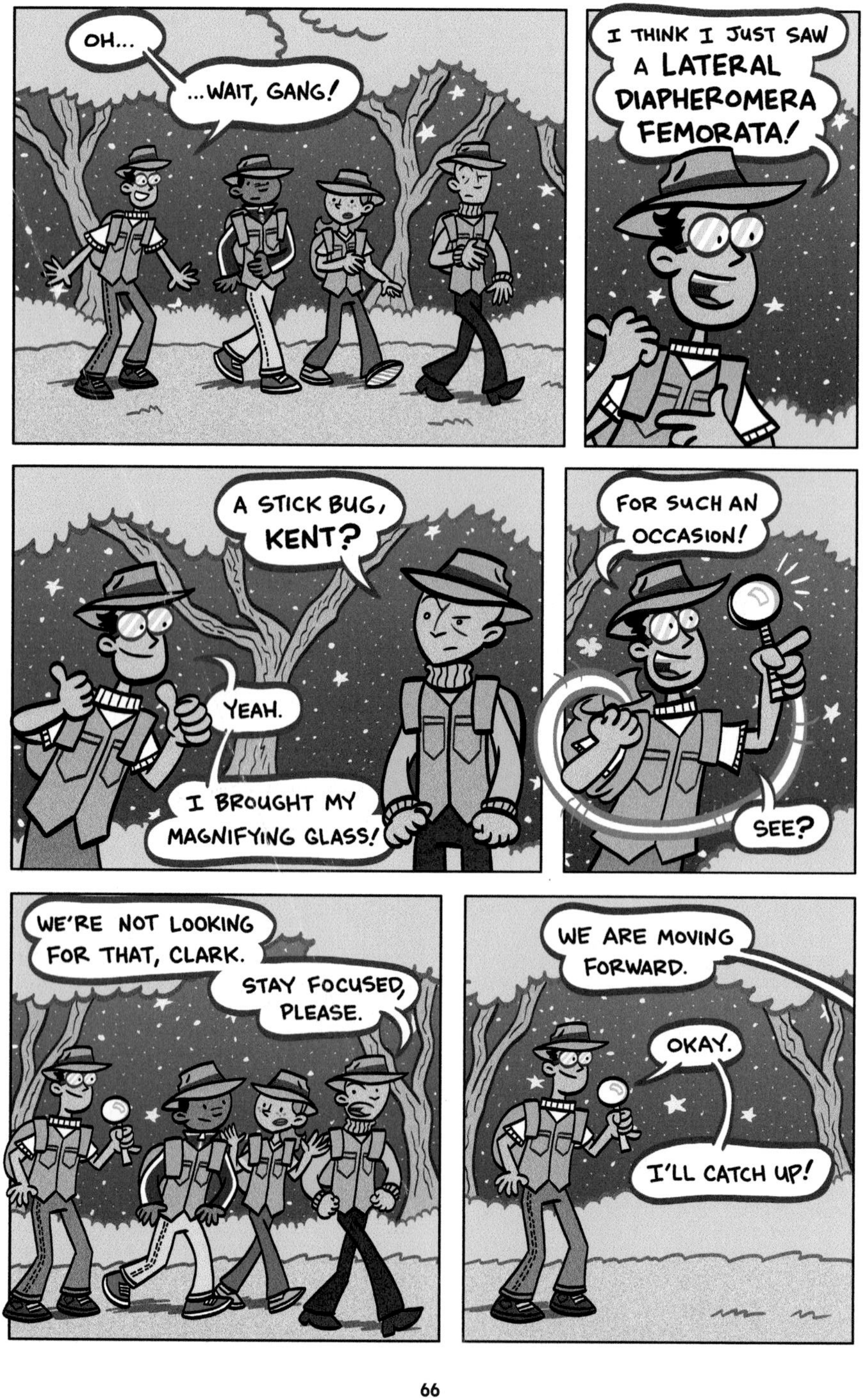
OH...
...WAIT, GANG!
I THINK I JUST SAW A LATERAL DIAPHEROMERA FEMORATA!
A STICK BUG, KENT?
YEAH.
I BROUGHT MY MAGNIFYING GLASS!
FOR SUCH AN OCCASION!
SEE?
WE'RE NOT LOOKING FOR THAT, CLARK.
STAY FOCUSED, PLEASE.
WE ARE MOVING FORWARD.
OKAY.
I'LL CATCH UP!

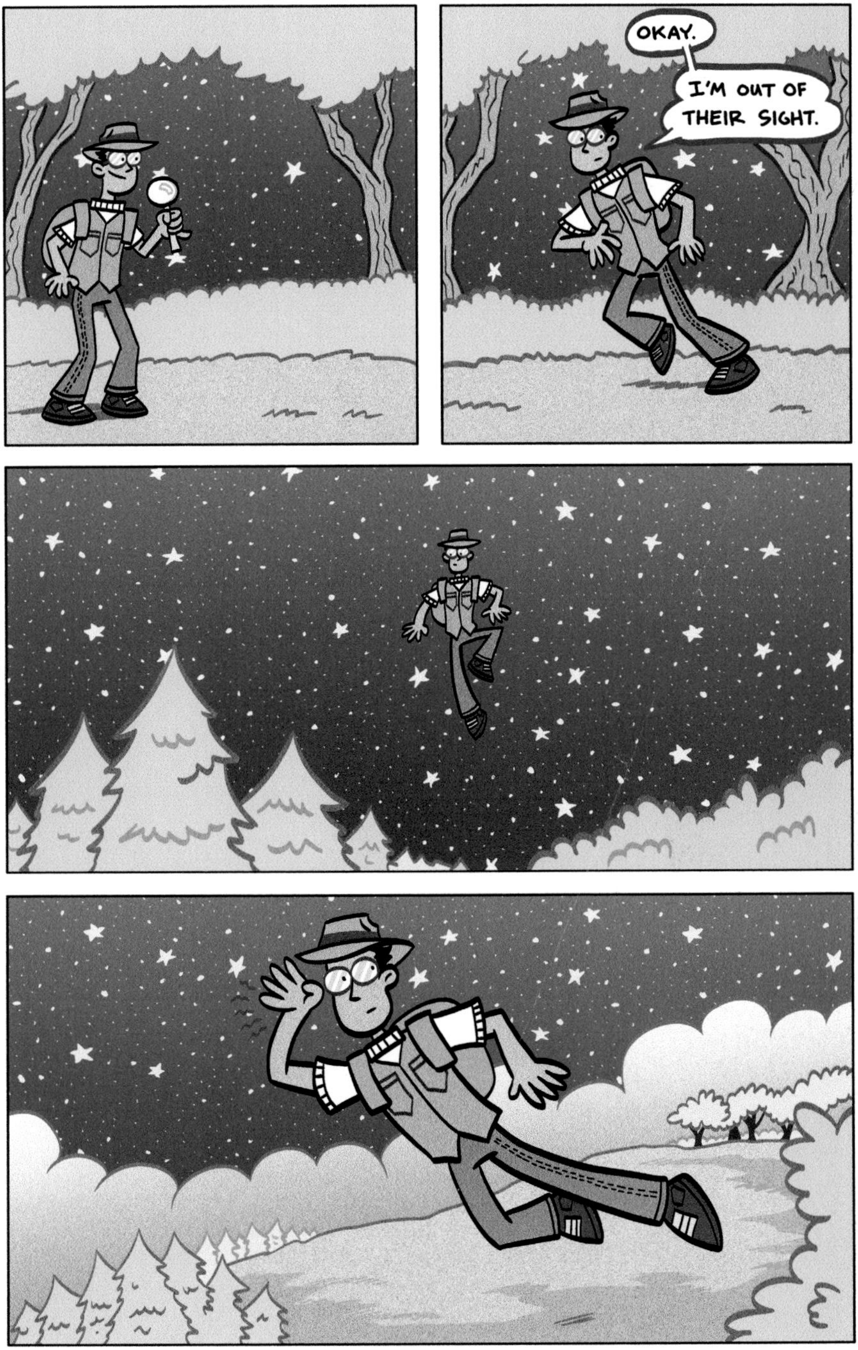
OKAY.
I'M OUT OF THEIR SIGHT.

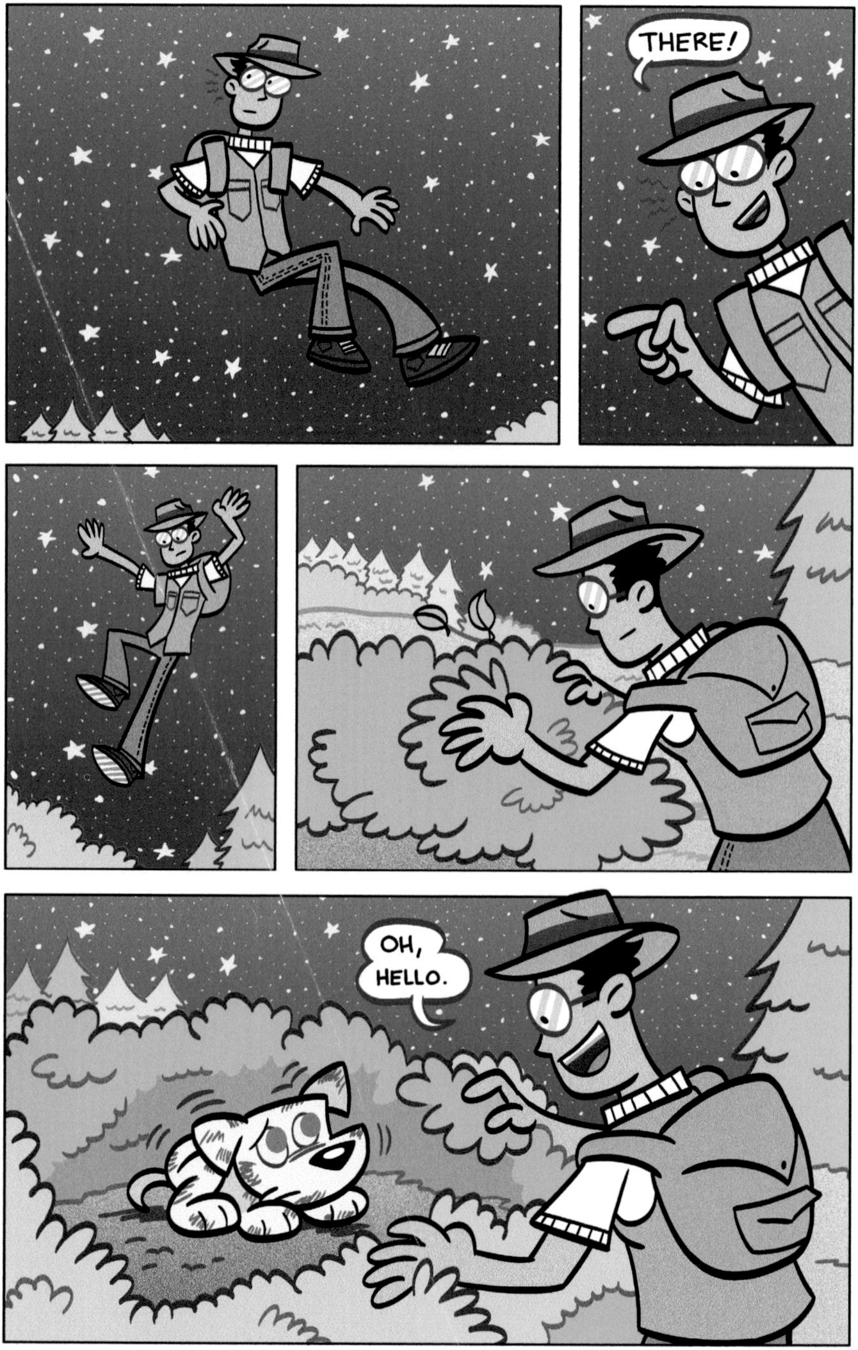
THERE!
OH, HELLO.

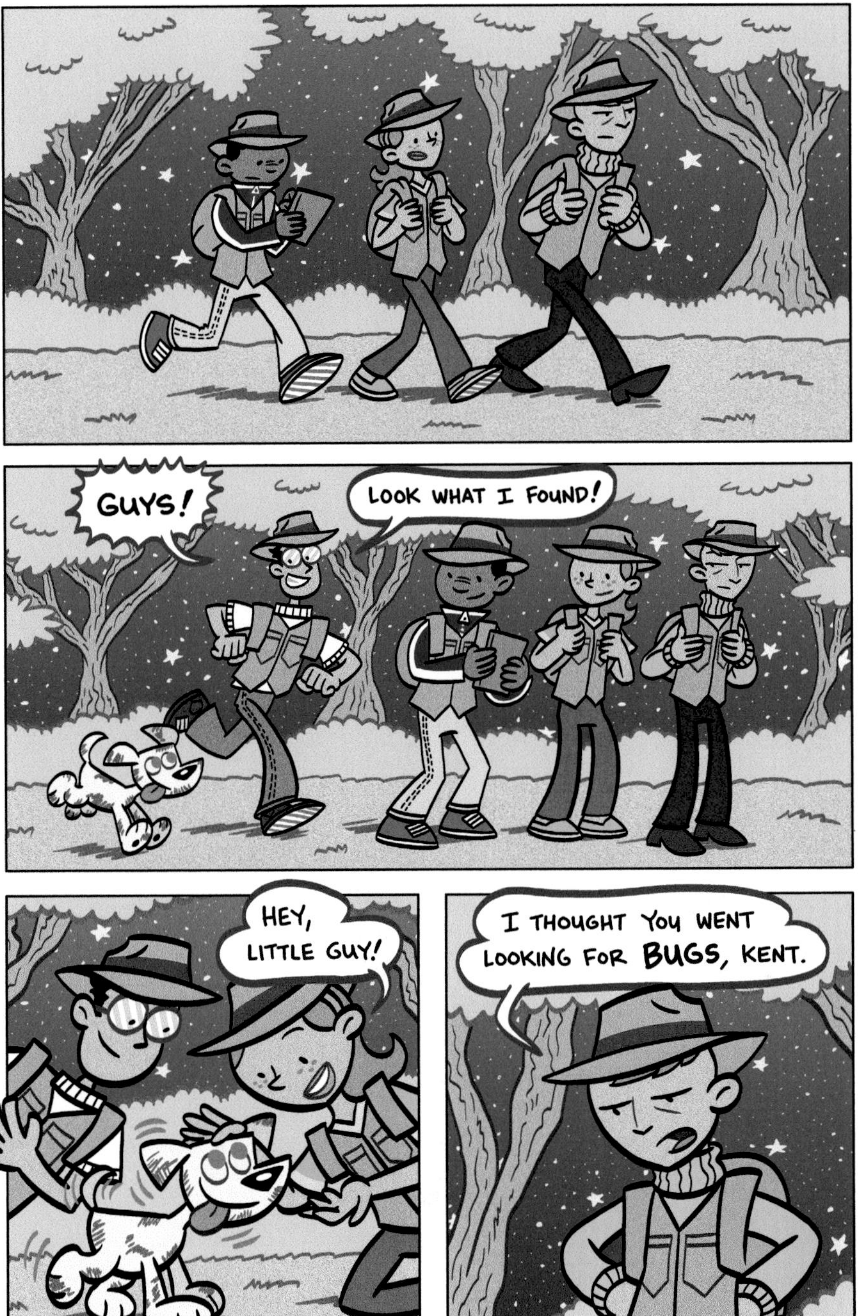
GUYS!
LOOK WHAT I FOUND!
HEY, LITTLE GUY!
I THOUGHT YOU WENT LOOKING FOR BUGS, KENT.

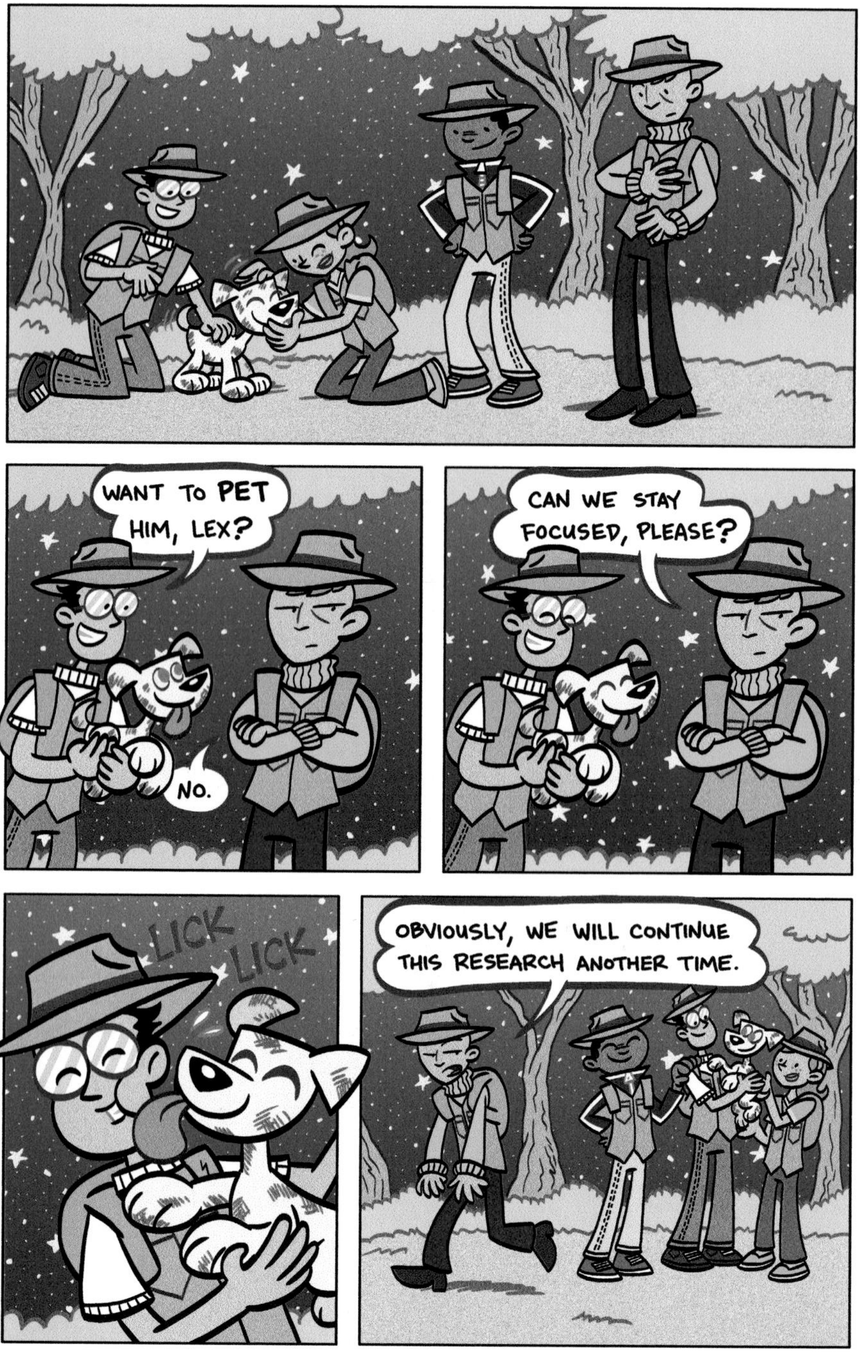
WANT TO PET HIM, LEX?
NO.
CAN WE STAY FOCUSED, PLEASE?
LICK LICK
OBVIOUSLY, WE WILL CONTINUE THIS RESEARCH ANOTHER TIME.

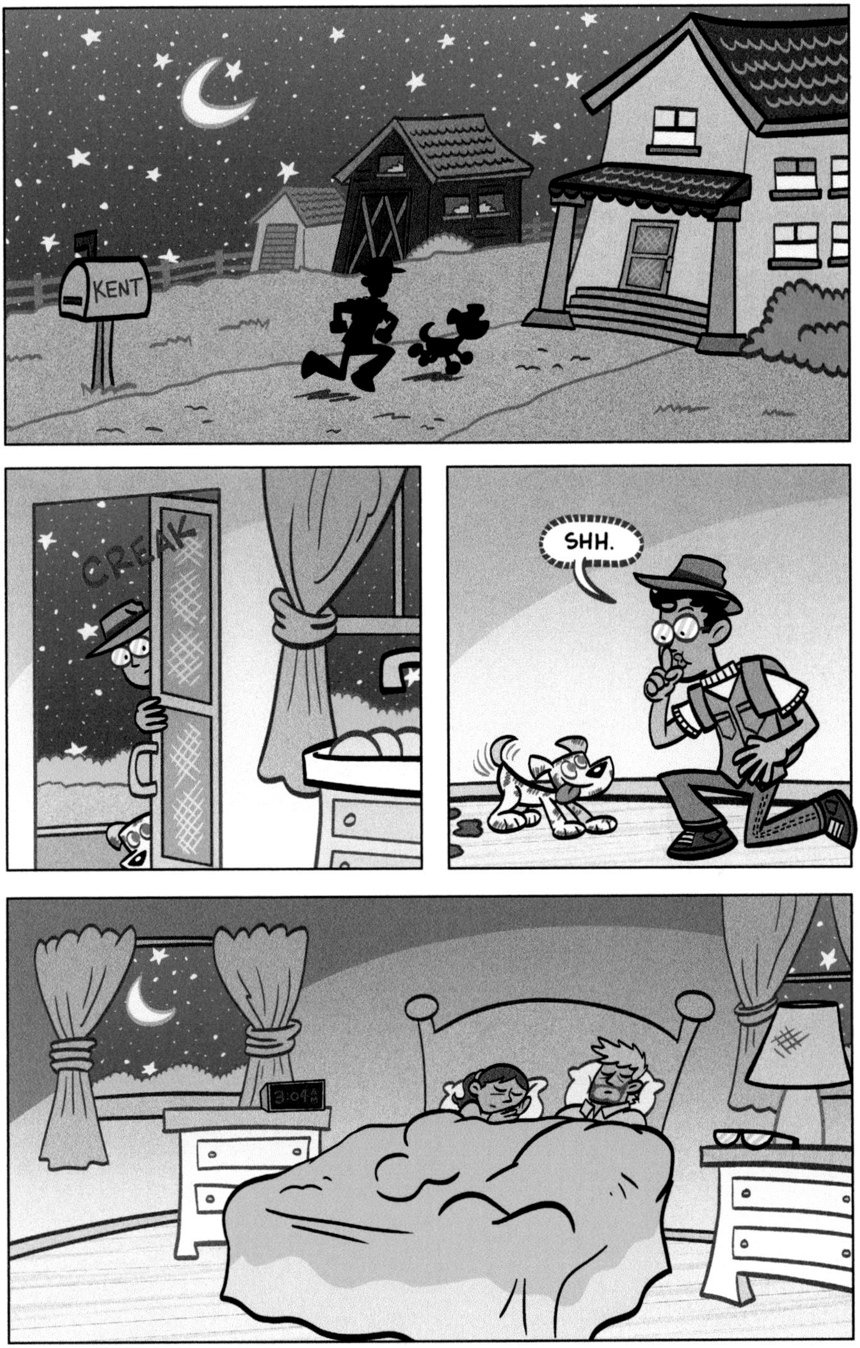
KENT
CREAK
SHH.
3:04 AM

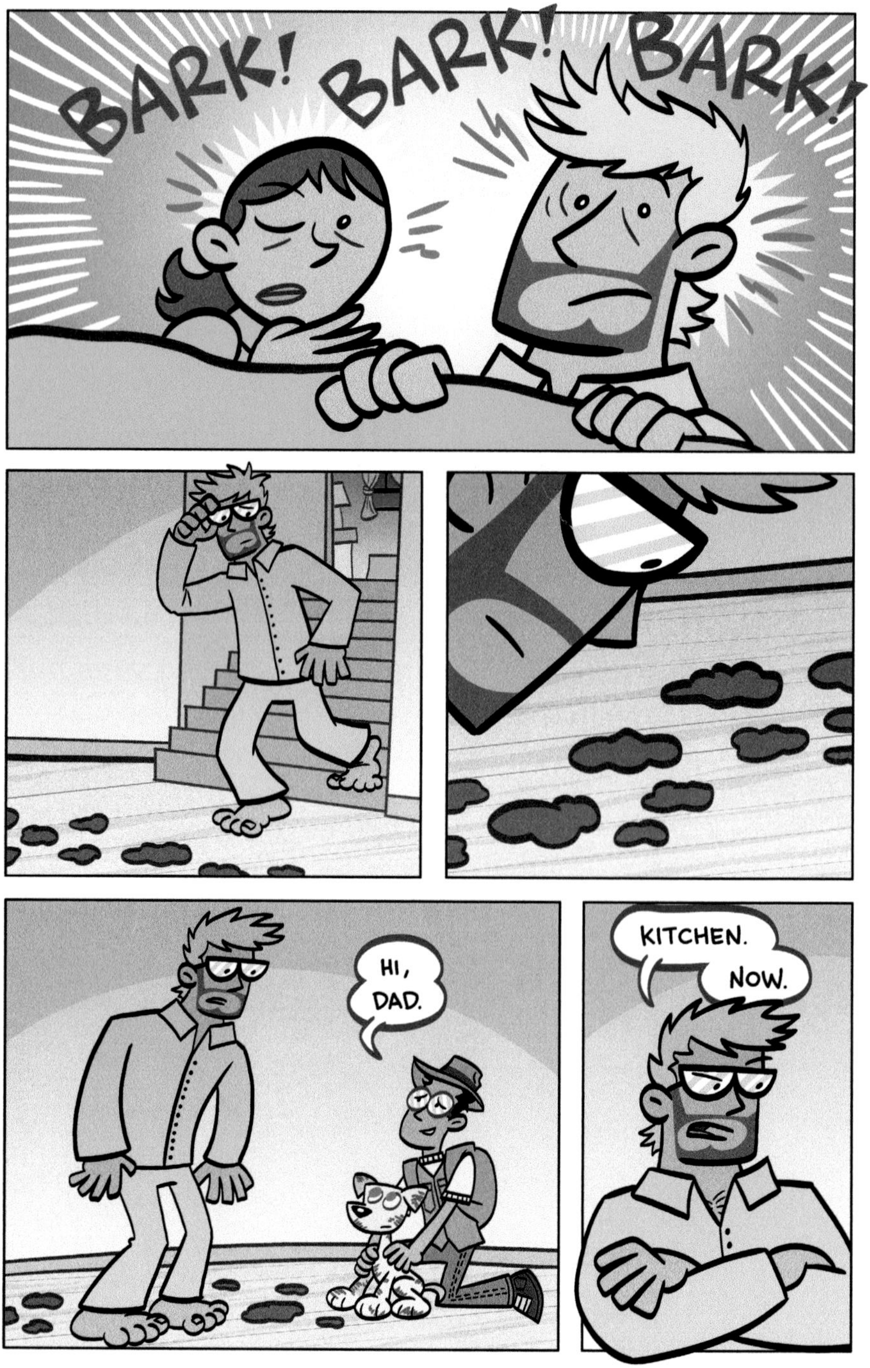
BARK! BARK! BARK!
HI, DAD.
KITCHEN. NOW.

CHAPTER THREE

SUPER GROUNDED

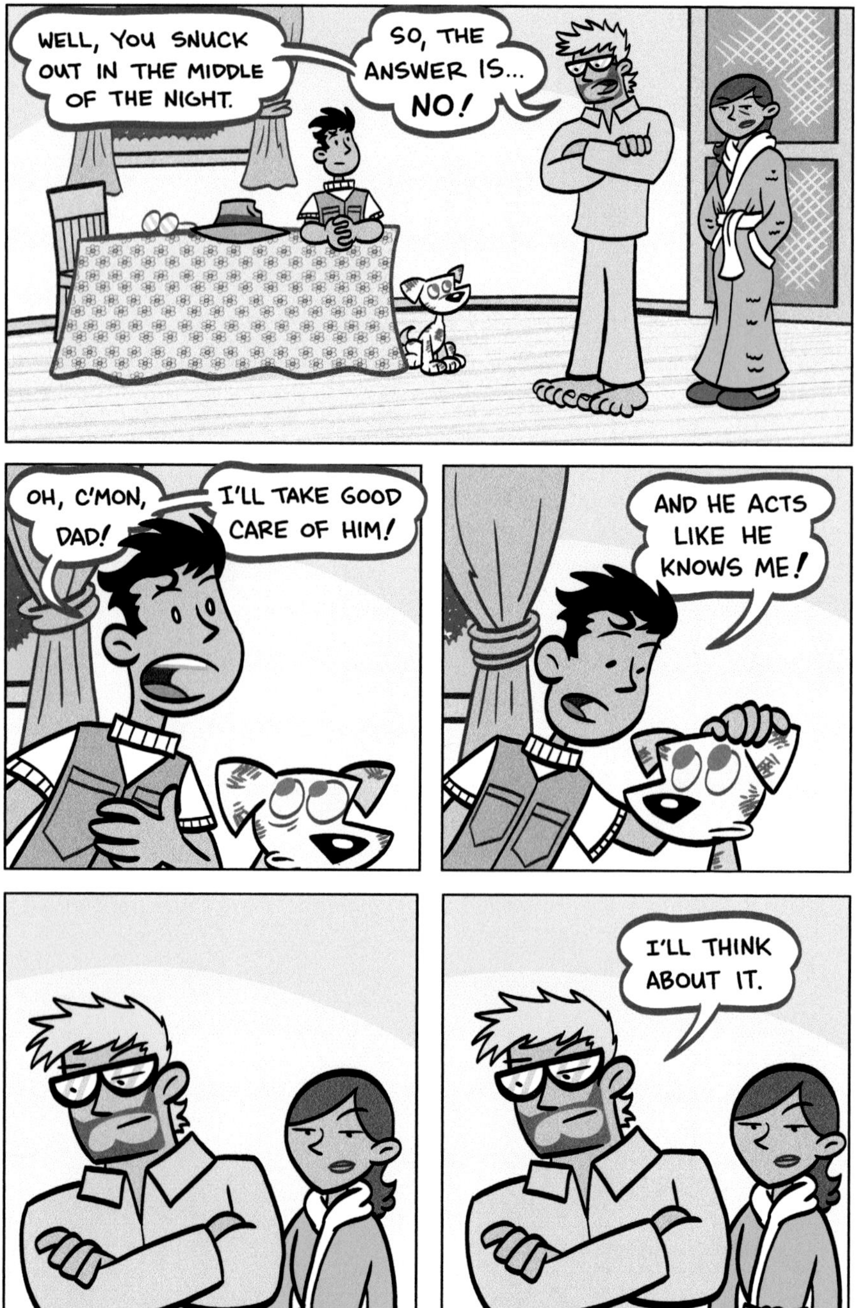
WELL, YOU SNUCK OUT IN THE MIDDLE OF THE NIGHT.
SO, THE ANSWER IS... NO!
OH, C'MON, DAD!
I'LL TAKE GOOD CARE OF HIM!
AND HE ACTS LIKE HE KNOWS ME!
I'LL THINK ABOUT IT.

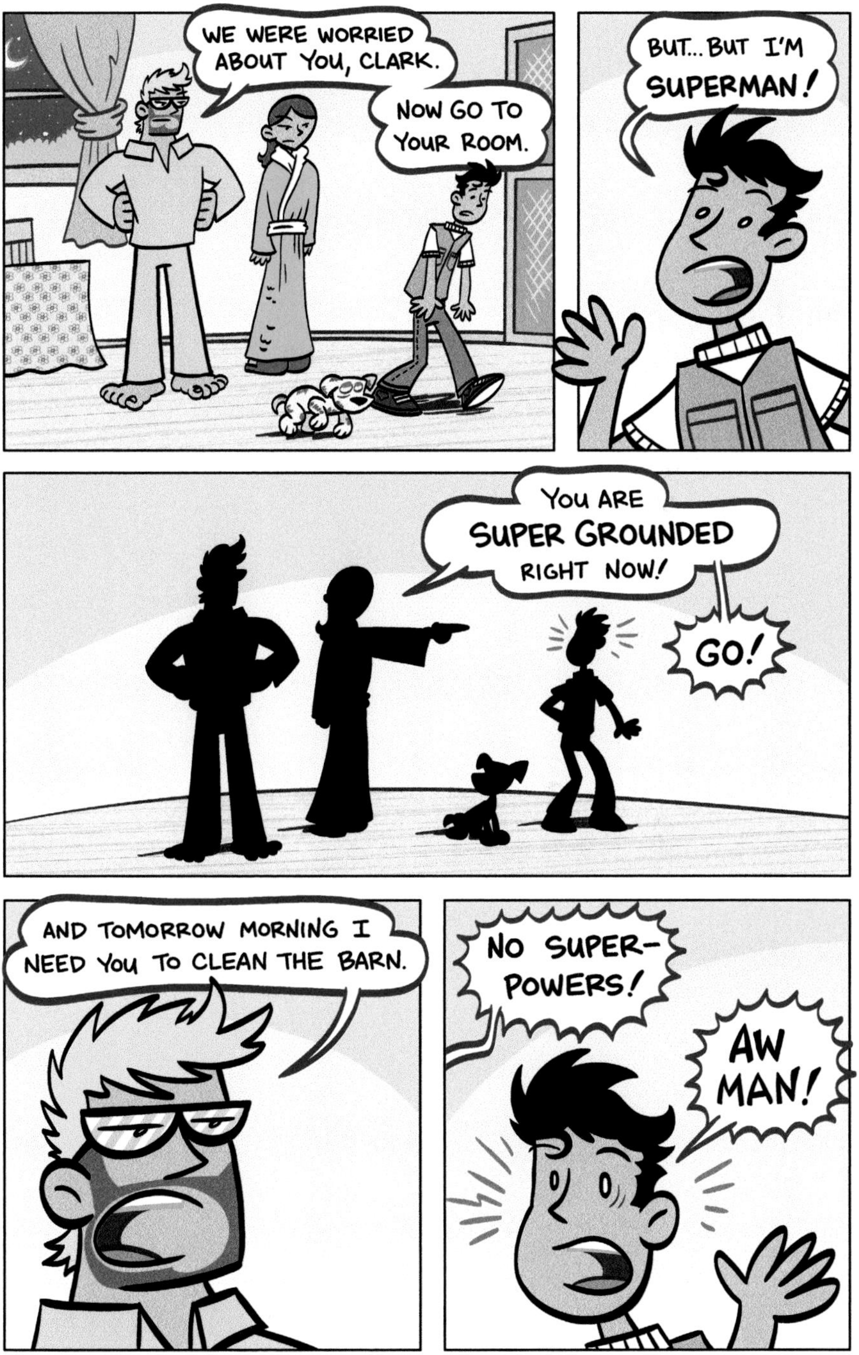
WE WERE WORRIED ABOUT YOU, CLARK.
NOW GO TO YOUR ROOM.
BUT... BUT I'M SUPERMAN!
YOU ARE SUPER GROUNDED RIGHT NOW!
GO!
AND TOMORROW MORNING I NEED YOU TO CLEAN THE BARN.
NO SUPER-POWERS!
AW MAN!

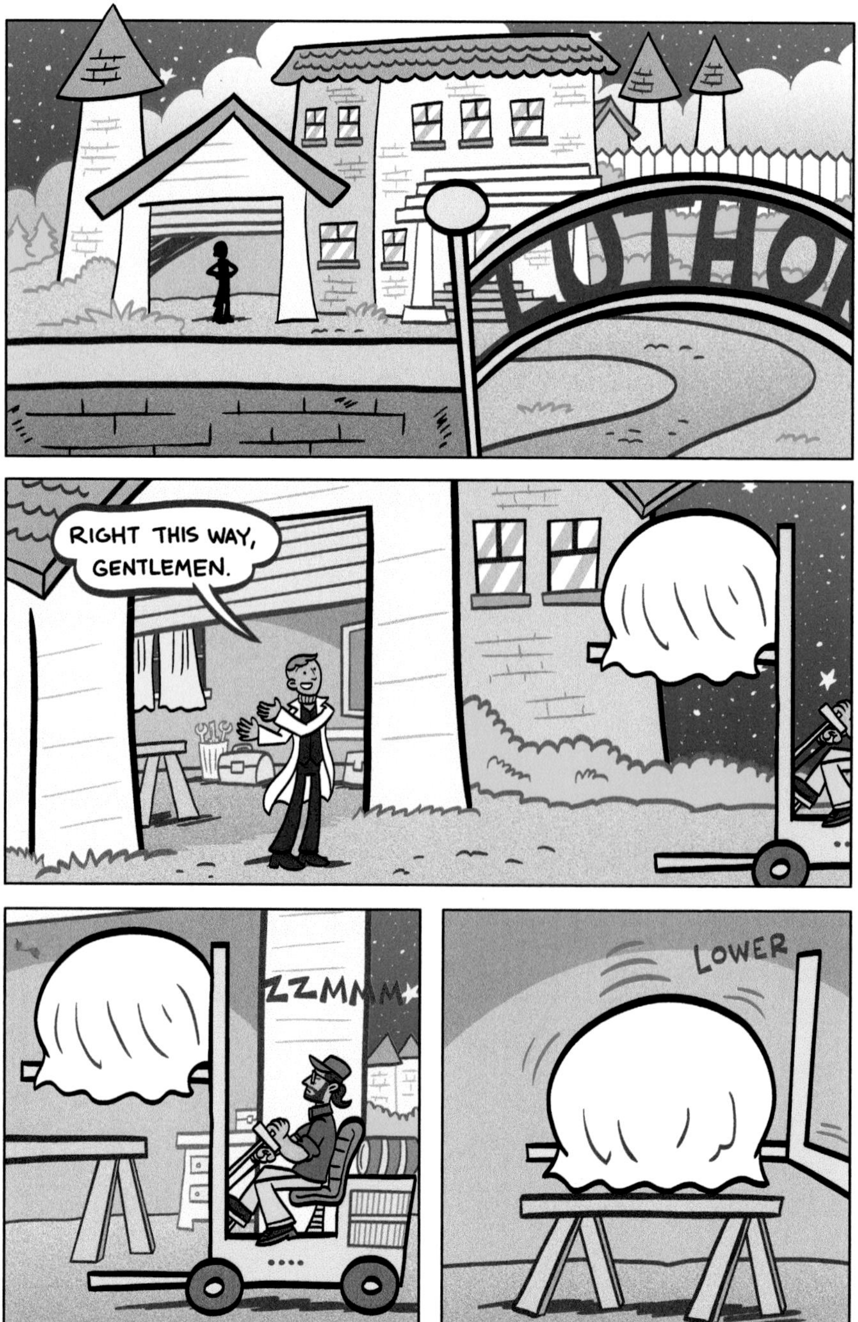
LUTHOR
RIGHT THIS WAY, GENTLEMEN.
ZZMMM
LOWER

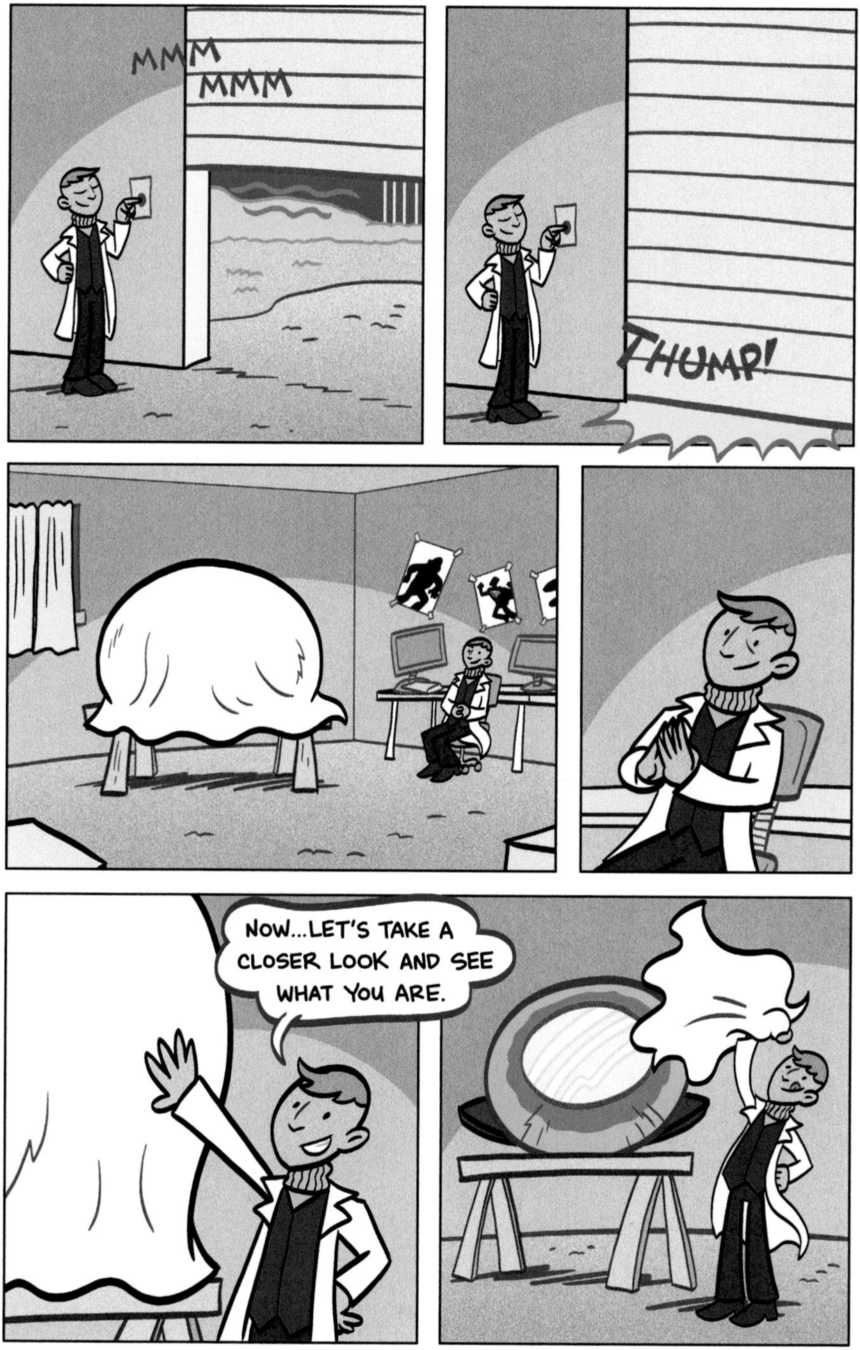
MMM
MMM
THUMP!
NOW...LET'S TAKE A CLOSER LOOK AND SEE WHAT YOU ARE.

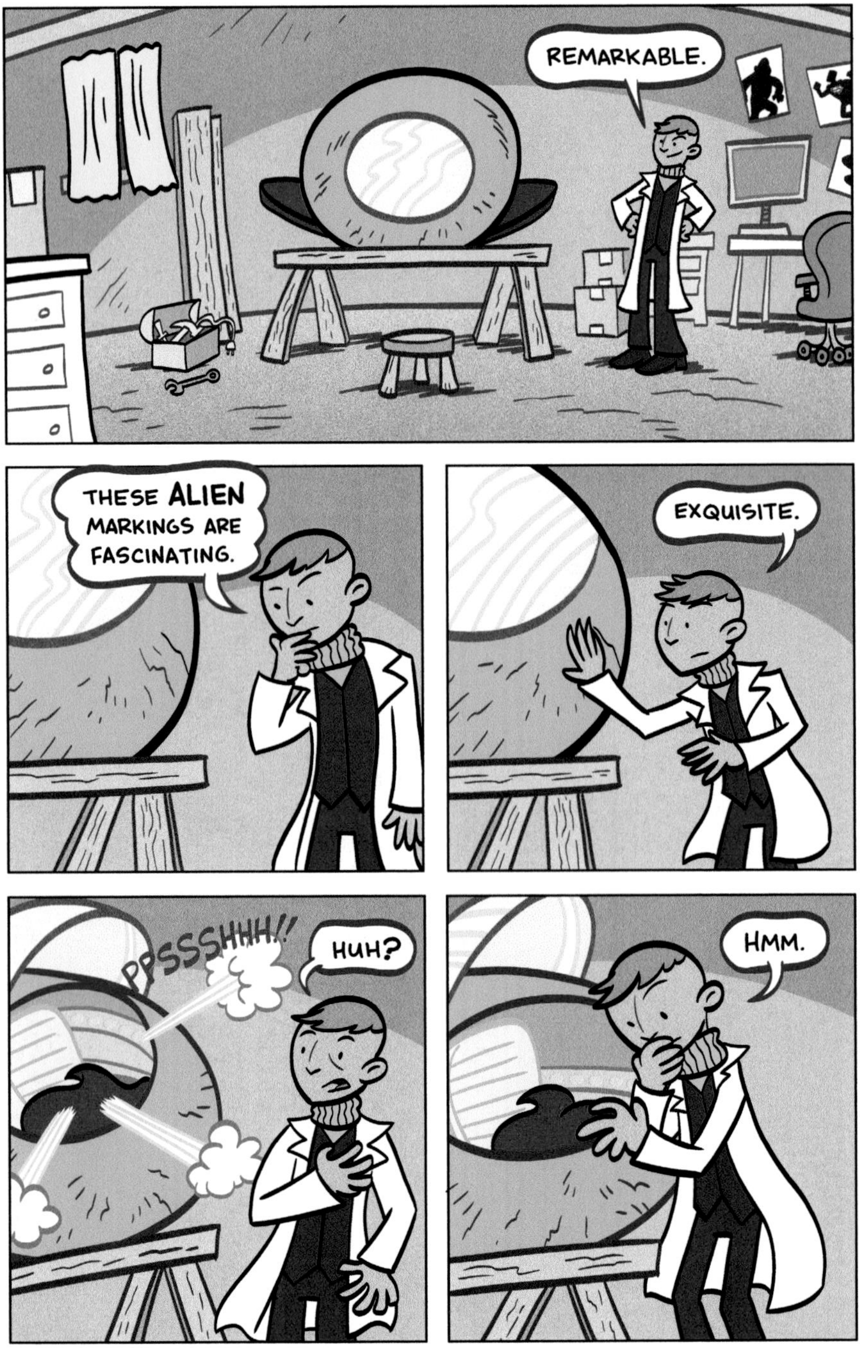
REMARKABLE.
THESE ALIEN MARKINGS ARE FASCINATING.
EXQUISITE.
PPSSSHHH!!
HUH?
HMM.

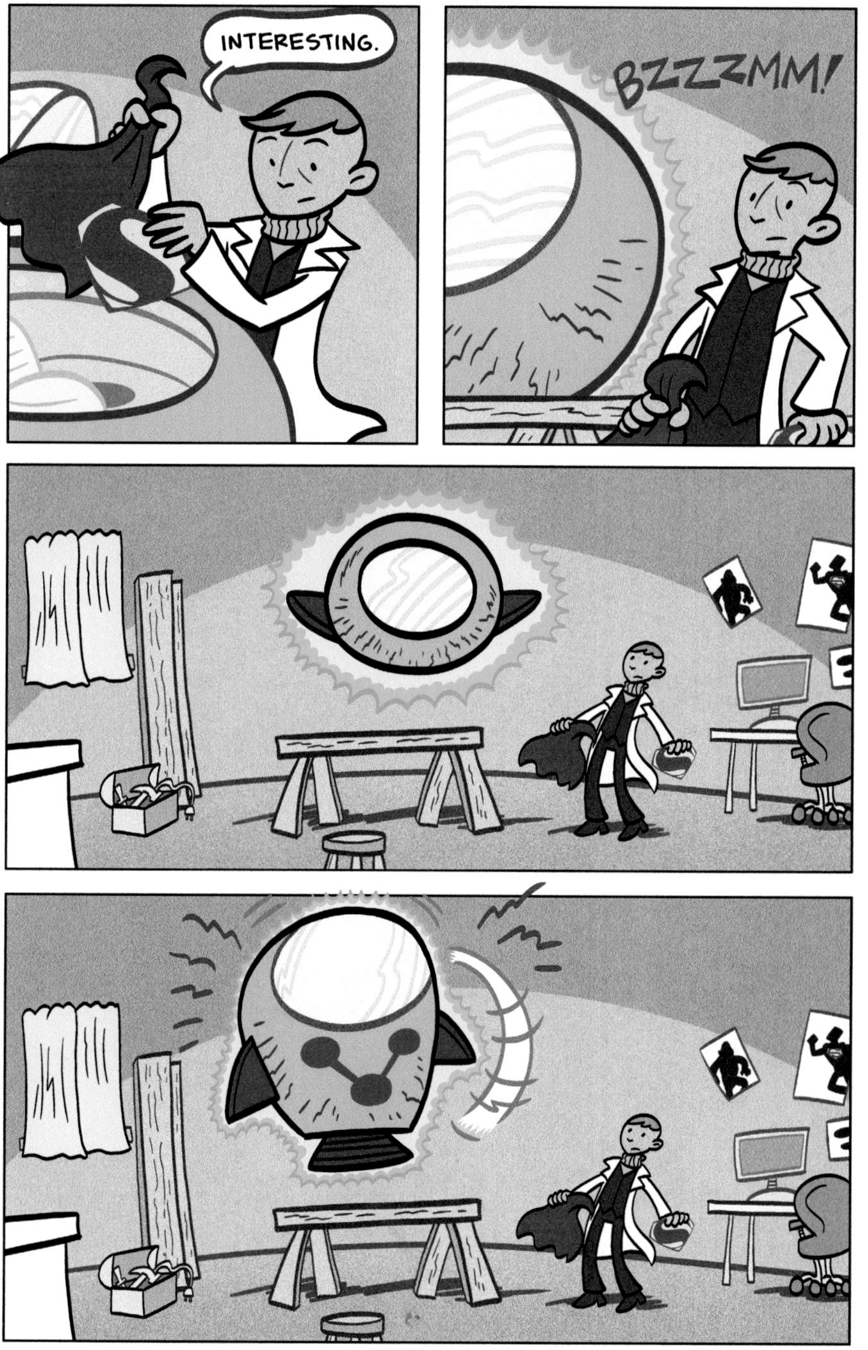
INTERESTING.
BZZZMM!

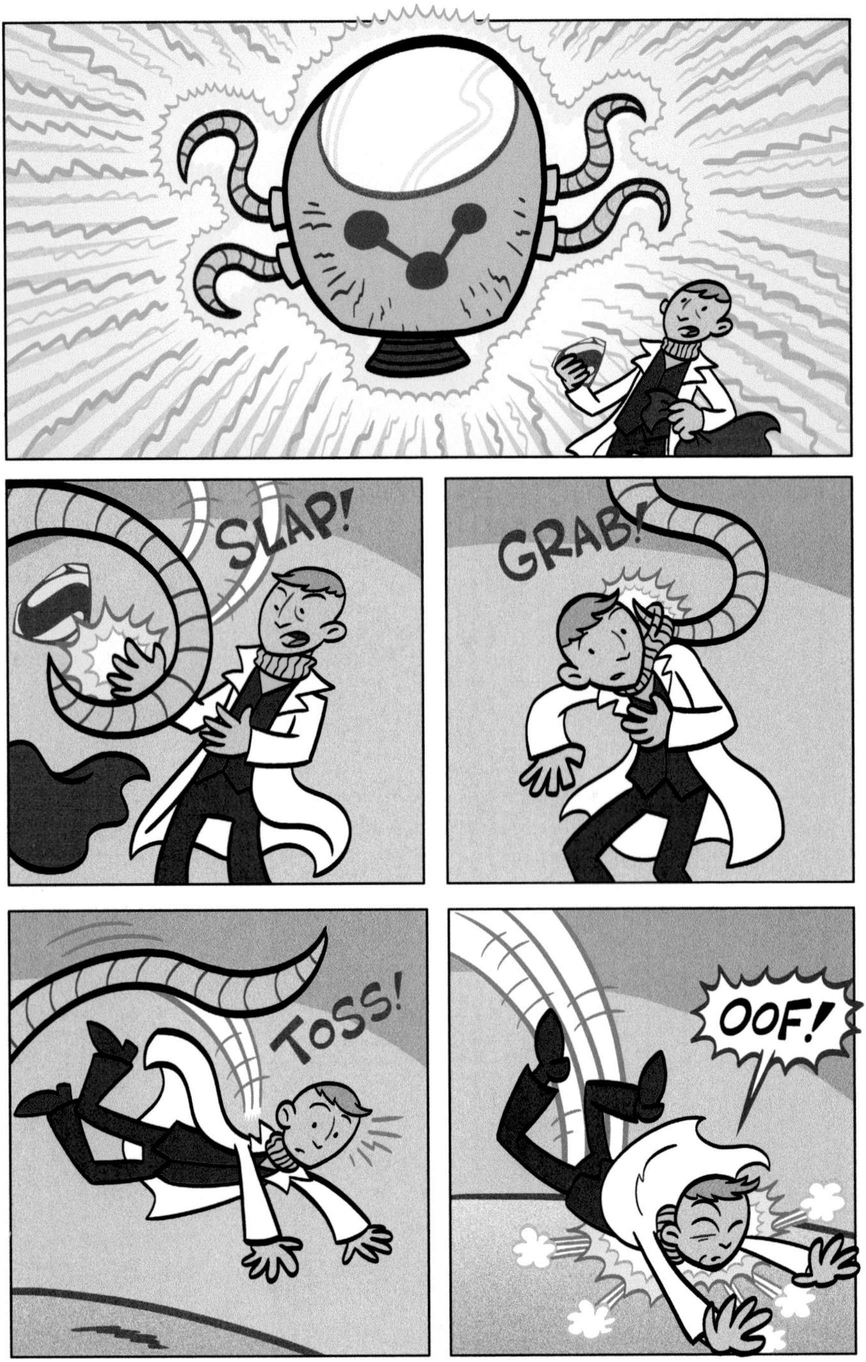
SLAP!
GRAB!
TOSS!
OOF!

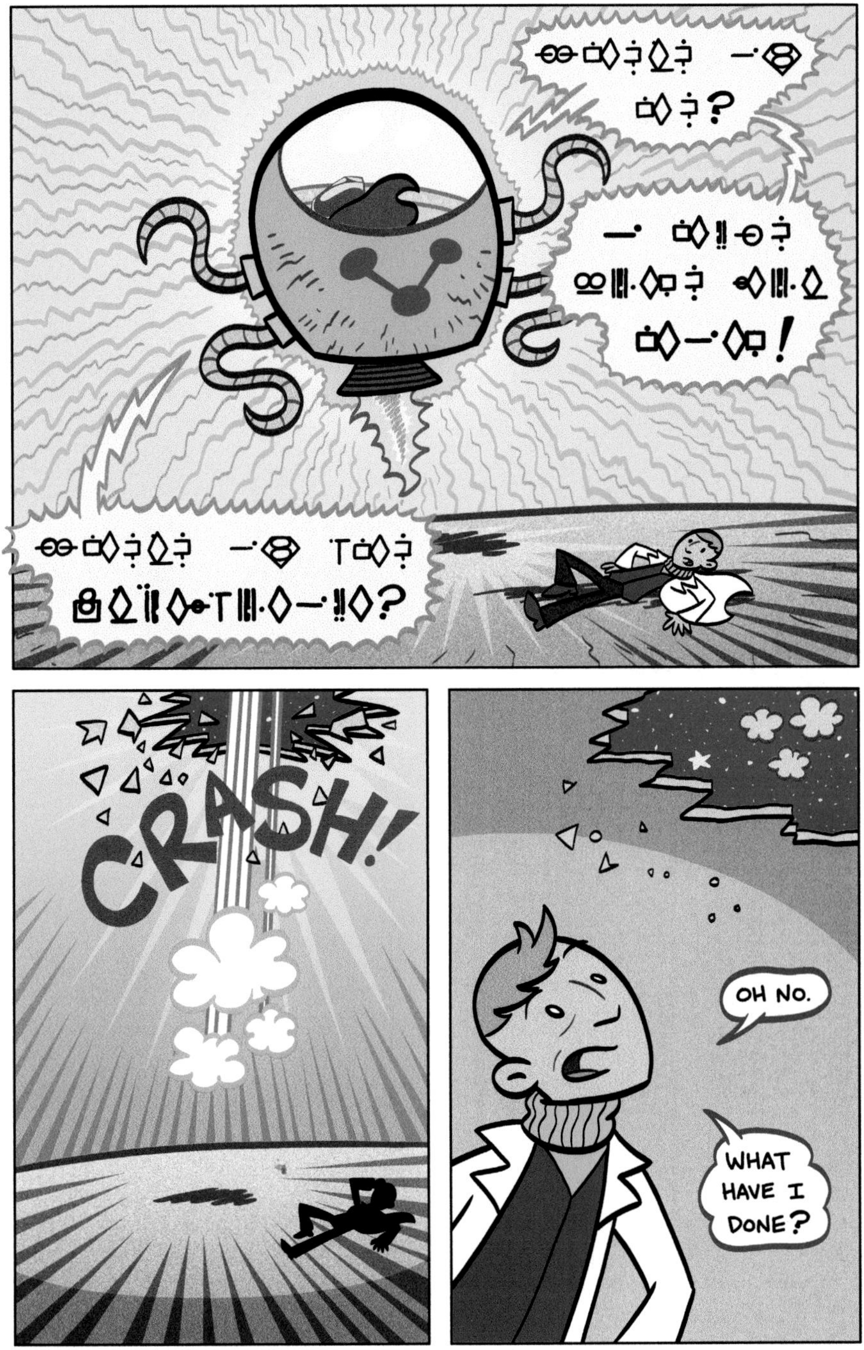
CRASH!
OH NO.
WHAT HAVE I DONE?

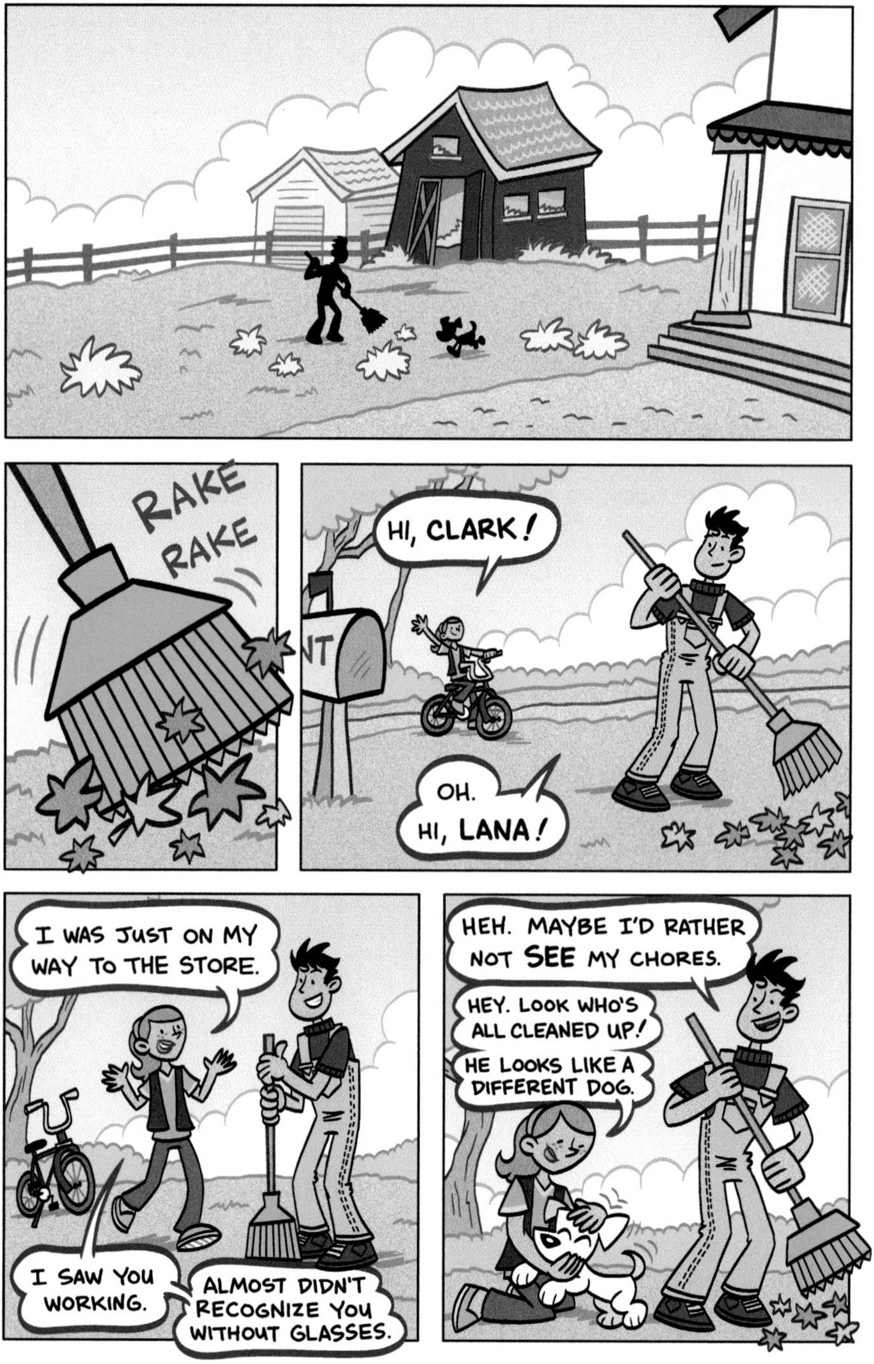
RAKE
RAKE
HI, CLARK!
OH.
HI, LANA!
I WAS JUST ON MY WAY TO THE STORE.
I SAW YOU WORKING.
ALMOST DIDN'T RECOGNIZE YOU WITHOUT GLASSES.
HEH. MAYBE I'D RATHER NOT SEE MY CHORES.
HEY. LOOK WHO'S ALL CLEANED UP!
HE LOOKS LIKE A DIFFERENT DOG.

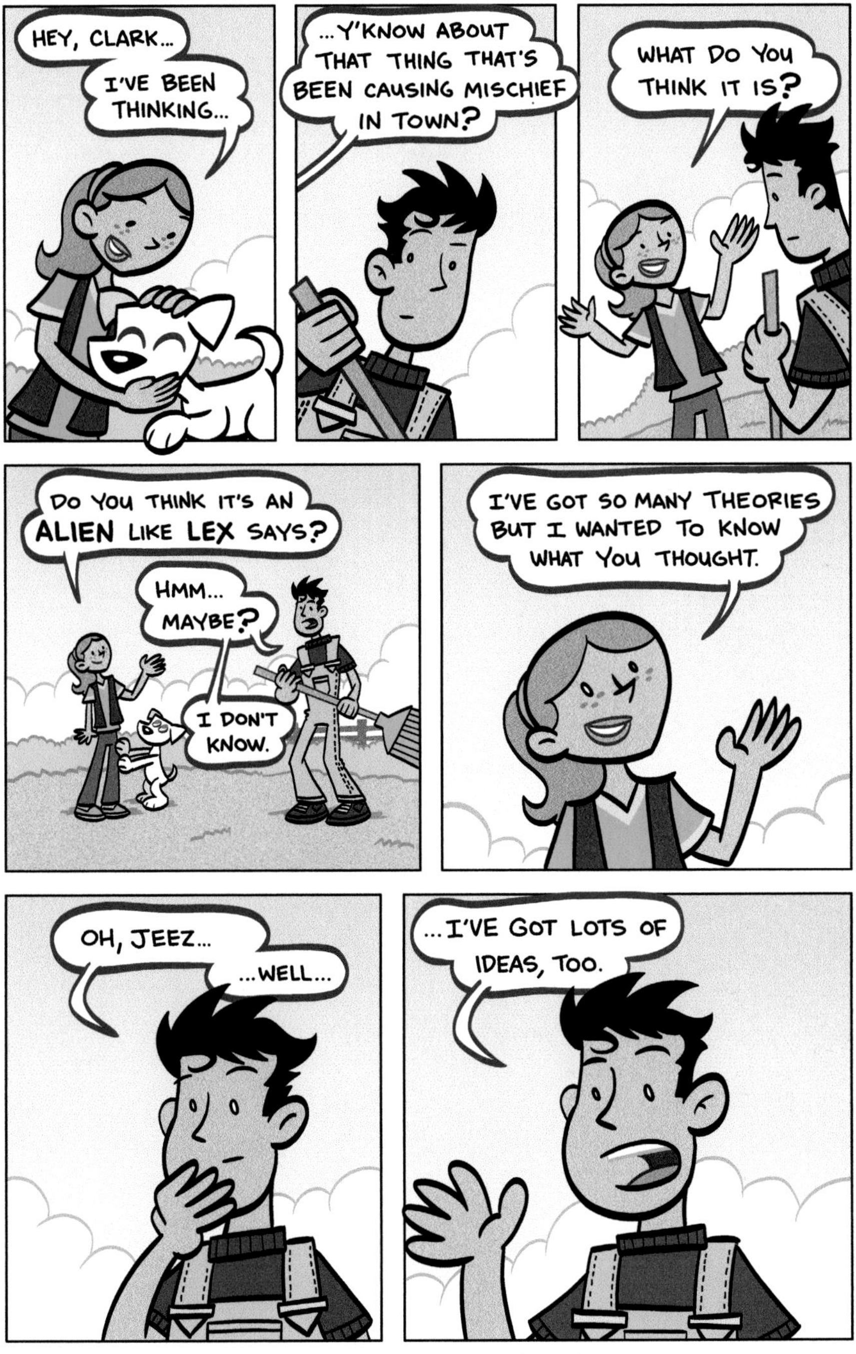
HEY, CLARK...
I'VE BEEN THINKING...
...Y'KNOW ABOUT THAT THING THAT'S BEEN CAUSING MISCHIEF IN TOWN?
WHAT DO YOU THINK IT IS?
DO YOU THINK IT'S AN ALIEN LIKE LEX SAYS?
HMM... MAYBE?
I DON'T KNOW.
I'VE GOT SO MANY THEORIES BUT I WANTED TO KNOW WHAT YOU THOUGHT.
OH, JEEZ...
...WELL...
...I'VE GOT LOTS OF IDEAS, TOO.

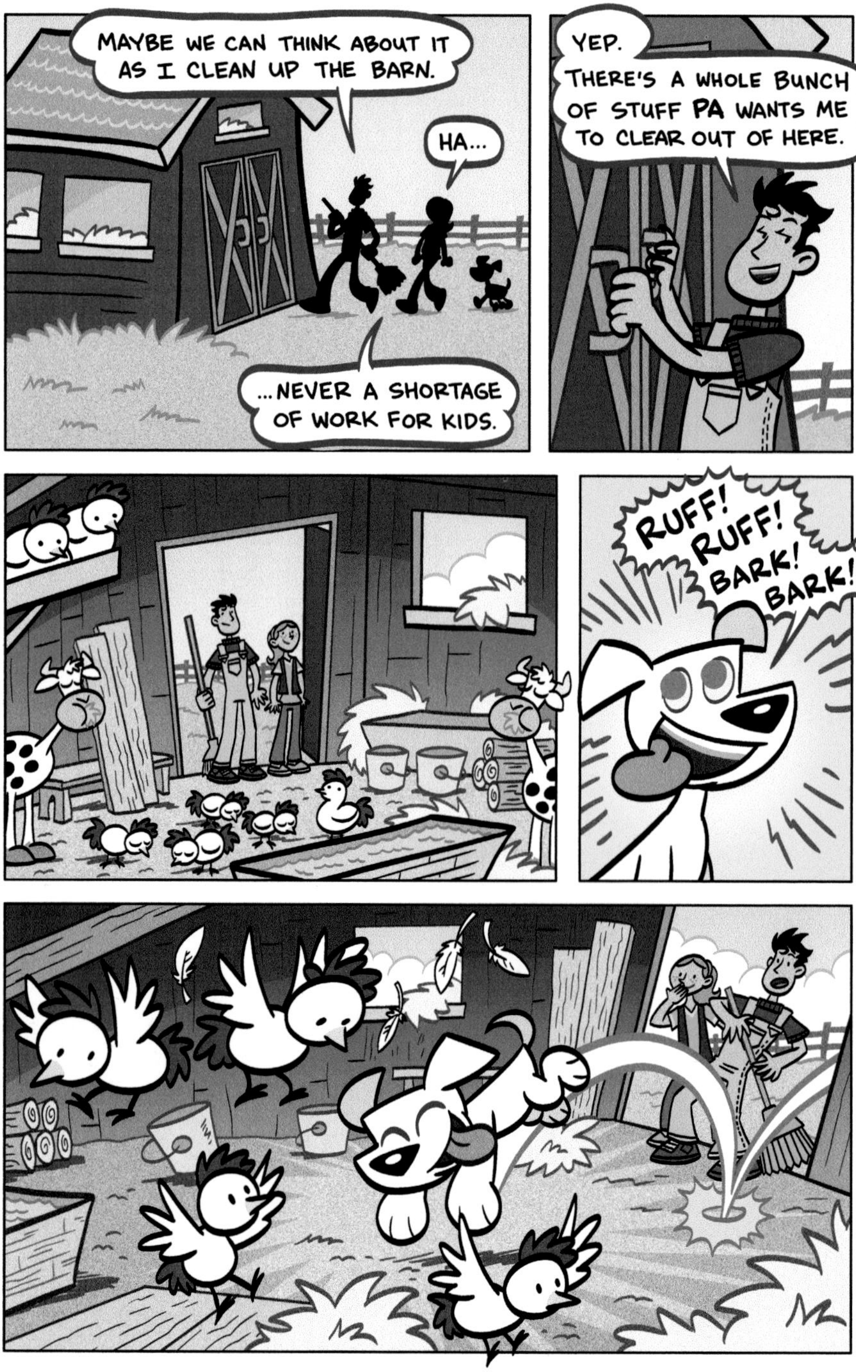
MAYBE WE CAN THINK ABOUT IT AS I CLEAN UP THE BARN.
HA...
...NEVER A SHORTAGE OF WORK FOR KIDS.
YEP.
THERE'S A WHOLE BUNCH OF STUFF PA WANTS ME TO CLEAR OUT OF HERE.
RUFF! RUFF! BARK! BARK!

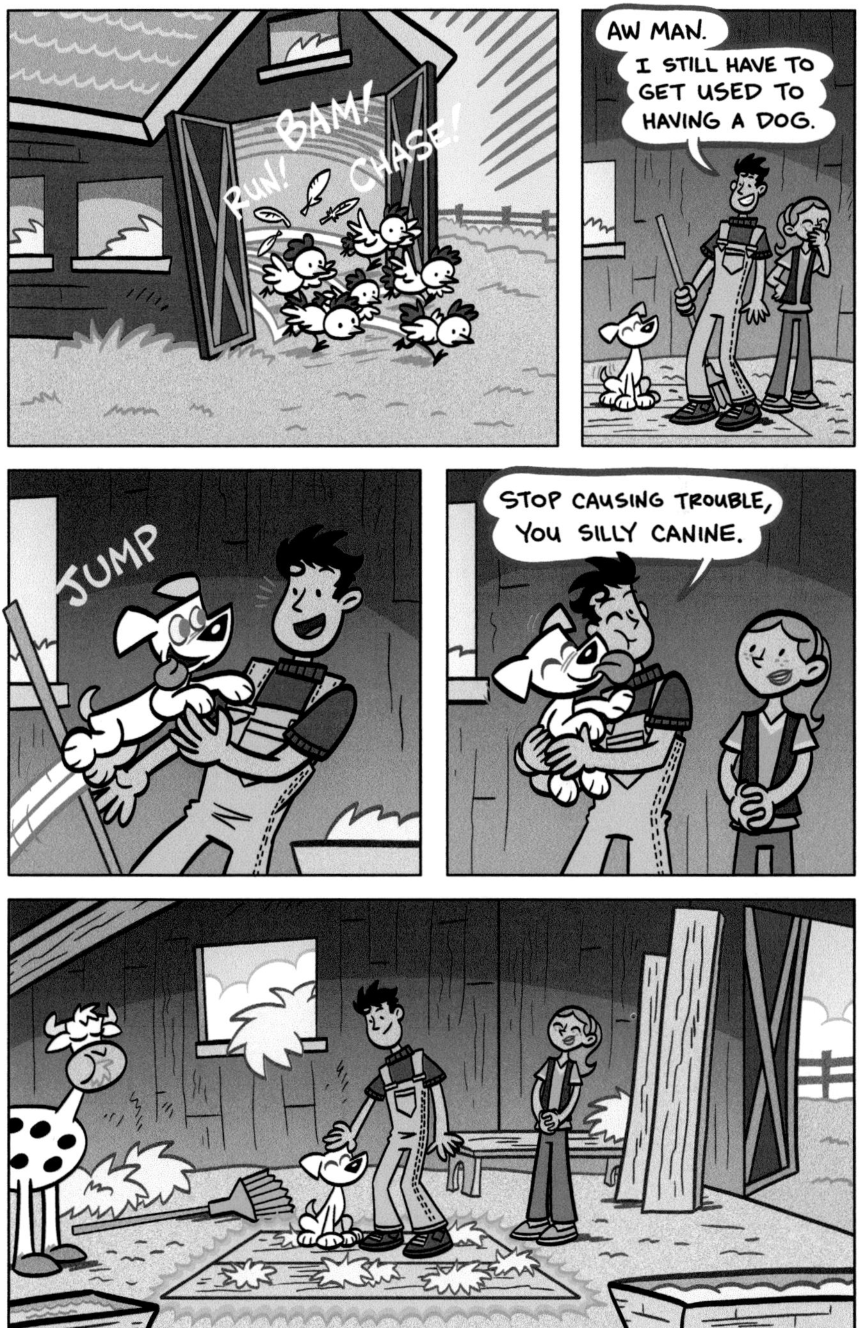
BAM!
RUN!
CHASE!
AW MAN.
I STILL HAVE TO GET USED TO HAVING A DOG.
JUMP
STOP CAUSING TROUBLE, YOU SILLY CANINE.

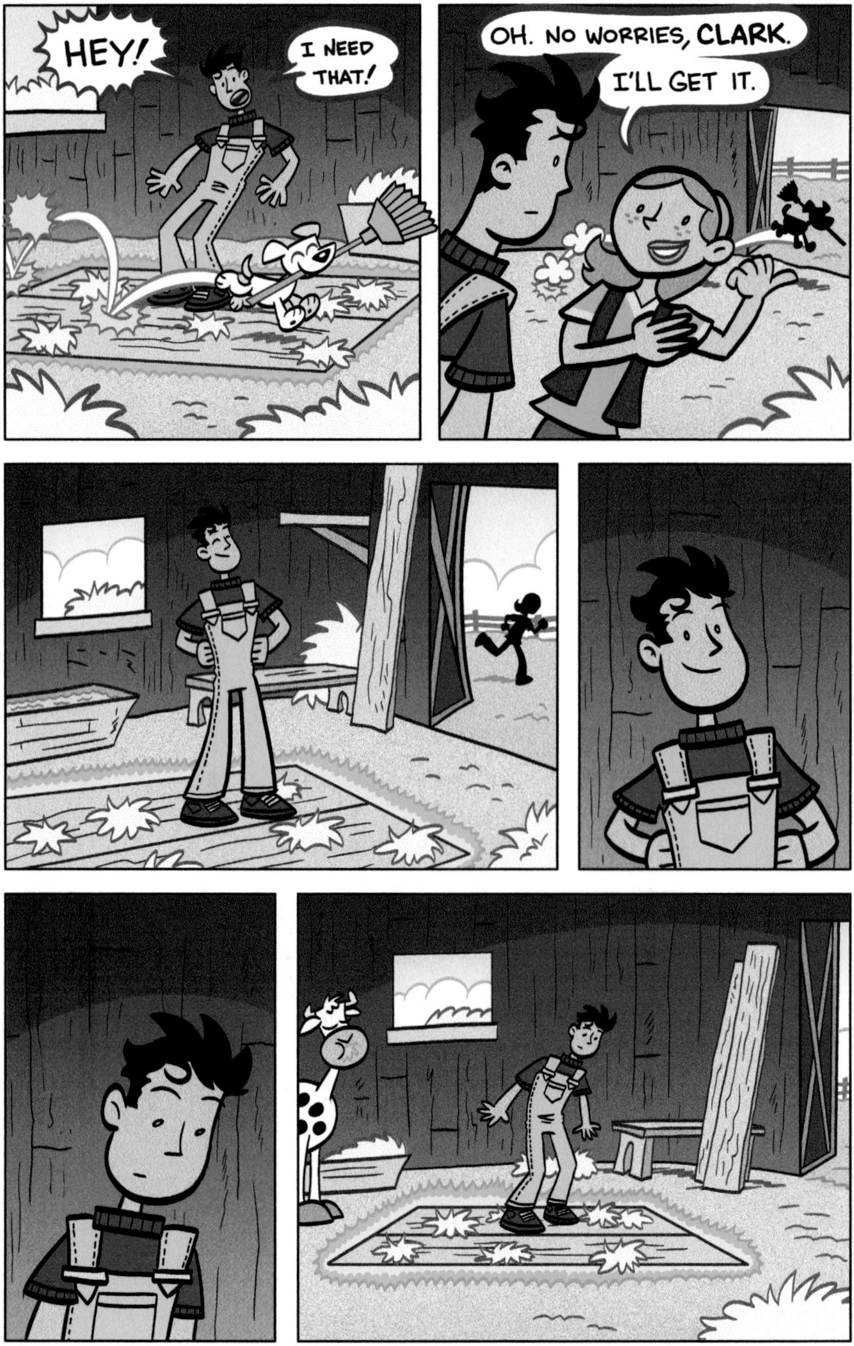
HEY!
I NEED THAT!
OH. NO WORRIES, CLARK.
I'LL GET IT.

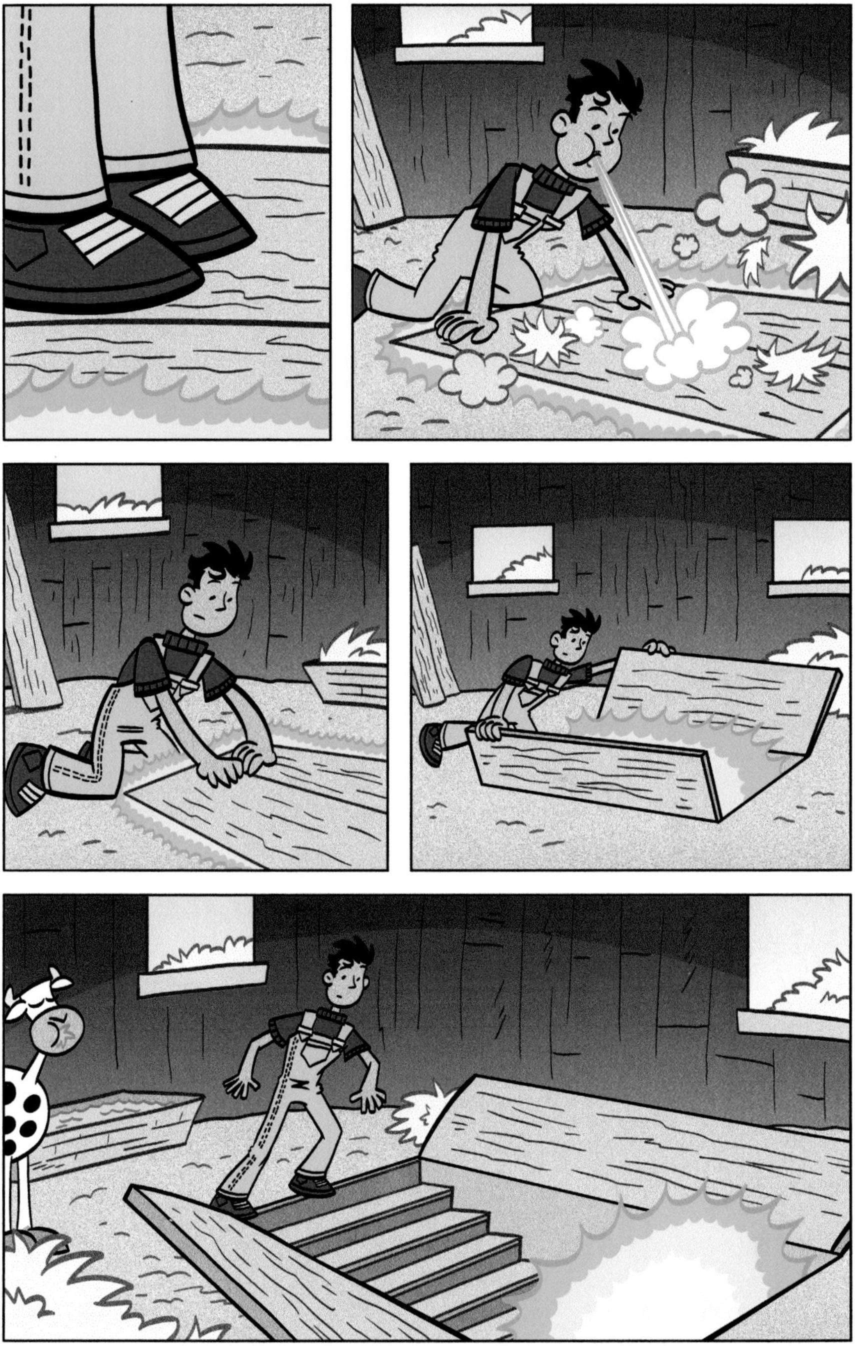

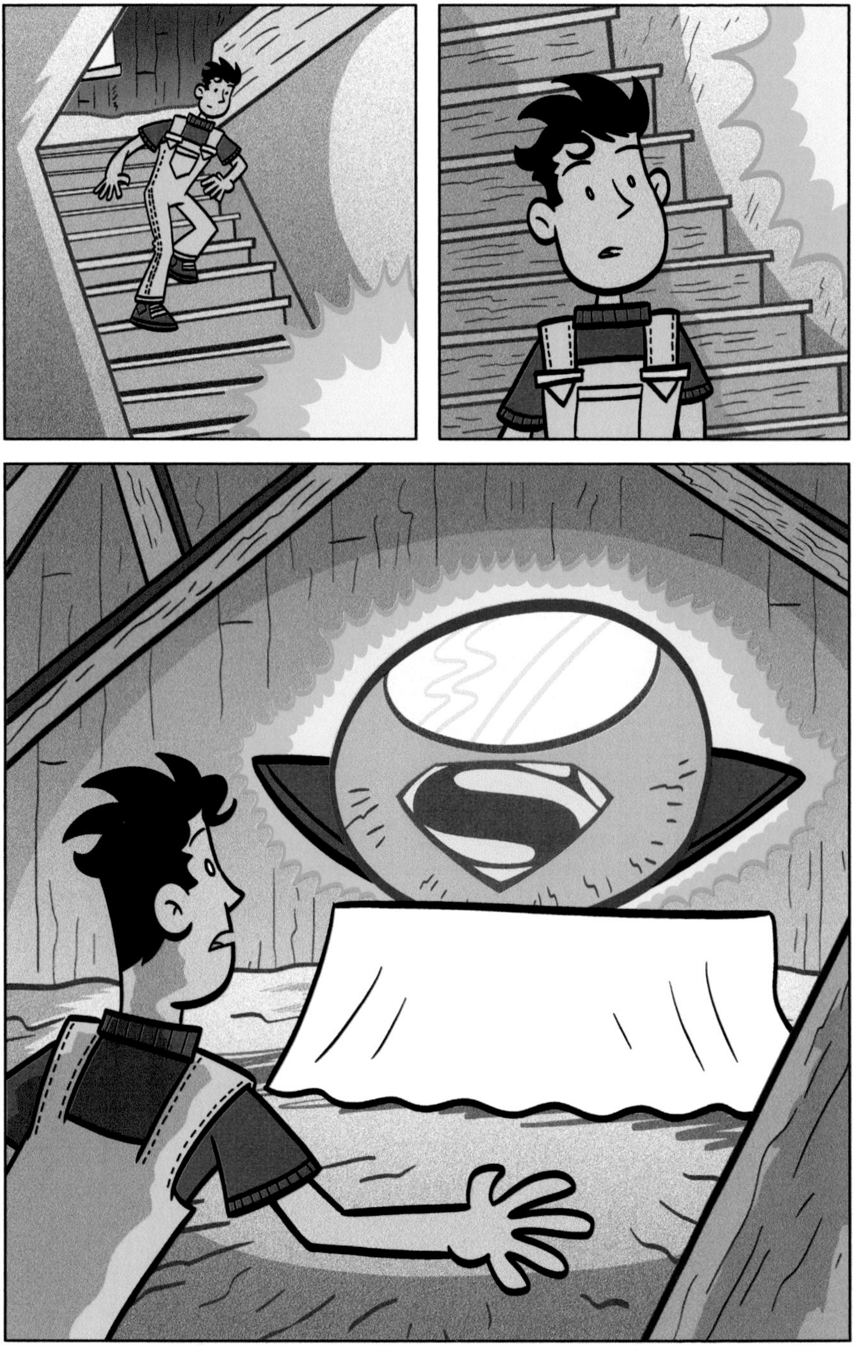

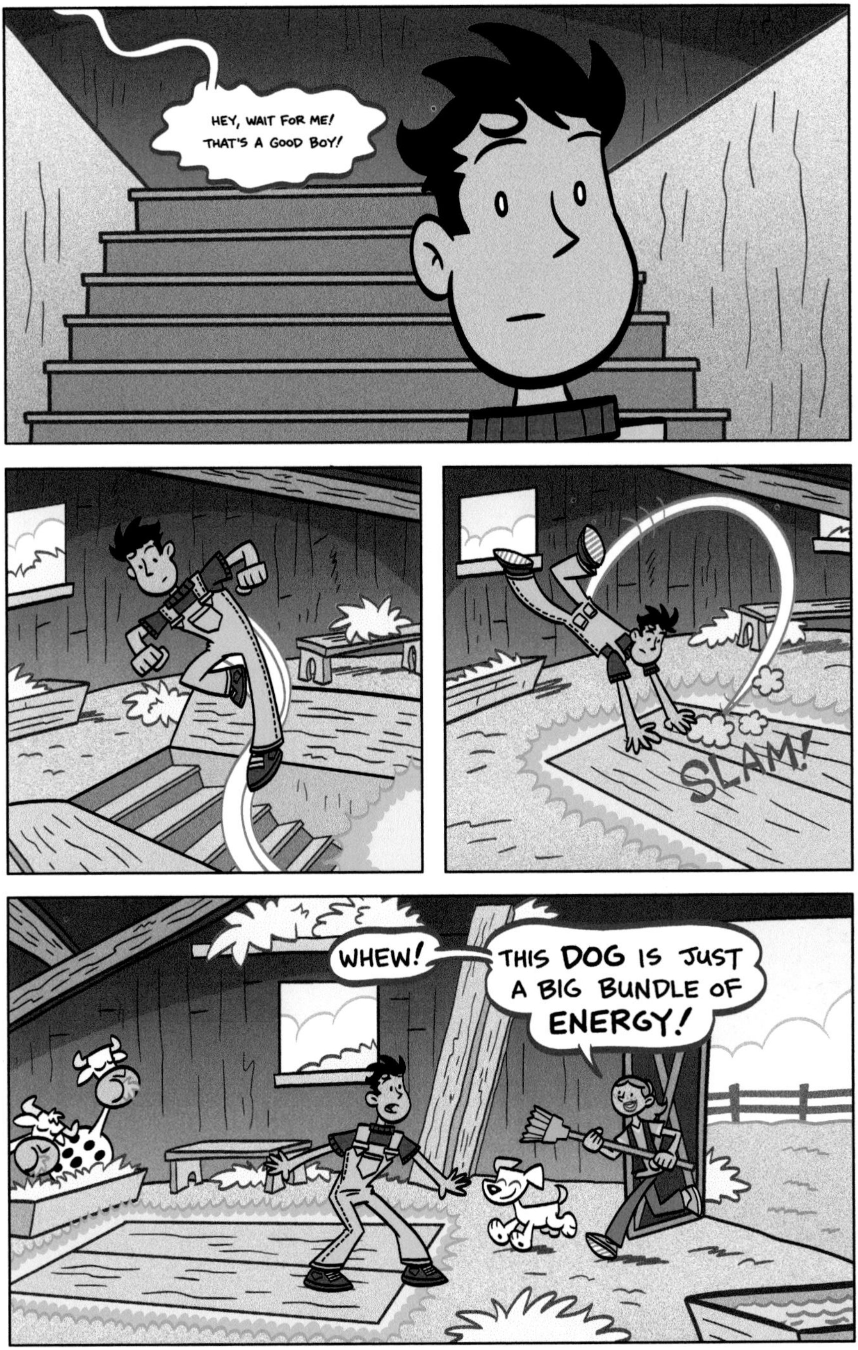

HEY, WAIT FOR ME! THAT'S A GOOD BOY!
SLAM!
WHEW!
THIS DOG IS JUST A BIG BUNDLE OF ENERGY!

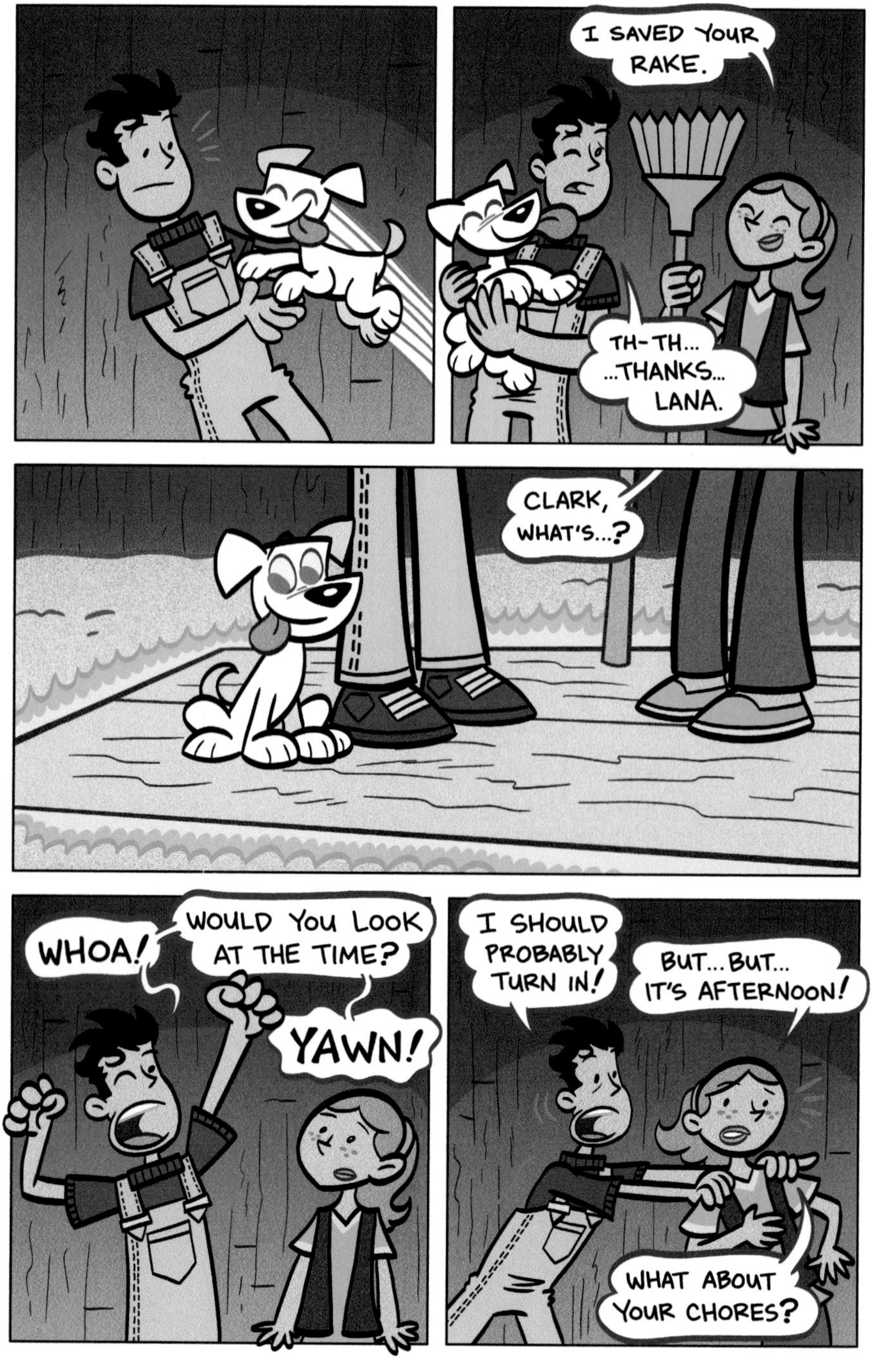
I SAVED YOUR RAKE.
TH-TH... ...THANKS... LANA.
CLARK, WHAT'S...?
WHOA!
WOULD YOU LOOK AT THE TIME?
YAWN!
I SHOULD PROBABLY TURN IN!
BUT... BUT... IT'S AFTERNOON!
WHAT ABOUT YOUR CHORES?

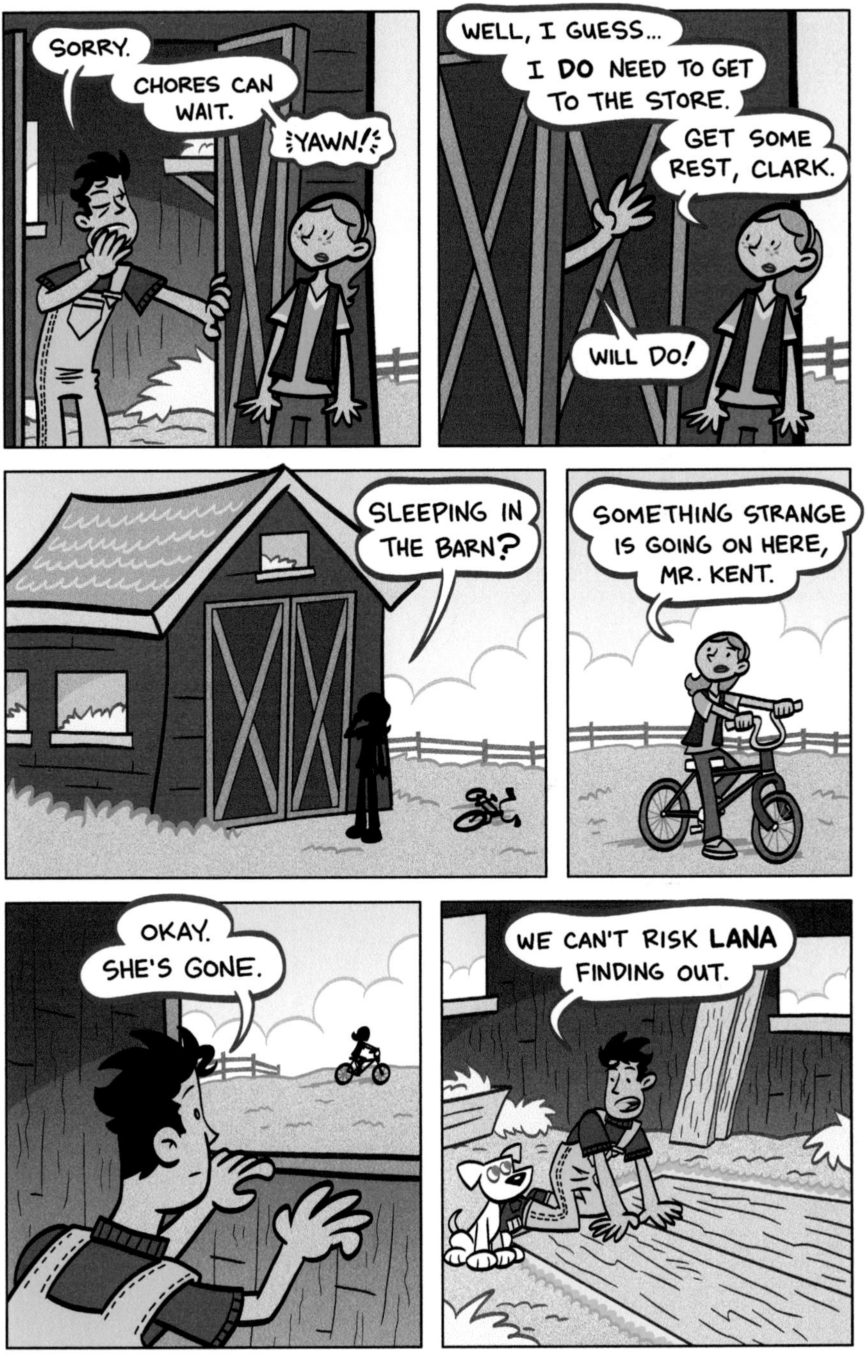
SORRY.
CHORES CAN WAIT.
YAWN!
WELL, I GUESS...
I DO NEED TO GET TO THE STORE.
GET SOME REST, CLARK.
WILL DO!
SLEEPING IN THE BARN?
SOMETHING STRANGE IS GOING ON HERE, MR. KENT.
OKAY. SHE'S GONE.
WE CAN'T RISK LANA FINDING OUT.

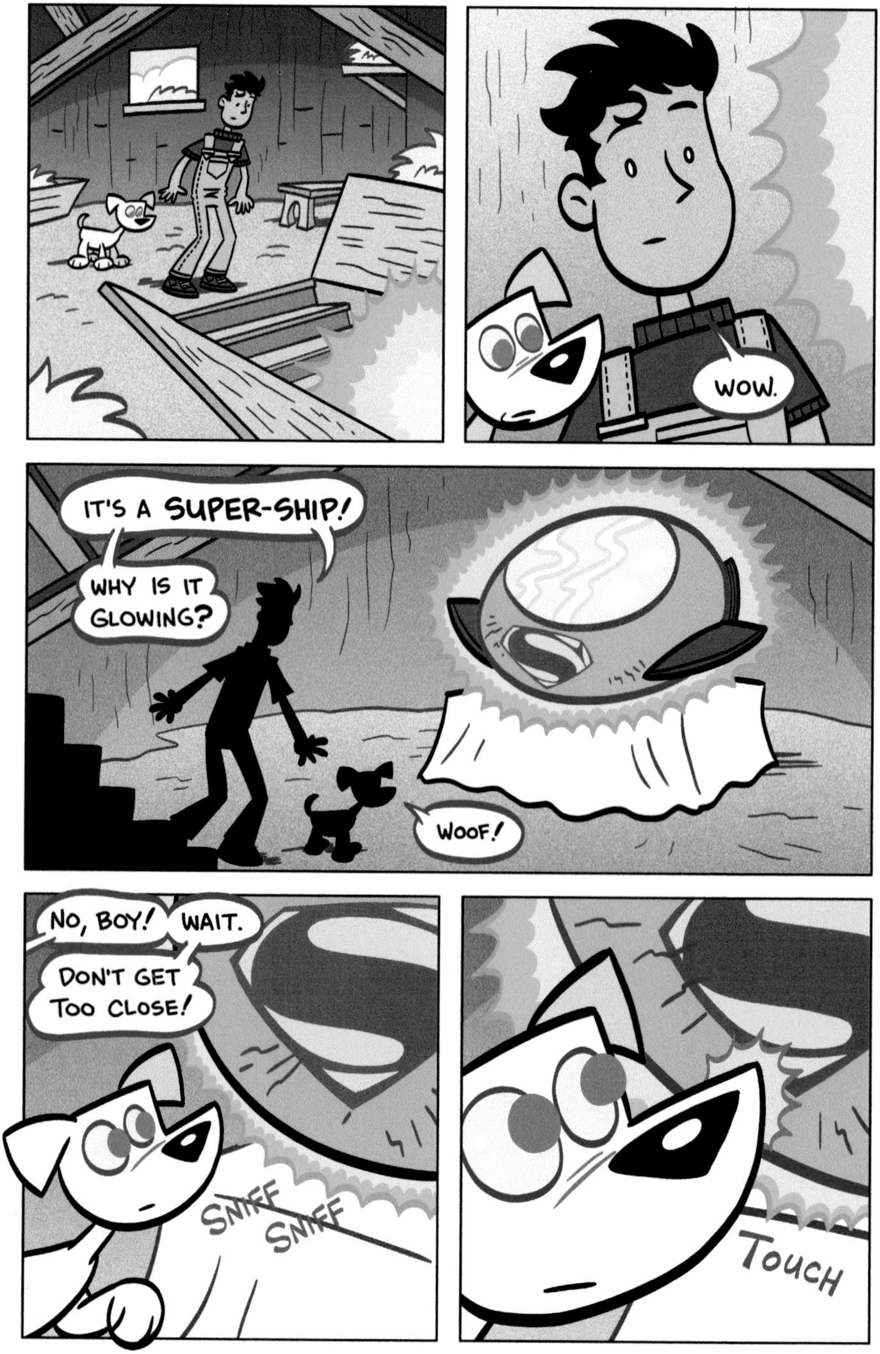
WOW.
IT'S A SUPER-SHIP!
WHY IS IT GLOWING?
WOOF!
NO, BOY!
WAIT.
DON'T GET TOO CLOSE!
SNIFF SNIFF
TOUCH

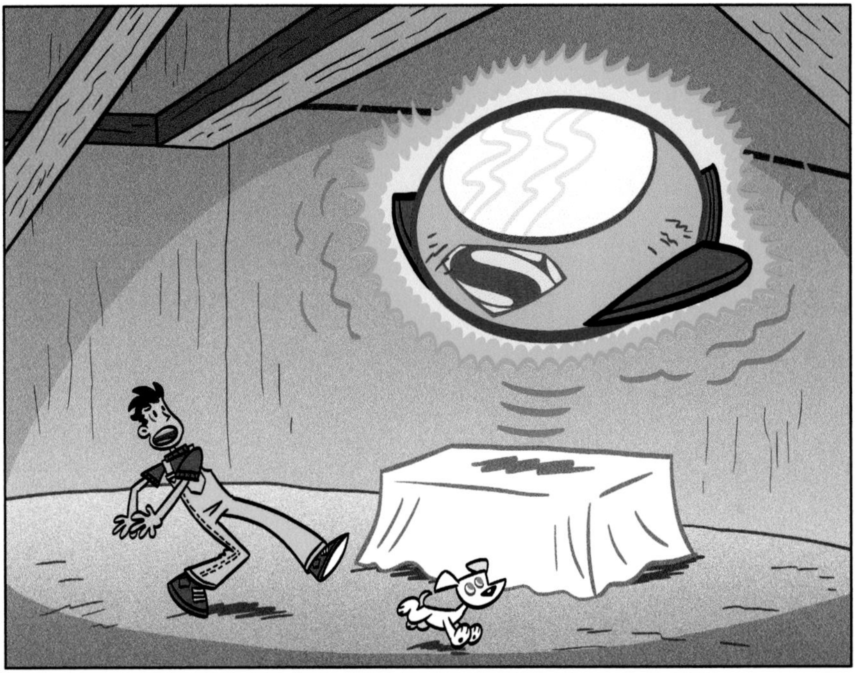

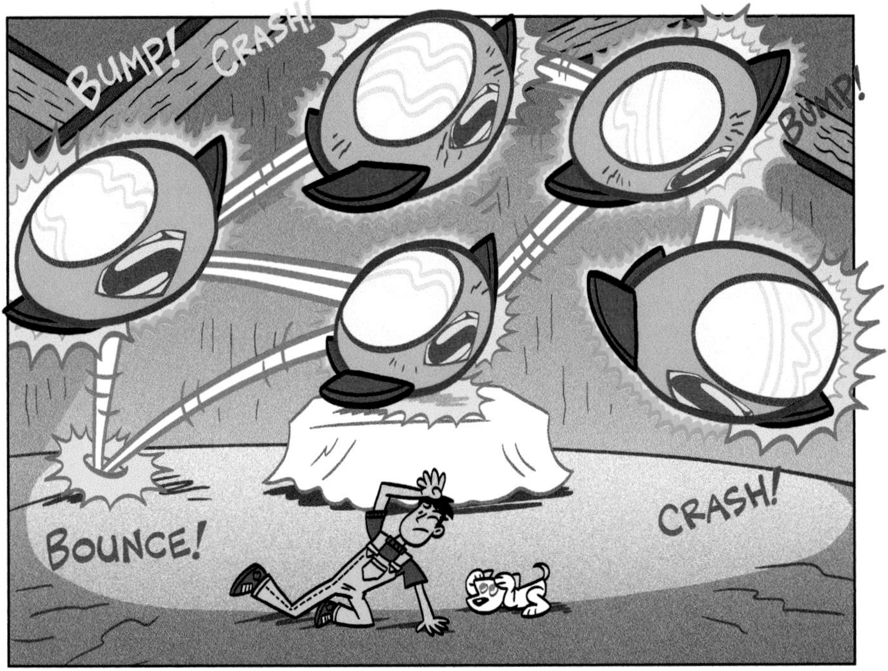
BUMP!
CRASH!
BUMP!
BOUNCE!
CRASH!

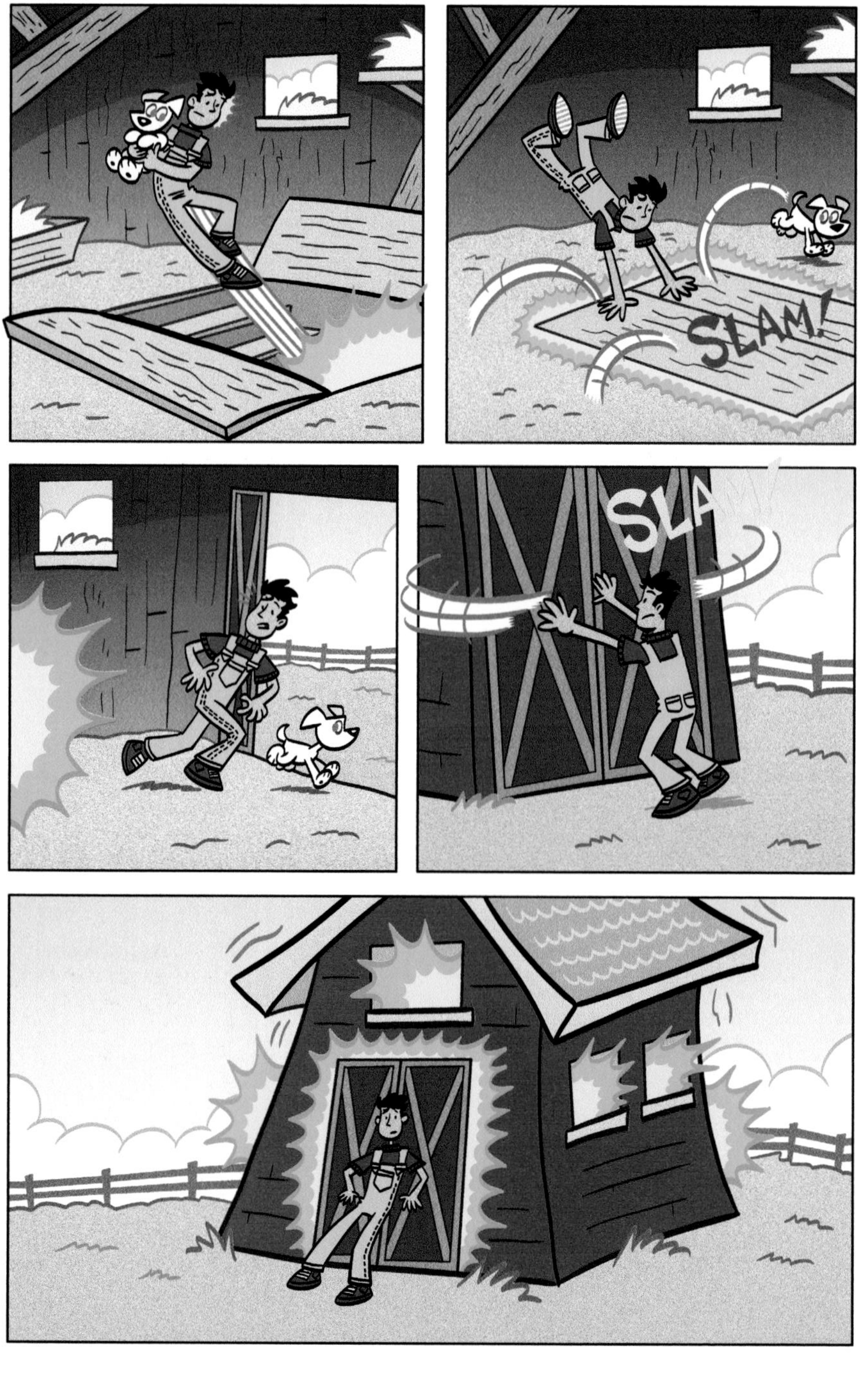
SLAM!
SLA

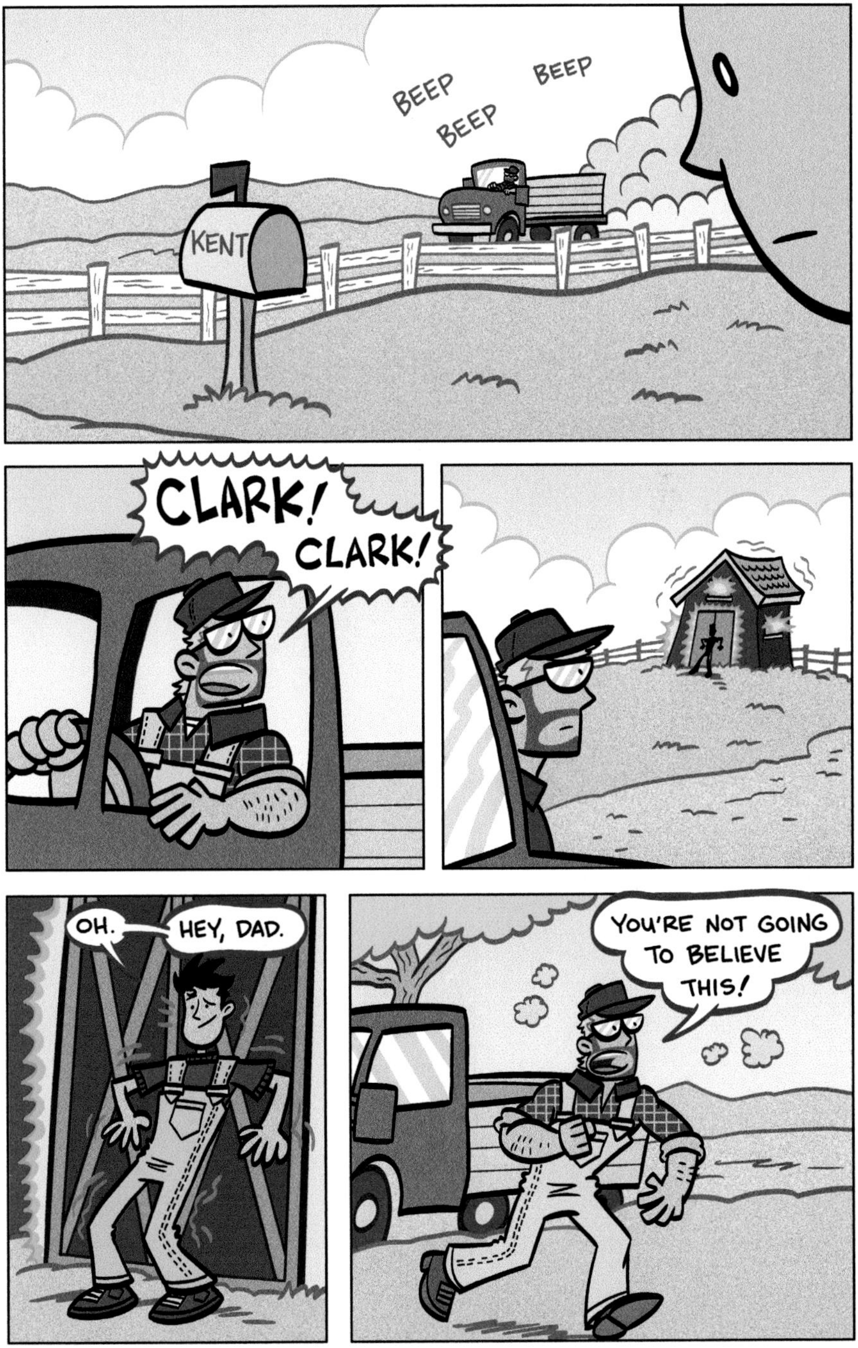
KENT
BEEP
BEEP
BEEP
CLARK!
CLARK!
OH.
HEY, DAD.
YOU'RE NOT GOING TO BELIEVE THIS!

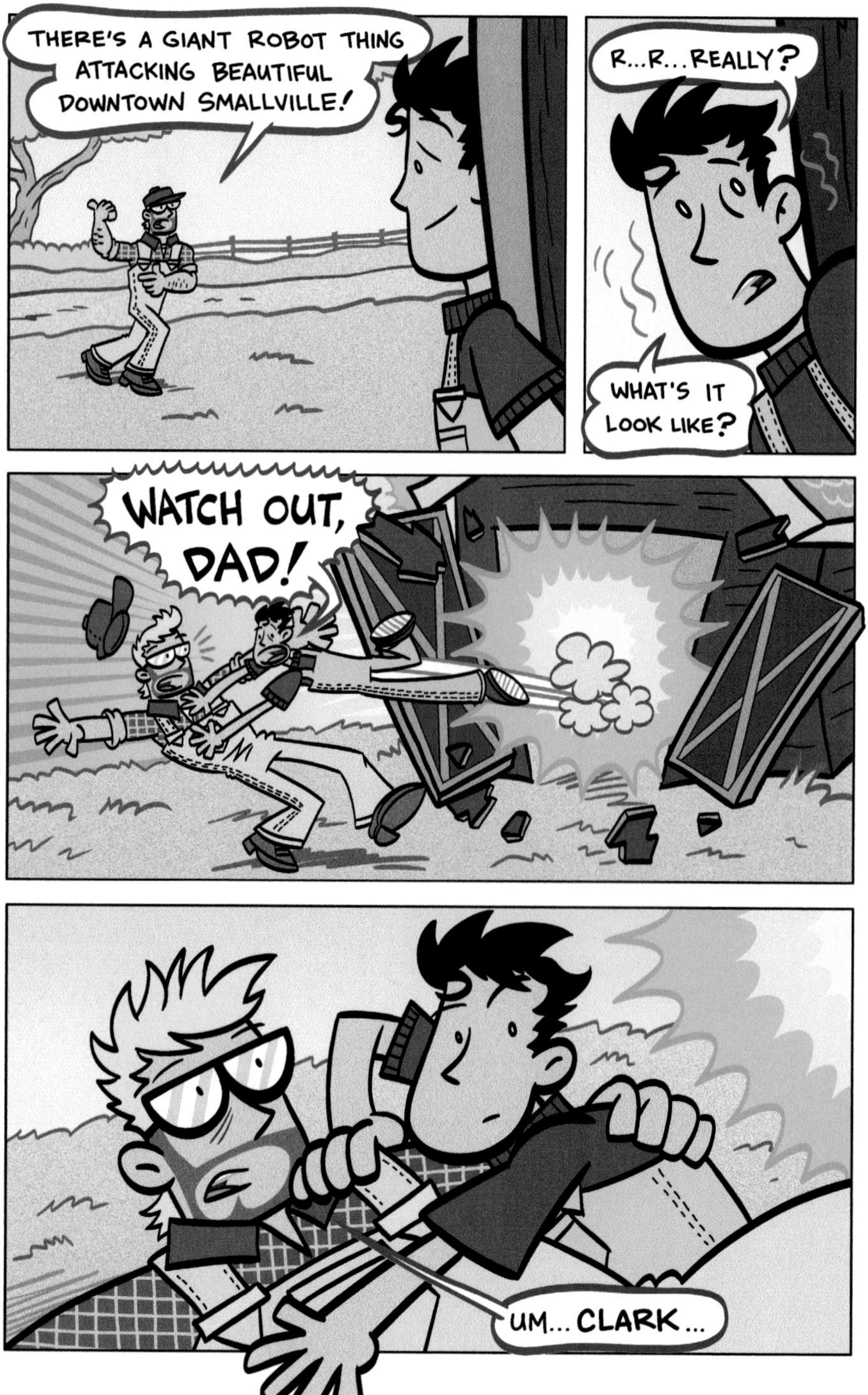
THERE'S A GIANT ROBOT THING ATTACKING BEAUTIFUL DOWNTOWN SMALLVILLE!
R...R...REALLY?
WHAT'S IT LOOK LIKE?
WATCH OUT, DAD!
UM...CLARK...

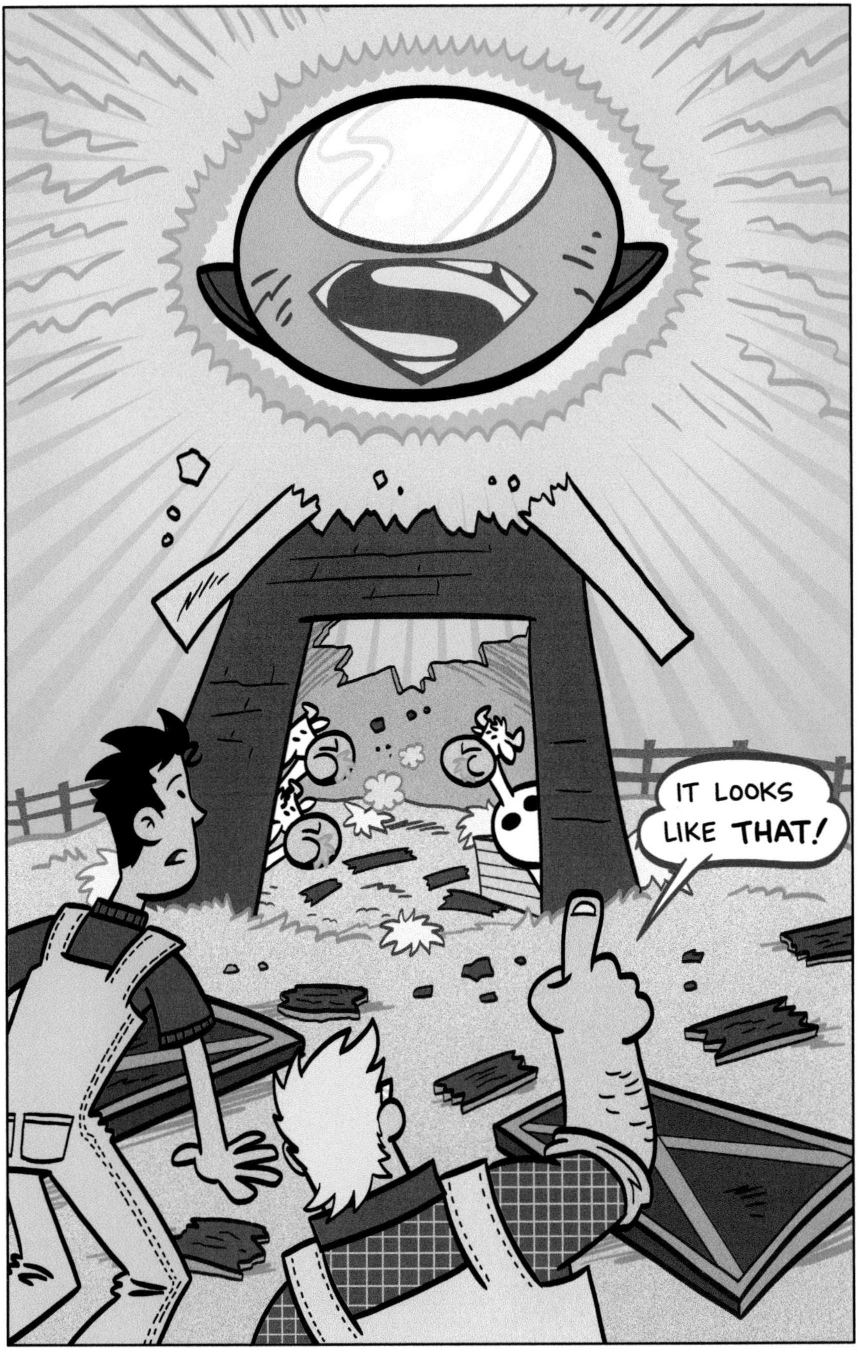
IT LOOKS LIKE THAT!

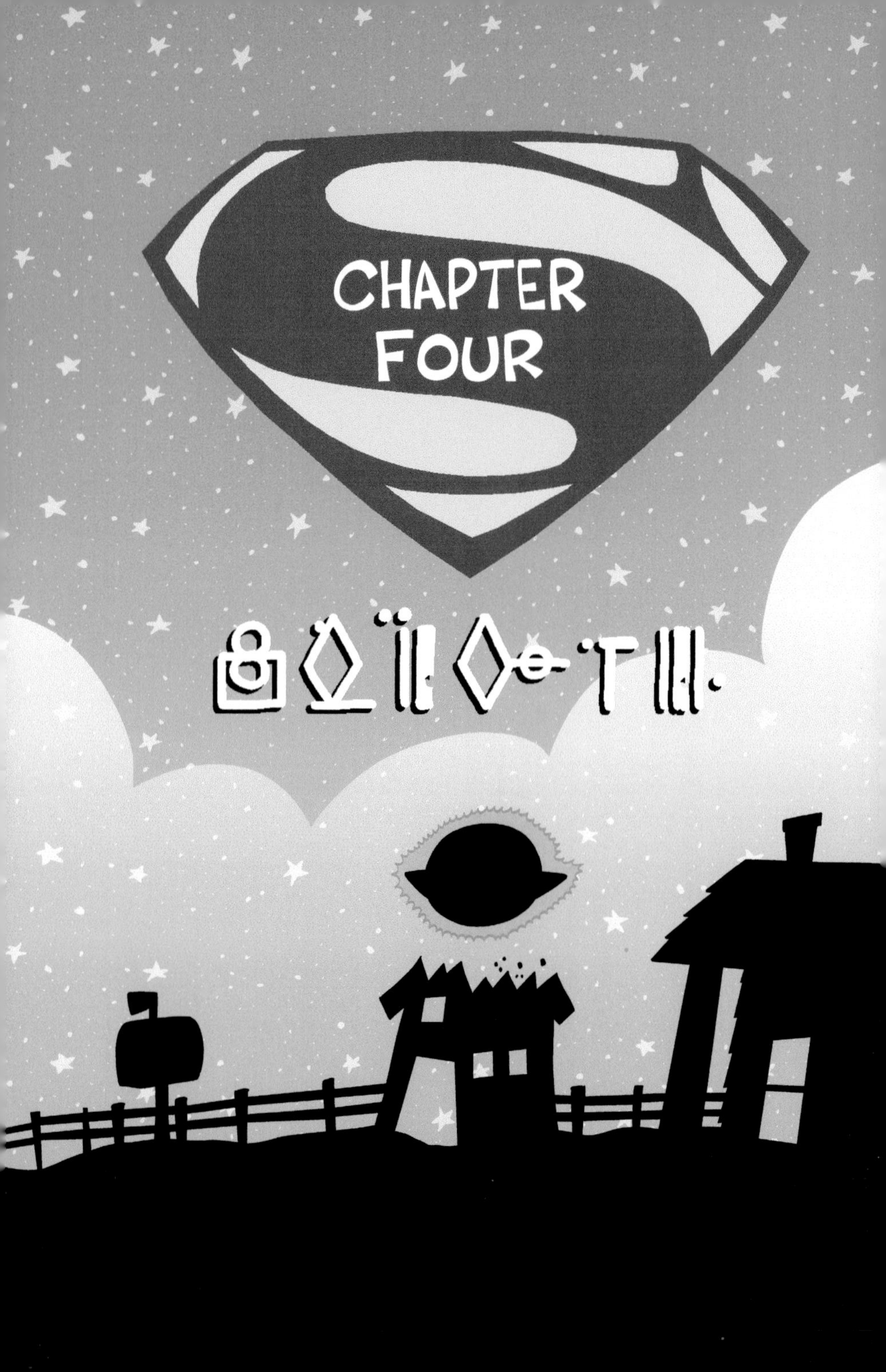
CHAPTER
FOUR

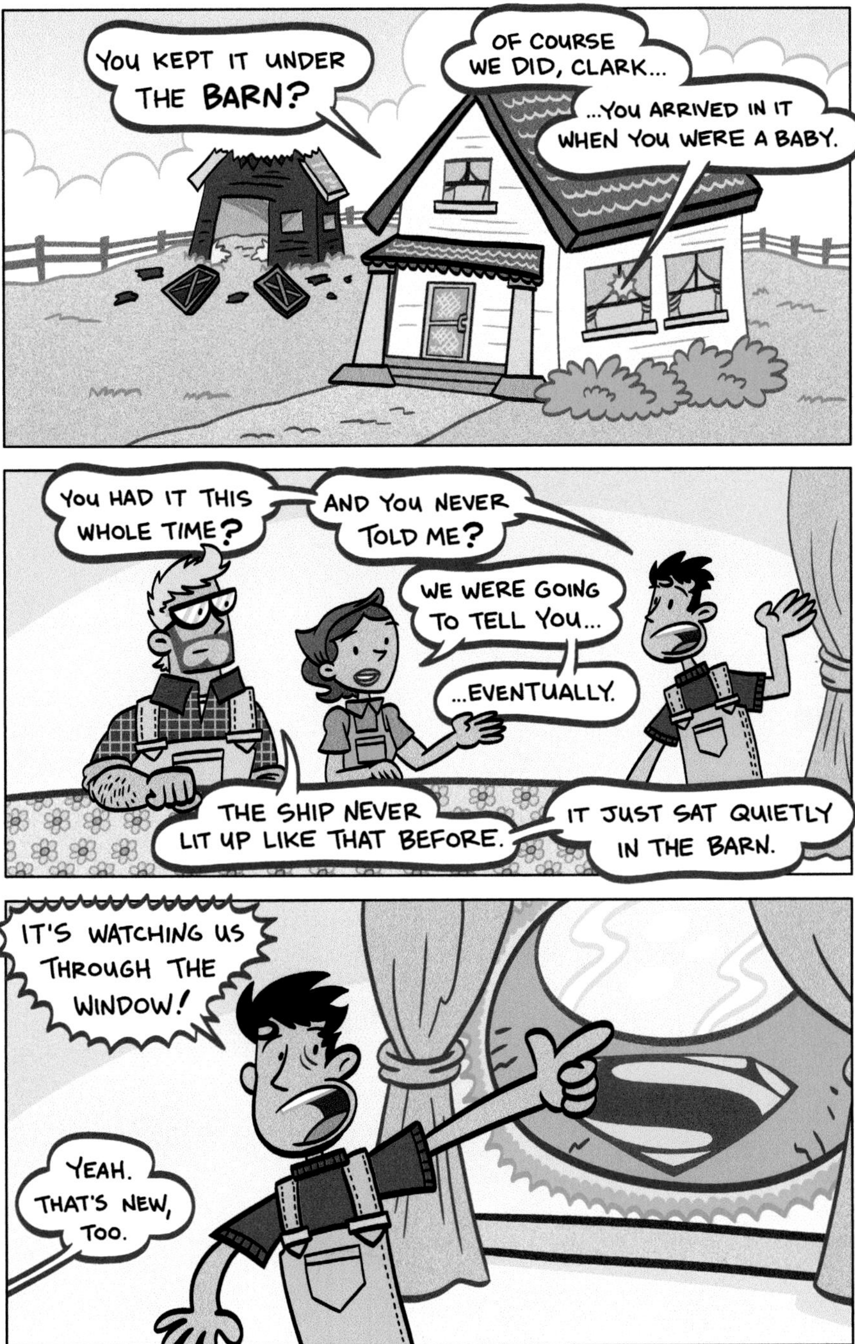
YOU KEPT IT UNDER THE BARN?
OF COURSE WE DID, CLARK...
...YOU ARRIVED IN IT WHEN YOU WERE A BABY.
YOU HAD IT THIS WHOLE TIME?
AND YOU NEVER TOLD ME?
WE WERE GOING TO TELL YOU...
...EVENTUALLY.
THE SHIP NEVER LIT UP LIKE THAT BEFORE.
IT JUST SAT QUIETLY IN THE BARN.
IT'S WATCHING US THROUGH THE WINDOW!
YEAH. THAT'S NEW, TOO.

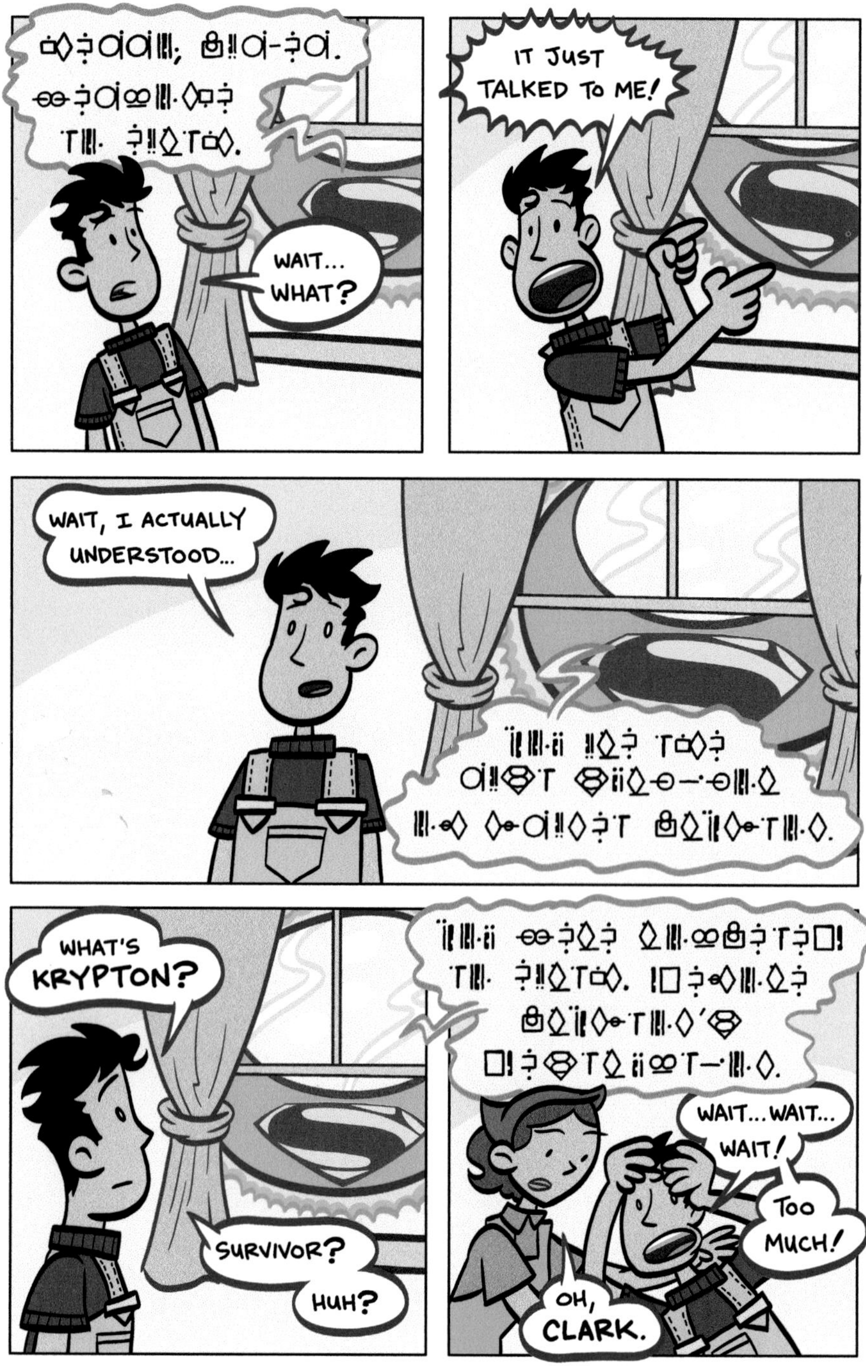
WAIT... WHAT?
IT JUST TALKED TO ME!
WAIT, I ACTUALLY UNDERSTOOD...
WHAT'S KRYPTON?
SURVIVOR?
HUH?
WAIT... WAIT... WAIT!
TOO MUCH!
OH, CLARK.

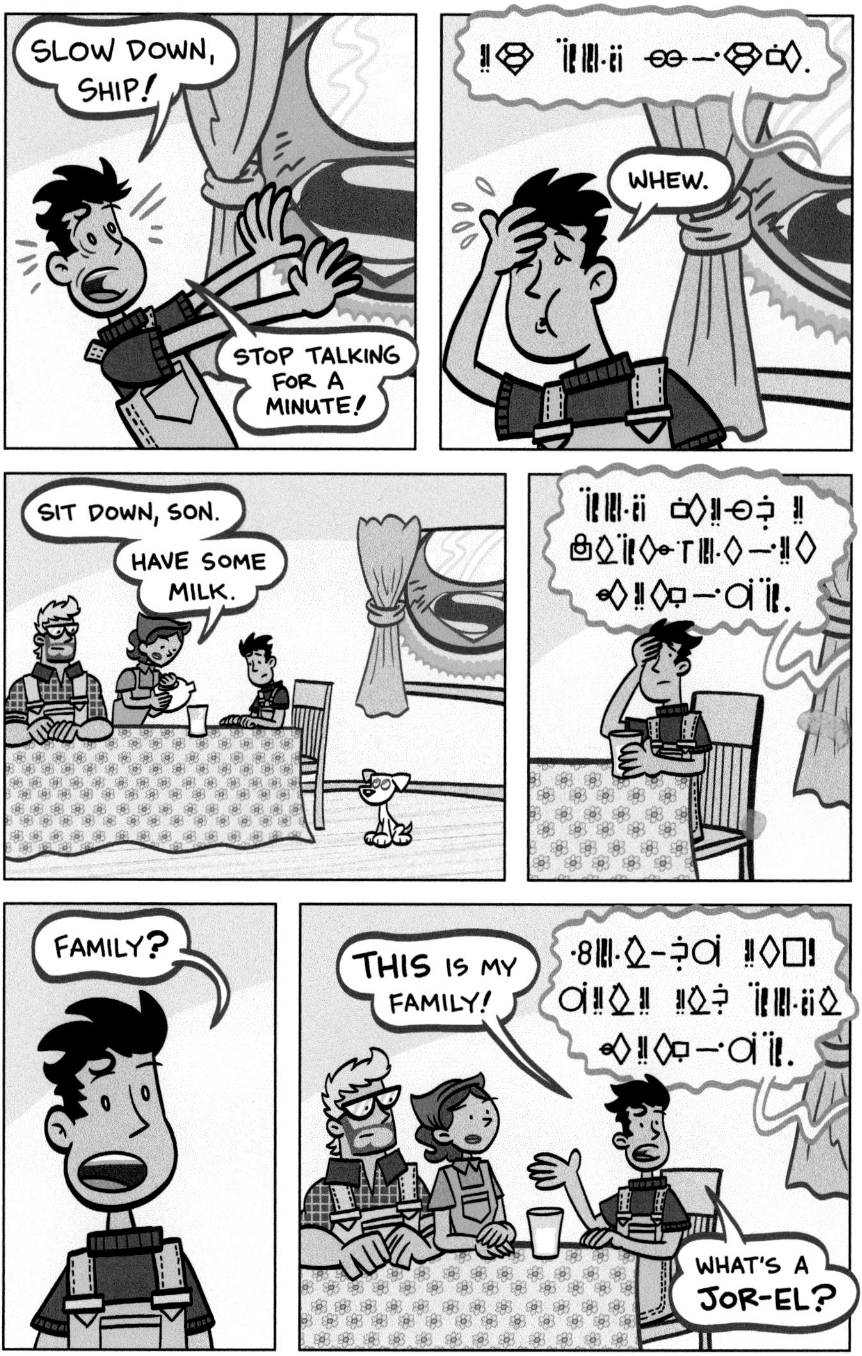
SLOW DOWN, SHIP!
STOP TALKING FOR A MINUTE!
WHEW.
SIT DOWN, SON.
HAVE SOME MILK.
FAMILY?
THIS IS MY FAMILY!
WHAT'S A JOR-EL?

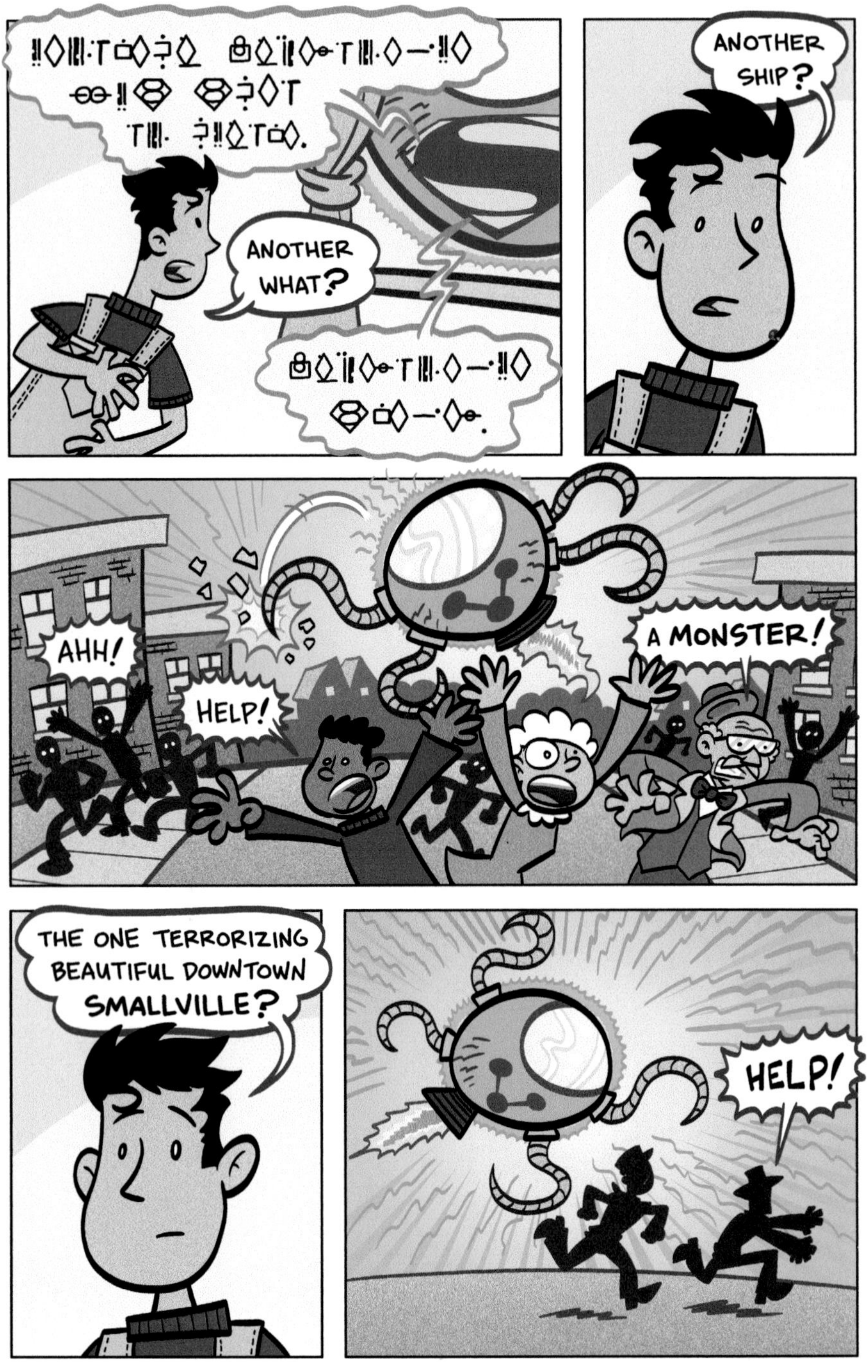
ANOTHER WHAT?
ANOTHER SHIP?
AHH!
HELP!
A MONSTER!
THE ONE TERRORIZING BEAUTIFUL DOWNTOWN SMALLVILLE?
HELP!

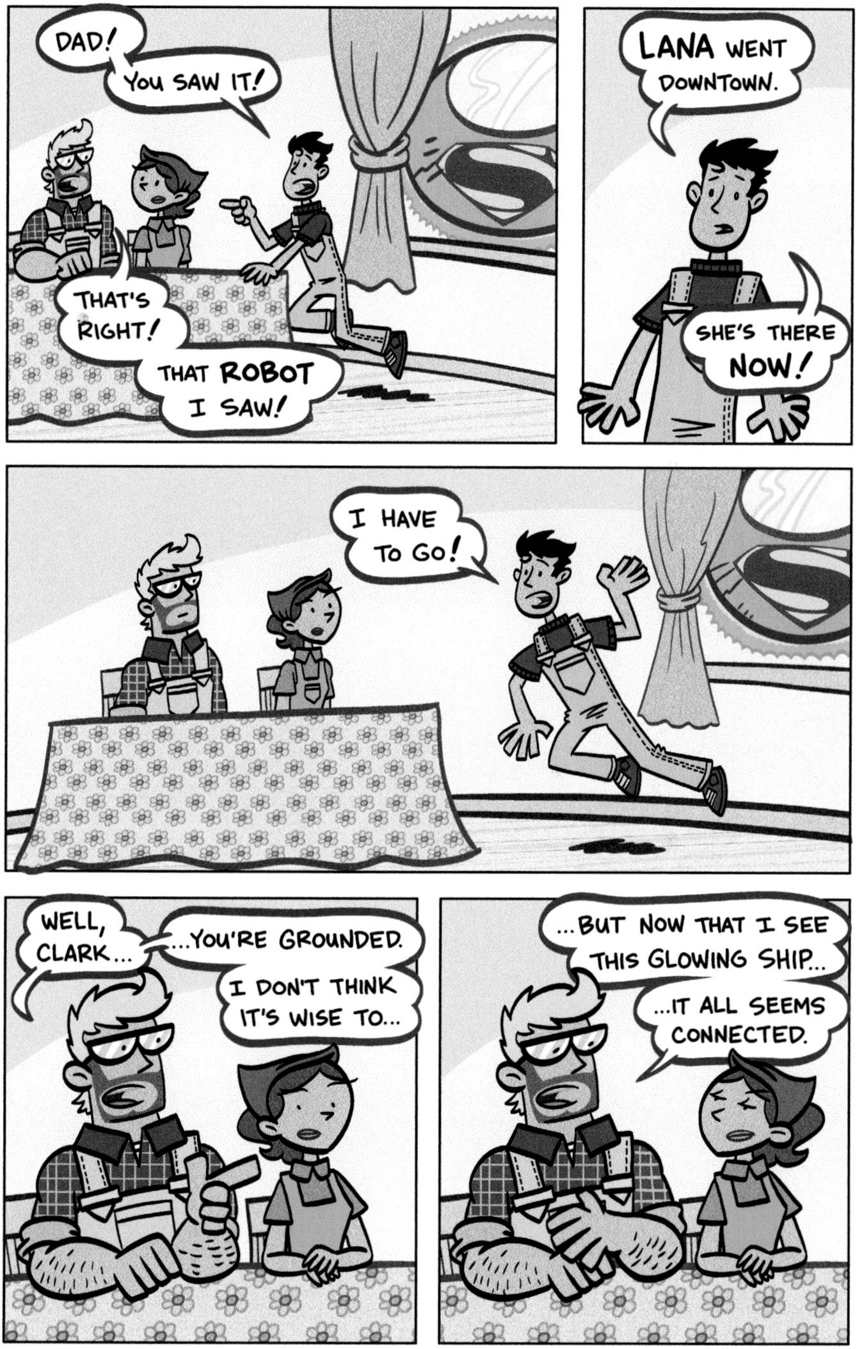
DAD!
YOU SAW IT!
THAT'S RIGHT!
THAT ROBOT I SAW!
LANA WENT DOWNTOWN.
SHE'S THERE NOW!
I HAVE TO GO!
WELL, CLARK...
...YOU'RE GROUNDED.
I DON'T THINK IT'S WISE TO...
...BUT NOW THAT I SEE THIS GLOWING SHIP...
...IT ALL SEEMS CONNECTED.

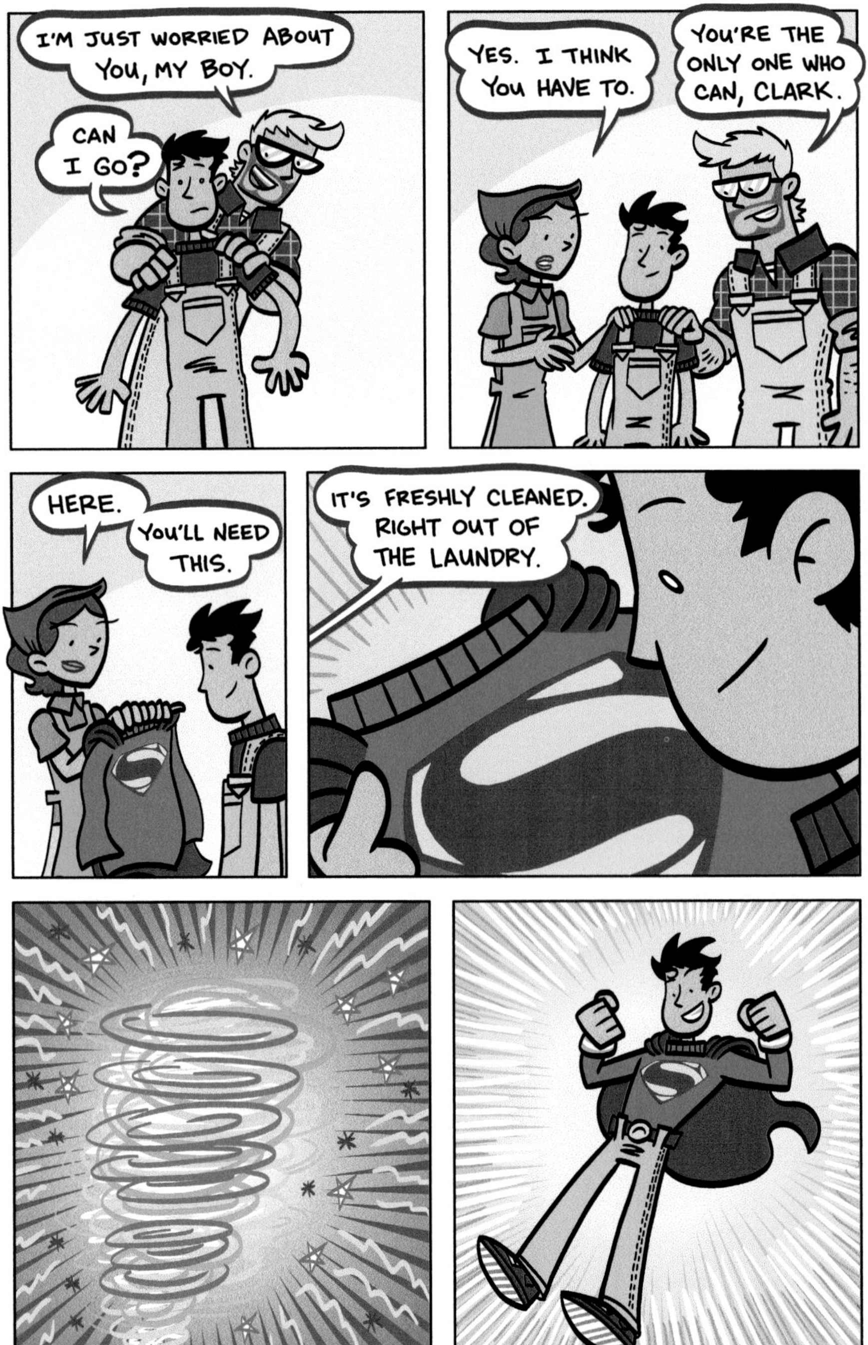
I'M JUST WORRIED ABOUT YOU, MY BOY.
CAN I GO?
YES. I THINK YOU HAVE TO.
YOU'RE THE ONLY ONE WHO CAN, CLARK.
HERE.
YOU'LL NEED THIS.
IT'S FRESHLY CLEANED. RIGHT OUT OF THE LAUNDRY.

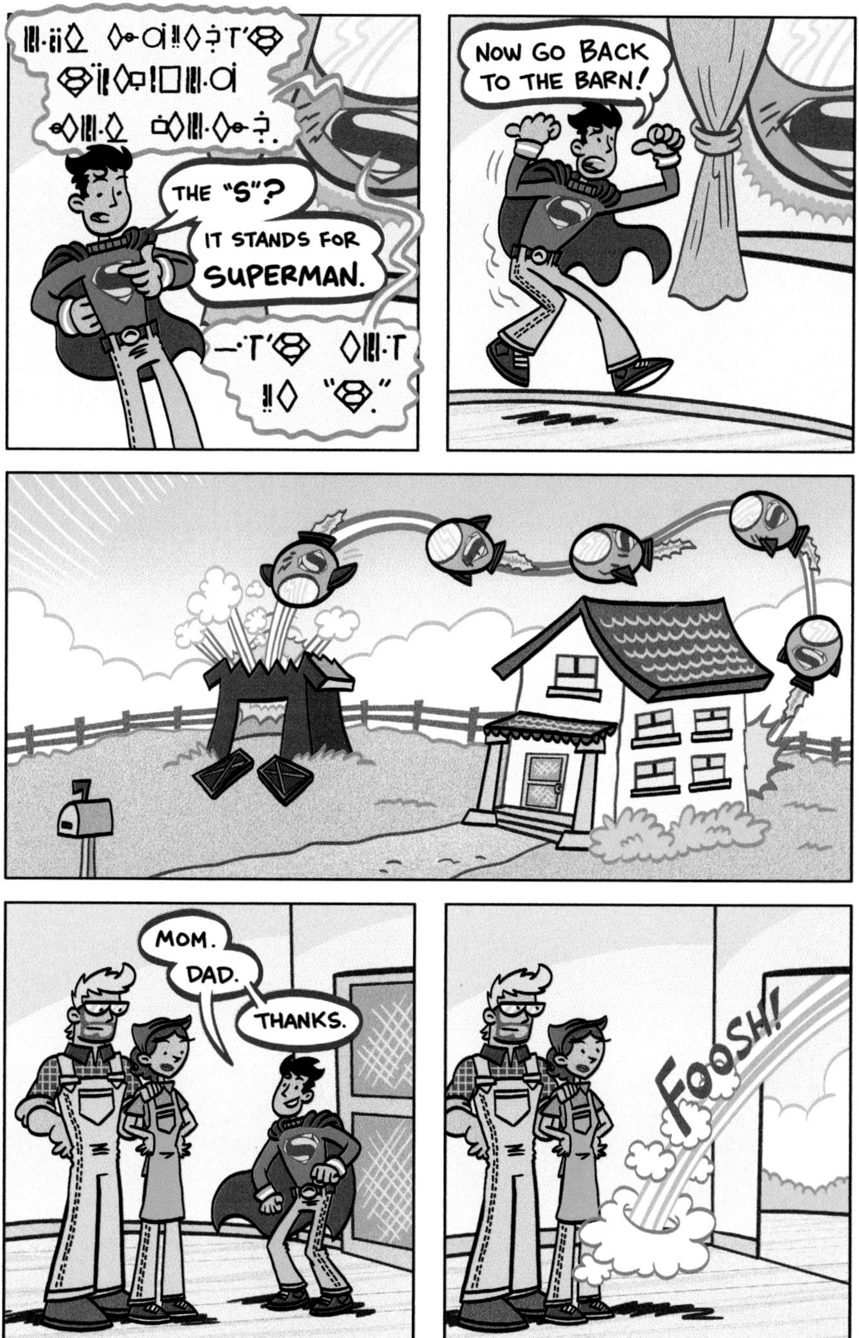
THE "S"?
IT STANDS FOR SUPERMAN.
NOW GO BACK TO THE BARN!
MOM.
DAD.
THANKS.
FOOSH!

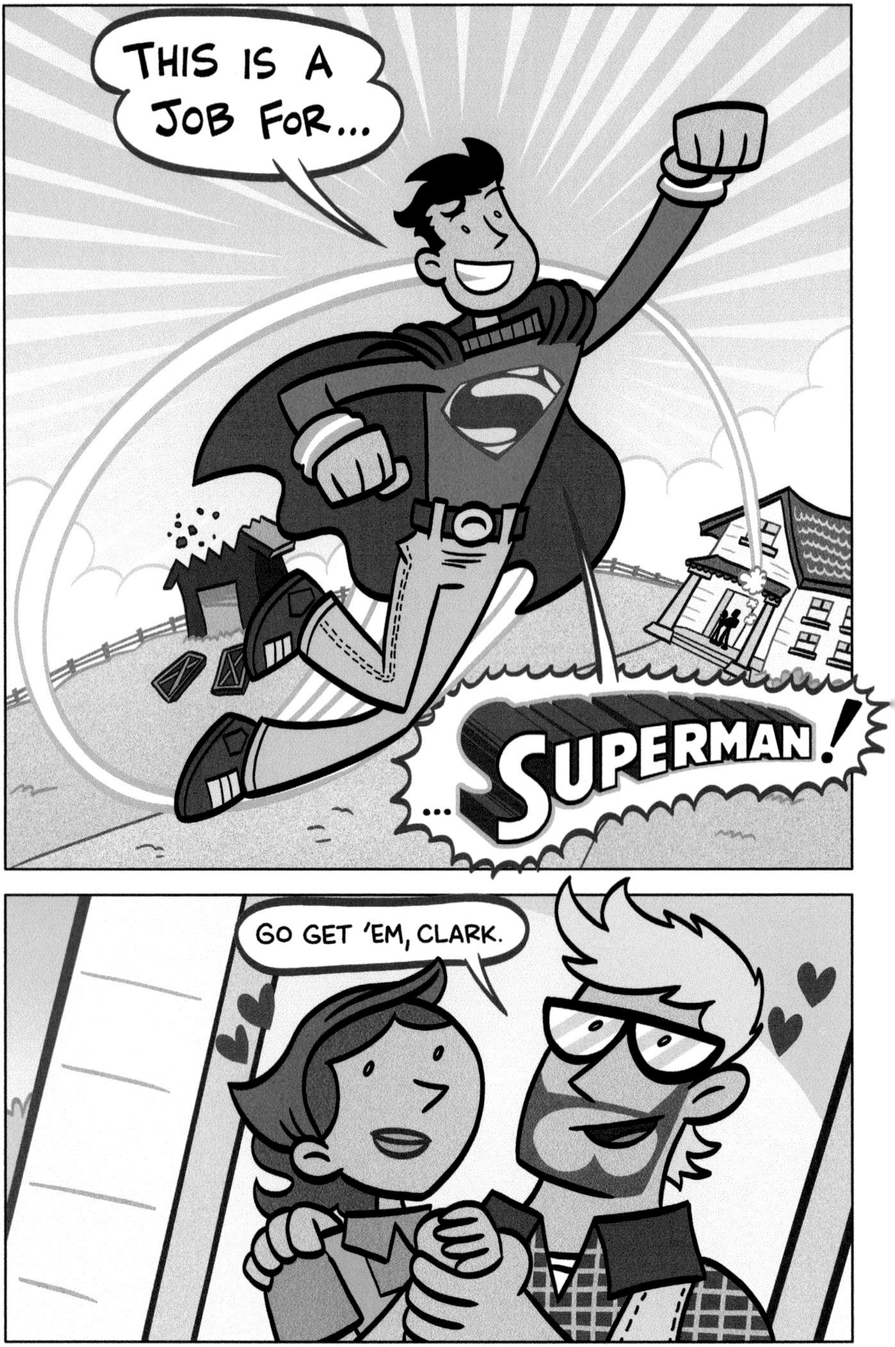
THIS IS A JOB FOR...
...SUPERMAN!
GO GET 'EM, CLARK.

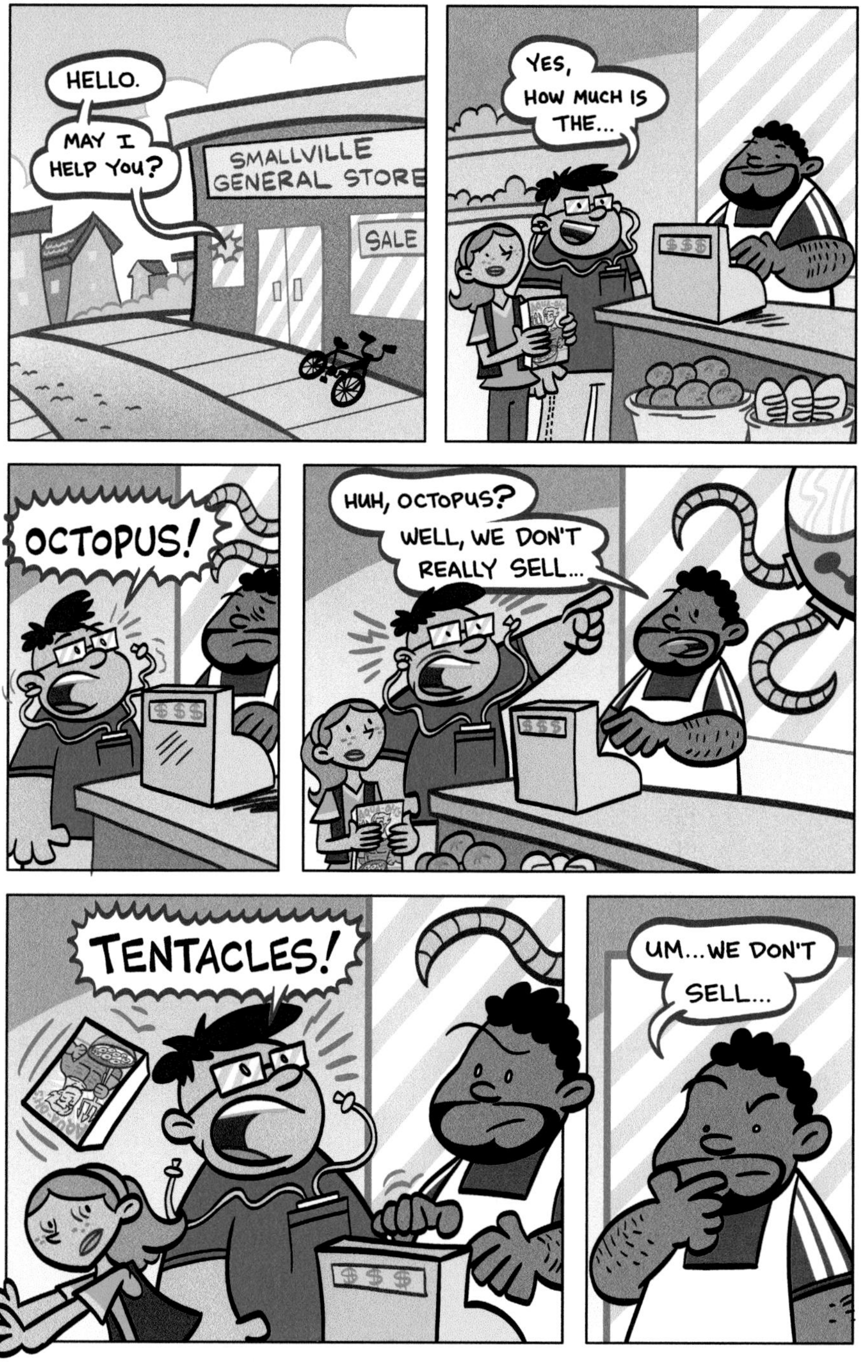
HELLO.
MAY I HELP YOU?
SMALLVILLE GENERAL STORE
SALE
YES, HOW MUCH IS THE...
OCTOPUS!
HUH, OCTOPUS?
WELL, WE DON'T REALLY SELL...
TENTACLES!
UM...WE DON'T SELL...

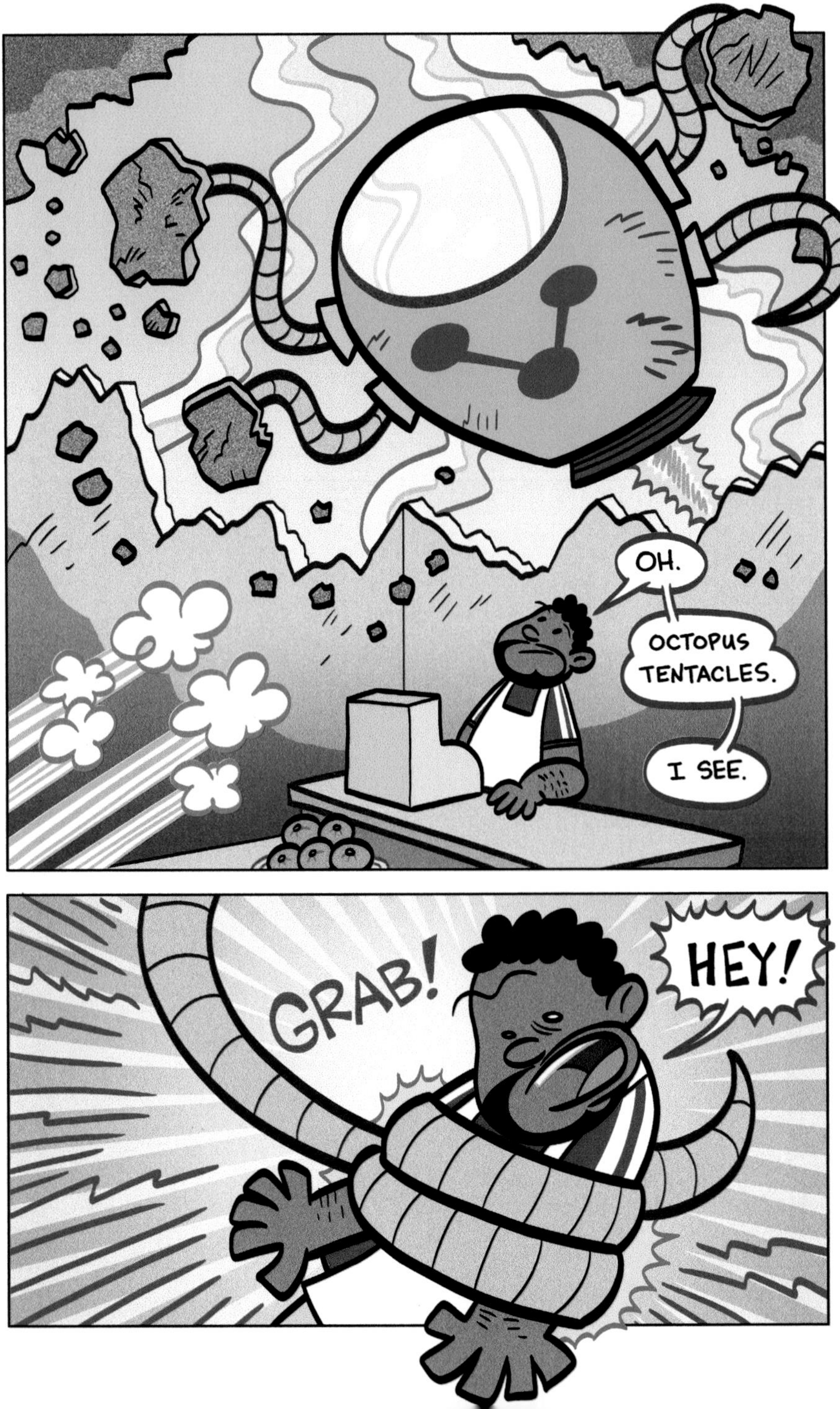
OH.
OCTOPUS TENTACLES.
I SEE.
GRAB!
HEY!

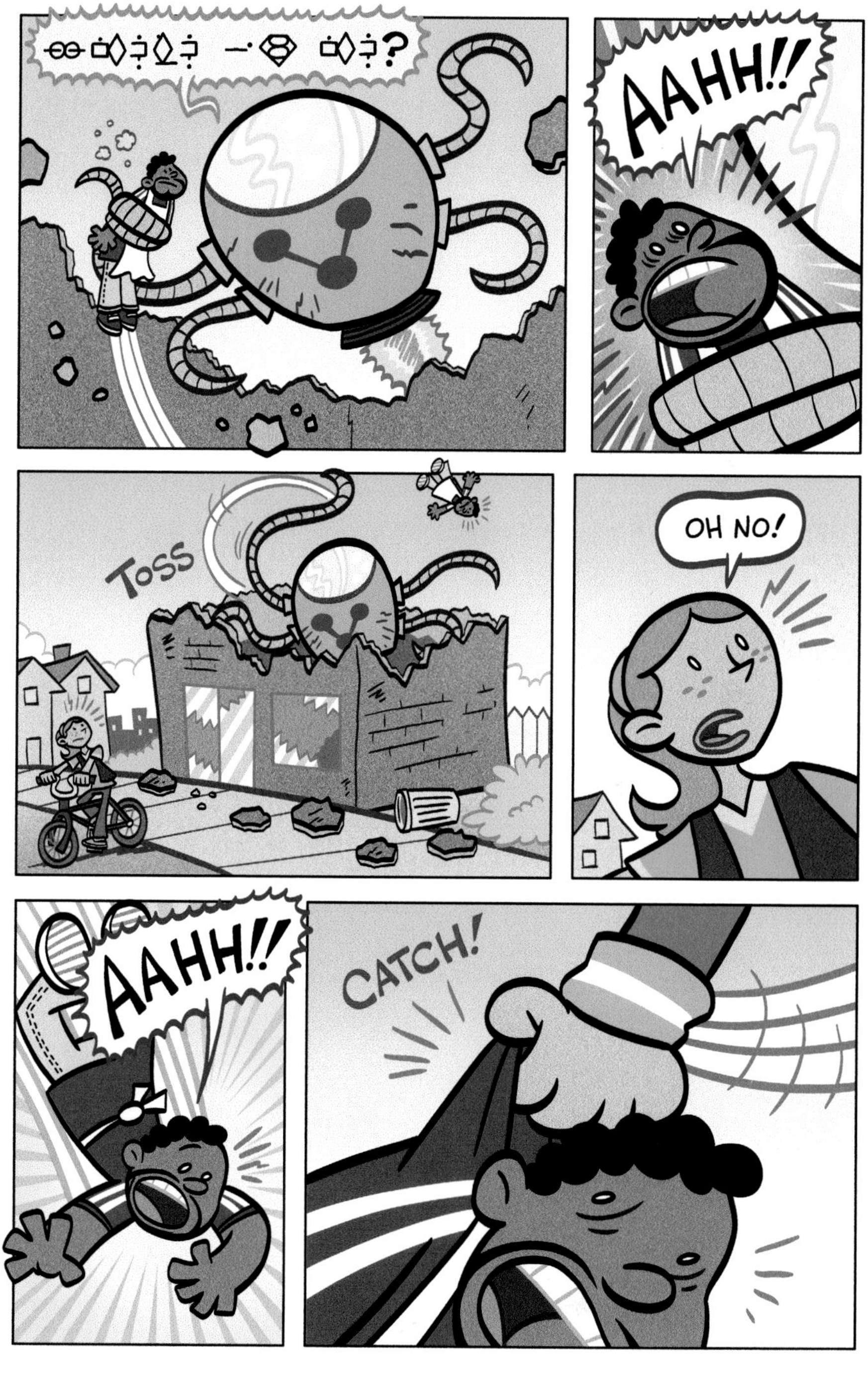
AAHH!!
TOSS
OH NO!
AAHH!!
CATCH!

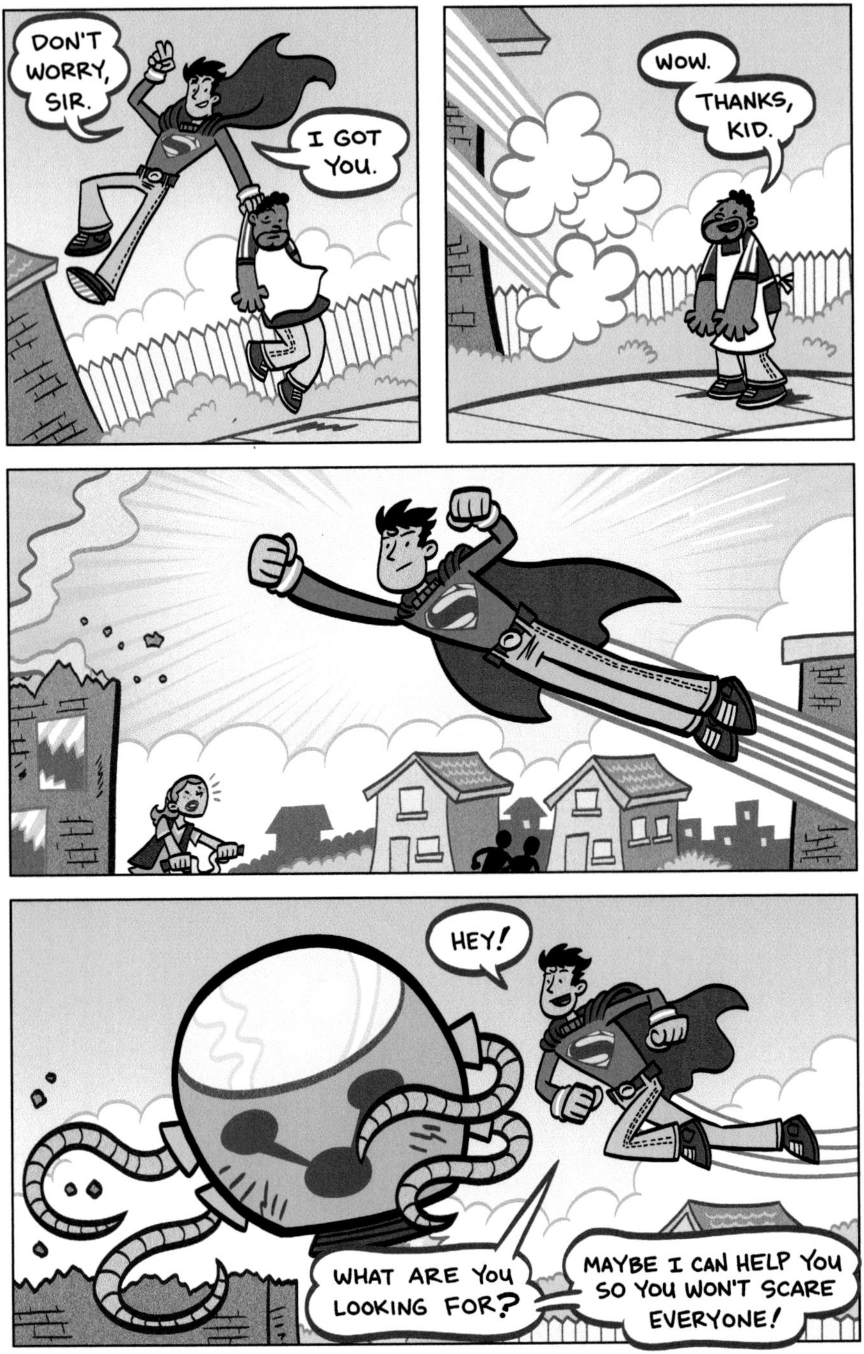
DON'T WORRY, SIR.
I GOT YOU.
WOW.
THANKS, KID.
HEY!
WHAT ARE YOU LOOKING FOR?
MAYBE I CAN HELP YOU SO YOU WON'T SCARE EVERYONE!

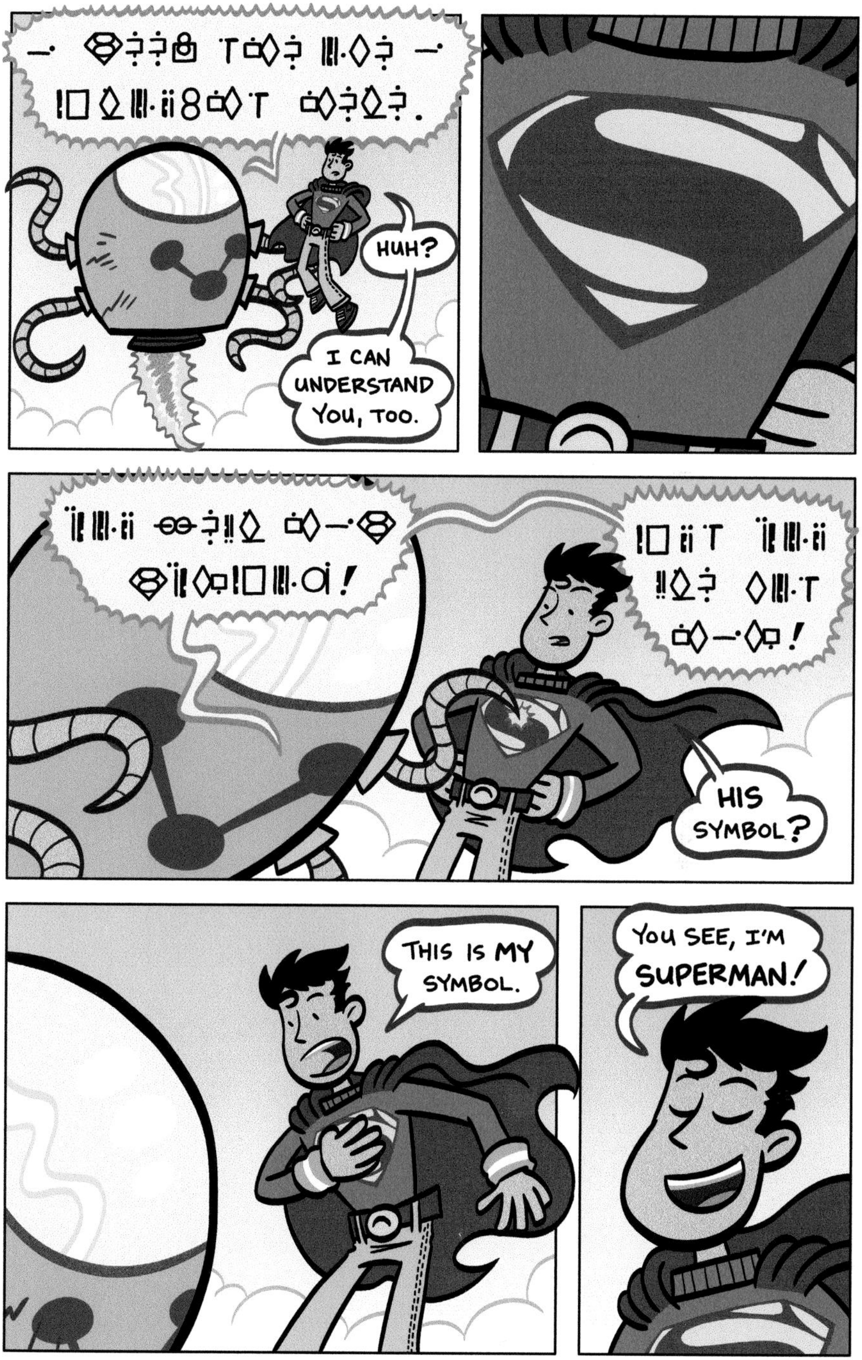
HUH?
I CAN UNDERSTAND YOU, TOO.
HIS SYMBOL?
THIS IS MY SYMBOL.
YOU SEE, I'M SUPERMAN!

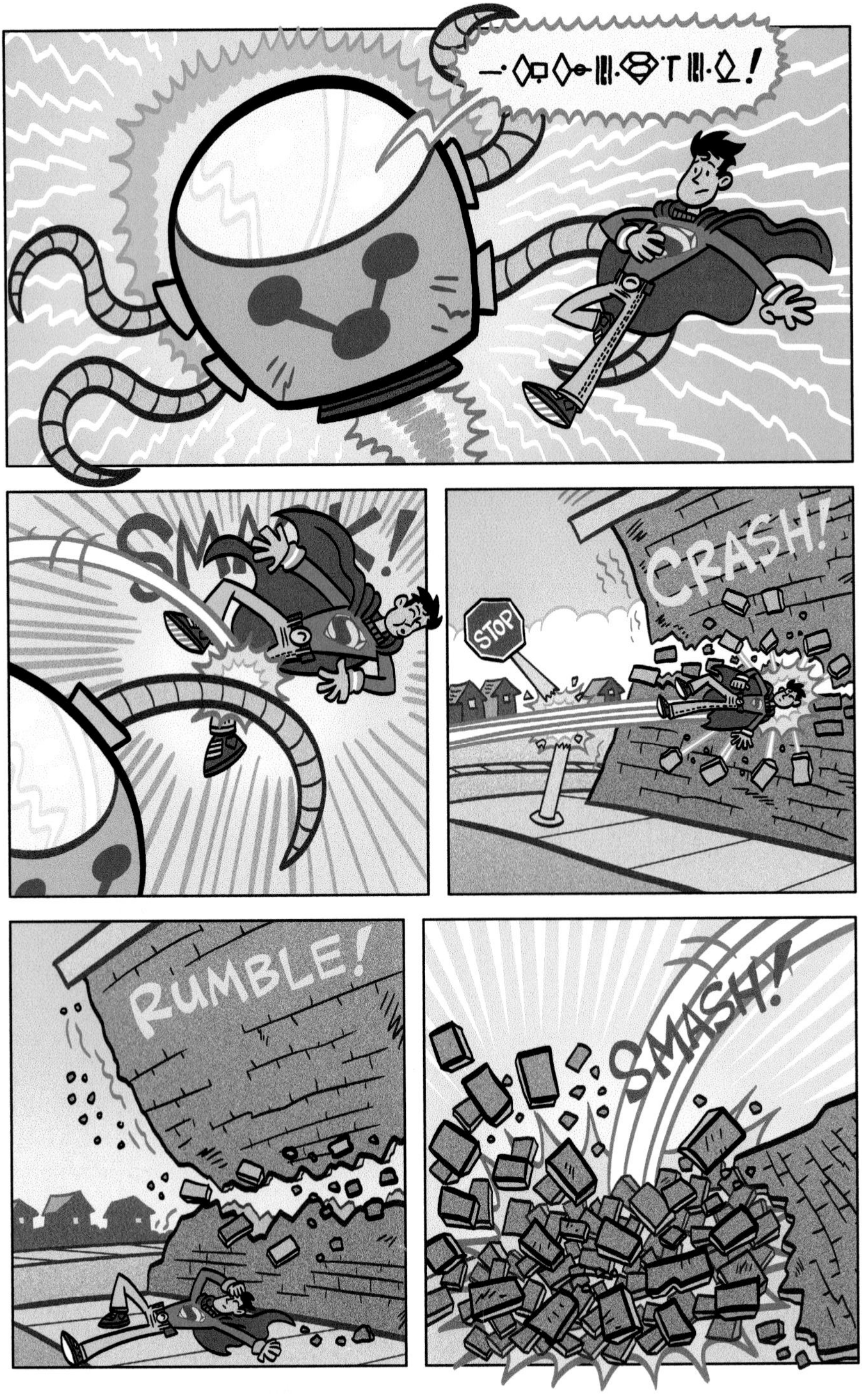
CRASH!
STOP
RUMBLE!
SMASH!

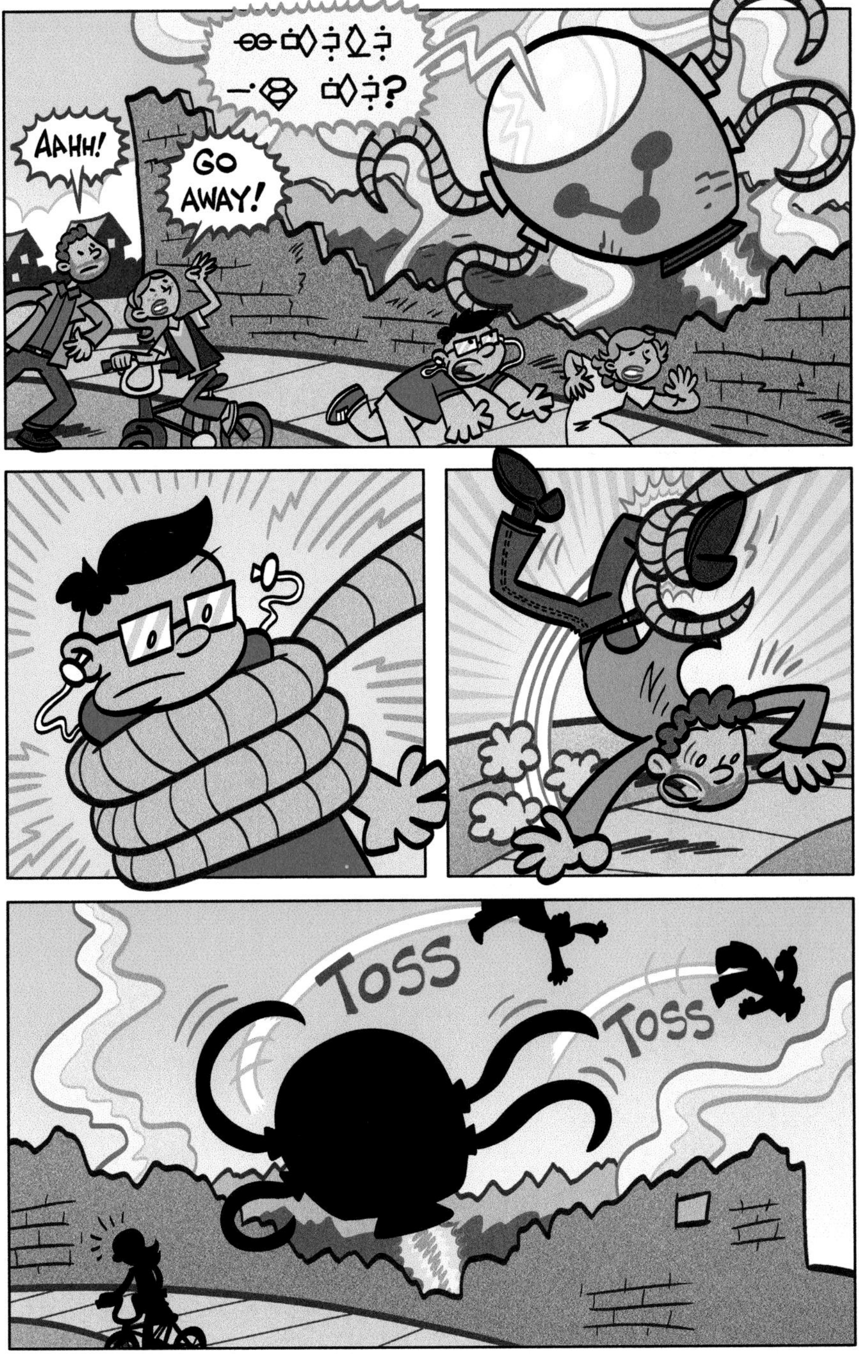
AAHH!
GO AWAY!
TOSS
TOSS

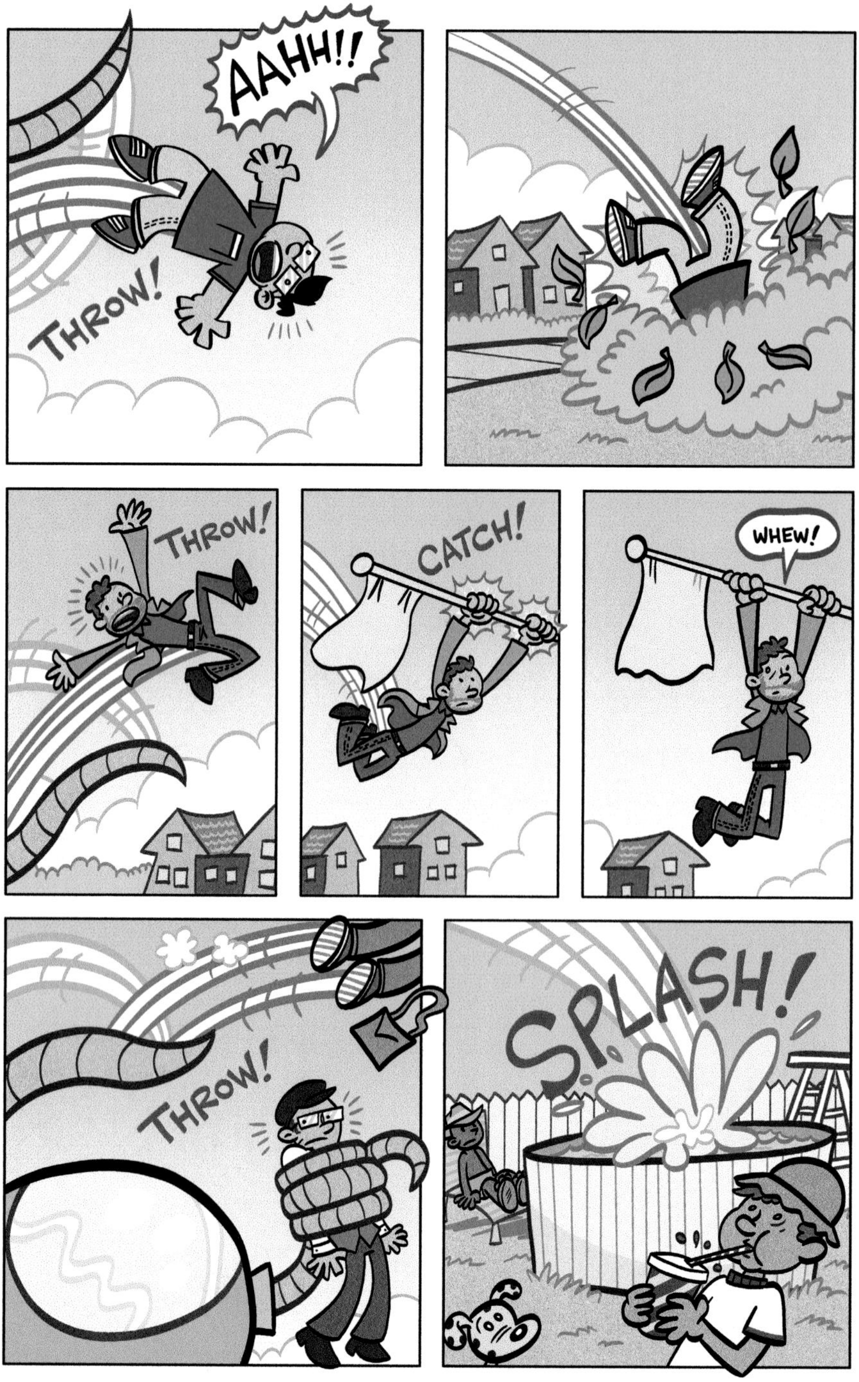
AAHH!!
THROW!
THROW!
CATCH!
WHEW!
THROW!
SPLASH!

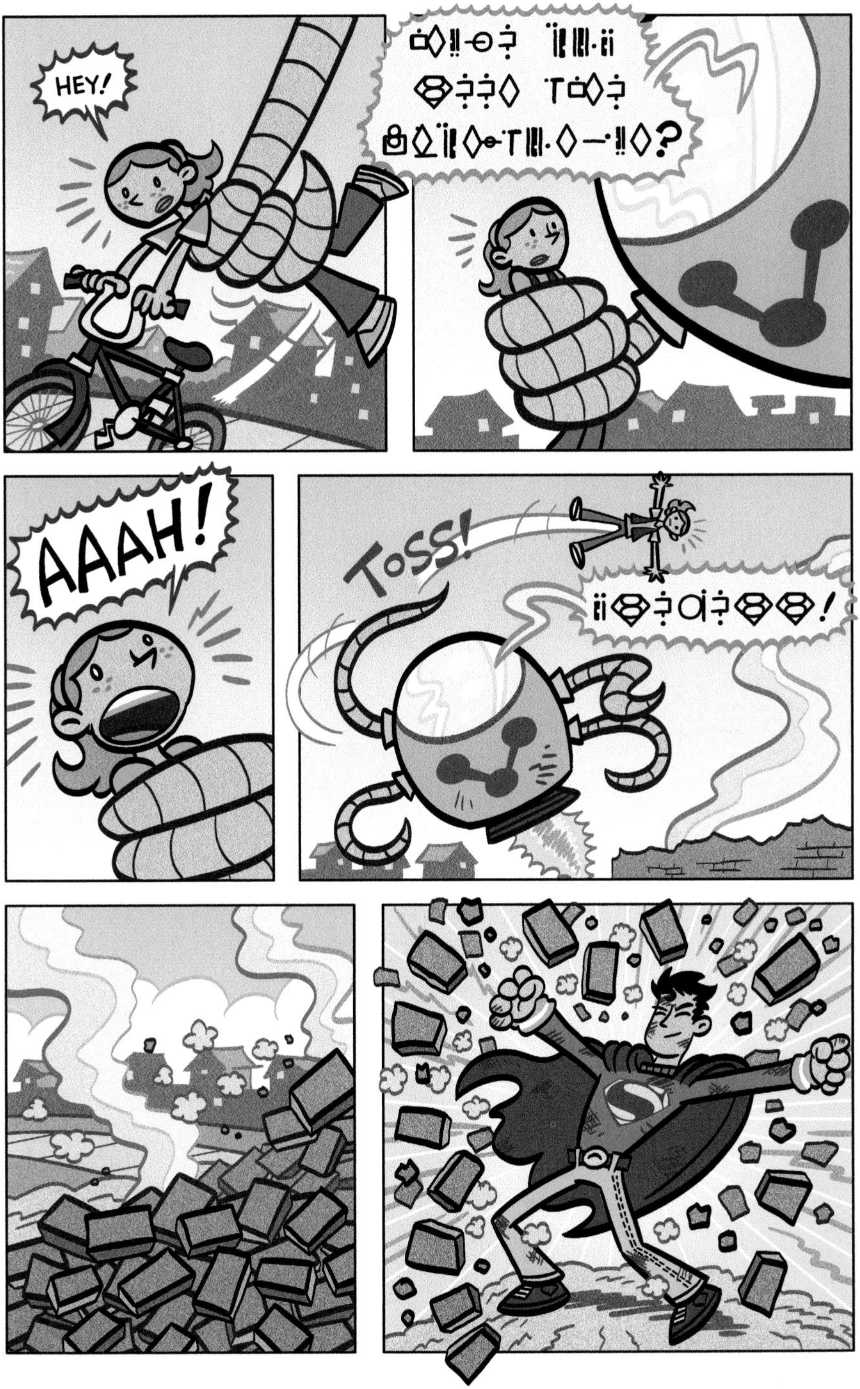
HEY!
AAAH!
TOSS!

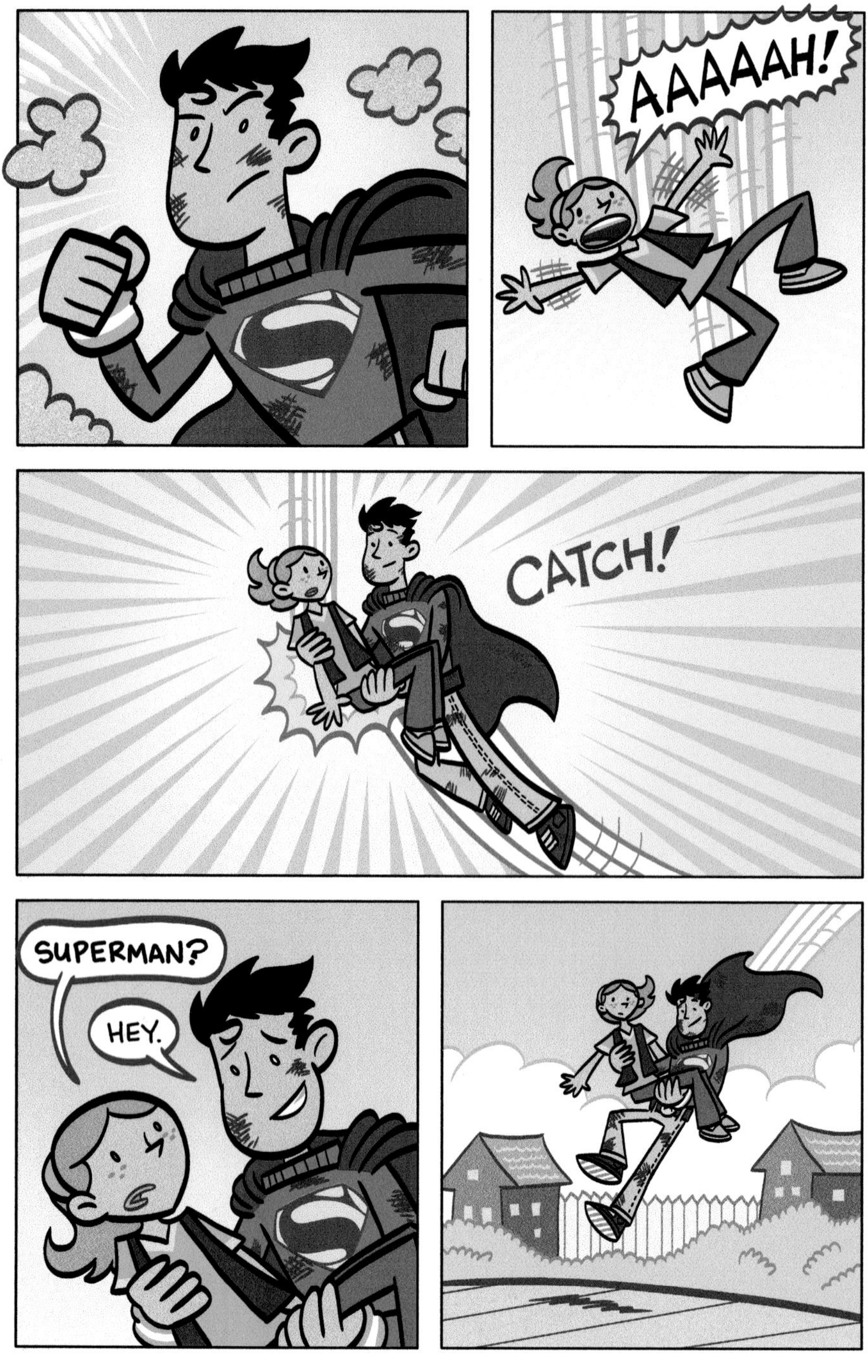
AAAAAH!
CATCH!
SUPERMAN?
HEY.

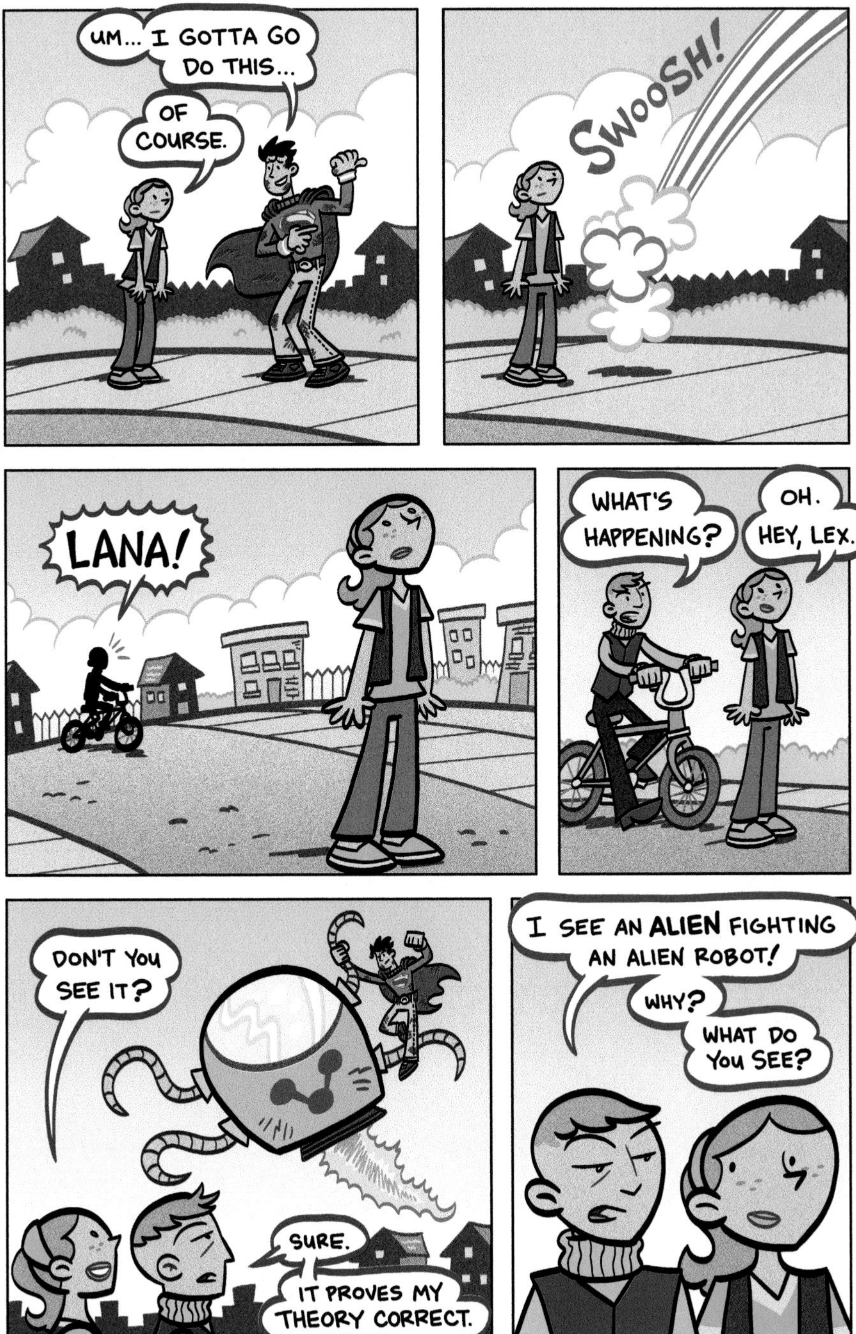
UM... I GOTTA GO DO THIS...
OF COURSE.
SWOOSH!
LANA!
WHAT'S HAPPENING?
OH. HEY, LEX.
DON'T YOU SEE IT?
SURE.
IT PROVES MY THEORY CORRECT.
I SEE AN ALIEN FIGHTING AN ALIEN ROBOT!
WHY?
WHAT DO YOU SEE?

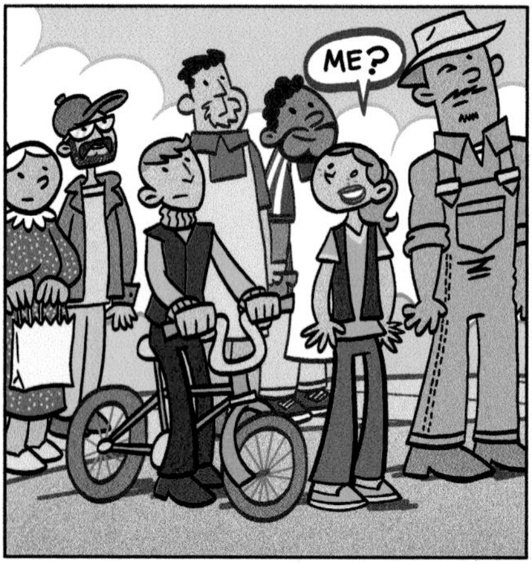
ME?

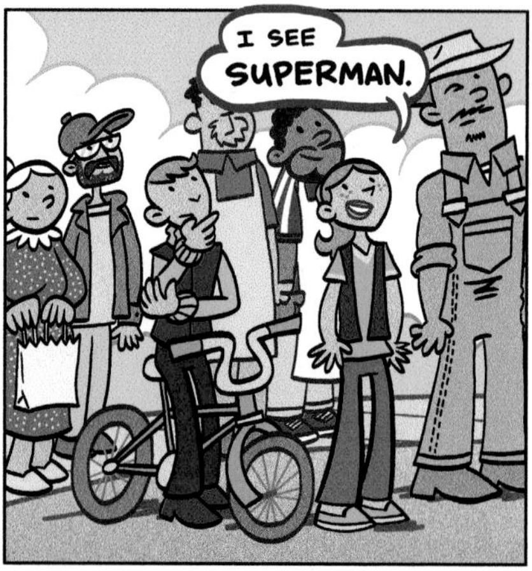
I SEE SUPERMAN.

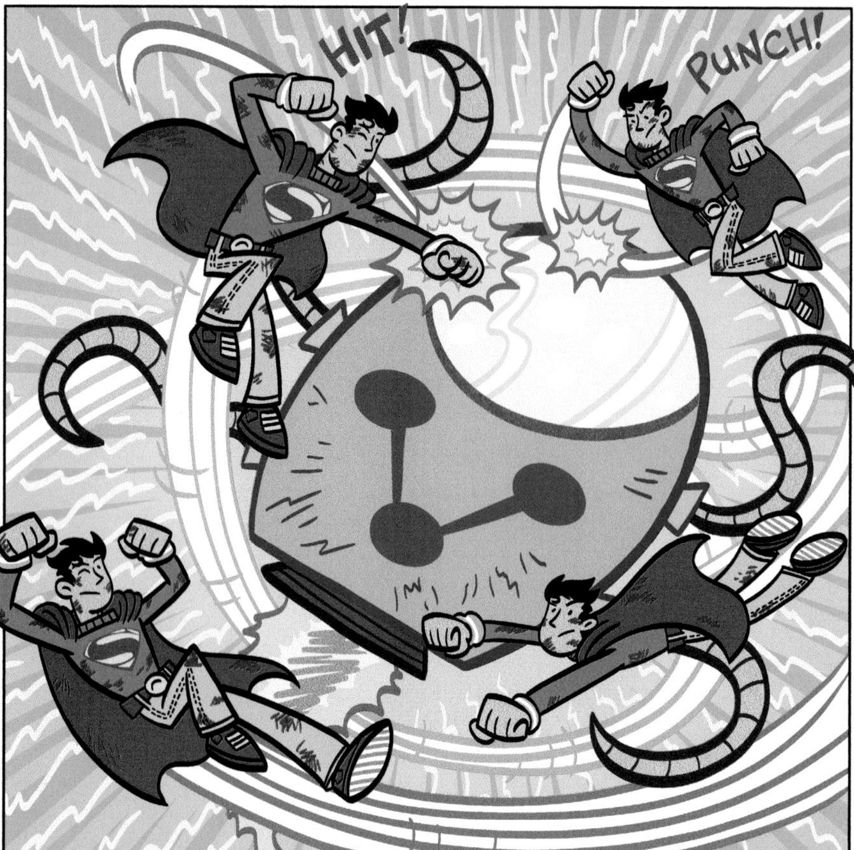
HIT!
PUNCH!

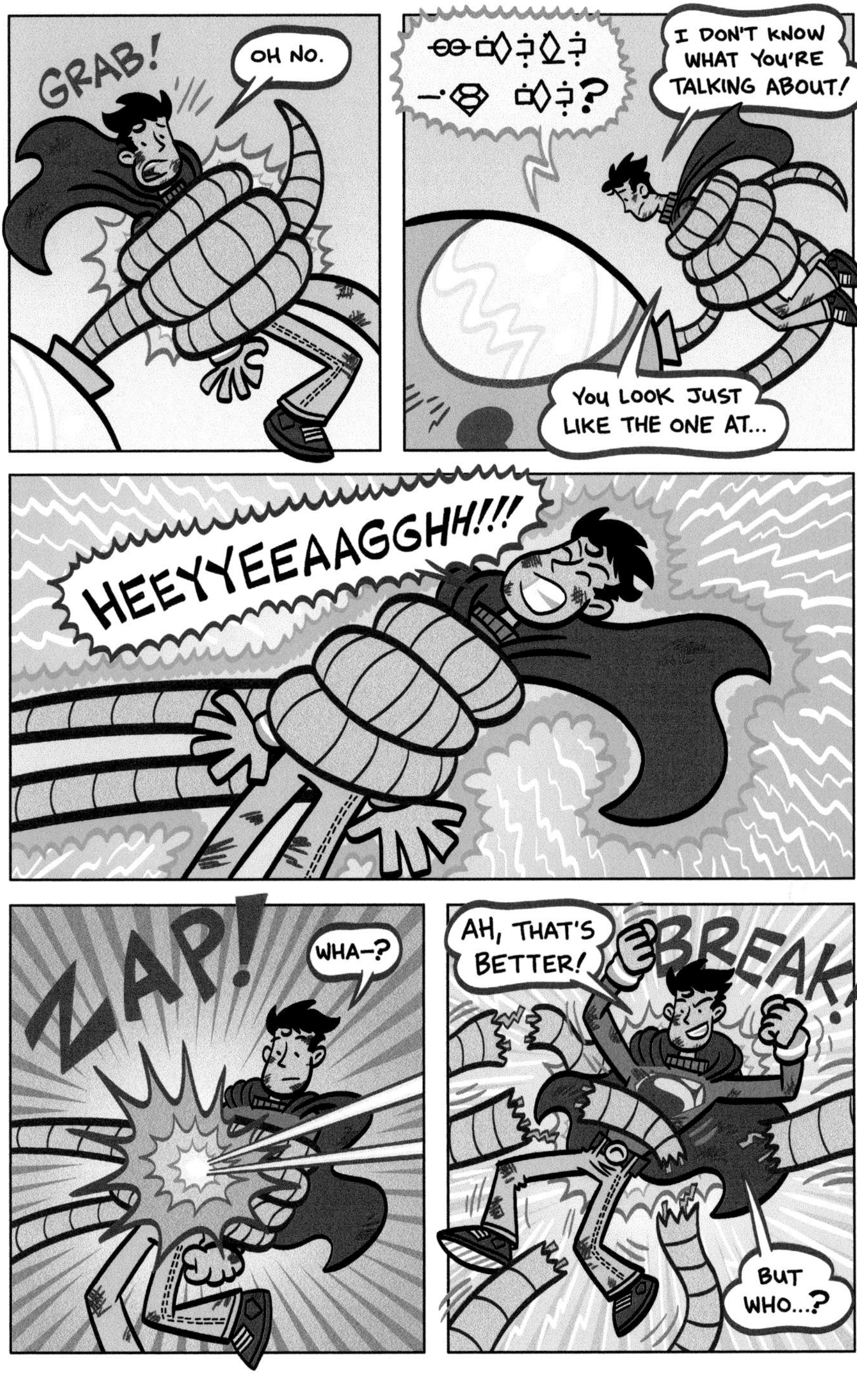
GRAB!
OH NO.
I DON'T KNOW WHAT YOU'RE TALKING ABOUT!
YOU LOOK JUST LIKE THE ONE AT...
HEEYYEEAAGGHH!!!
ZAP!
WHA-?
AH, THAT'S BETTER!
BREAK!
BUT WHO...?

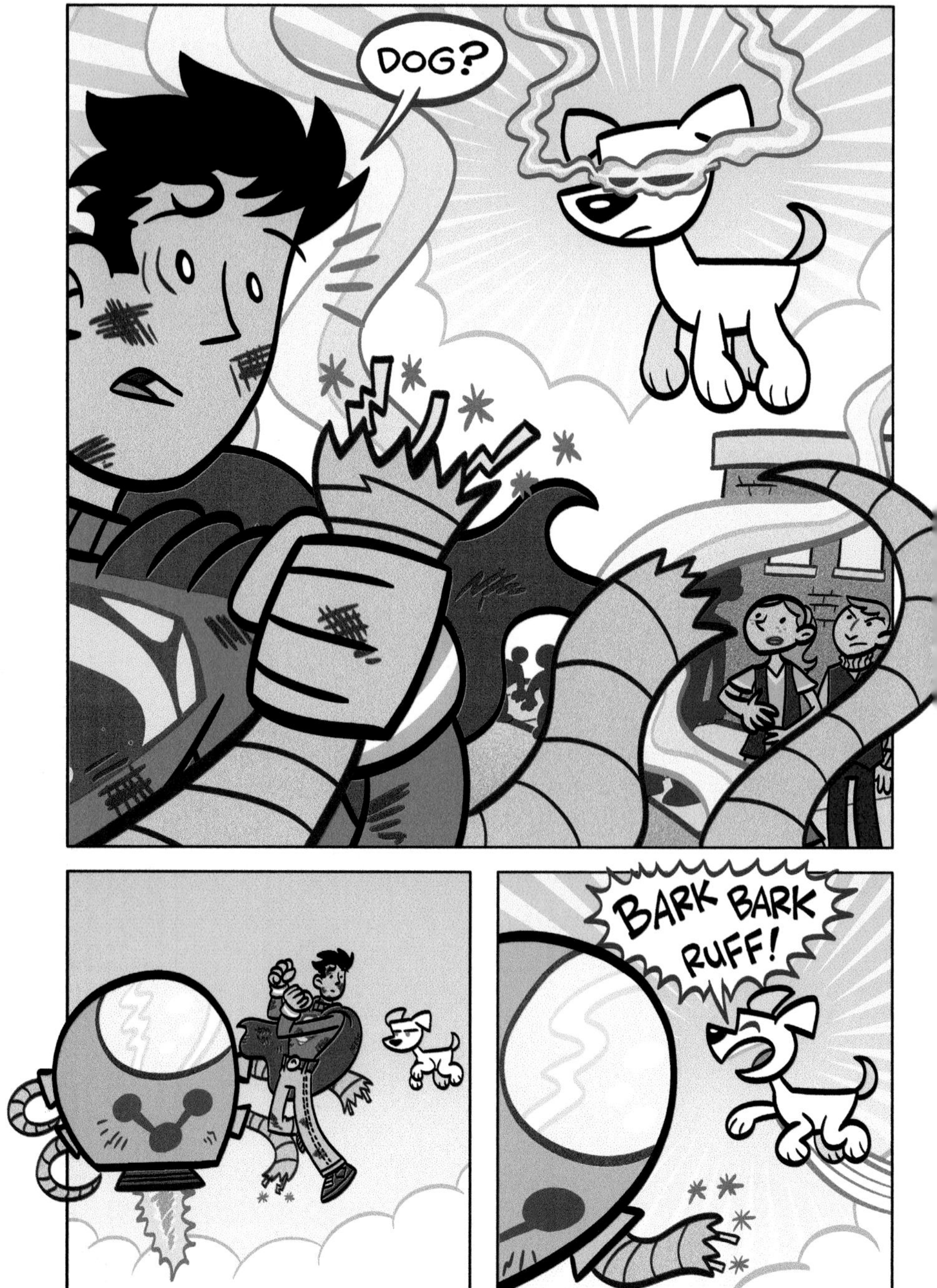
DOG?
BARK BARK RUFF!

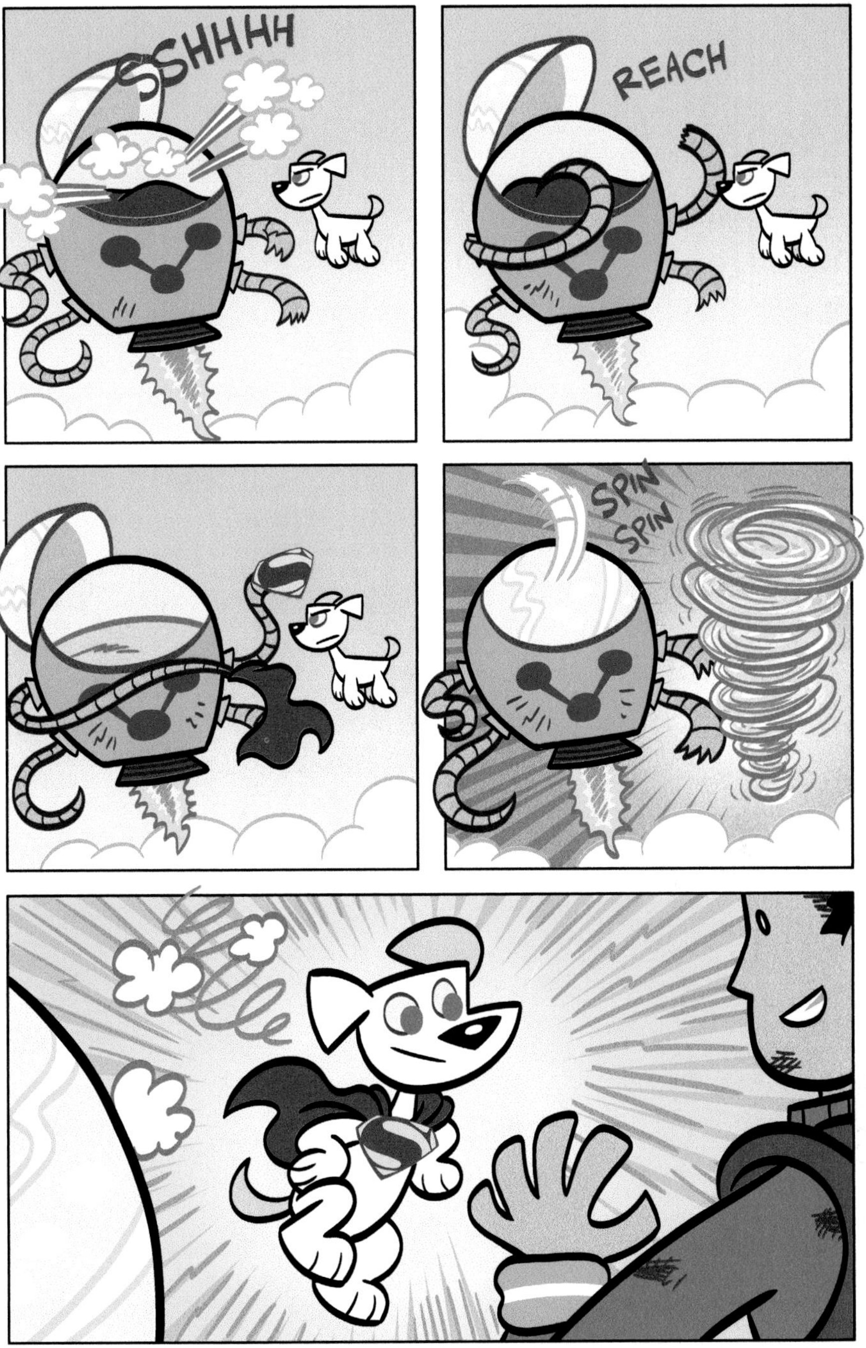
SSHHHH
REACH
SPIN
SPIN

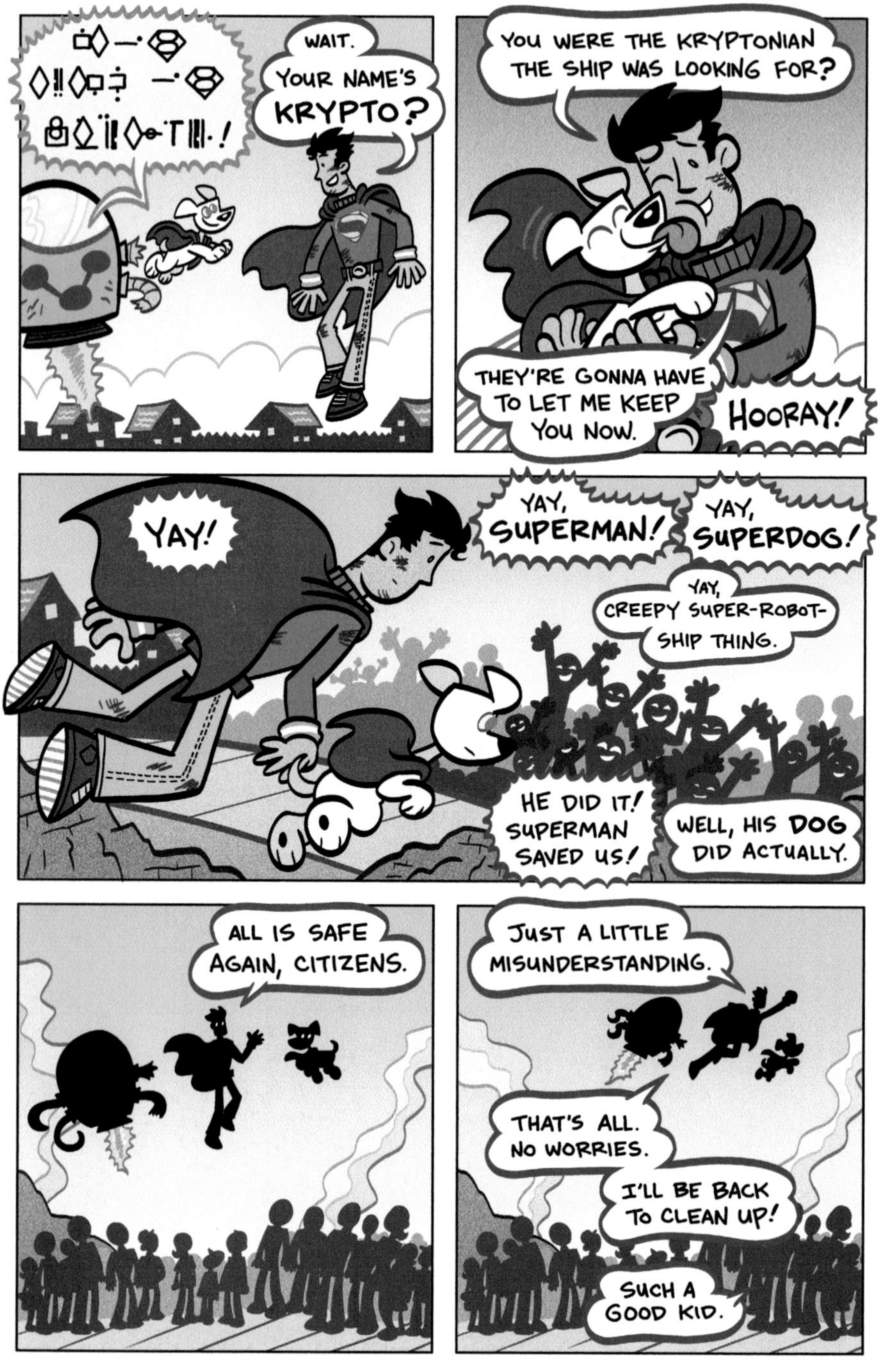
WAIT.
YOUR NAME'S KRYPTO?
YOU WERE THE KRYPTONIAN THE SHIP WAS LOOKING FOR?
THEY'RE GONNA HAVE TO LET ME KEEP YOU NOW.
HOORAY!
YAY!
YAY, SUPERMAN!
YAY, SUPERDOG!
YAY, CREEPY SUPER-ROBOT-SHIP THING.
HE DID IT! SUPERMAN SAVED US!
WELL, HIS DOG DID ACTUALLY.
ALL IS SAFE AGAIN, CITIZENS.
JUST A LITTLE MISUNDERSTANDING.
THAT'S ALL. NO WORRIES.
I'LL BE BACK TO CLEAN UP!
SUCH A GOOD KID.

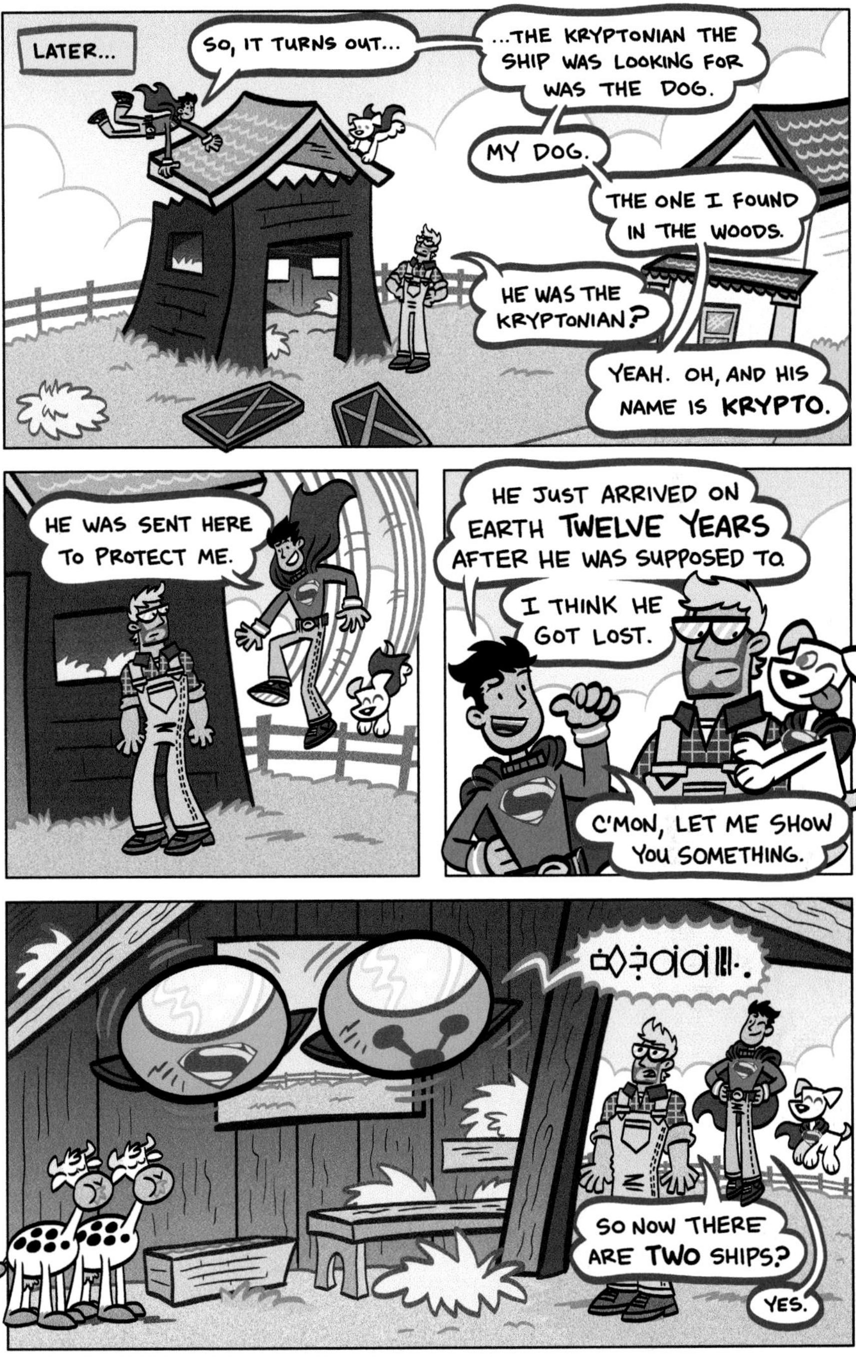
LATER...
SO, IT TURNS OUT...
...THE KRYPTONIAN THE SHIP WAS LOOKING FOR WAS THE DOG.
MY DOG.
THE ONE I FOUND IN THE WOODS.
HE WAS THE KRYPTONIAN?
YEAH. OH, AND HIS NAME IS KRYPTO.
HE WAS SENT HERE TO PROTECT ME.
HE JUST ARRIVED ON EARTH TWELVE YEARS AFTER HE WAS SUPPOSED TO.
I THINK HE GOT LOST.
C'MON, LET ME SHOW YOU SOMETHING.
SO NOW THERE ARE TWO SHIPS?
YES.

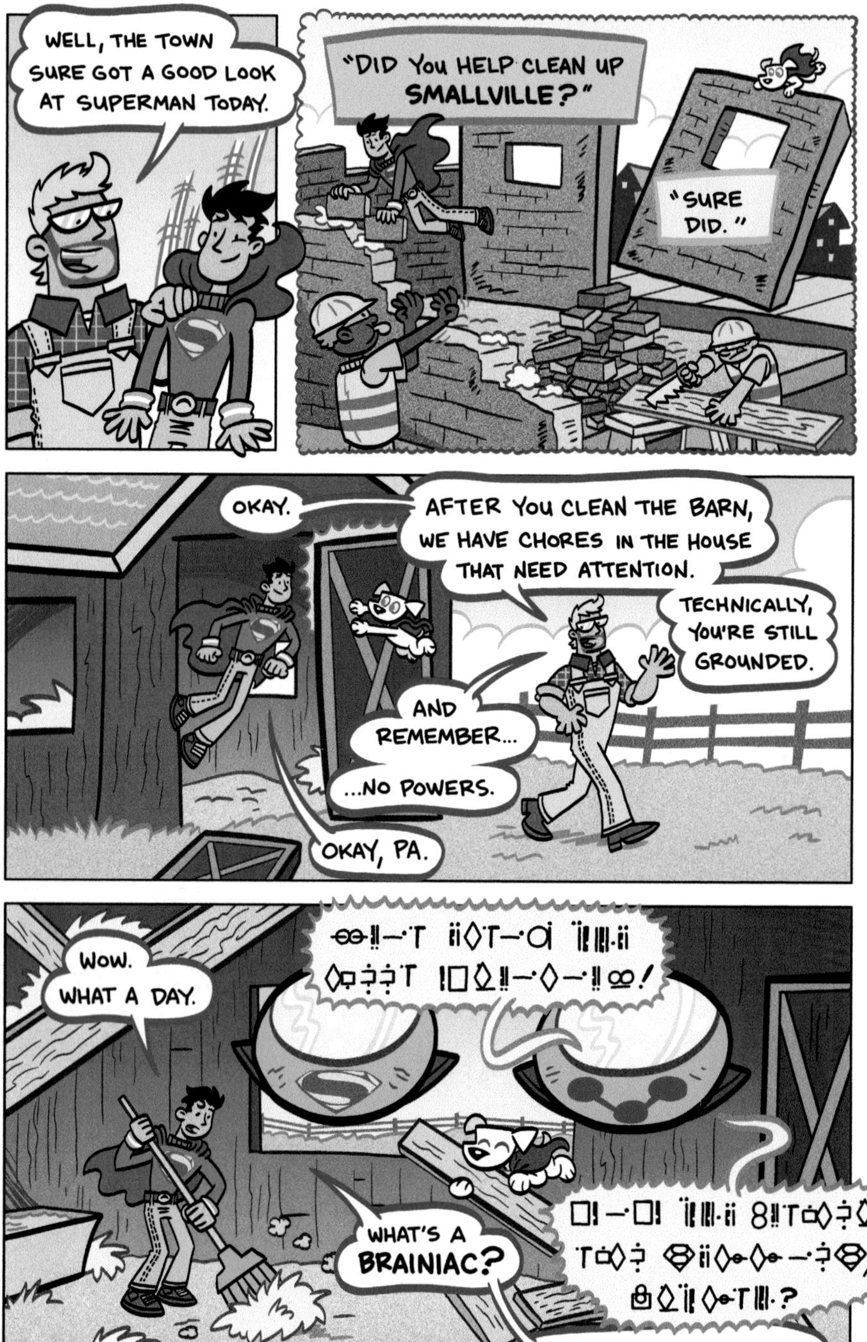
WELL, THE TOWN SURE GOT A GOOD LOOK AT SUPERMAN TODAY.
"DID YOU HELP CLEAN UP SMALLVILLE?"
"SURE DID."
OKAY.
AFTER YOU CLEAN THE BARN, WE HAVE CHORES IN THE HOUSE THAT NEED ATTENTION.
TECHNICALLY, YOU'RE STILL GROUNDED.
AND REMEMBER...
...NO POWERS.
OKAY, PA.
WOW. WHAT A DAY.
WHAT'S A BRAINIAC?
WAIT, WHAT SUPPLIES?

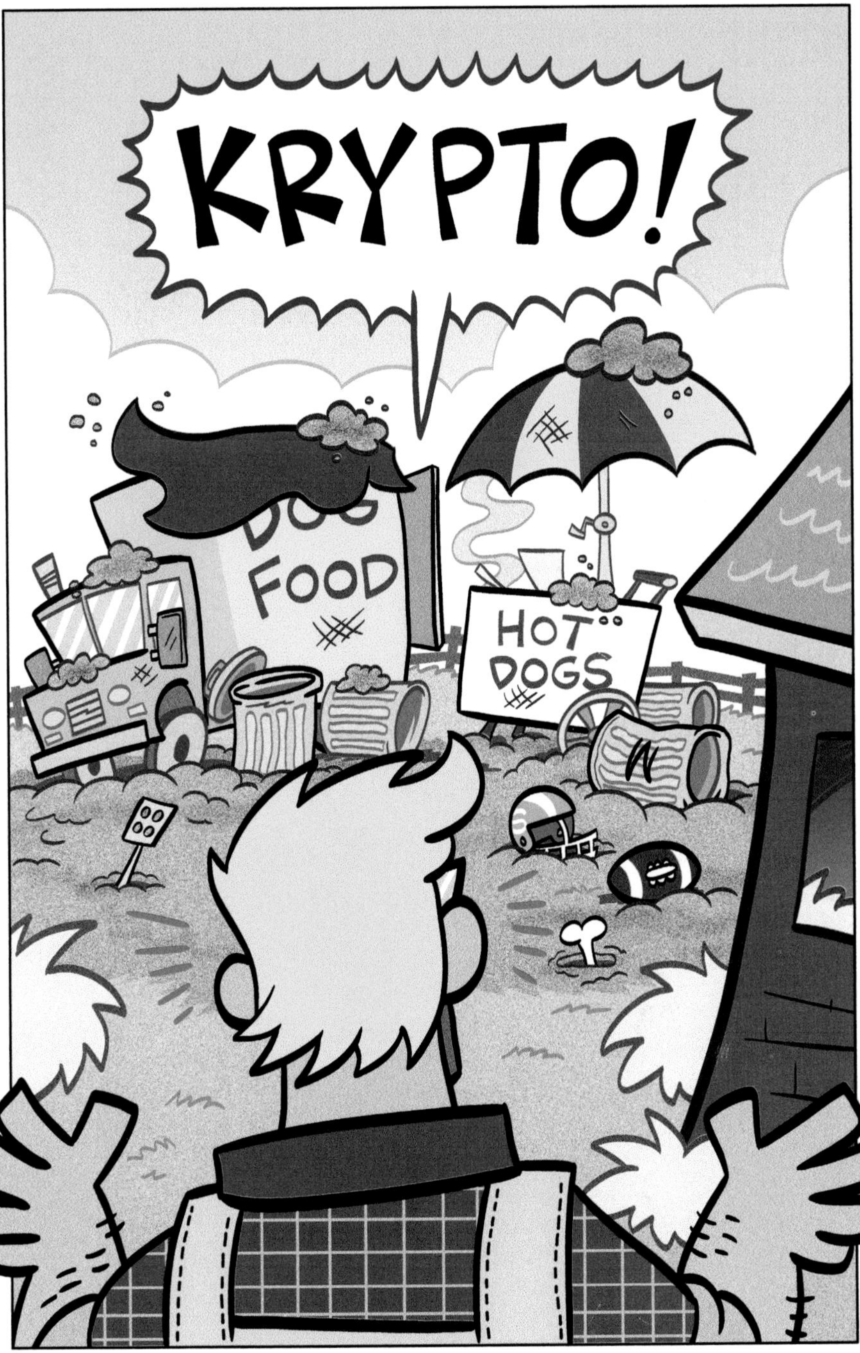
KRYPTO!
DOG FOOD
HOT DOGS

Kryptonian Key

A= ‼	B= ▯	C= ∞	D= ▯!	E= ÷	F= ◈	G= 8
H= ⬠◇	I= ⌐	J= ·8	K= 🔒	L= Ọ	M= ◇⊡	N= ◇
O= ⫴·	P= ◇⊶	Q= ♀	R= ◊	S= ◈	T= ⊤	U= ⅱ
V= ⊝	W= ⊝⊝	X= ▢	Y= ‖	Z= ⌐	AW	YEAH

HEY, **SUPER** AWESOME **READER!**

CHECK OUT THIS SUPER SECRET **KRYPTONIAN** DECODER.

YOU CAN USE IT TO GO BACK AND INTERPRET EVERYTHING THE SHIPS TOLD **KRYPTO** AND **ME.**

FRANCO AURELIANI is an Eisner Award-winning writer and artist and co-creator of *Patrick the Wolf Boy* and AW YEAH COMICS! Franco has worked on the Dino-Mike book series, and on critically acclaimed comics like SUPERMAN FAMILY ADVENTURES, YOUNG JUSTICE, BILLY BATSON AND THE MAGIC OF SHAZAM, and the *New York Times*-bestselling, multi-Eisner Award-winning series TINY TITANS and SUPER POWERS for DC Comics. He has also worked on *Grimmiss Island* and *Itty Bitty Hellboy* with Dark Horse Comics. Franco is also one of the principal owners of Aw Yeah Comics retail stores. When he is not working on comics, Franco can be found shaping young minds as a high school teacher.

ART BALTAZAR is one of the creative forces behind the *New York Times*-bestselling, Eisner Award-winning DC Comics series TINY TITANS. He is also the co-writer for BILLY BATSON AND THE MAGIC OF SHAZAM, YOUNG JUSTICE, the GREEN LANTERN: THE ANIMATED SERIES comic, and is the artist/co-writer for the awesome TINY TITANS/LITTLE ARCHIE crossover, SUPERMAN FAMILY ADVENTURES, SUPER POWERS, and *Itty Bitty Hellboy*. Art is one of the founders of the Aw Yeah Comics comics shop, and he's also the co-creator of the ongoing comic series of the same name. He stays home and draws comics and never has to leave the house where he lives with his lovely wife, Rose, sons Sonny and Gordon, and daughter, Audrey. AW YEAH, living the dream!

Check out the latest and
strangest book from DC ZOOM!

You are about to turn the page into
THE SECRET SPIRAL OF SWAMP KID by
writer and illustrator Kirk Scroggs.

WARNING!

You will never look at middle school the same way again.

In stores and swamps near you 10/1/19

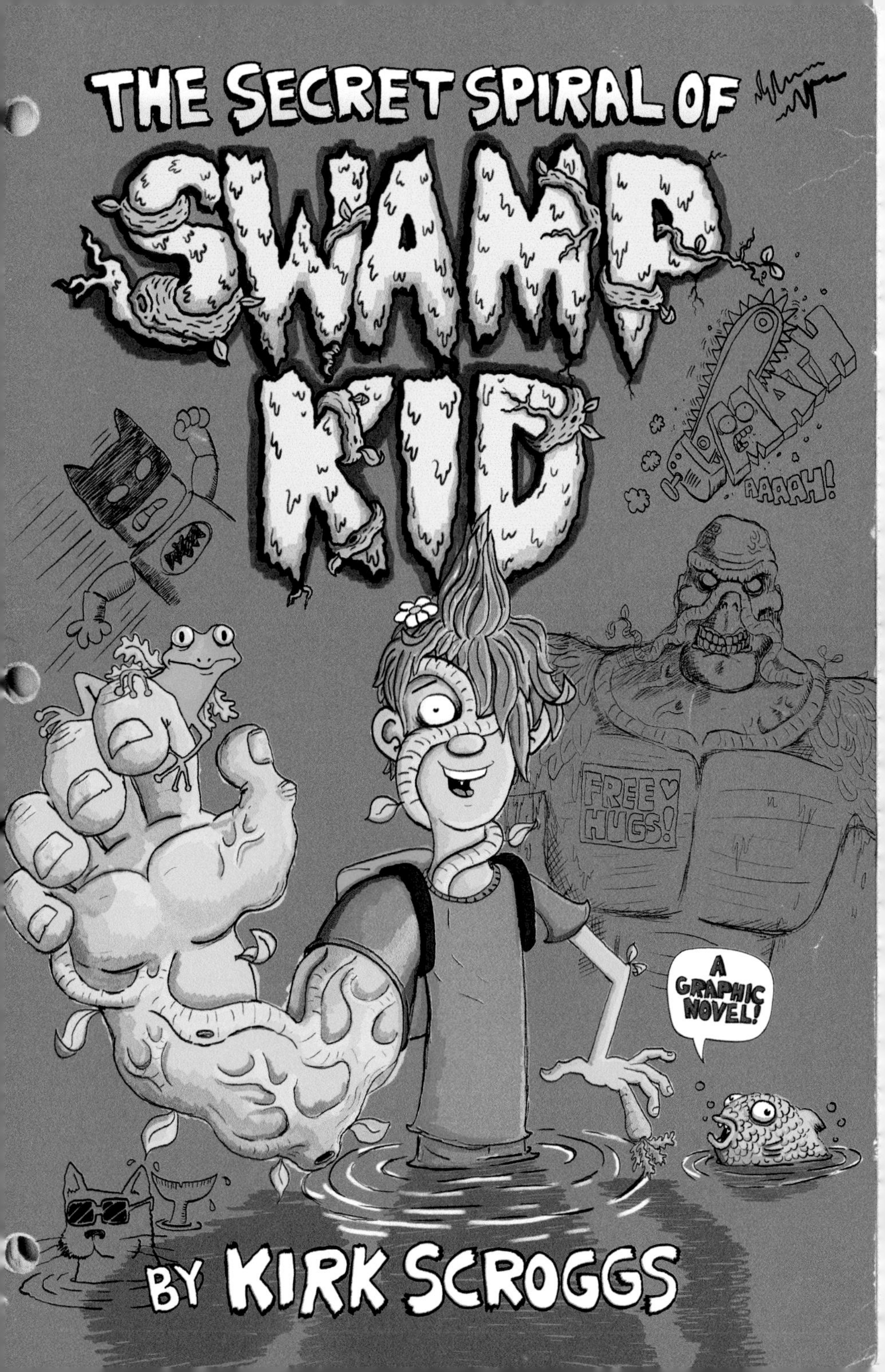
THE SECRET SPIRAL OF
SWAMP KID
AAAAH!
FREE HUGS!
A GRAPHIC NOVEL!
BY KIRK SCROGGS

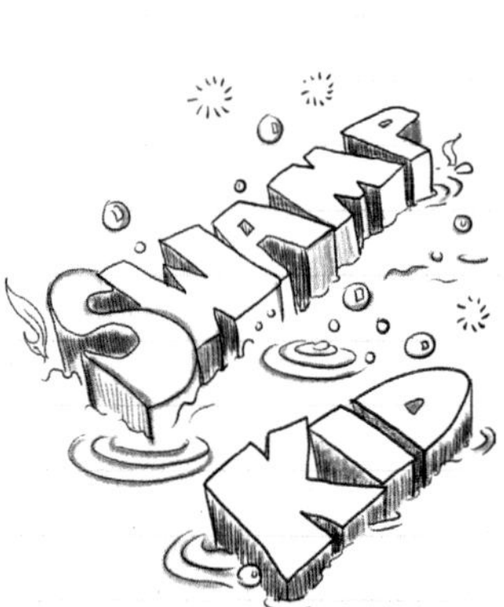
SWAMP
KID

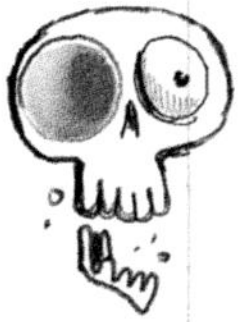

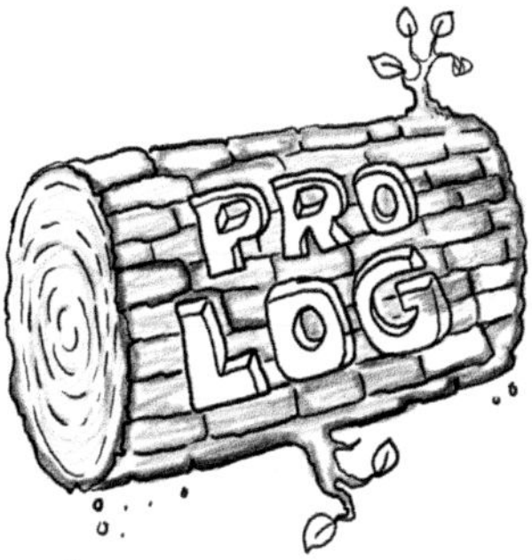
PRO
LOG

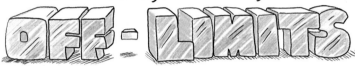

WARNING! Unless you have received explicit permission from Russell Weinwright, this scientific journal (NOT a diary!) is strictly

OFF-LIMITS

To make sure you comply certain pages have been written in toxic ink.

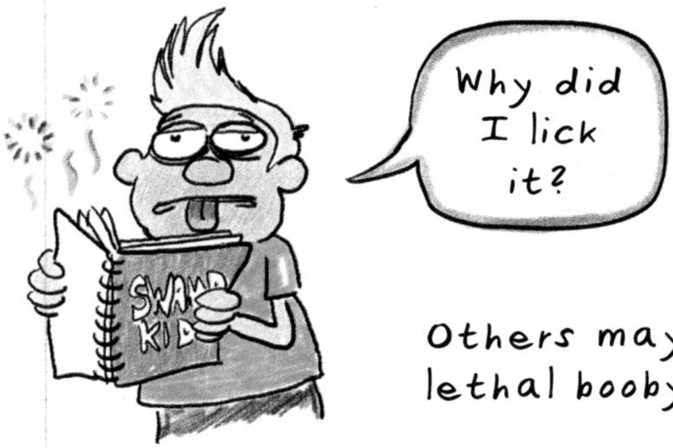
Why did I lick it?
SWAMP KID

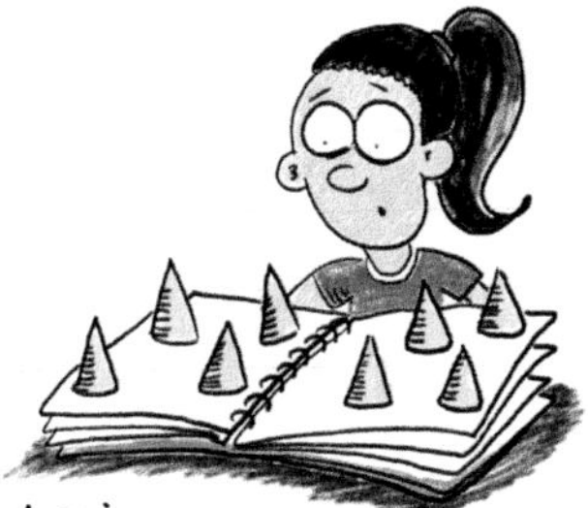

Others may contain lethal booby traps!

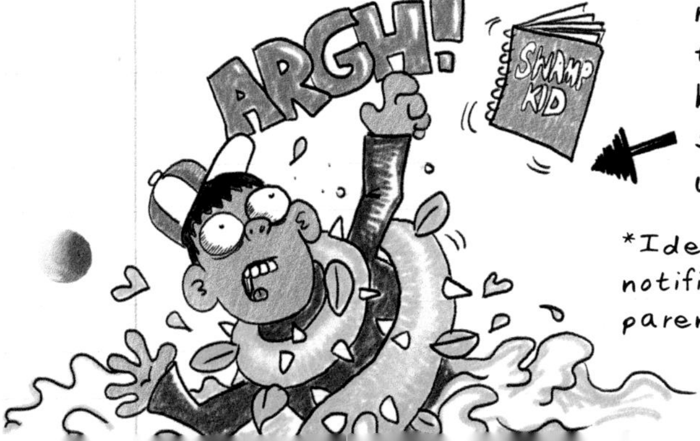
ARGH!
SWAMP KID

And should you read all the way to the end you could be pulled into the swamp like this unfortunate kid.*

*Identity withheld pending notification of distraught parents.

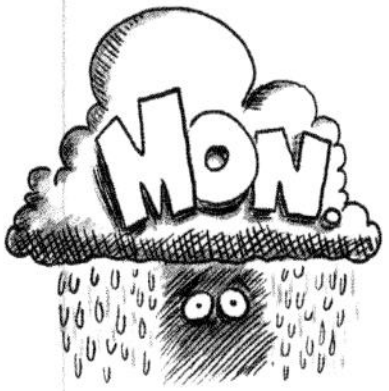
MON.

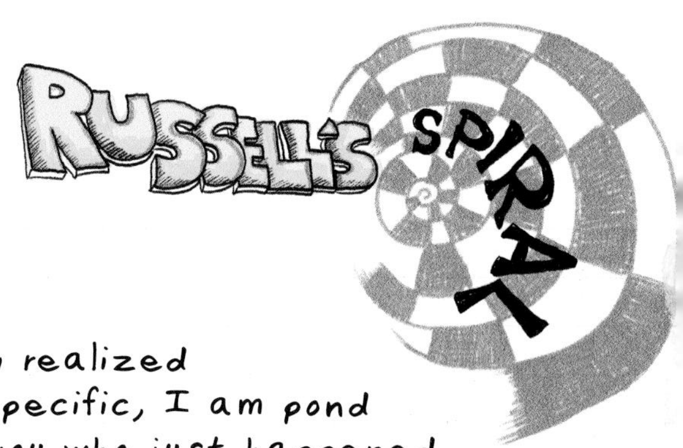
RUSSELL'S SPIRAL

Yesterday I finally realized I am scum. To be specific, I am pond scum. For those of you who just happened across this notebook, maybe because you are snooping where you don't belong (that means you, Mom!) don't worry. I'm not in a depressed tailspin, about to lock myself in my room and devour ten gallons of mint chocolate chip. I'm just stating the facts—I am pond scum. Literally: 50% cellulose, 50% human.

When most folks hear there's a half-swamp monster/half-human student at Houma Bayou Middle School they probably picture something like this:

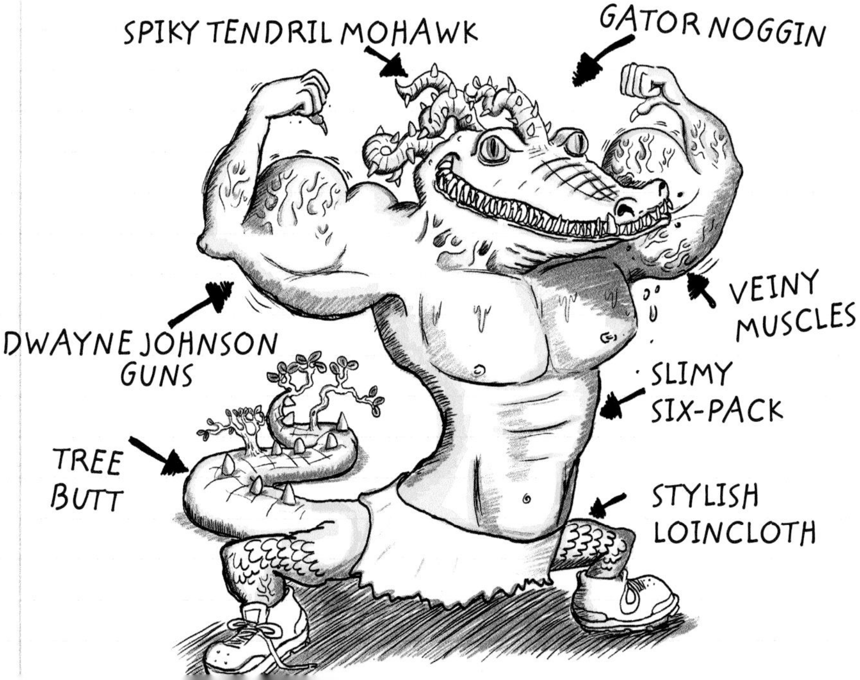
SPIKY TENDRIL MOHAWK
GATOR NOGGIN
DWAYNE JOHNSON GUNS
VEINY MUSCLES
SLIMY SIX-PACK
TREE BUTT
STYLISH LOINCLOTH

Of course, THIS is what I really look like...

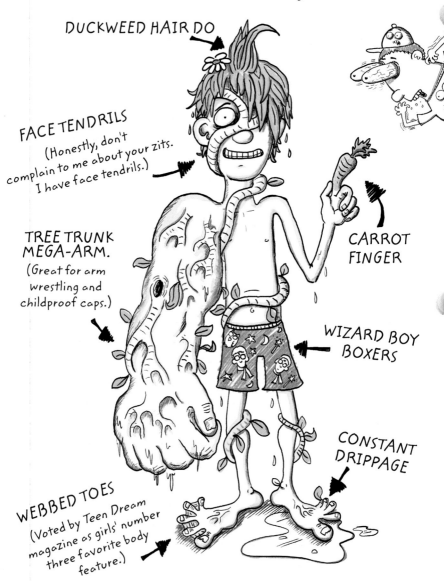

DUCKWEED HAIR DO

FACE TENDRILS
(Honestly, don't complain to me about your zits. I have face tendrils.)

TREE TRUNK MEGA-ARM.
(Great for arm wrestling and childproof caps.)

CARROT FINGER

WIZARD BOY BOXERS

CONSTANT DRIPPAGE

WEBBED TOES
(Voted by Teen Dream magazine as girls' number three favorite body feature.)

That's me. Russell Weinwright. Handsome, huh? I've come to realize I possess what fashion blogs call the Wet Algae look.

I'm used to my veggie physique by now, but yesterday reality hit me like a truckload of fertilizer. Charlotte tried to set me up on a date with her cousin Tonya and you can imagine how that went.

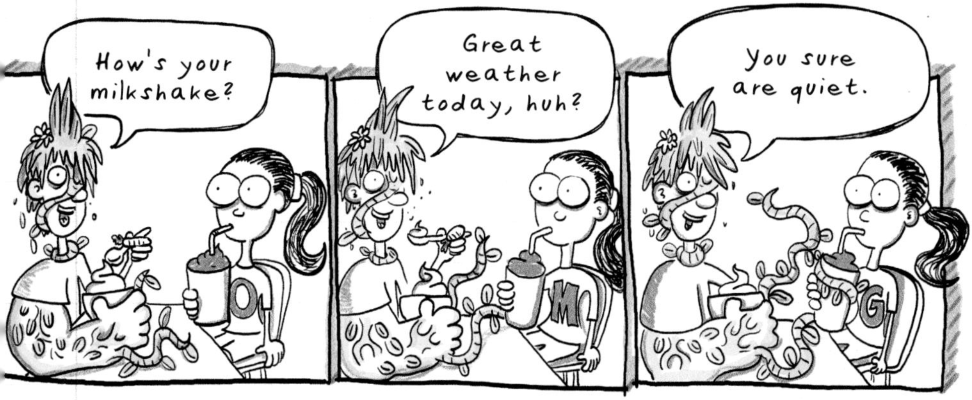
How's your milkshake?
Great weather today, huh?
You sure are quiet.
O
M
G

So, yeah, that happened. Like I said, pond scum. Charlotte was just trying to help, I suppose. She's my best friend at school...uh, scratch that. She's my ONLY friend at school. She's full of Cajun-spiced words of encouragement when I'm feeling sorry for myself.

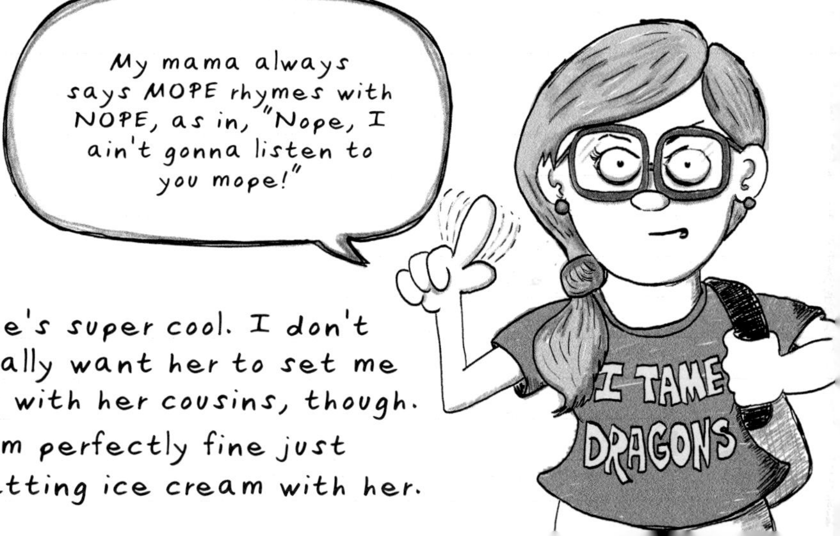
My mama always says MOPE rhymes with NOPE, as in, "Nope, I ain't gonna listen to you mope!"
I TAME DRAGONS

She's super cool. I don't really want her to set me up with her cousins, though. I'm perfectly fine just getting ice cream with her.

Right now, as I write this, Charlotte is totally staring at me from across the classroom, making some weird motion with her eyes.

Oh wait!

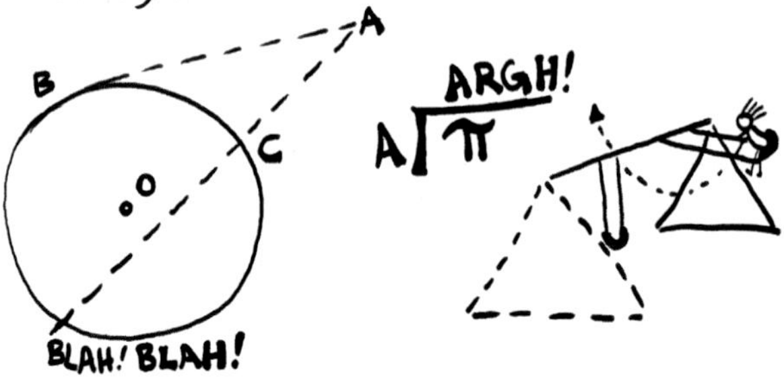

A
B
C
O
BLAH! BLAH!
ARGH!
A
π

Sorry, had to pretend to take notes there for a second! Charlotte must have been trying to warn me that Mr. Finneca was walking up right behind me! Dude's always busting me for doodling in science class.

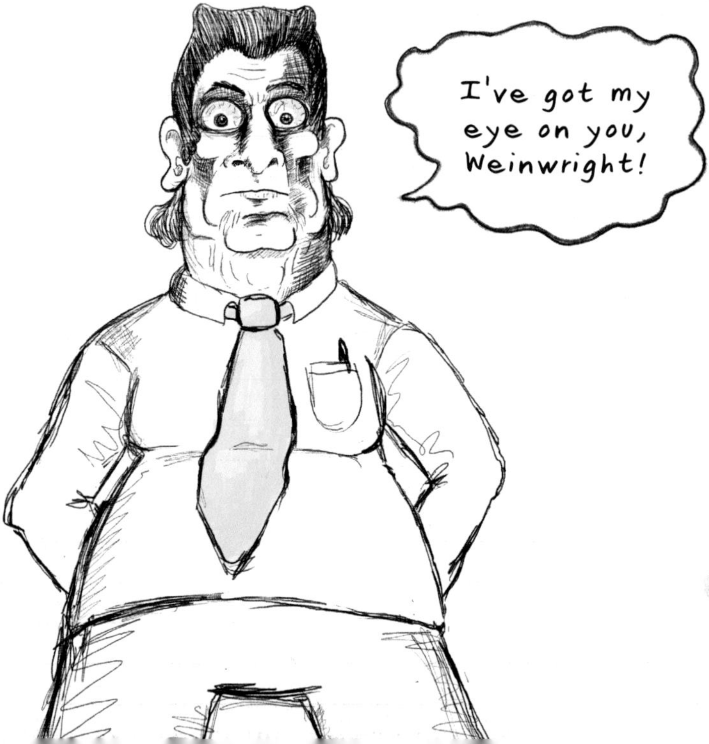

I've got my eye on you, Weinwright!

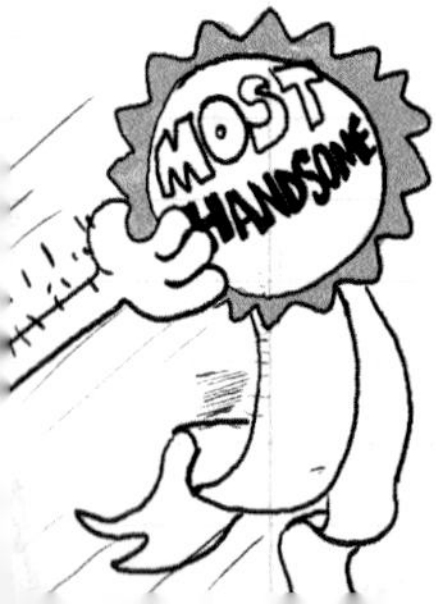

MOST HANDSOME

He's got a right to be cheesed. I do draw in his class 98% of the time, but it's almost always pictures of him. I draw him as evil vampires, evil space lords, deformed monsters... he should be honored!

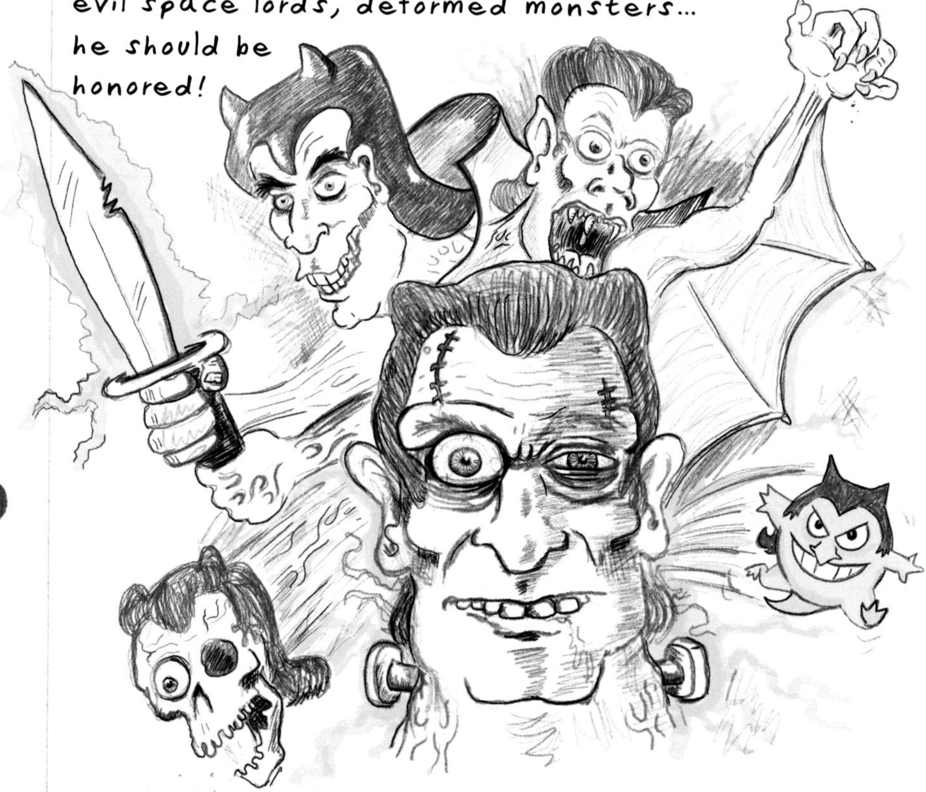

Okay, I guess my pics aren't very flattering, although he did seem strangely impressed when I drew him as a great white shark.

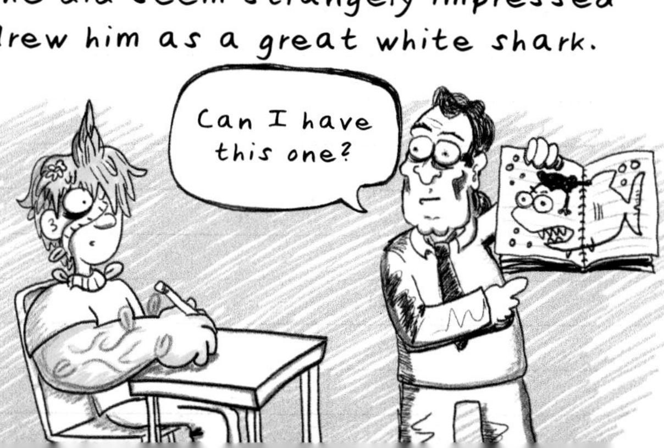
Can I have this one?

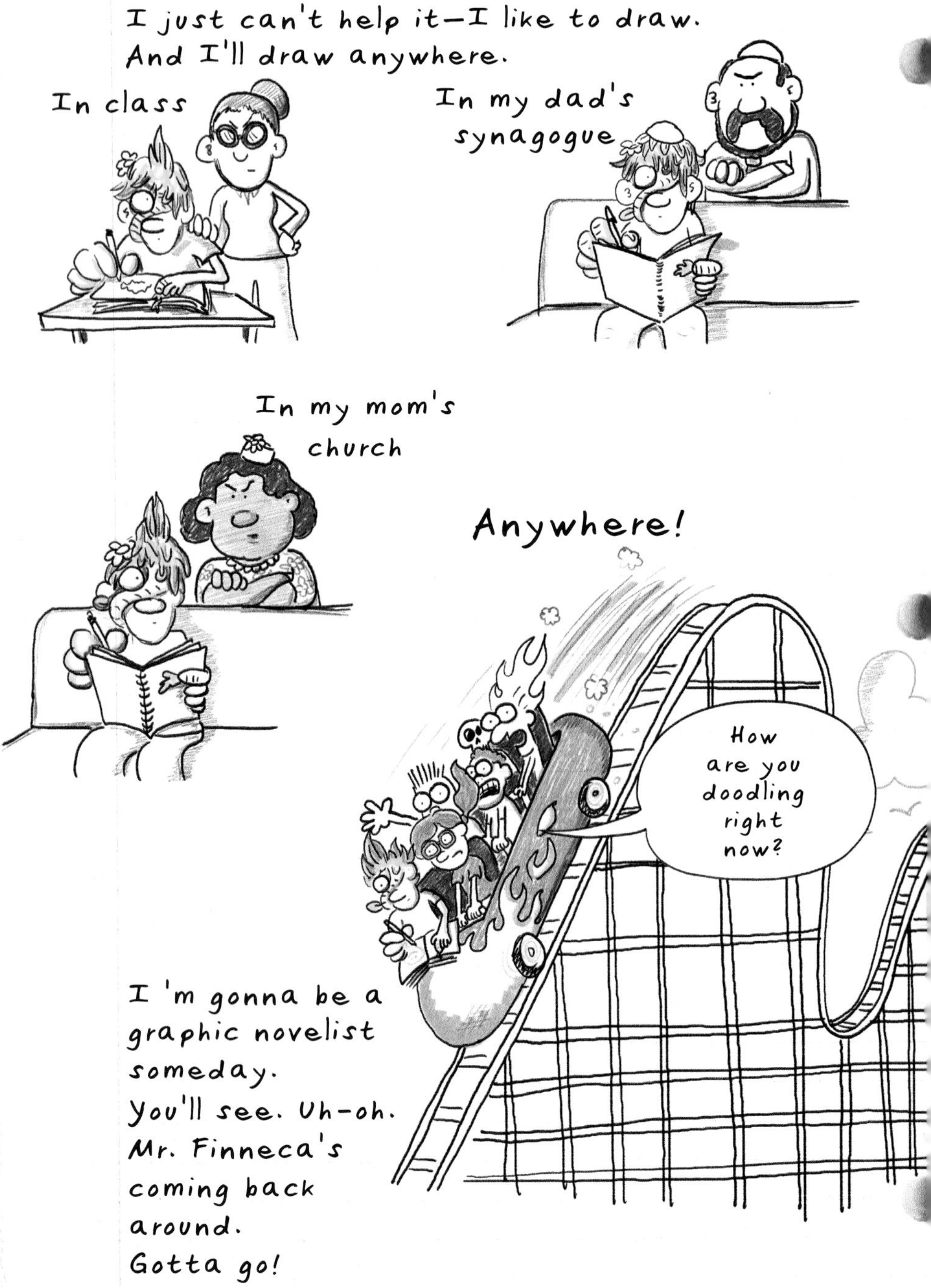
I just can't help it—I like to draw.
And I'll draw anywhere.
In class
In my dad's synagogue
In my mom's church
Anywhere!
How are you doodling right now?
I 'm gonna be a graphic novelist someday.
You'll see. Uh-oh.
Mr. Finneca's coming back around.
Gotta go!

MON. LUNCH

Lunch period. A.k.a. Last Meal of the Condemned.
Dad says my weekly allowance is bigger than the
whole Bayou Bend lunch budget for the year, which
explains the subpar cuisine. If you don't believe
me, just take a look at this pic of
today's spaghetti and meatball special...

HARD PASS!

Fooled you. It's actually a garden salad.

Today I decided to eat my lunch outside.
It's something I do a lot, mainly to escape
the stench of the lunchroom, the endless stares
from my classmates, the bullies trying to read my
spiral without my authorization, and, oh yeah...
I eat sunlight.

What did he just say?

He said he eats sunlight!

Is there gluten in it?

BULLIES

LADIES AND GENTLEMEN,
PHOTOSYNTHESIS!

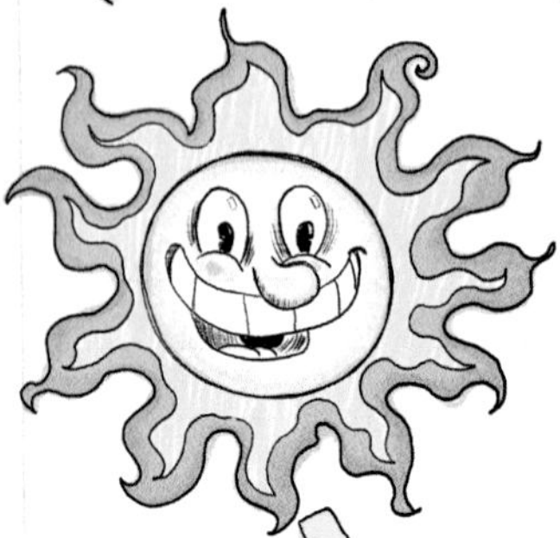

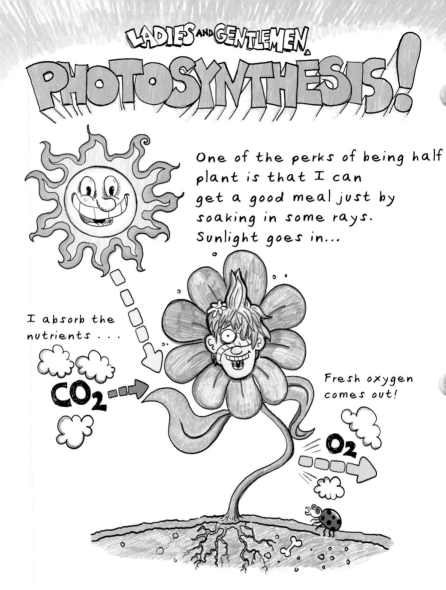

One of the perks of being half plant is that I can get a good meal just by soaking in some rays. Sunlight goes in...

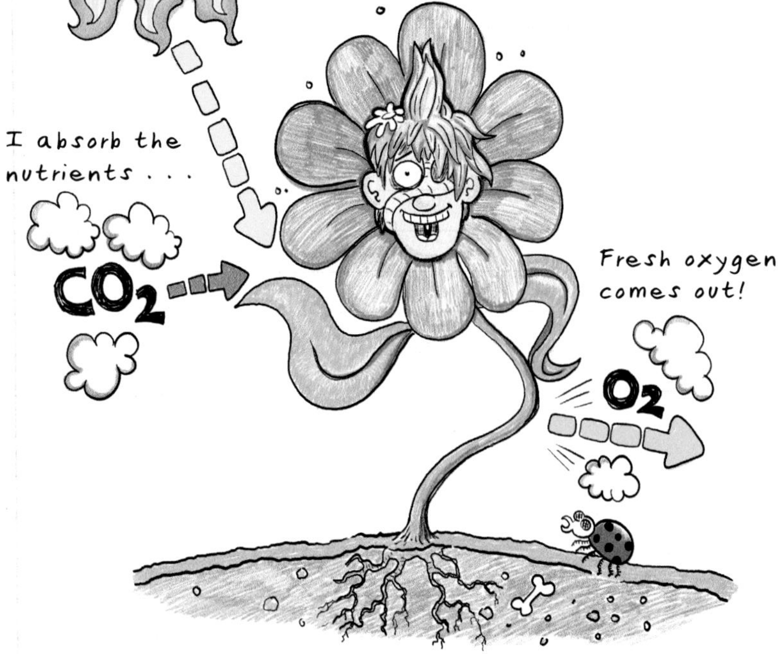

I absorb the nutrients . . .
CO_2
Fresh oxygen comes out!
O_2

Don't get me wrong, I still like a good pizza, but it's mostly the sun's warm rays that give me energy.

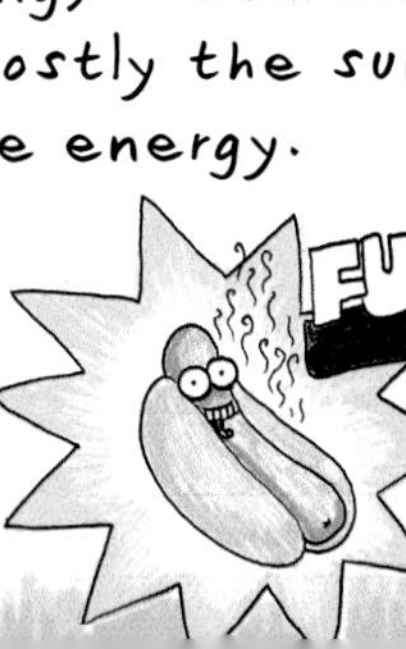

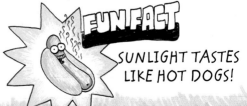

FUN FACT

SUNLIGHT TASTES LIKE HOT DOGS!

I also convert carbon dioxide pollution into oxygen, which helps you all breathe easily, so...

YOU'RE WELCOME!

Of course, this unique feature can cause confusion. Especially when it comes to my folks...

Be sure to get lots of sunshine, son. You're a growing boy and need your nourishment!

And wear sunscreen. You don't want melanoma!

Okay... Wait, what?

SPF 500

But, anyway, what was I talking about again? Oh yeah, eating outside. It's peaceful out here. I can draw my comics and write in my spiral while I absorb lunch. And I can avoid the other students asking me annoying questions. There's this one kid in particular who keeps following me around with his old school video camera and pelting me with personal questions that I just don't feel like answering...

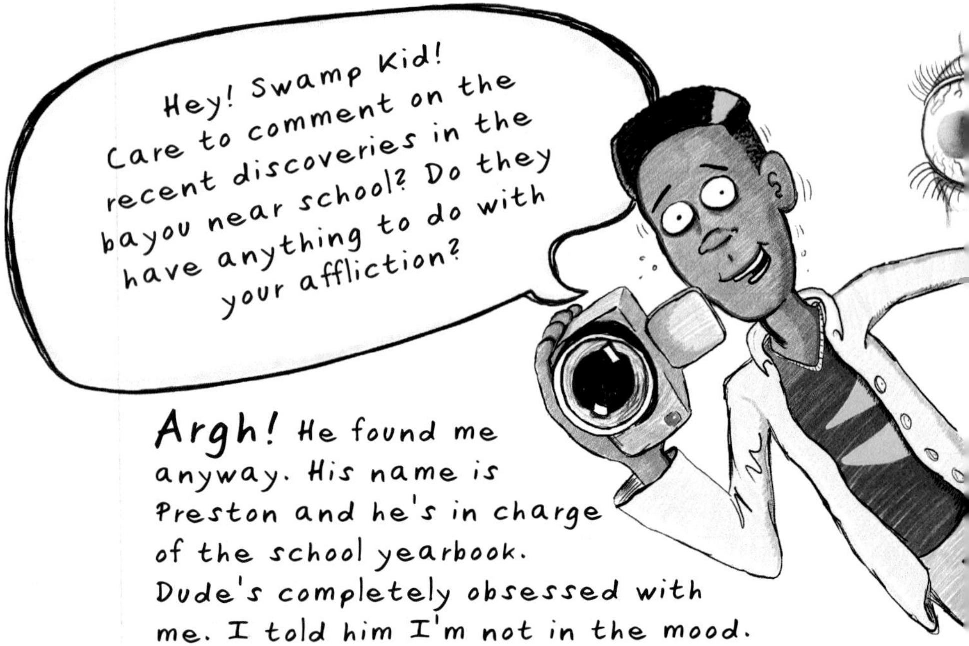
Hey! Swamp Kid! Care to comment on the recent discoveries in the bayou near school? Do they have anything to do with your affliction?

Argh! He found me anyway. His name is Preston and he's in charge of the school yearbook. Dude's completely obsessed with me. I told him I'm not in the mood. But that never deters Preston.

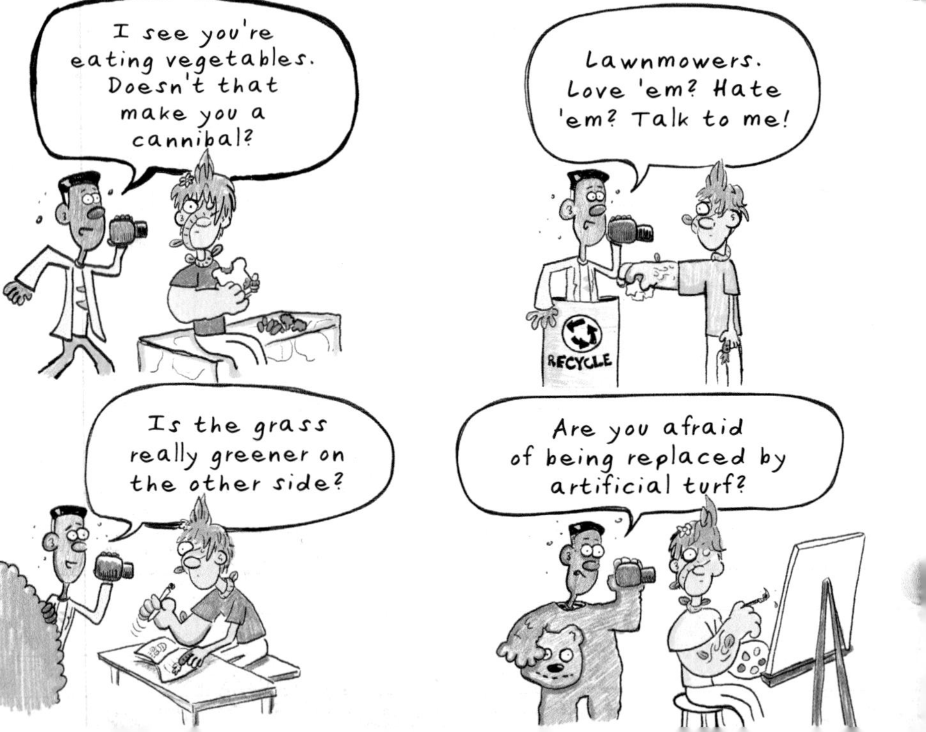
I see you're eating vegetables. Doesn't that make you a cannibal?
Lawnmowers. Love 'em? Hate 'em? Talk to me!
RECYCLE
Is the grass really greener on the other side?
Are you afraid of being replaced by artificial turf?

Luckily for me, Charlotte popped up out of nowhere and took care of business.

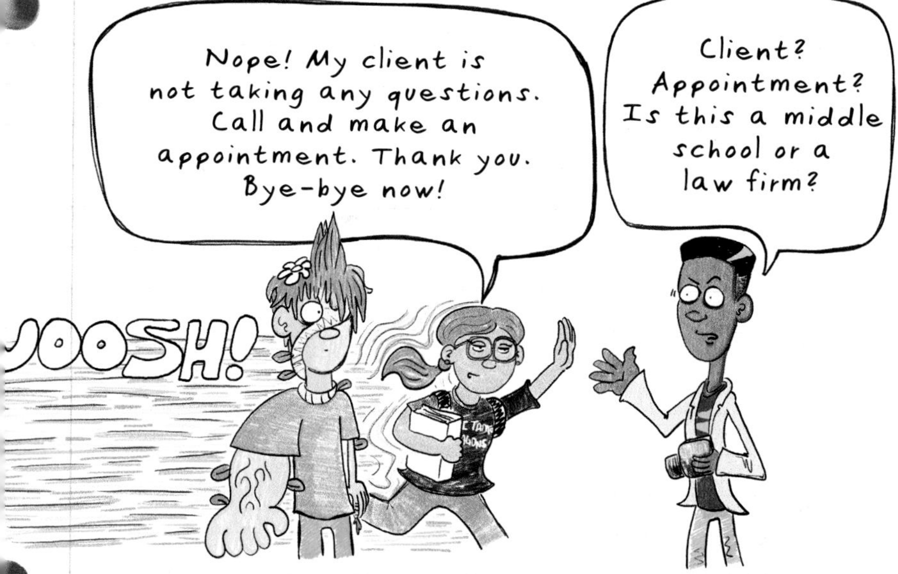
Nope! My client is not taking any questions. Call and make an appointment. Thank you. Bye-bye now!
Client? Appointment? Is this a middle school or a law firm?
OOSH!

Preston left in a huff. I thanked Charlotte for protecting her "client." She said she'd bill me later.

I couldn't help but think about what Preston had said. You know, about the discoveries in the swamp. It had been all over the news. Remnants of an old science lab scattered about in the bayou. I kinda wanted to go check it out, but not by myself. Good news, though. All I had to do was say one word to get Charlotte interested...

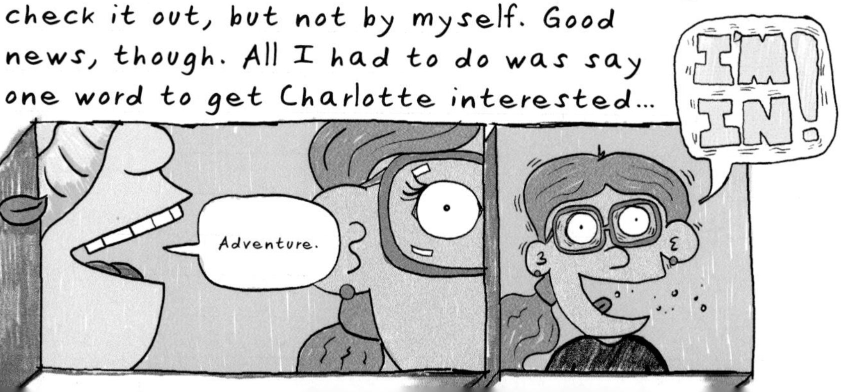
Adventure.
I'M IN!

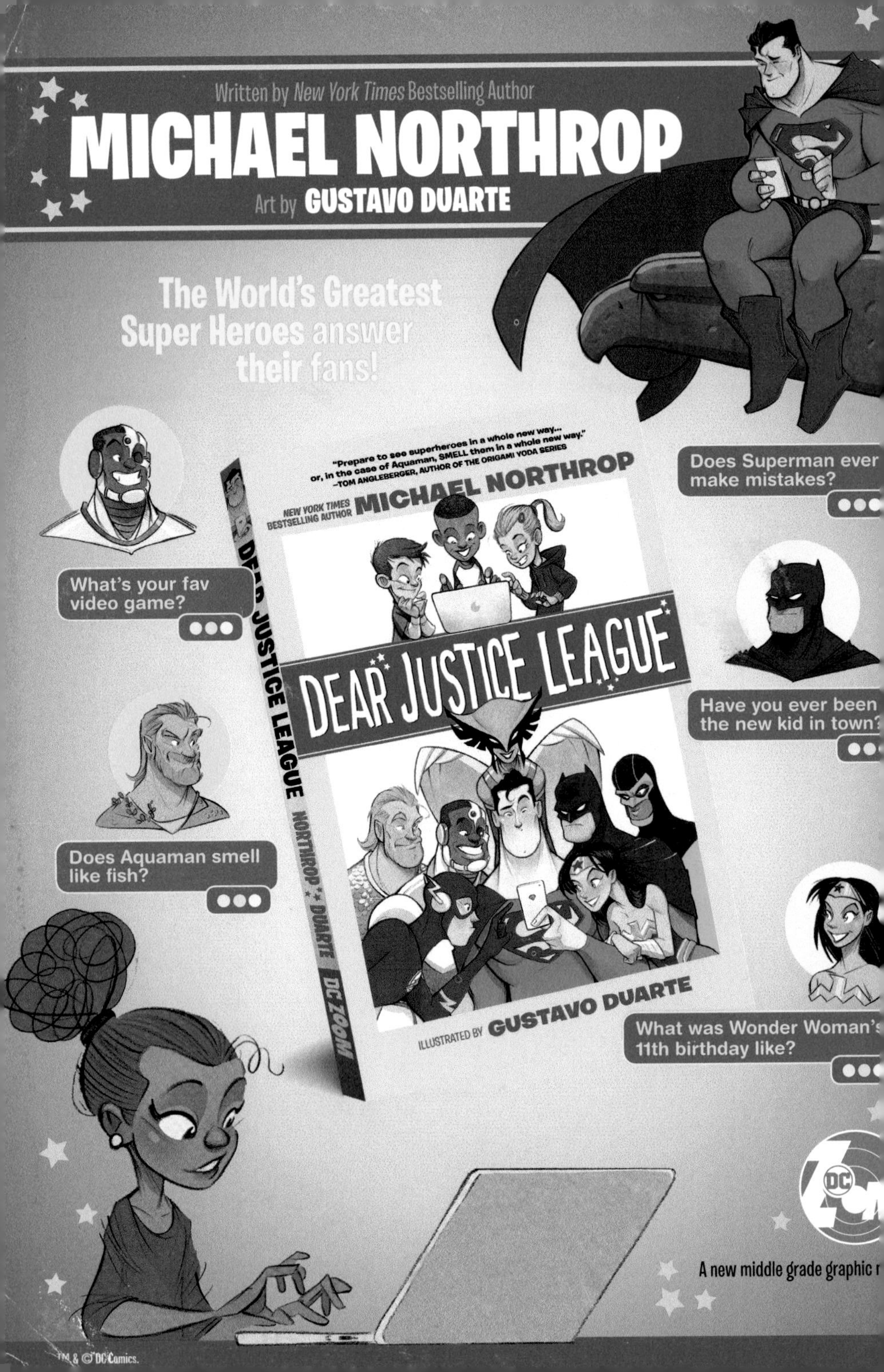

Written by New York Times Bestselling Author
MICHAEL NORTHROP
Art by GUSTAVO DUARTE
The World's Greatest Super Heroes answer their fans!
"Prepare to see superheroes in a whole new way... or, in the case of Aquaman, SMELL them in a whole new way." —TOM ANGLEBERGER, AUTHOR OF THE ORIGAMI YODA SERIES
NEW YORK TIMES BESTSELLING AUTHOR MICHAEL NORTHROP
DEAR JUSTICE LEAGUE
ILLUSTRATED BY GUSTAVO DUARTE
DEAR JUSTICE LEAGUE NORTHROP DUARTE DC ZOOM
What's your fav video game?
Does Aquaman smell like fish?
Does Superman ever make mistakes?
Have you ever been the new kid in town?
What was Wonder Woman's 11th birthday like?
A new middle grade graphic
TM & © DC Comics.